Deep Blue

KRISTY MCCAFFREY

DEEP BLUE

THE PATHWAY SERIES BOOK 1

KRISTY MCCAFFREY

A PATHWAY NOVEL

The Pathway Series

Deep Blue
Cold Horizon
Ancient Winds
Sapphire Waves

Blue Sage (related novella)

Deep Blue Australia*
Deep Blue Réunion Island*
Deep Blue Cocos Island*
Deep Blue Hawai'i*
Cold Horizon Telluride*
Shark Reef*

*Short stories in the Pathway universe

Praise for *Deep Blue*

"A sexy adventure packed with spine-tingling suspense … and sharks!" ~ Ann Charles, *USA Today Bestselling Author*

"An…engaging tale…McCaffrey has clearly done her research… [she] effectively increases the tension every time Grace enters the water; readers will never know what will happen next." ~ *Kirkus Reviews*

"A hunky filmmaker and great whites, what's not to love?" ~ Lynne Bryant, *InD'tale Magazine*

"Once I started reading, I couldn't put it down." ~ Robin, *Romancing the Book*

"This book has it all … danger, intrigue, romance, scientific fact and a fast-paced plot …" ~ Allison Brady, *Love Books Group*

"I truly recommend this great read." ~ *Night Owl Romance*

"… a powerful story …" ~ D. Donovan, Senior Reviewer, *Midwest Book Review*

"… a mix of romance, thriller and sharks …" ~ Donna M. Maguire, *donnasbookblog*

"… like shark week in a book …" ~ Rachel H., reader

2019 Write Touch Readers' Award – Second Place in Long Contemporary
2019 Carolyn Readers' Choice Award – Finalist in Contemporary Romance
2019 I Heart Indie Contest – Finalist

Cover Design: Okay Creations - okaycreations.com

Illustrator: Penny Fournier - instagram.com/penny.illustration

Editor: Mimi The Grammar Chick – merrelli.wixsite.com/grammarchick

Line Editor: Melissa Maygrove – truelovepress.com

Proofreader: Diane Garland – yourworldkeeper.com

Author Photo: Katy McCaffrey – instagram.com/katymccaffreyphoto

E-book ISBN-13: 978-0-9980907-4-0

Print ISBN-13: 978-0-9980907-5-7

kmccaffrey.com

kristy@kristymccaffrey.com

❀ Created with Vellum

In Memory Of

Ranger McCaffrey

October 9, 2004 – October 17, 2017

Beloved dog and dearly missed.

"We need another and a wiser and perhaps a more mystical concept of animals… For the animal shall not be measured by man. In a world older and more complete than ours they move finished and complete, gifted with extensions of the senses we have lost or never attained, living by voices we shall never hear. They are not brethren, they are not underlings; they are other nations, caught with ourselves in the net of life and time, fellow prisoners of the splendor and travail of the earth."
~ Naturalist Henry Beston, *The Outermost House*

"I don't believe in taking foolish chances, but nothing can be accomplished without taking any chance at all."
~ Charles A. Lindbergh

Carcharodon carcharias – Great White Shark

CHAPTER 1

Monterey, California
August

Alec Galloway leaned back in his seat and shifted his gaze from Dr. Grace Mann, who stood onstage beside a podium, to the auditorium's wide screen showcasing a photo of a shark. He'd been looking forward to this lecture all week.

"Since 2005, we have had five great white sharks in captivity at the California Marine Institute." Dr. Mann adjusted her dark-rimmed glasses and clicked to a new slide picturing a shark inside a large tube. "The first was a young female found entangled in a fishing net off Huntington Beach. Initially, we kept her in a special-ized ocean pen to assess her stress levels and to ensure that she would take food from us. One of our criteria was that she needed to eat three meals before transport; if she didn't do that then we would release her. Luckily, she did eat fish that was lowered to her on lines, and the female great white was subsequently brought to CMI.

"To transport her, we designed a special vehicle we dubbed the

'Fish Mobile.' Made of fiberglass, it held 3200 gallons of sea water and circulated filtered water with an oxygen injection."

Dr. Mann continued to click through photos of the captive shark as she spoke. A spotlight followed her as she stepped away from the elevated platform, the beam of light glinting off her blonde hair that was tucked into a loose bun at the base of her neck. Alec knew of Dr. Mann by reputation but seeing her in person had only increased his esteem. He hoped that she would agree to work with him.

"We were, of course, concerned about her well-being," Dr. Mann continued. "Before this, the longest a great white had survived in captivity was only sixteen days, but to our extreme delight she settled right into our exhibit."

A photo of a majestic female great white flashed onscreen, taken from an angle beneath the fish, showcasing its youth and vigor. A smile tugged at Alec's mouth. It must have been exciting to be so close to such an extraordinary creature for an extended period. He'd had many close encounters with great whites in the wild, but there was never time to strike up a friendship.

Dr. Mann moved away from the screen and tilted her head back to gain a better view of her own presentation. Her lithe figure—draped by a gray pinstriped suit and ivory blouse—was further accentuated with black heels, the ensemble presenting a very busi-ness-like demeanor. Alec had followed her research over the past year, but photos of her in journal articles usually showed her wearing a ball cap and sunglasses. It was damn nice, seeing her in person at last.

"We were even more astounded," she continued into the wireless microphone attached to her right ear, "when she lasted for 198 days in our care. We believe that she was born sometime in the twelve months prior to capture, and she initially measured four feet seven inches long and weighed 62 pounds. Upon release, she was six feet one inch and 162 pounds.

"Although she'd become quite popular in her exhibit at CMI, we remained committed to returning her to the wild. We chose the date of release based on two things—she'd become increasingly aggressive with other sharks in the exhibit, and her steady growth meant that if we waited much longer, we wouldn't be able to transport her safely.

"We released her into the Pacific Ocean with an electronic tag that was programmed to pop free thirty days later. From that, we learned she had traveled 200 miles south on a journey that took her more than 100 miles offshore and to depths greater than 800 feet below the surface."

Dr. Mann scanned the audience. Alec's cursory glance showed the auditorium to be packed. People were fascinated with sharks, especially great whites.

"So what information did we compile from our time with her?" Dr. Mann clicked to a graphic with bullet points.

"We learned a great deal about how to care for a white shark. We collected the first ever data on the metabolic rate of great whites—from the amount of oxygen the sharks consumed during transport in the Fish Mobile to the correlation of their food intake while on exhibit in relation to their growth, giving us insight into how much energy they require for swimming and life support.

"Our shark showed a strong capacity to swim in the exhibit, and therefore thrive. She had an impressive ability to heal from injuries. She preferred eating salmon over mackerel, and vitamins that we administered to other shark species also worked well on her. We modified our feeding and handling techniques to keep her healthy, and as she grew, we observed behavioral changes.

"Now, I'll share briefly what we learned from the four additional great white sharks that we were able to keep in captivity before also releasing them back into the wild."

Alec had come to the lecture at the urging of Stewart Smith, Grant Administrator at the California Marine Institute. Smith was part of the team that had offered Alec the job of filming a documentary on Dr. Mann this fall during an expedition to Guadalupe Island, located off the coast of Baja California Sur. She and her team, which included Brad Michaels, an old surfing buddy of Alec's, were developing a sonar array to track the movement and location of sharks within a specified grid area. They one day hoped to employ this at beaches around the world. However, it seemed Dr. Mann wasn't keen on Alec's participation and wanted to hire a different filmmaker. Smith thought if Grace met Alec, she might change her mind. There was a gala to attend the following night in Pebble Beach—a fundraiser for the Institute—and since Alec was in town for the event, Smith had nudged him to attend Grace's talk.

Alec couldn't deny that he'd been curious about Dr. Mann's work. And about her.

"In conclusion," Dr. Mann said, "sharks are over fifty million years old and protecting them is an urgent matter today. Millions of sharks are slaughtered each year for their fins, while many are killed as by-product when they're caught in commercial fishing gear. It is imperative that we understand the biology of these fish, as well as where they go and why, so that we may better protect them. To this end, it is our aim at CMI, in partnership with other researchers and scientists, to document the migrations of adult and juvenile white sharks in the Eastern Pacific. Great white sharks are apex predators at the top of the ocean's food chain. Without them, we simply won't have a healthy ocean. Thank you."

Applause resounded.

The lights came on, and a moderator, an older woman, walked onstage and fielded questions from the audience for the next thirty minutes. Dr. Mann answered each inquiry with a thoughtful and thorough answer. She clearly knew her stuff.

When the presentation finally ended, Alec was grateful to stand and stretch his long legs as the crowd began to disperse. He headed toward the stage, but was cut off by a student of the high school where the talk had taken place.

"Can I help you, sir?" the stout young man asked, his ruddy face sporting a smattering of acne.

"I was hoping to speak with Dr. Mann."

"I think she's already left."

Damn.

"Thanks," Alec said, and quickly exited the auditorium out a side door and headed toward the parking lot. A quick search showed a throng of people, although it wasn't as jammed as Alec had thought it might be. He caught a glimpse of Dr. Mann near a light-colored hatchback.

Alec jogged to catch her. "Dr. Mann."

At the sound of her name, she turned, and Alec's gaze locked on her face. She wasn't wearing her glasses. The admiration he'd quietly nurtured for her these past months suddenly sprang loose, making him tongue-tied. He cleared his throat to shake it off.

"I'm glad I caught you." He held out his hand. "I'm Alec Galloway."

Her expression went from flat to a frown.

This isn't going well.

She shook his hand, but the movement was as stiff and formal as her outfit. "Stewart didn't tell me you were here."

"I came for the fundraiser tomorrow. He mentioned your lecture this evening, so I thought I'd come by and introduce myself. Great talk, by the way."

"Thanks." She offered no crack in her armor.

"Listen, would you like to grab a drink?"

"It's late, and I have work tomorrow."

Alec smiled and rubbed a hand behind his neck. He was starting to sweat beneath his blazer, despite the chill in the air.

He took a breath. "Look, I'm trying to be considerate here. Stewart has offered the documentary job to me, and from what I gather, you're not excited to have me along, but I'm trying to make peace. We're both after the same thing—a film showcasing the sonar array so that more funding can be secured, and your message of saving sharks can be shared with the world. I'm not trying to be a stumbling block."

She watched him, her cool gaze filled with shadows from the

low lighting in the school parking lot. "Fine. I know a place. Follow me in your car."

Without any further talk, she turned, unlocked her car, and was settled behind the wheel before Alec had moved. Snapping out of his daze, he walked quickly to his rental vehicle, two rows over, and jumped behind the wheel before Dr. Mann drove off and left him in her dust. He guided his vehicle behind hers, cutting off a carful of students in the process.

Stewart had told him she'd said no to Alec's name on the film-maker shortlist, not once but three times. Why did Dr. Mann dislike him so much? They'd never even met until today.

Alec followed her down to Cannery Row, stopping at a bar with a half-filled parking lot. He maneuvered into a spot and joined her at her car. She didn't speak and instead walked around to the front of the establishment, clutching a big purse that hung from her right shoulder, her heels clicking in a steady rhythm on the asphalt.

She was fast, and Alec had to surge forward at the last minute to grab the entrance door, holding it open for her as she went inside. She acknowledged him with a curt nod.

The darkened room wasn't busy.

A hostess appeared. "You can sit wherever you want."

Alec was thinking a booth—it would be quieter—but Dr. Mann immediately settled on a barstool. Alec took a seat beside her.

The bartender approached, a young woman wearing a pink tank top.

"I'll have a glass of Malbec," Dr. Mann said.

"Give me whatever lager you have on tap."

The woman nodded, quickly went to work, and then deposited the drinks before them.

"Where are you from, Mr. Galloway?" Dr. Mann kept her body faced forward as she took a sip of her wine, although she did glance in his direction, offering a glimpse of her very blue eyes.

Alec didn't usually have to work so hard charming a woman. He was beginning to think this job might not work out. "The Bay area. I have a place there, near my parents, but I'm not home much of the time."

He'd heard a few whispers about Dr. Grace Mann, and the nickname "Bulldog" had been bandied about. His eye landed on the restaurant menu—she'd brought him to a pub called *The Bulldog*. Perfect.

She was the daughter of famed shark researcher Eddie Mann and had apparently inherited his single-minded focus when it came to the creatures of her work. Alec was beginning to appreciate the uphill battle before him in trying to gain the biologist's approval.

"Weren't you just in South Africa?"

She was keeping tabs on him. He suppressed a grin by taking a swallow of beer. Maybe she was more interested than she let on. About the job, of course. If he wanted to get laid, the boss lady was the worst possible choice.

"Yes. I was filming at Seal Island. We got the usual footage of great whites breaching for seals, but I was working with two scientists who wanted to monitor the pinniped population as well."

"How did that go?"

"Good. It was a pretty intense shoot with the whites always on the hunt. We only did cage diving."

Grace took another sip of wine and pursed her lips together. "You're referring, of course, to my photo."

Alec laughed as he set his glass down, trying to shake off the nerves that were drumming a tune in his chest. He was like a boy meeting his favorite leading lady. "It's a hell of a shot. Mind sharing how you got it?"

Earlier this year, a photo had gone viral on social media outlets along with several news sources of Grace freediving with a great white shark. Alec had been both envious of the photographer and stunned by the image. Grace had been holding onto the shark's dorsal fin, the massive fish dwarfing her petite frame, triggering a deep-rooted survival instinct in Alec. His reaction still rang in his ears: *Holy fuck, this woman is nuts.*

Grace's shoulders became less rigid, and if the beaming look on her face was any indication, a link in her armor had dissolved. "In January, I went to Oahu to visit some friends. We went diving off the North Shore to see Galapagos and sandbar sharks, and maybe a few tigers, but it got even better when a lone male white showed up. Of course, as soon as he appeared, all the other sharks fled, but he wasn't aggressive, just curious." A smile flitted across her face. "It took a while, but he eventually let me get close. My friend Sam had his camera along, and he shot incredible footage of the interaction. And the rest, as they say, is history."

"You certainly gained a bit of fame."

She shook her head, releasing a combination grunt and sigh. "It wasn't my goal. There was certainly some backlash from those who thought I was nuts."

Alec flinched, thinking of his own reaction.

"People condemned me for being reckless," she continued. "But if you'd been in the water with him, it was anything but. Have you ever been to Guadalupe Island?"

The abrupt change in the conversation jerked his attention back to the present. "No."

"There are a lot of sharks there."

"I guessed as much," he said cautiously, wondering if he was walking into a trap, unable to tell if she was being humorous or not.

But her tone made him think she was speaking not only of the fish but *him* as well. He racked his brain. Had he slept with her in a drunken stupor and completely forgotten? Maybe back in his college days something like that could have happened but not lately. He was nearly thirty and liked to think he'd matured since those days of occasional recklessness.

Besides, if he'd been with a woman like Grace Mann, he never would have forgotten it.

Did I hook up with one of her friends?

Shit, he hoped not. He had to believe that he hadn't scorned the wrong woman at some point in his past. Despite his enjoyment of the opposite sex, however, he was no player, so the odds were in his favor.

"Can I ask you something, Grace?"

She squinted at him, clearly annoyed he'd used her first name.

He didn't wait for an answer. "How hard have you worked to get where you are?"

She arched an eyebrow and pinned him with those blue eyes. "And your point is?"

"I can help you. I'm good at what I do."

"Why, exactly, are you so determined to be on this expedition?"

Accusation simmered in her voice. He really couldn't tell her the truth—that he was a Grace Mann fanboy; that while her work was exemplary, it was her persona that had snagged his attention, whether through a paper she co-authored or a post on her social media accounts. The picture of her with a great white shark may have flooded him with bone-deep terror, but it also had intrigued the hell out of him. She was in a category of daredevil reserved for a very few. Grace didn't just appreciate the creatures she studied; she blended herself with them. He had a hell of a lot of respect for that. He had a lot of respect for *her*.

But, damn. He hadn't expected her to be so wary of his company, so absolutely closed-off to him. He was an easygoing guy, and it pricked his pride that she hadn't succumbed to at least a sliver of his charm.

"I respect your work," he said, opting for a partial truth, "and I've known Stewart for a long time. He cares about you and your research. I'd like to be a part of that."

She took another drink of her Malbec. "All right. I'll think about it." She reached for her purse, retrieved her wallet, and dropped a twenty-dollar bill beside her half-finished glass of wine. "I really need to be going."

He stood as she did.

She waved him back to his seat. "No, stay. Finish your beer. My treat." She shook his hand. "I'm guessing I'll see you tomorrow at the fundraiser."

He nodded, and she walked away before he could utter a response.

He settled back on the stool.

"Would you like another?" the bartender asked.

"No." He needed to keep a clear head.

Dr. Grace Mann was as sleek and sharp as the sharks she studied. If Alec expected to go head to head with her, nothing short of his A-game would do.

CHAPTER 2

G race exited the taxi and adjusted the navy sheath dress she wore, tugging at the lace sleeves that ended just above her elbows. She hung the strap of the small matching purse on her shoulder and fingered the simple stud earring on her right ear. Her hair was pulled back into her usual bun, although she'd tried to make it look flowing and pretty. And she'd opted for a dark lipstick instead of her usual pale pink.

Brad would likely be here.

But it wasn't her ex who'd been on her mind earlier, as she'd gotten ready for the evening. Her thoughts had wandered instead to Alec Galloway.

A dark haze of gray hung in the sky, and a gust of ocean wind blasted against her. She turned her face away to avoid getting dust in her eyes and hurried toward the reception area of the Monterey Peninsula Country Club in Pebble Beach, taking short steps because of the heels she wore.

Once inside, she paused to check the state of her hair with multiple pats of her hand. *As if that ever fixed anything.* She was contemplating a trip to the lady's room when Missy Rembert approached.

Grace grinned at her friend, the knot in her stomach lessening, and admired Missy's outfit—a snug sequined bodice with a flared black skirt.

"Gracie, I love your makeup."

Grace brushed her fingers over the smooth silk of Missy's skirt, then gave it a playful tug. "Snazzy. And you did curls tonight. You look cute."

Missy's brown hair was swept away from her face and landed in soft waves on her shoulders. She emitted a low growl. "Cute wasn't what I was going for, but I guess I'll take it."

Grace pressed her lips together. "You know that these events are a terrible place to meet a guy. Most of them are already married."

"A girl can dream, can't she? I can't live with fish forever." Missy also worked in marine sciences, except she was based in San Francisco. "And why the dramatic makeup?"

"Just trying to change it up," Grace said.

"Please don't tell me it's for Bozo Brad's benefit."

Grace smiled. "No, but maybe for whatever bimbo he'll have on his arm tonight." That had been the case for previous work dinners, which was essentially what this was.

Grace scanned the crowd milling about.

"He's inside already," Missy said.

For a crazy moment, Grace thought Missy was referring to Alec Galloway, but she hadn't told her friend that the lanky filmmaker with California surf-boy good looks would be here this evening.

Missy means Brad, shark researcher and asshole ex-boyfriend.

Grace now understood why workplace relationships were frowned upon. She would be perfectly happy never to interact with the man again.

Missy didn't wait for Grace to respond. "I heard from Stewart that he hired Alec Galloway to film your doc, but I thought you'd said no to him."

Grace brought her attention back to Missy. "I did."

"You never did tell me why."

"He knows Brad." Or so Michaels had told her. Repeatedly.

Enlightenment dawned on Missy's face. "Got it. Birds of a feather flock together, right?"

"Something like that. I didn't feel like going on an expedition with Brad *and* a Brad clone." As soon as she said it, however, she knew she was wrong. Galloway wasn't like Brad. The first five minutes with him had told her that.

But striking Galloway off her list of potential filmmakers had seemed easier than hashing out whether he might be another jackass she would have to work with. This expedition was too important to muck it up with people who might have other agendas. It was bad enough dealing with Brad.

"He's inside as well, you know." Missy nodded toward the banquet room, visible through two open doors. "I wonder if he has a girlfriend."

"Why?"

"I'm single. He's hot."

"What if he's just like Brad?" Grace asked, irritation rising across her skin like an outbreak of hives. The hot flash of jealousy struck her like a wayward thunderbolt. What the hell? She barely knew Alec Galloway.

"Your mistake with Brad was that you tried for a relationship with him. He's only good for short-term hooking up."

Grace's mistake had gone deeper than desiring a commitment from her ex. Brad was worse than a bad boyfriend; he was a professional snake. It still galled her that she was forced to work with him, but if she played her cards right, this expedition would change that.

"So you're looking for a quickie with Galloway?" Grace's voice squeaked, annoying her.

Missy shrugged. "I've been having a dry spell lately."

Grace took in her friend's appearance and, for one brief wild moment, wondered if Galloway would find Missy attractive. Where Grace was slender and athletic, Missy was shorter and more rounded. They were both strong—their work in the water demanded a level of fitness—but Missy was a bit more fun-loving, and in Grace's eyes, that made her appear more feminine. They'd met several years ago in the Bahamas while interns at the Shark Lab in Bimini, and Missy had been more of a partier than Grace.

Grace shook off the green-eyed monster. Why should she care if Missy had a fling with the rather compelling filmmaker? Missy was always supportive of Grace's romantic highs and lows; the least Grace could do was return the favor.

"I suppose a quickie would be just the ticket with Galloway," Grace said, forcing her voice into a neutral cadence. "He admitted to me that he's never home."

"You've talked to him?" Missy asked in surprise.

"Yes, last night. He came to my lecture."

Missy tucked a strand of curly hair that had drifted loose behind her ear and laughed. "I guess he heard of your reputation as The Bulldog and wanted to interview with you directly."

Grace glared at her and asked in exasperation, "Do people really say that about me?"

Missy made a face and shrugged. "Just a smidge, Gracie. You're rather obsessed about your little shark babies."

Grace exhaled in frustration. "I don't go on expeditions to make friends. Getting drunk and rubbing elbows seems like a waste of time. I've got a job to do. And I don't have time to entertain so many acquaintances. It's too much work."

"Hmm, thanks, I think."

"You know I don't include you."

Missy tugged on Grace's arm. "C'mon. Let's get inside and start mingling. I want you to introduce me to Galloway."

ALEC TOOK a drink of his beer as he considered the man opposite him. It had been almost ten years since he'd last seen Brad Michaels. It was Michaels who had phoned him a few months ago to catch up and present the opportunity of filming a documentary for the Institute. Dark-haired and more compact in stature, Brad had always been cocky, and that blustery demeanor was still in full-swing. Alec hadn't cared for it back in high school, especially when Brad's cowardice at Mavericks had left Alec banged up on the rocks, his surfboard broken in three pieces.

"Looks like you got the job," Brad said as he sipped a whiskey on the rocks.

"Looks that way." Stewart had informed him this morning that CMI had approved the contract with Galloway Films, but Alec feared that Dr. Mann still wasn't on board. And he wanted her to be.

Brad leaned forward. "It's going to be a fantastic expedition. The sonar array is going to be a game-changer in shark conservation. You'll be glad you're a part of it. And if Grace Mann gives you a hard time with shooting, just let me know. She's such a freaking perfectionist. Personally, I think she's one of those women always on their period."

Alec slid a sympathetic look to the very young woman trying hard to appear at ease at Michaels' side—the one he'd not even bothered to introduce. Apparently, Brad hadn't outgrown being a dick.

Alec extended his hand. "I'm Alec Galloway."

The doe-eyed girl with porcelain skin smiled in gratitude. "I'm Sidney."

"Is your dad still surfing?" Brad asked.

"When he can." Alec swung his gaze to the right and froze. Headed straight for them was Grace Mann, looking damned impressive in a form-fitting dress the color of the deep blue sea and a face that put him in mind of supermodels. He took another swallow of his drink to douse the impulse to stare at her curves.

"Big Jim Galloway," Brad said. "He was such a legend."

Alec reluctantly returned his focus to Michaels. "He still is." His old man wasn't in the grave yet. He felt the heat of Grace's presence as she came to a stop beside him.

"Why is your dad a legend?" she asked.

Alec gazed at Dr. Mann and, for a moment, let his admiration for her show. "He was one of the original big wave surfers."

Her cheeks flushed a pinker hue.

Pleased that she'd read his signal, he let a half-smile reach his lips, adding, "It's nice to see you again, Dr. Mann."

She gave a nod and cleared her throat, her elegant brows slightly furrowed as she shifted her attention to Brad and his date. Grace reached her hand to the girl. "I'm Grace Mann. It's nice to meet you."

"This is Sidney," Brad cut in, his tone brusque.

"Brad," Grace acknowledged, her voice devoid of inflection. She stepped to the side as another woman joined them. "This is Missy Rembert."

Missy leaned around to shake Alec's hand. "Mr. Galloway, it's always a pleasure to meet an underwater filmmaker. Didn't you work in the Cocos Islands a few years ago?"

"I did. I was part of a team doing a project for IMAX."

"I thought so. It was very nice." Missy turned to greet Sidney.

Grace turned to Alec. "I heard that you and Brad were surfing buddies."

"We were both on the competition circuit when we were kids," Alec replied, "and then we progressed to big wave surfing." He wanted to add that they weren't really buddies but let it go.

"Wow," Missy said. "That must be exciting. Any big wipeouts?"

"A few," Alec conceded.

Brad finished his drink and waved the bartender over. "What were you and your brother called?" He snapped his fingers. "T and A, that was it."

Sidney giggled.

Missy raised an eyebrow. "How risqué."

Alec chuckled. "Not really. My brother's name is Tyler. It was just shorthand for Ty and Alec. I seem to recall your nickname was Frog," he said to Brad.

Brad took hold of a new drink. "Yeah, yeah. That was bullshit."

"Let me guess," Grace said. "You rode the waves like a frog."

Alec leaned toward her. "That's about right. When we were kids he'd do this weird thing with his legs bowed out."

Everyone laughed while Brad cursed under his breath, the ice in his glass clinking as he took a large swallow.

"Can I get you ladies a drink?" Alec asked.

"I'll have a Miami Vice," Missy replied with a bright smile.

When Grace didn't answer, Alec looked at her and asked, "A Malbec?"

A smirk of laughter escaped Brad. "Galloway's got you figured out already, Grace."

Brad's proprietary tone made Alec want to step between the man and Grace.

"I'll have a shot of tequila," Grace said, the statement clearly meant to defy Brad.

Michaels was a burr under Grace's skin, and Alec wondered why. He caught the bartender's attention and ordered the drinks.

"What do you do, Sidney?" Missy asked.

"I'm an exotic dancer."

For a moment, everyone was silent.

Finally, Missy blurted, "I've never actually met a woman who does that. You must be in fantastic shape."

"Yes, I work pretty hard at working out. Do you both research sharks like Brad?"

Grace nodded.

Missy shook her head. "I study cephalopods." At the girl's clearly confused expression, Missy added, "Octopus."

Sidney's head bobbed up and down, and her mouth formed an O-shape. "Do you have one of those doctor titles too?" she asked Missy.

"Yes."

"Octopus are kind of creepy, huh?"

"Actually, they're quite intelligent." Missy softened her answer with a smile.

Brad set his glass onto the bar and unbuttoned his suit jacket. "Gracie's not really a shark researcher."

Alec narrowed his eyes as Sidney gifted Grace with an inquisitive look. If the suddenly chilly atmosphere and the tension coming off Grace were any indication, Alec half-expected her to punch Michaels in the stomach.

"If we're going solely off academics," Grace replied, her voice as edgy as a razor blade, "then Brad's right. I only have an undergraduate degree in Marine Biology. My doctorate is in Computer Science."

Her announcement surprised Alec. "How did your dad feel about that?" If he remembered correctly, Eddie Mann had passed away several years ago.

Grace's rigid stance lessened a bit when she answered him. "He died before I finished high school, but I think he would've been proud. He was a closet programmer and got me hooked young. I was taking college-level programming classes when I was in the 12th grade." Her eyes shifted back to Michaels. "I wonder how well your array would work without me, Brad."

"It's just programming. There's a dozen people who could do your job."

Alec was certain he heard Missy mutter *dickhead* under her breath.

"Then give it a go," Grace challenged.

Brad grimaced. "Just don't screw it up, Gracie."

"I could say the same to you."

The discord between Grace and Brad was palpable. It appeared filming the sharks would be the easiest part of this project.

With the discomfort level peaking, it was, oddly enough, Sidney who sought to defuse it. "Brad says he'll take me diving to see a shark up close soon. I'm so nervous. What if it bites me?"

"It's always the shark you don't see that does," Grace murmured.

Concern pinched Sidney's face.

"It's very safe," Brad said. "Right, Alec? You've been in the water with all types of sharks when you're filming."

"Grace is right," Alec said to the girl. "Be aware of your surroundings at all times. If a shark bites, it's because he's curious. Sharks are ambush predators, so if you see one coming, you can easily avoid them. If you make eye contact, most sharks will divert." Elliott Marsh flashed in his mind, and he took a steadying breath to put the memory back in the basement.

The bartender set the drinks that Alec had ordered on the counter. As Alec handed Missy her colorful red-and-white concoction, she smiled and angled toward him, despite Grace being positioned between them. She thanked him as both of her hands closed over his to take the glass. The flirty behavior wasn't lost on him, but she was clearly a friend of Grace's. He wasn't about to enter that arena, not when his job with Grace was still possibly hanging in the balance.

He stepped back and motioned for Grace to take his place at the bar so that she could have access to the tequila shot as well as the lime and the salt. Spurred by an urge to protect her from Brad, he indulged a brief touch at the base of her back, noticing the edge of a scar on her neck that peeked out of the fabric of her dress.

He didn't linger, and she didn't pull away as she made fast work of the tequila. Alec reached in front of her to grab his beer on the far right, close enough to enjoy her scent—a subtle, flowery aroma that made him think of sunny days, blue seas, and gentle swells.

Apparently, he *was* in the mood to flirt, and the woman on his radar wasn't friendly Missy, but instead a prickly blonde.

"All ready to head to Guadalupe?" Grace asked.

"Of course," Brad quipped.

"Where's that?" Sidney asked, an earnest expression on her face.

A knowing glint in the girl's eye, however, made Alec realize the young woman was purposely taking hold of the conversation.

Michaels was in over his head and didn't even realize it.

"Guadalupe Island is off the coast of Baja California," Grace replied. "Starting in October, a large great white population migrates to feed on the seal colony that resides there. It's also thought that the sharks mate and that many of the females give birth, although most scientists suspect they swim into the Sea of Cortez for that. Neither activity has ever been witnessed, let alone recorded, so we keep returning in the hopes of learning more. There're also several outfitters who take tourists to the area."

"That sounds extraordinary."

Grace shifted her attention across the room. "I really should speak with Stewart. If you'll all excuse me." She stepped out of the circle and left them. Alec debated whether to follow, since she'd likely be discussing his position on the expedition, and whether she would let him stay.

"Let's go eat," Sidney said, tugging on Brad's arm and thankfully he relented. The buffet on the far side of the room appeared open for business.

"Let's catch up more later," Brad said to Alec.

Alec gave a nod but hoped to avoid it. Now it was just him and Dr. Rembert.

"How long are you in town?" Missy asked.

"Just until tomorrow."

"Too bad."

Alec didn't take the bait. "What's the problem between Grace and Michaels?"

Missy gave a slight roll of her eyes. "Oh, that. Sorry it slid out of control. Usually Grace is able to keep her claws retracted."

"Is there something I should know?"

"Well, they *are* at odds professionally, but I guess the real problem is that they used to date."

Alec wasn't too surprised by the news, but it still chafed. "I'm guessing he moved on, and Grace hasn't?" Damn. He didn't like his conclusion. "Did he dump her for that toddler with him tonight?"

Missy laughed. "Brad's got a different girl for every event, and they keep getting younger and younger; although an exotic dancer is a new one." She took a sip of her drink. "But I don't think Grace is still hung up on him. She's the one who broke it off. I have to admit I never understood what she saw in him in the first place."

Hope sprang back to life. "Why do you think she's against me filming her? Does it have something to do with Brad?"

Missy wrinkled her nose. "I plead the fifth. But I'll be on the expedition, so maybe I can put in a good word for you."

Alec set his empty glass on the bar. "I appreciate the help, but I've a feeling Grace makes up her own mind."

CHAPTER 3

G race made every effort to hide her annoyance.

"I've already offered Alec the job," Stewart said, his eyes level with hers and unflinching. Stewart Smith's love of the ocean was vast, almost child-like in its enthusiasm, but he hadn't earned his position at CMI without a backbone of steel.

A frown crept onto Grace's face. "I thought you said I could have final approval."

Stewart tempered his gaze, the wrinkles around his eyes relaxing. He was seventy-five, but he appeared as young and fit as a fifty-year-old. "I did," he replied, "but your second and third choices are no longer available, and truthfully, he's far and above the best there is. You sound almost suspicious of him. Is there something you haven't told me?"

Despite feeling the effects of the tequila shot, a voice of reason cautioned her to remain silent. If she stated her reason—that Alec knew Brad, and Brad had proven to be a heartless backstabber, and by association she'd developed an immediate distrust of Galloway —she would sound like a woman scorned. The last thing she wanted was to appear unprofessional to her colleague and mentor. Besides, Stewart had agreed to keep her recent employment contract negotiation with the CMI board confidential, even allowing her the added insurance of an attorney present. He'd already jumped through hoops for her.

Pick your battles, Gracie, her father would say. *Always keep your eye on the buoy in the distance and not the hell-fight in your own backyard.*

"No." She took a settling breath. "I had no idea you thought so highly of him."

"I do. I've known his family for a long time. His uncle, Simon Galloway, is a philanthropic powerhouse, and I won't lie—I'm hoping for a bit of funding to be thrown our way. Alec's parents, Jim and Lily, are good people, and their children are as well. Alec's younger brother, Tyler, is a promising mountaineer and writer, and his sister, Brynn, is an archaeologist. I think Alec will do a great job for us." Stewart paused and cleared his throat, amusement in his gaze. "Maybe you're worried that you'll fall in love with him."

She laughed to deflect his ridiculous statement. Never mind that Alec Galloway was proving to be a fascinating package. But fascinating had led to misjudgment before, and Grace liked to think she was smarter these days.

She'd fallen for Brad in the beginning, and what a stupid mistake that had been. She had no intention of a repeat, especially not now, when she was so close to getting the sonar array off the ground.

Even a man as attractive as Alec Galloway couldn't compete with her work.

"You know me better than that," she said. "And I'm sure he has a sweetheart, or two or three, somewhere."

He sighed. "I do know you. And he's single. Perhaps a little fling is just the ticket."

"Why would you say that?" Her face heated. Had she leaned too much on Stewart this past year, as a daughter might a father? It had been eight years since losing her dad, but there were still days where it felt as raw and painful as if it had just happened. She couldn't deny that she'd grown attached to Stewart and his wife, Helen.

"You work too much. You seem so stressed much of the time."

"I like to work. It's important to me." *It was important to Dad.*

He nodded. "I know, but you're a beautiful woman who is spending her life alone."

She and Brad had broken up before either of them had come to work at CMI, and thankfully, Brad had been as determined as she to keep their past dead and buried.

Stewart knew of her professional issues with Brad, but did he know the rest? He'd never said anything directly to her, even if idle gossip had reached his ear. But if he knew, then why on earth was he suggesting she take up with Galloway? Was Stewart trying to sabotage her career?

She shook off that thought. "And you think a man who travels the world, who has no roots, is the answer to me being so uptight?"

Stewart chuckled. "It's just a suggestion. I should add that Alec lobbied very hard for this job."

"Did you tell him what I plan to do?"

"No. We've only discussed the sonar array in broad strokes. I thought I'd leave the details to you. I think he admires you, Grace. He's a man very connected to his work—much like you. I think you have a lot in common."

She'd thought the very same thing about Brad. And look how that had turned out.

Alec Galloway. A flutter passed through her belly, bringing her dormant hormones to life. For God's sake, she didn't need sex. She needed a kick-ass filmmaker who wouldn't make any waves.

Her accelerated heartrate and general giddiness every time Galloway looked at her would need to stay firmly in the backseat.

"I may be old, but Helen is my life," Stewart added.

Grace willed her stiff shoulders and tight posture to relax. Alec Galloway would be her filmmaker. Time to accept it and move on. One thing sharks had taught her—don't waste unnecessary energy. And be a grown-up. Well, fish hadn't taught her that, but it was her new mantra. She was twenty-six. No whining, no complaining. Time to be an adult and jump in and get the work done. One never knew how much time was left. Watching her father die from cancer had taught her that.

"I don't know why she puts up with you," Grace teased, but she did know. Helen loved Stewart with a passion that hadn't waned in over fifty years. Much the way Grace's mom had loved her dad, difficult as he'd made their life together. Maybe there was hope for Grace yet.

She glanced over her shoulder to where Galloway was still chatting with Missy. Just the two of them.

Oh crumb.

Grace didn't like it.

GRACE SET her plate of hors d'oeuvres and a glass of red wine on the small round table and then took a seat beside Missy, two chairs still open.

"Did you score a date with Galloway?" Grace asked, trying to keep her tone light.

Missy popped a cucumber canapé into her mouth and raised an eyebrow. "I didn't get anywhere, and there's a very good reason why."

"What's that?" Grace took a *prosciutto crostino* in hand and eyed it, Missy's response filling her with relief.

"You," Missy said around her food. "Once he and I were alone, all he did was talk about *you*."

Grace's stomach took a nervous tumble. "Why?" She set her food back onto her plate, her appetite gone.

"Well, I think he's trying to figure out why you don't want to hire him, but he also wanted to know what was going on between you and Brad."

She probably shouldn't have allowed Brad to get her hackles up, but better for Galloway to know that if he were Camp Brad, then he was definitely not welcome in her world any way other than professionally. She chided herself for *thinking* about Galloway romanti-

25

cally. The expedition hadn't even started, and already there was too much interpersonal conflict.

Grace shook her head. "My mom was right."

"About what?"

"I'm too stubborn." Determined to stop worrying about how the chess pieces were lining up, she nudged Missy's shoulder. "I'm sorry he didn't offer you roses and mimosas and the best sex of your life."

"May I?" a deep, male voice asked.

Grace jumped, flooded with embarrassment, as Alec stood over her. Had he overheard what she'd just said?

With a response clogging her throat, she nodded and waved at one of the empty seats. He pulled the chair out and sat, his presence looming large. From the corner of her eye, she had to admit he cleaned up nicely. While he hadn't looked shabby during their brief talk the day before, tonight he cut a striking figure in an upscale dark-gray suit, blue shirt, and a darker blue tie, reminding her of a European businessman. She'd always had a weakness for a man in a suit.

Alec looked at her. "What's it like to be the daughter of Eddie Mann?"

Missy released a playful laugh. "It means all her friends growing up were sharks. Is it any wonder she still hangs out with them?"

Grace nursed her wine glass. "I'll admit it wasn't a traditional upbringing, but I'm not that weird, am I?"

"Hah." Missy grinned.

"I've overheard you talking to your octopus subjects," replied Grace.

"Then that makes me just as nerdy as you. They are exceedingly more interesting than most of the men I've dated."

Grace dipped a petite carrot into a pile of ranch dressing and started crunching away.

"So, your dad was based in the Bay area," Alec said. "Where-abouts did you live?"

"Orinda."

"I know it. I grew up around San Mateo. My dad's a software engineer in Silicon Valley. I'm sure the two of you would hit it off. My mom's eyes glaze over when he starts talking about computers."

"I thought he was a big surfing legend," Grace countered.

He popped a square piece of cheese into his mouth. "He's that, too. Taught me everything he knows."

"Do you still surf?" Missy asked.

"When I can."

"And what does your mom do?" Grace asked.

"In her youth, she was a formidable mountain climber, but then she met my dad and gave it all up. Mostly. These days, she does a little travel writing, painting, and some photography. My brother, Ty, takes after her."

Grace pushed the food around on her small plate. "Did you get into filmmaking because of her?"

"Not really," Alec said. "I started in high school with some of my surfing buddies."

"Like Brad?" she asked.

Alec settled back in his chair and stretched his legs out. "Yeah. Listen. I don't know what Brad's been saying, but he and I were never that chummy. It's been years since I've seen him." He cleared his throat. "In case that makes a difference with me taking the doc job."

Missy released a sing-song whistle, and Grace threw her an annoyed look, then turned back to Alec. "Thanks for the clarification."

"And furthermore," he continued, "I've never minded girls who talk to fish."

"Then you'll love Gracie's sister, Chloe."

"Does she study sharks, too?"

Grace popped another carrot in her mouth. "No. Cetaceans."

Missy sighed. "She's picked a godawful subject for her dissertation. She's trying to crack the language of the sperm whale."

Skeptical surprise marched across Galloway's features. "For real?"

Grace nodded. "My little sister is even more of a bulldog than I am."

"Must run in the family."

The praise in Alec's voice crept beneath Grace's armor and zapped her heart, and she found herself basking under his masculine attention. For a moment, all she could do was stare. Then she mentally shook herself and broke the spell.

Did I just swoon? What a freaking distraction he'll be on expedition.

"I wonder what they say," Alec said. "'Let's eat the big squid first, then the little ones'?"

Grace uncrossed her ankles, dislodging one of her heels in the process. "I imagine it's something like that. Scientists have been intrigued by the language of dolphins and orcas for a long time. I admire Chloe's dedication. If she can do it, it could have far-reaching consequences."

"Such as?"

She angled her right foot to retrieve the wayward shoe. "Well, at the very least it will allow humans to better protect the creatures of the ocean. And what about intelligent life elsewhere?"

"Now you're talking about outer space."

"If we can talk to whales, it might help when the aliens arrive one day."

Alec pinned his gaze on her.

Missy pushed away her now-empty plate and leaned her elbows on the table. "I'm shocked she showed this side of her so soon in your relationship, but yes, Grace believes in aliens."

"Quit acting like it's so farfetched," Grace defended. She peeked under the table, exasperated that she'd somehow lost the shoe.

"But you're a scientist, Gracie," Missy said. "You're supposed to be ruled only by *science*."

Success. Grace slipped her toes into the footwear then returned her focus back to the table.

Alec gifted her with a twinkle in his eyes. "For what it's worth, I don't think we're alone in the universe either."

"Oh, God," Missy moaned. "I'm not sure I can sit here and listen to this." She turned to Grace. "Let me know if you want a ride home." Missy stood and merged into a crowd of people near the bar.

"Don't you have your car?" Alec asked.

"I usually take a taxi to events like this, in case I drink too much."

Alec eyed her with a look of disbelief. "Do you ever drink too much?"

He made it sound like she was incapable of having a good time. He was probably right, but she was loath to admit it. "Sometimes," she hedged.

"Let me drive you home. In fact, if you're up for it, we can leave immediately."

And now the handsome filmmaker was making a pass at her. Wasn't he? Grace's brows pushed together as indecision battled in her head. Should she accept?

It had been two hours, and she'd made the rounds in the room, dutifully chatting with potential donors and sponsors. She was weary of socializing.

"You don't mind driving me?" she asked.

"I'd be happy to, Grace."

As if she suddenly stood outside herself, she observed as stupidity took over the higher functions of her brain. "Okay, thanks."

Alec stood and pulled her chair out as Grace rose as well, wobbling a bit on her heels. He probably already thought she was tipsy. She should tell him that it was simply that she wasn't comfortable in fancy shoes, and she had dressed up more than usual this evening. And maybe it had been for him.

I certainly can't admit to that.

She led him from the banquet room and then tried to keep up with his long stride as they walked side by side through the reception area.

Leaving with Galloway was no doubt a bad idea, but they were both consenting adults. She didn't need anyone's permission. And

29

she ought to get to know him better. For professional reasons, of course.

She spied Stewart across the room and gave a modest wave in his direction. When he smiled, she shook her head in mock chagrin. She wasn't planning to invite Galloway into her house in Pacific Grove or into her bed. They would soon be in close proximity on the boat at Guadalupe Island, and it would be awkward and distracting to attempt hooking up during that time. The rocky island was remote and had few permanent residents, and there were no hotels to be had if anything went south.

As she and Alec exited through a rotating glass door, the chilly evening air greeted them, and Grace rubbed her arms.

Alec removed his jacket and set it onto her shoulders.

"Thanks," she said, feeling a bit bashful as the heat from his body transferred from the coat to her. The subtle scent of Galloway's aftershave engulfed her, an enticing mix of soothing pine alongside the spicy and nutty aroma of cardamom and cloves, and she inhaled like a puppy who'd just discovered the wonders of bacon.

Damn, he smells nice.

She silently chastised her traitorous self.

They came to a stop in front of a truck.

"What happened to your car?"

"It was a rental. A friend in town loaned me this."

He unlocked it and opened the passenger door. The cab was higher than normal, and with the tight dress Grace wore, along with the heels, she found it impossible to climb in. Without warning, Galloway scooped her into his arms and set her on the seat.

"You seemed to be struggling," he said, then stepped back and shut the door.

Grace sought to compose herself as his touch left a lingering, heated imprint. He rounded the vehicle and took the driver's seat.

"Listen, it's still early. You wanna go somewhere?"

He made it sound as if he planned to go park and make out with her. "Like where?" she asked cautiously.

"I know a barbecue joint near Cannery Row. A friend of mine

owns it. I could buy you a beer, and we can talk about the expedition."

She should say no. This was beginning to feel too much like a date, and no good could come of it. But before she could decline, her inner stupid-brain spoke up.

"Sure, why not?"

CHAPTER 4

Alec navigated the truck along the windy road from Pebble Beach, watching the woman beside him from the corner of his eye. Grace's hair was starting to fall from where it was secured, and her expression had relaxed. Alec liked her in this unguarded state, and he'd enjoyed the feel of her in his arms when he'd swooped her up and deposited her into the truck cab.

They spoke little. Something about that physical contact seemed to linger in the air; Alec could feel the tense awareness emanating from Grace.

Or maybe it was just him.

He managed to squeeze the truck into a parking space a block from the barbecue joint. He was lucky—spots were hard to find since Cannery Row was only a few streets down, always bustling with an ever-present throng of tourists.

He dashed around to the passenger side, but Grace had slid from the truck before he arrived, her heels striking the road before he could touch her again. She'd returned his jacket, but rather than put it back on, he draped it over his shoulder as he followed her inside.

"Alec!" John Peters greeted him, still sporting the same bushy beard and hearty smile that he'd worn when he'd run boat charters out of Monterey Bay several years ago.

"John, it's good to see you." He shook his friend's hand.

"I didn't know you were in town. Where's Ty? You both still owe me a photoshoot for that last charter I took you on."

"I remember," Alec replied. "You looking for a portrait of yourself?"

"Hell, no. I want Ty to write up my restaurant in one of his magazines." He wiggled his brows and gestured to the bustling, one-room eating and drinking establishment. "I can always use more business."

Alec smiled. "I'll let him know." He brought a hand to Grace's lower back to include her in the conversation. "I'd like you to meet Grace Mann. Grace, this is the owner, John Peters. He and I go way back."

John stepped close and grasped her hand, beaming like a school boy playing hooky. "I know you. You're Dr. Grace Mann, aren't you?"

She glanced at Alec, bewilderment in her gaze. "Yes," she replied, her answer almost a question.

Grinning, he pointed over her shoulder. On the wall hung an 8x10 photo in a simple black frame of Grace's famous dive with the male great white shark. She wore overly-long flippers and a black wetsuit that hinted at the contours of her breasts and hips, and a weight belt hugged her narrow waist. Blonde hair framed her diving mask like a halo. Other than that, there was no equipment, not even a snorkel.

Floating parallel above the shark, her hand was a tiny speck as she clasped the dark gray dorsal fin, hitching a ride on one of the most feared and dangerous predators on earth.

All over again, Alec felt the audacity of the act, the ballsy nerve of Grace to even attempt it. He couldn't deny there was an elegance to the shot, but once his eyes dropped to the great white, viewing the creature in all its wicked glory—dark eyes, rows and rows of serrated teeth, the powerful body and caudal fin that could turn the shark on a dime—the temperature of his blood dropped several degrees.

The shark was twice as long as Grace. If it had decided to investigate the wisp of a woman clinging to it like a tiny sucker fish, she wouldn't have stood a chance.

She certainly wouldn't be standing beside him right now.

"It's a real pleasure to meet you," John said. "You must have nerves of steel."

Grace laughed. "He was never threatening, just curious. In fact, he was actually kind of shy."

John slid his gaze to Alec. "My God. You've found the perfect woman."

"Yeah, yeah. You got a table we can use?" He didn't feel like setting John straight about Grace since his friend looked about ready to hit on the pretty Dr. Mann himself. Time to get Grace alone.

John bellowed with laughter. "I've got something quiet and romantic. Follow me."

He led them across the room to a corner spot. Once Grace was settled in a chair, John leaned toward her. "Will you autograph my photo before you leave?"

Looking a bit perplexed by her celebrity, she said, "Sure."

"Hot damn. I got to meet the Shark Lady." He gripped Alec's shoulder. "It's always good to see you, buddy. Tell Ty to get his ass down here."

"Will do," Alec said.

John waved a waitress over. "This table is on the house," he told her. He left before Alec could thank him.

The perky young woman with a bobbing brown ponytail smiled. "Can I get you both something to drink?"

Alec looked at Grace.

"I'll have whatever you're having," she said.

Alec ordered two beers, then shifted his attention to his new boss. "Tonight, it's my treat."

She nodded, a wary countenance overtaking her composure. "Considering it's on your friend, John, I'm not sure how to take that."

He laughed.

If it's easy, it's not worth it. His mom's words echoed back to him. Usually she was lecturing him about work and life in general, but he supposed the advice applied equally well to women.

"You and Brad used to be a couple," he said, unable to stop himself. His mom had also cautioned him on his impulsiveness.

Right on cue, Grace appeared to grow cactus needles right from her skin.

She narrowed her eyes. "Ancient history. I'm sure you've got a few relationships you could've done without."

True. "I'm not forced to keep working with them, though."

The waitress appeared and set the tall glasses of amber liquid on the table. "Would you like to order any food?"

"No, I'm good," Grace said.

"Me, too," Alec said.

Grace took a big drink. "I'm sure you already know, but you've got the job."

"Don't look so excited."

She took another swallow of the brew. "Sorry if I appeared rude before. I didn't realize how much Stewart liked you."

He raised an eyebrow. "And that makes a difference?"

She released a partial laugh, strangled and reluctant. "Yeah, it does."

"Have you ever been filmed before?"

"For a full-blown feature?" She lifted her glass to her mouth again and downed a big gulp. Either she was very thirsty or nervous. If it was the latter—and he hoped it was—then maybe she wasn't immune to him after all.

All the bullshit about workplace romances circled inside his head for a brief, annoying moment. If she gave him a chance, would it be worth the risk of screwing up their professional relationship? Would he have the strength to say no to a woman like her?

"No." She answered her own question.

Shaking off his randy thoughts, he said, "I'll want to film just about everything you do, and we'll likely need to set up shots as well. And I'll do direct interviews as we go."

"Just like *The Bachelorette*."

"I do want you to speak openly about your feelings for every shark," he teased.

"I don't know. It's usually better not to show all your cards at once."

Alec loosened his tie. "But then you might lose that one special fish." He unbuttoned his left cuff link and rolled the sleeve to his forearm.

"There're plenty more where he came from."

He repeated the action on his right arm. "The best ones are always endangered."

He enjoyed the sparkle in her eye as she gave a slight smirk and a blush crept up her face.

She definitely wasn't immune to him. He couldn't keep the shit-eating grin from his face.

"Don't get too happy, Galloway." She leaned back in her seat and crossed her arms. "Stewart said he hasn't told you everything about the expedition."

"And?"

She paused, pressing her lips together. "I'm planning to do something I've never done before at Guadalupe. I'm going to free-dive with the whites. I know you have a lot of experience filming sharks, but this will be different. You'll likely have to leave the cage. I need to know that you're up for it."

Alec watched her. The dark burgundy lipstick was long gone, and she hadn't bothered to replace it. He preferred women without a lot of fluff, but when Grace cleaned up, she was nothing short of stunning. But what really grabbed him, especially now, was the gleam in her eyes as she spoke about her work.

"My partners and I can use rebreathers." The lack of bubbles and noise from a rebreather was exactly why Alec used one for long dives, but they were riskier than normal scuba equipment, so he didn't operate one unless needed. "And I've been outside the cage before. How many times have you freedived with whites?"

Grace cleared her throat and licked her lips. "Including my famous photo? Once."

Alec moved forward so Grace could hear him over the din from the crowded restaurant. "Then why do it? Do you think you need a wow-factor for the doc? This isn't a reality show."

She flashed him a frosty glare. "I agree." The prickles were back. "I'd like to meet the sharks on their own terms. No chumming, no noisy cages, no scuba bubbles. It will be a chance to observe a more natural behavior. I'm prepared for the risk."

Anxiety tightened Alec's gut.

"What's wrong?" she asked. "Did I find your deal-breaker?"

He gave a slight shake of his head and scrubbed a hand down his face, shying from the memory of that fateful expedition one year ago. "Where'd you get that scar on your neck?"

She raised both eyebrows, her blue eyes darkening. "A shark bite. Surely, you've got a few war stories as well. Maybe even a bite from an ex-girlfriend." Her voice rang with amusement.

The tension in Alec's shoulders began to ease. He only allowed himself to revisit the death of Elliott in moments of deep despair; he was never inclined to spend much time facing the dark demons that, despite his best efforts, had taken up residence in his head these past twelve months.

"I've only had one ex who drew blood," he said. "How'd you get the bite?"

The waitress reappeared with two more tall beakers of beer. She also set a basket of wings on the table. "It's from John."

"Thank you," Grace said, a hungry glint in her gaze as she looked at the food.

The waitress grabbed the previous glasses, now empty, then left them alone once again. Grace unrolled her napkin and removed the silverware tucked inside, then pushed the edge of the white cloth into the neckline of her dress. She grabbed a wing, dipped it into the accompanying cup of ranch dressing, and ate like a ravenous teenage boy.

"Why didn't you say something?" Alec said.

"What do you mean?" Barbecue sauce smeared her upper lip.

"I'll buy you dinner if you're hungry."

"This isn't a date, Galloway."

No, it wasn't. "Got it," he said, annoyed by the sting of her comment.

Apparently with Dr. Mann it was two steps forward and one step back. He snatched a wing since she was already on her second one. At the rate she was going, he'd be lucky to get another.

"So?" he prompted, biting into the spicy meat. "The scar?"

"Right. It was a great white."

"But you said you only freedived that one time in the presence of a white."

She dropped a carcass of bones back into the basket and licked her fingers. "It happened when I was a kid. My dad spent several months each year stationed at the Farallon Islands researching the whites." She removed the napkin at her neck, wiped her mouth, then her hands. "Once Chloe and I were old enough, he'd bring us along for a week or two at a time." She laughed. "My mom hated it. She didn't think it was safe. My dad and I agreed never to tell her how bad it was when I got bit, but Chloe eventually spilled it. After that, Mom threatened to never let us go again, but Dad eventually wore her down."

Alec stared at her, slack-jawed. The Farallones—a collection of granite peaks jutting from the Pacific Ocean and known as the Devil's Teeth—were just a hop, skip, and a jump from San Francisco Bay. The water was undeniably cold year-round, not to mention murky, and the weather was hell most of the time. "You got in the water around the Farallones?" he uttered in stunned disbelief. "When you were a kid?"

She'd finally wiped most of the wing sauce from her appendages, although a faint smear still rested on her cheek. When she looked at him again, she paused, noticing his shock. "It wasn't on purpose. I was out with Dad on the small outboard he used to visit shark attacks on the seals when the love of his life bumped us. I was perched on the gunwale. It was entirely bad luck."

"No shit," he choked out.

"I fell in, and a big beautiful sister sideswiped me, ripping off my lifejacket like it was a piece of tissue. Her teeth grazed my neck enough to slice it open, but thankfully it wasn't a deep wound."

"A sister?"

"It's what the researchers call the large females, the twenty-footers. There's only ever been a handful of them documented over the years. They generally travel alone and always dominate the feeding grounds." Her eyes went glassy. "There's nothing like them anywhere on earth. They're a sight to behold."

"How old were you?"

"Twelve. Dad yanked me out before Bonnie came around for another pass."

Where had he heard that name before?

Recognition surfaced. "I think I know your shark."

"Really?" Excitement animated her face.

Overcome with an urge to touch her, Alec grabbed his napkin and wiped the sauce from her face. She immediately brushed her fingers across both cheeks, attempting to find anything else left behind.

"You're good," he muttered, reluctantly withdrawing his hand.

"Well?" she prompted, her complexion flush in a rosy glow.

But he knew it wasn't for him. If he'd learned anything about Grace Mann in the last day and a half, it was that it wasn't just her father who'd had a love affair with great whites—his daughter was head over heels as well.

"I dived the Farallones once, and only once, two years ago. Even now, it still makes my heart skip a beat and my palms sweat."

Her focus, filled with excited anticipation, tugged at him in a physically uncomfortable way—there was certainly no outlet for such a response.

"I was part of a team filming a guy named Bertie Nichols, who was one of the few divers with enough nerve to continue harvesting abalone near the islands. Over the years, most have abandoned the practice because there are so many white sharks in the area.

"The sharks were on us almost immediately. Nichols was used to it, but we had to keep a constant vigilance. It's one thing to watch out for one shark, but we had three big, aggressive females who weren't happy about our presence. It was a pain in the ass to get the footage. I was scared shitless the entire time, waiting for one of them to ambush us."

"And one did," Grace concluded.

"It was like being hit by a bus. At that point, survival instinct took over. There were three of us with Bertie, and we all flailed to the surface in a frantic bid for the boat."

"Did anyone get bit?"

"Thankfully, no. Those sharks didn't want to eat us. They were just pissed we were in their territory."

"Did you get the footage?"

"No one wanted to get back in the water. Except Nichols, of course. We discussed at great length how he might film himself with a selfie stick and a go-pro, but it just wasn't going to work."

Grace watched him with rapt attention. "So, you went back in."

"Somebody had to. I told Nichols to get in quick. We'd shoot some footage, then get the hell out. We slipped in the water as quiet as can be, and to our surprise, the three females that were harassing us had disappeared." He took a long swallow of his beer hoping it would slow down his surging heart rate. "Then a new shark showed up—a leviathan that triggered every nightmare scenario I could imagine." Alec exhaled a long breath. "She put the others to shame."

"Bonnie," Grace whispered.

Alec nodded. "Nichols told us her name later. He had contact with the researchers on the island from time to time, and they must've swapped stories about her. She wouldn't leave us be. She circled and circled—she had to be well over twenty feet. Maybe she was the top sister?"

Grace's lips curled into a smile at his question.

"I was shaking as I shot Nichols," Alec continued. "Bonnie showed up in some of the footage—a gigantic dark shadow lurking in the background. As we ascended, I never took my eyes off her. I know that most sharks, even whites, are generally curious and shy like you described your famous photo partner, but Bonnie was a big angry woman who couldn't be reasoned with. I still have dreams about her." He rubbed the back of his neck. "Dark dreams where I'm deep below the surface, with no light, and I know she's out there, watching, waiting to pounce when I least expect it." Exactly what had happened to Elliott.

"You say this was two years ago?"

"Yeah, give or take a month."

"The last known sighting of her was six years ago. Dad always wanted to tag her, but she eluded him. Instead he had to rely on visual sightings. She has a rather unusual jagged scar that runs along her left side, as if a drunk toddler took a white marker and tried to draw a very bad straight line."

"I can't verify that, since I was more interested in her mouth and those razor-blade teeth, but I can dig up my footage, and you can have a look, if you like."

Grace beamed. "I'd like. Can you do this soon?"

"I'll burn you a CD and put it in the mail as soon as I get back to San Francisco."

"Thanks." Grace took a sip of her second beer. "I feared she might have died, maybe even been killed, but this means she could still be alive." A wistful yearning overtook Grace's features.

"It was two years ago, Grace."

"I know, but the females generally skip a year migrating to the Farallones or Guadalupe Island. We believe it's to give birth. Maybe she'll turn up this year. Does Bertie Nichols still dive?"

"As far as I know," Alec said. "I have no idea why. His wife certainly doesn't like it. He goes out alone, but I think the researchers on the island keep an eye on him, just in case. I can't help but think that one day his luck will run out."

"Maybe."

"I take it you have a theory on this."

"I do. I know that sharks are wild, dangerous, and at times, highly unpredictable; but I also believe that a type of communication can occur between individual sharks, and also between sharks and humans. An unspoken communication."

"Ocean whispering?" he countered.

"Well, yes, for lack of a better term. When you're in the water, don't you just *know* things about the creatures you encounter?"

"I get where you're going with this. Some people are better at it than others."

"People like Bertie Nichols."

"And you?"

She raised her shoulders in the barest hint of a shrug. "I'm not so full of myself to think I'm completely in sync with an animal, but I try. Why else are we here?"

Alec raised an eyebrow. "You mean on earth?"

"Yes, that, but also why do we study them, why do we try so hard to understand them?"

"To preserve nature. Humans have proven quite adept at wide-scale annihilation of certain species."

"Yes, some humans. But not all. I think I study sharks because I'm always seeking a communion of sorts with them. And what if they want the same?"

"What're you talking about?"

"What if, despite Bonnie's sometimes grumpy disposition, she's developed a connection with Nichols, maybe even a little bit of tolerance for his presence. Perhaps a grudging respect even."

"That still doesn't mean that Bonnie's reptilian brain won't override her good manners one day. She'll take a bite out of Nichols, go her merry way, and never think twice about it. It's survival, Grace."

"You think I'm anthropomorphizing."

From the tone of her voice, Alec suspected someone else had accused her of the same. "Is this an old argument with Brad?"

Surprise flashed in her eyes. "Maybe you have a little whisperer in you, too. Yes, Brad loves to cut down my theories on animal consciousness and intelligence. He likes it almost as much as talking about himself."

Alec didn't like being grouped with her ex-boyfriend, despite Michaels being an old surfing buddy. He also didn't like the idea that Grace would let her guard down, for even one second, while in the water with Jaws. "They aren't puppies, Grace. They could cut you in half in less than a second, and you'd never see it coming. Unfortunately, I've seen it face-to-face."

"Really?" She sobered. "I'm sorry. What happened?"

Alec immediately regretted his words. He wasn't ready to rehash the incident with Elliott. "Maybe I'll tell you sometime," he said, his voice tight.

She silently acknowledged his statement, compassion reflected in her eyes.

"Every day is a gift," she murmured.

"Did you read that on a magnet?" he teased, trying to lighten the mood.

"No. My dad would say it to Chloe and me. He truly believed it."

"Do you?"

"There are definitely days I could do without, but mostly, yes."

Her face glowed and delight crept into her eyes. Alec could imagine this was what she had looked like as a girl—determined, curious, a dreamer.

The waitress dropped off two more glasses of beer.

Grace shook her head. "I really can't drink another one, otherwise you might have to carry me home."

It had merit, but Alec didn't say it aloud. Grace was no one-night stand, and he didn't want her to be. He wished he didn't have to leave in the morning. He wouldn't be able to see her again until the expedition. Six weeks from now.

Damn.

A checklist of thoughts swirled in his head—he needed to clear his work schedule, he needed to begin planning the logistics of a lengthy and complicated shoot, he needed to beg his mom to watch his dog again—but one beamed louder than the rest: He hadn't expected to like Grace Mann so much.

CHAPTER 5

San Diego
October 1

Alec deposited the last of his gear—fifteen bags worth—onto the flat rectangular dolly near the shuttle van that had brought him, his assistant cameraman, Dan Donovan, and photographer, Stephanie Kim, from the airport to a dock at the Americas Cup Harbor in San Diego Bay. Thankfully, it had only been a ten-minute ride.

"What's the name of the boat?" Donovan asked, grunting as he pushed the luggage transport forward. The man had the look of a wrestler and the strength of a bull, but was apparently whipped by a dolly laden with filmmaking equipment.

Alec swung a daypack over his shoulder. "The *Mercado*."

The sun was barely over the horizon, but Alec pulled a ball cap on his head nevertheless.

They had prepaid for the ride so no tip was needed, but Stephie still bounded over to the driver to thank him, her petite frame dwarfed by the man, her tone sincere and all-business. At 5'1", the young Asian woman was usually the smallest human on any expedition. She was reliable, organized to the point of anal, and a damned fine underwater photographer.

Donovan stifled a yawn as the van left. "I'll take the rear, as always."

It had been a pre-dawn flight out of San Francisco, so sleep the night before had been cut short. It hadn't mattered—Alec had been too busy making sure he had all his equipment in order; he also hadn't been able to quiet his eager anticipation of seeing Grace again.

"That way I can pick up your crumbs," Donovan added.

It was an old discussion. Donovan claimed that Alec's good-looks drew the women in, and Donovan's job was to trail behind and choose the choicest morsels from Alec's castoffs.

Alec shook his head as Stephie went to the front of the dolly to guide it. Donovan was like a giant oak tree, with a shock of dark hair that left Alec convinced the man's ancestry was Russian. Donovan had always denied it, claiming he was nothing but English, and that his mother's family hailed from the very proper corners of Britain.

Alec marveled at the man's maneuverability in the water despite his size, and he trusted him to have his back. He'd done just that for the last five years. And Stephie was every bit Donovan's equal. They were a combination of Jack from *Jack and the Beanstalk* and Tinkerbell from *Peter Pan*.

His colleagues guided the precious cargo down the ramp and then onto a floating pathway that led to the watercraft currently berthed at the harbor—a collection that ranged from fishing vessels to sailboats to catamarans. There were several houseboats and yachts as well.

Alec headed toward a collection of larger vessels on the south end, guessing the *Mercado* would be with the bigger boys.

Via emails during the past six weeks, Grace had filled him in on all the particulars of crew and itinerary, the correspondence professional and businesslike. They'd only spoken once by phone, shortly after Grace had received a copy of the Bonnie-footage he'd sent, a thirty-minute reel he'd filmed in a state of complete anxiety. She'd excitedly called him, exclaiming that it had indeed been Bonnie that had stalked him and Bertie in the waters off the Farallones two years ago.

Thrown for a loop by her happy, gushing response, he had gone out on a limb and offered to take her diving at the Farallon Islands later this fall. She'd readily agreed, and he took comfort that he'd have an excuse to see her again after this expedition. Then, once he'd ended the call, he'd sat at his desk, stupefied by the overture he had just made.

He *never* wanted to get into those murky Northern California waters again. At least, he hadn't until blue-eyed, flaxen-haired Grace Mann had showed up in his life. Perhaps she was a sea siren, luring him to his death.

Unlike some of his fellow filmmakers who relished the thrill of a new and dangerous project, Alec was usually gripped with apprehension. His mountain-climbing mother told him it was his way of managing risk, but his father—never fully alive unless gambling on the edge, whether surfing hazardous waves or navigating the volatile software market—chided his oldest son about his nervous-Nellie tendencies.

Alec hadn't known that Grace would be diving cage-free with one of the most fearsome predators in the ocean, and frankly, with anyone else, that would have been a deal-breaker. He didn't need a repeat of what had happened to Elliott. But Grace's approach to her work and her connection to the sharks struck him as deeply genuine. He sensed that Grace was on the precipice in her shark research, about to make a big splash. She had intelligence and drive, and the charisma to widen her reach beyond scientists and conservationists. The viral nature of her one-on-one photo with Jaws itself had opened a door, and if all went well, Alec's film could propel her to the next level, possibly on a world-wide scale.

And Alec wanted to be a part of it.

He spied a boat in the distance with "Mercado" written in block letters on the hull, and anticipation thrummed through him.

Missy materialized beside them, a duffle bag slung on her shoulder, and her dark hair pulled into a tight ponytail.

She flashed a beaming smile at him. "Hey, you made it."

Alec glanced behind her. "Is Grace with you?"

"Are you kidding? At this point, we're all late. I'm pretty sure Gracie slept on the boat last night while the rest of us stayed in town. One last hurrah before being stuck on a tin can for three weeks." Her eyes slid to Alec's companions.

"Sorry," Alec cut in, "this is my crew, Dan and Stephie."

Missy reached over with a free hand and greeted them both with a brief handshake. "That's a lot of gear you've got."

"If the boat sinks, we want to make sure we're to blame," Donovan said.

"Double D breaks a lot of equipment," Stephie said coolly, not breaking her stride.

"Double D?" Missy asked.

"Only the biggest cup size for me," Donovan answered.

Missy laughed then flicked her head toward the gangplank as they reached the walkway to the *Mercado*. "Let's see what muscle we can find to help load your stuff."

Stephie slung a backpack onto her shoulder, and Alec grabbed two bags.

Donovan grasped two large hardcover cases in each hand and gave Alec the once-over. "You're slacking off."

Alec wasn't of a mind to be all hot and sweaty when he first saw Grace. "No. I'm just getting my money's worth, considering what I pay you."

"Not enough, that's for damned sure."

Stephie preceded them on the gangplank.

The liveaboard vessel was over one hundred feet in length, with a white hull and a large boom crane tucked against the port side where they now boarded. Alec caught a glimpse of three diving cages secured on the aft deck, a winch on each side.

They followed Missy through a doorway on the main deck into a salon that had been outfitted with scientists in mind—the makeshift office was crowded with computers occupying most of the counter space. Stacks of notebooks, research books, and papers stood at the ready near the large desktop screens that were black and silent for now.

At the center of the lounge area was a U-shaped couch hugging a table and facing a big screen TV on the wall. A coffee station offered easy access to caffeine, and Alec hoped the adjacent mini-fridge was stocked with something stronger than soda. After spending hours in the water with great whites, he had no problem indulging in a beer or two, or three.

Grace appeared from a corridor on the left, carrying a cup of something hot. She was clad in khaki pants and a lavender fleece zipped to her neck. Contrasted with the top she was wearing, her eyes appeared bluer than usual. They widened, and the barest hint of a smile came and went on her lips, and Alec reined in his own urge to grin at her.

"Look what I found," Missy said.

"It's about time," Grace replied. "We thought we might have to leave without you."

"You wouldn't leave without *me*, would you, Gracie?" Missy asked.

"I think she means us," Alec said. "Looks like we made it just under the wire."

He tried not to gawk, but with Grace's hair down and no makeup on her face, she was the epitome of a California girl.

Grace's eyes shifted to Stephie, and Alec shook himself free of staring. "This is Stephie Kim. She's the still photographer."

Stephie's face beamed with a smile that filled her eyes with adoration as she gave Grace a firm handshake. "It's an absolute honor, Dr. Mann."

Alec did a double-take on his assistant. He'd never seen the diligent young woman idolize anyone.

Warmth reflected from Grace's gaze. "It's nice to meet you, Stephie. Welcome aboard."

"I'm thrilled to be working with you."

Alec leaned closer. Was Stephie blushing?

"And this is Dan Donovan," he said.

Donovan dropped a large piece of gear, and Alec flinched. There'd better not be camera equipment in that one.

Pushing past Alec, the man shook Grace's hand. "You can call me Double D."

"I like your nickname better than mine," she replied, stepping back now that the introductions had been made.

"Shark Lady?" Donovan raised an eyebrow. "What's wrong with that?"

Grace gave a slight shake of her head. "Not that one."

"What could anyone possibly call you but that?" Alec asked.

Missy chuckled. "Ice Queen has been mentioned in certain circles."

"I think I prefer Bulldog," Grace said, crossing her arms.

"Then Bull Shark Lady it is," Donovan said.

Grace suddenly laughed. "Just don't call me bullshit."

An older man with a curly beard and swarthy complexion stepped inside.

"This is Captain Alan Bellamy," Grace said.

More introductions were exchanged.

"I hear you boys know the drill," Bellamy said, "but just in case, no one gets in the water unless I say so."

"Understood," Alec responded.

Two more men joined them, both young and fit and tan.

"These are my deckhands, Erik Westfall and Pete Drummond," Bellamy said. "Erik is also co-captain. We'll keep things running smoothly for you so you all can concentrate on your work. The final crew member is Chris Dillon. He's our cook but helps with other chores when needed. He's around somewhere." Bellamy looked at Grace. "Is everyone aboard?"

She nodded.

"Then let's get underway."

Double D nabbed Erik and Pete to help load the rest of their gear.

Before Alec left to join them, he turned to Grace. "You ready to be a superstar?"

"That was never my intention."

"I know. Just promise me one thing."

As her eyes focused on him, he came to appreciate the force of nature that was Grace Mann. Perhaps Ice Queen and Bulldog weren't too far off the mark.

"You'll listen to your gut," he said.

"You don't think I do?"

"That's not it. I'm pretty sure you've got spot-on radar when it comes to sharks, but...." He lifted his hat, scratched his head, and then pulled it back on.

Her face relaxed a bit, and she gave a nod. "I know what you're saying, and thanks for being concerned about my welfare. I appreciate it."

Alec released the grin he'd been suppressing since he'd boarded the boat. "Toward the unknown we go."

She gifted him with a double-wattage smile that, for a moment, left him stunned.

"You'd better help get that gear on board," she said. "I'm eager to get underway."

He nodded and made his way onto the outer deck.

A rush of expectation filled him. Pushing aside his worries of what could go wrong, he basked in the promise of the unknown, the plain old thrill of a new adventure.

Was he thinking of the great white sharks they'd encounter or Dr. Grace Mann?

∼

GRACE STOOD at the railing and watched the San Diego dock fade away as the *Mercado* headed out to open sea. As always, ambivalence filled her.

Fieldwork was always a boon to her spirit. She loved the sea and was more at home in its waters than any place on land, and being near the creatures of the ocean filled her heart with so much happiness she nearly burst from it. At the same time, living in close quarters on a boat filled with people always made her claustrophobic and antsy. It wasn't that she didn't get along with the crew or her colleagues, but her need for solitude often left her peevish within days of an expedition.

Usually after a trip ended, she would hide away in her house for several days, eating take-out pizza, watching movies on her couch while wrapped in a fuzzy blanket, and poring over the data that had been acquired. Only after she had her hibernation period would she emerge to interact with the human race once again.

But this trip was different. Not only would she test the algorithm she'd worked eighty-hour weeks to perfect, but she'd be interacting with the whites in a wholly different way. She could be hurt. She could die. But it was a low risk, in her mind. At the end of the day it would be worth it, and she wanted to try.

Galloway.

He would definitely be a distraction.

Perhaps it was fate that he was on this trip since she was attempting two bold moves—get the array functioning, putting her one step closer to developing an effective early-shark warning system for crowded beaches, and spend one-on-one time with whites without the encumbrance of scuba gear and cages. Perhaps he was meant to facilitate the change that was coming—not just in her work life, but her personal life as well.

She gave a slight shake of her head.

Chloe often said she was too philosophical. During times of stress, her sister went outward, getting physical. Chloe had always been the more athletic Mann daughter. Grace went inward, always trying to figure out the universe's motivation. Why, always why.

Frank Fowler sidled up to her, and she wrinkled her nose at the cigarette in his hand. The wind shifted, blowing smoke into her face.

"You really ought to do that at the back of the boat." She moved away from him and squinted at the horizon where ocean met bright blue sky. As the sun crept higher in the east, she wondered where she had left her sunglasses.

Brad had introduced the co-owner of Benchmark Films to her the previous day in San Diego, saying Fowler's company was interested in possibly distributing the documentary when it was completed. But apparently Frank had little experience with marine films and had decided to tag along to see what the fuss was about.

Grace didn't appreciate Brad's last-minute crew addition, and it made her suspicious of both Michaels and Fowler.

"Of course," he answered, and threw the cigarette into the water. She seethed.

Asshole.

"And you shouldn't do that either." She strained to keep her voice neutral. "Some poor fish could eat it."

Enlightenment lit his blue-gray eyes, and his mouth shifted to a smirk amidst the forest of his salt and pepper beard. "Didn't mean to offend the shark lady."

She didn't trust herself to speak and was glad when Dan Donovan—or Double D, as he liked to be called—approached.

"Frank Fowler," Dan bellowed, putting Grace in mind of an angry *Shrek*, "what the hell are you doing here?"

"It's no crime to be interested in the latest shark research."

Double D snorted, his dark long-sleeved nylon shirt straining across his thick chest.

Grace looked back and forth from one man to the other. "Do you know each other?"

"You could say that." Double D leaned against the railing and said to Fowler, "Alec know you're here?"

The tension between the two men stretched across Grace like a taut rubber band. She caught sight of Alec walking toward them from the aft of the boat. She allowed a brief indulgence of his t-shirt clad broad shoulders and narrow hips covered by khaki shorts until he was close enough to notice.

Alec stopped beside Fowler. "Nice to see you, Frank." His tone was far from friendly.

"Always a pleasure, Alec."

They were quite a cozy foursome crammed onto the narrow pathway.

Grace peeked at Alec. A slight grimace crossed his face, and then it was gone. He tugged on the tawny-colored baseball cap embroidered with GALLOWAY FILMS in black, dislodging the sunglasses perched on the brim.

"Have you all worked together before?" she asked.

"We have," Frank replied. "It was the only marine film Benchmark has distributed so far and was a rather tragic expedition. But we managed to get it into the European market for a nice payout."

Grace looked at Alec. "What happened?"

His jaw flexed and his gaze darkened. "I lost a good friend."

"Elliott Marsh got caught in a bad place." Fowler shook his head.

In a rush, understanding filled Grace. "That was your film?" she asked Alec, as if it were just the two of them conversing.

He nodded but didn't elaborate.

Grace had heard the story when it broke. Marsh, a biologist based out of Australia, had been diving in the Neptune Islands; he'd left his cage and been decapitated by a white. Had it been last year? She couldn't recall.

She resisted the urge to touch Alec's arm, but only because they had company. "I'm so sorry."

She hadn't watched the film but had heard the details from others in the shark community. The consensus was that Marsh had been partially hidden in a kelp forest, and the shark had mistaken him for a seal. It had been an ambush strike, typical of white sharks, and unfortunately, Marsh had had no time to react. The assault had been fast, precise, and devastating.

Attacks like that were rare, but that meant little to Marsh's family and friends.

Had Alec been there? Had he witnessed it? Her heart squeezed painfully for him.

Grace generally made a concerted effort not to dwell on such incidents. Allowing terror and panic to take up residence in her psyche would only destroy her composure, and along with it, her career.

But fear was a tricky monkey. Violent deaths perpetrated by great whites did occur—the movie *Jaws* hadn't been entirely inaccurate.

She took a steadying breath.

Double D turned from the railing and faced them. "Well, that nice payout of which you speak never trickled back to Galloway Films, and you did a shit edit on the film to make it more sensational."

"I'm sorry to hear you didn't receive adequate compensation." Fowler crossed his arms, the odor of cigarette smoke wafting off his shirt—his brand-new, quick-dry shirt, if the deep creases on the sleeves were any indication. "Contract negotiation is vitally important, I say. As for the edit, I did what I had to do. I had a distributor breathing down my neck."

"Bullshit," Donovan uttered under his breath, then said more clearly, "That footage should never have been made public."

Grace sensed that Alec wanted to say more, but he remained rigid.

"I imagine it was difficult for Mr. Marsh's family to see that dive," she said.

Double D sucked in a breath and silently agreed.

"What exactly are you doing here, Frank?" Alec asked, his tone lethal.

"Well, Benchmark Films is interested in what's happening on this expedition, so Brad Michaels invited me along to observe. Maybe it's true that I didn't have enough compassion or understanding for what happened with the Marsh film. I thought maybe I should be here to see it all unfold for myself, a sort of work vacation."

"You're on a fucking holiday?" Dan's chuckle held little humor.

Frank shrugged. "There's no denying that Grace here has charisma and is about to go swimming sans cage with the most fearsome beast in the ocean. Who wouldn't want to see that?" He smiled. "I think I'll grab a cup of coffee." He turned and headed to the back of the boat.

Double D's mouth curled into a snarl. "That's just fucking great."

"Where's our contract?" Alec asked.

Dan sighed. "Probably back at the office. I didn't think to pack a copy."

"Why?" Grace looked from Alec to Double D and then back. "Do you think Fowler is here to steal the doc from you?"

Alec narrowed his eyes. "In simple terms? Yes."

"He did when Elliott died," Donovan said. "There was a loophole, and we got blindsided."

Alec crossed his arms. "I'll get my mom on the satellite phone and see if she can dig it up for us."

Grace rested her hands on her hips. "Aren't you more careful now?"

Alec's forehead sloped lower over his eyes. "Yes, of course. But...."

"But what?" Grace asked.

Double D clapped Alec on the shoulder and gave him a shake. "Our boy here was so excited about this project that when the chance came to sign on, he ran toward it like a kid in a candy store."

Alec wouldn't look at her. It was both endearing and troubling. Time to change the subject.

"I'm sure the shoot will go smoothly, with nothing eventful happening that Fowler can twist around," she said.

Alec lifted his gaze and stared at her.

Double D glared at her. "You *have* been on an expedition before, haven't you? These things never run smoothly. That's what makes this work so damned exciting. And frustrating." Then he said more quietly, "God rest Elliott's soul."

Grace tucked a loose strand of hair behind her ear and wet her dry lips. "I can't imagine how horrible that must've been. But the water around Guadalupe has good visibility, and the chances of a shark sneaking up on any of the divers is very low. Nothing will happen."

A flash of pain and then concern crossed Alec's eyes. "It better the hell not."

His gaze bored into her, then it was over. Her grad student and diving partner Antonio Costa appeared on the walkway, his flip-flops clacking against his feet as he moved toward them.

Embracing the distraction, Grace introduced the young man to Double D and Alec. "Tony's a strong diver and has been working with us for the last year."

"Have you freedived with whites before?" Alec asked, bracing his legs against the gentle swaying of the boat on the ocean swells.

"No, sir." Tony grinned, his teeth extra-white against his tan skin. "But I'm looking forward to it."

Dan gave a grunt of satisfaction. "A young, tasty Italian boy to dangle as a sacrifice. Smart."

The remark diffused the somber atmosphere.

"I'll be all right," Tony replied. "Dr. Mann is a shark whisperer. The creatures seem to flock to her and do her bidding. She'll keep me safe."

Double D raised an eyebrow and asked Tony, "Does your mother know what you're about to do?"

Tony shrugged. "I'm not stupid. I didn't mention the part about no cage." He turned to Grace and added, "But Missy seems a bit skittish."

Grace nodded. "I know. And while I appreciate your faith in me, I want you to know that you can change your mind at any point about being in the water. Or at the very least, you *can* use the cage."

"Are you kidding? I already posted on Facebook about my exploits."

"Then your mother already knows," Alec said.

"Nah. She's not on social media. She thinks it's the bane of society."

Double D snorted. "Son, you underestimate your mama. They *always* find out."

"I think it's time to break out the equipment," Alec said to Dan.

"I'm on it." Donovan pushed away from the railing and strolled down the narrow walkway.

Alec's focus landed on Grace. "Stay close. We'll set up and take some practice footage."

"I'm not going anywhere."

He squinted and pressed his lips together. "I wouldn't put it past you to hop in the water."

"He knows you too well, Dr. Mann," Tony said. "I'm convinced she's secretly got a set of gills."

"If only that were true." Grace couldn't hide the longing in her voice. As a girl, she'd yearned to be a mermaid.

"Can I check out your filmmaking stuff?" Tony asked Alec.

"Sure."

As the two of them headed inside, Grace rested her forearms on the railing and gazed out over the water. The boat swayed up and down, undulating in a steady rhythm, a primordial memory with roots in the womb. A light breeze whipped her hair against her cheek as the blazing sun warmed her skin.

The ocean blended with the sky, varying shades of blue that kept the planet alive.

Her gaze dropped to the waves adorned with frothy whitecaps. There was so much beauty hidden from view. As she often did, Grace imagined what was down below at this very moment, so near and yet a world apart.

Humankind fancied themselves the most important species on the planet, but Grace didn't believe that. Sharks had existed for the last fifty million years, remaining largely unchanged during that unfathomable timetable. Mother Nature didn't need to upgrade her design; God had gotten it right the first time. There weren't too many species that could say that. Crocodiles, maybe. Or cockroaches.

Studying cockroaches undoubtedly posed less risk, and she couldn't deny that crocodile research was probably vastly fascinating, but her heart belonged to sharks.

And it was the whites that awakened her soul with a force that never failed to take her breath away.

The company of *Carcharodon carcharias* activated her primitive brain, her nerve endings literally vibrating in their presence, and experience had taught her it wasn't from fear or terror.

They were kin.

They were her tribe.

CHAPTER 6

B y late morning Alec sat crammed on the U-shaped bench in the salon—Missy on his left, Frank and Tony on his right—a notebook on the table before him partially filled with preliminary commentary about the expedition. He had one for every trip. Initially it contained information about gear, supplies, and backup apparatus. He also sketched a storyboard for the doc. As the trip unfolded, he would record a diary of daily activity, which could be used as a reference during the editing phase. It also helped in packing for future trips. He always jotted down what he wished he'd brought with him, along with items that had been totally useless and should be left behind for the next job.

Double D had a camera recording on a tripod in the far corner, and Stephie periodically snapped photos from a spot on the opposite side.

The deckhands—dark-haired Pete and wiry Erik—crowded into the salon, along with Chris, the cook, who was sporting a serious collection of ocean-themed tattoos along his exposed arms. Everyone was present for the meeting called by Brad, Grace, and Captain Bellamy. Alec considered it fortuitous that he'd gotten a seat at the table.

"We'll be stopping shortly in Ensenada for our Mexican check-in, so have your passports handy," Captain Bellamy said. "Then it's full steam ahead. We should arrive at Guadalupe Island tomorrow morning. We'll anchor in Discovery Bay, which is on the northeast and lee side of the island. It'll offer calmer waters, and there's a seal colony nearby. It's a good spot to set up the sonar array, so long as there's not too many additional boats. We're required to maintain a distance of 450 meters with other vessels."

"The array consists of three buoys that will be deployed over one nautical mile," Brad said. "That will be the first priority. After that's complete, then we'll move forward with Grace, Missy, and Tony getting in the water."

"How long to deploy the buoys?" Erik asked.

"Hopefully just one day," Grace answered. "But at the most, two."

"And then what happens with the array?" Pete asked. "Do we have to do something?"

Brad shook his head. "No. We'll monitor it from the boat. Every few days we might want to do a check on the apparatus and make sure nothing is amiss. Sharks have been known to attack equipment. Since we have a special permit to dive outside the cages, this shouldn't be a problem."

"Who's gonna check it?" Pete asked, humor mixed with a bit of terror on his face.

Nervous laughter filled the room.

"Me, Missy, or Tony will do it," Grace said, her voice calm and reassuring.

"Or I'll do it," Alec added.

Grace gifted him with a clipped nod. She and Brad were playing nice, but Alec guessed that was only because Double D had them on film.

Brad uncrossed his arms. "I'll help, too. Don't worry. No one has to get in the water with the sharks if they don't want to."

"How does the sonar array work?" Alec asked.

Grace started to speak, but Brad interrupted her. "The array will identify creatures inside the grid space by using a convolutional neural network that will narrow down whether they're a fish, a seal, a turtle, etc., or a shark. Once a shark is identified, then further neural networks will compute type of shark, its mass, its speed, and its depth."

"Holy shit," Frank blurted. "What kind of computer program do you have?"

Alec tried to hide his frustration. Thanks to Frank's expletive, he and Donovan would need to edit around it since the goal was to make a PG-rated documentary.

Brad beamed with pride. "It's an ambitious undertaking, but we're committed to making it work."

Grace directed her gaze toward a point on the table only she could see, as if she were listening intently to Michaels, perfectly fine with his answers. But Alec didn't count himself a casual observer of Dr. Mann. Her rigid stance, her whitened knuckles as she leaned back and gripped the edge of the countertop near the door, and the vaguely dismissive look in her eyes told a different story.

Fowler pressed on. "Are you processing all this data real-time?"

"We are," Brad replied.

Frank glanced around at the handful of computers present along the edge of the salon. "Wouldn't you need a massive amount of computing power?"

Grace cut off Brad. "The algorithm is very efficient. The desktops we have will do the job."

"But we'll no doubt have bugs to work out," Brad interjected, his tone impatient, almost verging on bellyaching.

Grace turned to him and smiled, but it didn't reach her eyes. "I'm sure you can handle it."

Brad didn't respond to her and instead switched to a new topic. "We also have shark tags on hand."

"But no tagging around the boat," Grace said. With her hair now pulled back into a loose bun, the slight sunburn she sported on her nose was more noticeable.

Brad's chest puffed out as he inhaled a deep breath. He threw a glance in Grace's direction. "Once the tracking system is in place, there's no time to waste."

"If you start chumming, we won't get what we need from our dives. Give me at least a week. You can take the outboard and go somewhere else to tag."

"And who's gonna keep an eye on the buoys?"

"I will," she said. "I won't be in the water the whole time."

A fleeting look of annoyance crossed Brad's face. "I'll hang back a few days to monitor everything, then I'm tagging."

Without a doubt, Alec would need to interview the two of them separately.

Grace faced everyone. "Just so we're clear—I don't want any chum in the water. It'll change the behavior of the sharks."

"What's the harm in waiting?" Fowler asked.

Alec suppressed an eye-roll over the man's blatant attempt to bolster his street cred with Grace.

"Tagging whites isn't easy," Brad said. "You can't catch them on a fishing line and reel them in. They're far too big. They need to be lured close to the boat." He shook his head. "Three weeks may sound like a long time, but sometimes you get no sharks interested in you, even with the chum. I hate to blow an entire seven days."

"I might be able to tag a few," Grace said.

Alec frowned at the image of Grace swimming up to one of the beasts with a spear and stabbing the dorsal fin. Odds were high it could end badly. "Let's cross that bridge if and when we get there," Alec said. "You don't want to annoy a great white when one is so close to you."

Her eyes darted to him, but to her credit she tamed the flash of irritation quickly. "You, Dan, and Stephie will be in the submersible cage," she said.

"We'll have two," Captain Bellamy said, "so you should be able to get decent footage from one or both of them."

Stephie stepped closer and snapped a photo of Grace. "I may occasionally go in the surface cage to get a different angle."

Grace nodded.

"Who are your safety divers?" Alec asked, still watching Grace.

Grace folded her arms across her t-shirt. "Missy, Tony, and I will remain together with a 360-degree view of our surroundings at all times."

"What about Erik or Pete as backup?" Alec asked, glancing at the two young men.

"No offense," Pete answered, "but I have no desire to get in the water unless I'm in a cage."

Erik sighed. "Yeah, we can help in an emergency, but I have to agree. We're gonna be near the sea lion and elephant seal colonies. That makes the sharks more unpredictable."

"We were assured that you had a team with you for the dives," Captain Bellamy said.

"We do," Grace said, then looked at Erik and Pete. "Don't worry. You won't have to get in the water." Her voice held a steely edge.

"We'll make sure everything is working with the cages from up top," Pete said.

"The submersibles will have backup air tanks and scuba gear for Dr. Mann, Dr. Rembert, and Tony," Captain Bellamy said. "Hopefully with the cage away from the boat, you'll all be able to see any shark coming from a distance, but you'll still need to watch each other's backs while you're down there."

"What happens if one of you is bitten?" Fowler asked.

"Get back to the boat as soon as possible," Grace said. "Missy has EMT training."

"And so does Erik," Bellamy said, "but the Mexican coast guard is probably three hours away, give or take, so we'd do best to make sure no one requires serious medical treatment."

"Sharks aren't as aggressive as they're made out to be," Grace said to Frank.

"Has anyone ever met a mako?" Double D asked. "I like to call them rocket ships."

Missy bumped against Alec. "Grace knows all about makos."

Unsure whether the dark-haired woman was still attempting to flirt with him, he took the route of no encouragement and remained focused on Grace. "What happened?" he asked.

She wasn't doing a great job of hiding her displeasure about the meeting, and Alec suspected that he was as much on her shit list as Michaels.

Appearing to resign herself to the change of topic, she replied, "A group of us were diving offshore from Monterey, and I got clipped by one."

"You're being modest, Gracie," Missy said. "He sliced her open on the shoulder. You lost a lot of blood, from what I heard. You were lucky on that one."

Grace shrugged and took a sip from a white mug, a teabag string hanging over the side. She had a bite on her neck from a white and now one on her shoulder from a mako. Alec wondered how many more close calls she'd had over the years.

"If we're about to compare scars," Donovan interjected, "then I've got a doozy on my ass I'd love to share."

Alec turned around to glare at him.

Double D laughed. "Don't worry, I stopped filming. And if you want a shark attack story, then Alec's your guy. He's got one of the best."

Alec closed his notebook, thinking of Elliott. But that one had been in a class all its own. The one to which Donovan referred hadn't been so traumatic. "It wasn't exactly an attack."

Grace waited, her interest palpable. Shit list or not, he'd at least retained enough of her regard to get her attention.

"What happened?" she asked.

"We were off the New Jersey coast. We'd chummed the waters and had attracted several sharks, and had gotten some good shots. But then they got tired of us and left. It was a very hot day, so I decided to get back in the water without the cage. The threat wasn't high, and I had scuba gear on. Once I was in, one of the deckhands must've decided to go fishing off the front of the boat."

"Uh-oh," Grace murmured under her breath.

Although the incident had threatened his life, the memory no longer caused pangs of panic in Alec's chest. "Yeah. A longfin mako caught the line, and before I could react, he'd wrapped it around my ankle."

"How much blood?" Missy asked.

"Longfins are a rare sight," Grace said at the same time.

Alec responded to Grace first. "I know. It was a shame I didn't have a chance to film him." Then he said to Missy, "There was definitely enough blood to drive the shark crazy. He severed the line but the bait was still in his mouth and my ankle was still caught, so down I went. I honestly don't know how far he dragged me, and I wasn't sure if I'd be able to safely rise without getting the bends. He plowed through the water for what felt like forever, but during one brief lull, I managed to get my knife free and cut the line that was wrapped around my ankle. And in the blink of an eye, he was gone."

"Did you fire that deckhand?" Missy asked.

Alec gave a slight shake of his head. He hadn't wanted the man to lose his job, despite how easily it could have been a fatal lapse in judgment. "No, but I did try to instruct him about sharks, fishing, and diving, and why never to mix the three."

"You were lucky." Grace set her mug on a nearby counter.

"I like to carry a sawed-off broomstick. Why don't you take it when you dive with the whites?"

"Unfortunately, it's illegal to carry any type of weapon down in Guadalupe," Brad interjected.

"How's your right hook, then?" Double D asked Grace.

"I hardly think a great white would register a punch from a little woman like Grace," Missy said.

"Then go for the eyes," Alec said flatly.

"I don't anticipate them being aggressive," Grace said. "And I don't anticipate being close enough to reach an eye. And," she raised her voice so that everyone in the room would hear, "there's to be no fishing during the expedition. At all. Is that clear?"

"Aye-aye, Boss," Double D responded.

Captain Bellamy stepped forward. "I can assure you that we will follow all standard protocols and will take everyone's safety very seriously. If anyone breaks a rule, besides getting a tongue-lashing from me, a citation, and a fine, you'll be forbidden from getting in the water any further. Now, I need to get back to the bridge. Let me know if anyone needs anything."

GRACE SAT on a bench on the upper deck of the boat while Alec secured a video camera to a tripod. The stop in Ensenada had been brief and uneventful, and now the *Mercado* raced along the Mexican coastline.

She took a deep breath of the salty breeze blowing against her face.

Alec wanted to film a preliminary interview with her, and damn if she wasn't a little nervous. She tucked strands of hair behind her ear that had escaped the clip and cleared her throat, then sat ramrod straight. The fleece she had worn earlier was now replaced with a navy windbreaker. Maybe she should change back. What if the material crinkled and made noise that could be picked up by the microphone clipped on her jacket lapel?

Alec glanced up at her. "Ready?"

"Do you think I should change?" she asked.

He looked through the viewfinder. "No. Try to relax, Grace. It's not any different than the talk you gave onstage."

She nodded and pressed her lips together, dispersing the lip balm more evenly. She'd wanted to apply a bit of makeup to cover her rosy nose, but Alec had stopped her, saying she looked fine, emphasizing how her blue eyes would really pop on film.

Was that good?

She'd have to trust that he knew what he was doing.

"I'll give you prompts," he said, "and you answer. If you flub, just keep going. I can edit it down later."

She swallowed, her tongue suddenly two sizes too big. "Got it." She sounded like a toad. She cleared her throat one more time.

He held up his hand. "And we're filming. State your name and title."

"I'm Dr. Grace Mann. I'm an associate shark researcher at the California Marine Institute."

"Where did you grow up?"

"I grew up near San Francisco. My father was a shark researcher and devoted his life to studying the great white. I suppose his love of sharks rubbed off on me."

"What was your father's name?"

"Dr. Eddie Mann."

"What about your mom? How does she feel about you studying sharks like your dad?"

Grace's lips stretched into a smile, and she was glad she'd applied the lip balm, if only to avoid a painful crack in the skin. "She tolerates it. She loves the ocean—in fact she designs beautiful fused glass pieces with water themes—but she generally doesn't ask about any close encounters I've had with sharks."

"What's your background?"

Grace made a concerted effort to keep her gaze on the camera and not on Alec's unflinching eyes. "My Ph.D. is in Computer Science from the University of Miami, but I also earned a Bachelor's degree in Marine Biology at the same time."

"What's so special about Guadalupe Island in Baja California?"

"When it comes to the Pacific great white shark population, there are two major gathering areas starting in September. One is the Farallon Islands near San Francisco, and the other is Guadalupe Island, located off the coast of Baja California Sur. Because the conditions in Mexico are generally better than in Northern California, Guadalupe offers an excellent location for studying white sharks. It's here that the largest adults come, offering unprecedented opportunities for observation and tagging before they head back out to sea for several months."

"Tell me about the imaging system you and Brad Michaels are developing."

"For the past year, Dr. Michaels and I have been working to

create a 3-D imaging system that can be placed along heavily-used beaches to track the position of sharks in the area. Employing a buoy system of multiple sonar devices, it will take thousands of data points and run them through a deep learning program, outputting not only whether a shark is a shark, as opposed to some other marine creature, but also the type. As we know, certain species are more aggressive to humans, such as great white, bull, and tiger sharks.

"The goal of our program is to present real-time data to local life-guard and police stations so that swimmers and surfers can enjoy the water safely. These buoys will use no nets or lines that could entangle wildlife. It's a win-win for beachgoers and marine life. The shark isn't an enemy, but attacks on humans often lead to vigilante hunts that rarely solve the problem. Sharks are disappearing from our oceans at an alarming rate, and if something isn't done to stop it, one day there will be no more sharks. This would have devastating consequences on the ocean ecosystem, since sharks are apex predators and keep much of the other marine creatures in check."

"Tell me about your famous photo of freediving with a great white shark."

"Freediving offers a way to enter an underwater environment with little disruption. Scuba gear produces sounds and bubbles that often frighten wildlife, especially sharks. While my freedive with a male great white shark in the waters off Oahu wasn't planned, I'd been working with various shark species for years and knew what behaviors to watch for. This particular shark was quiet and confident and inquisitive. I was never afraid. He came near me at one point, and I carefully took hold of his dorsal fin. It was a moment I'll never forget."

"What would you say to someone who might want to attempt this?"

"I've been around sharks my entire life. My father used to take me on his research trips when I was young. So, first, I would say to get a lot of experience with their behaviors before ever getting in the water with one. I've done a fair amount of cage diving in addition to freediving. Great white sharks are wild animals, and it's important to understand their posturing actions. If they're annoyed by your presence, they'll let you know before making a move, with behaviors such as deliberate lowering of the pectoral fins, shaking of the head with an open mouth, or arching of the back. A particularly important gesture is known as gaping; they approach with an open mouth and show their teeth. This is considered aggressive, and you should exit the water immediately. I make sure I pay attention to such cues, and I take them seriously.

"Cage dive first and learn from someone who knows about the behaviors of sharks. Then freedive with other species—reef sharks and lemons are a good place to begin. There are dive spots in the Bahamas and Florida where you can interact with bull and tiger sharks. Once you're comfortable with that, then proceed to the great whites."

Her nose itched, but she fought the impulse to scratch. "It's a humbling experience to be so close to such an ancient and extraordinary species," she continued. "There's so much we don't know about them: Why do they migrate thousands of miles? What do they eat during these migrations that occur in very deep water? Where do they mate? Do they adhere to any type of social structure? And, while we have some idea of where the pupping nurseries are located based on sightings of baby sharks known as young of the year, no one has ever witnessed or recorded a live birth.

"We know they're solitary creatures, and yet, in places like Guadalupe Island they will congregate together. Do they hunt as a group? How do they communicate? There are so many questions, but before we answer them, we must first protect the whites—and all shark species—from unethical and detrimental fishing activities. Each year over one hundred million sharks are slaughtered. That's an unsustainable number, especially for great white sharks who don't reach sexual maturity until they're ten to twelve years old. We estimate the females to have an eleven-month gestation period, giving birth every other year. The species can't possibly recover with these numbers."

A rush of heat filled her, as it often did when speaking about the plight of sharks, and her nerves gave way to a steely resolve of purpose. "I encourage everyone to learn more about great white sharks, and all sharks, for that matter. While most people won't ever eat shark fin soup, many products we buy are made from the skin of sharks, such as handbags, wallets, and belts. Hunters prize the jaws and teeth of whites, some of which sell for thousands of dollars. It's a heartbreaking thing to kill an animal because you want a piece of it for yourself. That creature is worth more alive. Communities that poach sharks can shift their economies to tourism, and those sharks —alive—will bring unlimited income instead of a one-shot deal by dying."

Grace ended her passionate plea and kept the camera in her sights.

"Cut," Alec said.

Her shoulders sagged, and she shifted her gaze to the horizon, then glanced back at Alec. "Too much?"

Amusement danced in his eyes. "Yeah. But in a good way. If I were a shark, I'd be glad to have you in my corner."

"I'm only doing this for the animals, the earth, and all of humankind," she teased.

"Listen, about earlier during the meeting. I wasn't trying to be difficult about your dives. I'm just concerned for your safety."

"I know." But it had chafed that Alec had joined forces with Brad to put the brakes on what she could and couldn't do. She wasn't a child to be told what to do and when. The most important man in her life—her father—had instilled in her a dogged tenacity. *It's the only way to live,* he'd said. And she believed him.

Alec paused, resting a hand on the top of the camera, and watched her. "You don't do anything small, do you?"

"What's the point in living, if you don't at least try to do something amazing?"

"Your determination reminds me of a—"

"I know. A bulldog." She bit her lip, her tone harsher than she had intended.

To her surprise, Alec laughed, throwing his head back and showing lots of straight white teeth.

She stared at him, mesmerized by her effect on him. It triggered something warm and fuzzy deep in her abdomen, a tug that was definitely sexual. But there was more to it, and it was the *more* that scared her.

A vision of kissing the lanky, muscular filmmaker flashed in her head, and she worried that, at any moment, she might slide off the bench and become a puddle of goo on the boat deck.

Shit. I'm in trouble.

She scrambled to divert her attention from sex, and worse, attachment. "Maybe you should edit down my passionate speech. Too much lecturing and condemning causes people's ears to close up. It's better to try and reach them some other way."

The sides of Alec's eyes crinkled. "I can see I'll have my work cut out in the editing room. Just give me all you've got, Grace. I promise I'll make you look good."

The itch on the side of her nose returned, and she indulged herself, scraping her fingernail along the skin, then stopped abruptly, not wanting to leave a noticeable mark. Being on camera was going to take some getting used to, as was trying to act professional while staring into Galloway's blue-green eyes. She'd need the determined willpower she usually reserved for the whites.

She scrunched her mouth and shook her head. "You've got me all wrong. I'm not in this for me. I'm here to be an advocate among men *for* the sharks. Not to build myself up."

"I know," Alec replied, his voice quiet. The unmistakable resolution in his tone sent the tingling in her stomach straight up to her heart, to a place reserved for very few: her dad, her mom, Chloe, the sharks she studied. It was the only explanation for why she proceeded to open up in a way she normally kept hidden.

"I started cage diving when I was in grade school, and I immediately fell deeply in love with the shark interaction. Watching them swim by, looking into their eyes, coming to know them—it was all so unbelievably life-changing for me. They were so free and majestic, and it was so obvious what a clear intelligence they possessed. They saw me. I never doubted that." She chewed on her lower lip and watched low-lying fluffy-white clouds hovering on the horizon.

"They're quite aware of the humans who come into their world," she continued. "When I'm with them, I can *feel* them. The connection is real, and profound." She lowered her voice. "It's sacred. And while I know that the wrong move could end my life—and yes, in a very gruesome way—it's such a small fear that I hardly acknowledge it anymore. All I know is that I can't wait to get in the water with them."

She'd started crying. What the hell?

She swiped at her cheeks, then stood. "Please don't include that. Everyone will think I'm a loon."

"No. They'll respect you because you have an authentic connection. That's how you'll reach people."

She crossed her arms. "You filmed that, didn't you?"

"I wouldn't be good at my job if I missed gems like the speech you just gave. I found the altar at which you worship."

"And at what altar do you worship?" she challenged.

"I'll let you know when I find it."

CHAPTER 7

A lec balanced a plate holding a cheeseburger with all the fixings, French fries, and a generous helping of ketchup as he opened the door with the hand that held a beer. Thankfully, he managed to make it out onto the front deck without spilling either the food or the drink. Double D sat with Grace on a curved bench, their plates of food resting on their knees. Alec took an open spot, putting Donovan in the middle.

"Just in time, Galloway." Double D took a swig from a can of soda. "Gracie and I are comparing our battle wounds."

"Be prepared to start in Double D's childhood," Alec said to her. "He was very accident-prone."

"I grew too fast, and that made me a bit awkward." Donovan popped a large fry in his mouth.

Grace smiled then took a bite of her loaded burger, ketchup dripping down her chin before she wiped it away with a napkin.

"Very ladylike," Alec teased.

"You go first." Double D nodded in Grace's direction.

As she chewed her food, she unzipped her windbreaker, careful not to dislodge the plate resting on her knees, and shrugged her shoulders free of the jacket. Twisting, she tugged the back of her t-shirt collar down and let Double D have a peek.

What the hell?

Annoyance blanketed Alec.

"You've got a collection going back there," Donovan remarked.

She nodded, shrugging back into her jacket. "The big one is from a white shark named Bonnie, and you already know about the one on my shoulder from the mako. The scar in the middle of my back was from a bull shark. When I was in college, my sister, Chloe, and I decided to go to the Bahamas one summer and try to be beach bums and live on five dollars a day. We found work with a guy who had conditioned local bull sharks to take food from a spear in a certain area of the reef. Each day he brought tourists out to experience the closeness of the sharks."

She took a swig of water from a green plastic bottle adorned with a cartoon shark and the words *Will you be my chum?* below it. "One afternoon," she continued, "after we'd finished a dive, one of the customers wanted to go back in with his son. The boy had been too scared to go with the rest of us. The man was insistent and offered me a hundred dollars to do it. In the back of my mind, I knew it wasn't a good idea, but I needed the money.

"We were out of shark food, but I didn't think anything of it. I figured the bulls would be full anyway from the earlier feeding, so the three of us went down and got situated on the ocean floor."

Alec made fast work of his burger while Grace spoke.

She replaced the lid on her water bottle and set it on the deck near her feet. "At first, only one shark appeared, but he was aggressive, swimming in a tight circle around us. That's when I knew I'd made a huge mistake. Before I could signal that we needed to leave, at least eight more sharks showed up."

"Sonuvabitch." Double D enunciated each syllable as he shook his head, then gulped more soda.

Grace popped a French fry in her mouth. "Yeah, it got out-of-hand quickly. The sharks were expecting food. I indicated to the man to put his son between us so we could shoot for the surface, and just before we rose I purged my regulator, hoping the screen of bubbles would deter the sharks. When the dad saw what I was doing, he did it too, so we were able to make it topside. We both tossed his son onto the swimming platform."

Alec took a drink of his beer, then asked, "Where were the sharks?"

"Swarming, although I didn't know how bad. I wanted to make sure I saved that kid and then his dad. I yelled at the man to get out of the water, and just as he did, one of the bulls caught me from behind."

"Jesus," Double D said, dragging the word out.

"It actually wasn't too bad, but there was a lot of blood. I doubt that kid will ever swim in the ocean again, which is a shame."

"How deep is the scar?" Alec asked, since he hadn't had the chance to gaze down her shirt.

"Not very. Luckily, I didn't lose any major chunks of flesh or have any nerve damage." She laughed. "Chloe lucked out. Since I couldn't swim, she got paid double to handle the remainder of the tours for the summer, and I got to kick back and drink margaritas on the beach."

"I'm thinking maybe you got the better end of that deal." Double D stood. "I need something stronger than soda. I hope you girls packed some sauce."

Grace nodded. "It's in the galley."

Donovan scooped up his plate. "Any music requests?"

"Something with a beat," Grace said.

"The Bee Gees it is, then." Double D turned his back on them and headed to the salon door. "And when I return," he added over his shoulder, "I'm gonna tell you about the love bite on my ass."

Alec moved his empty plate to Dan's recently vacated spot. "Spoiler alert—it wasn't from a shark."

Donovan faced them as he backed through the doorway. "All I've got to say is that sea lions can be real peckerheads sometimes."

Grace laughed as Double D disappeared behind the closing door. "How long have you two been working together?"

"Going on five years now. I met him on a dive in Australia.

When I decided to form Galloway Films, he was interested in partnering with me."

Grace's eyebrows shot toward her hairline. "He's part owner?"

"Yep. I've got no hope of getting rid of him now."

Grace's forehead smoothed back into place. "He doesn't act like a boss."

"I'm pretty sure he'd do this job for free. I learned early on from my dad that if an employee was valuable, you do what you can to hang onto them. Galloway Films wouldn't be where it is today without Double D."

Alec leaned back, the boat rocking back and forth from an increasing collection of whitecaps. He glanced at the sun as it dipped toward the west. "We might have a green flash," he said, referring to the optical phenomenon that sometimes occurred at sunset.

"The perfect ending to our first day at sea, although those clouds on the horizon look a bit ominous."

Alec agreed with a nod and made a mental note to check with Captain Bellamy about the forecast through the night. "Did you know that my sister, Brynn, and your sister, Chloe, were roommates in college?" he asked.

"Really?" She wiped her fingers on her napkin, then tucked it beneath her thigh so it wouldn't blow away. The setting sun illuminated Grace's face in a soft orange glow. "Wait!" Her eyes widened. "I've met Brynn. Is she really your sister?"

"Yep."

"It's funny we didn't make that connection sooner," she said. "Stewart mentioned she was an archaeologist." She nodded vigorously. "Now I remember. Chloe had two roommates. I think Audrey was an archaeologist or an anthropologist too. How is your sister? What's she up to?"

He stretched out his right arm and rested it on the back of the bench seat. "She's good. She's been spending most of her time lately in Istanbul studying Sumerian tablets."

"I'll have to ask Chloe if they still keep in touch."

Donovan reappeared carrying three red plastic cups. "I didn't want to drink alone."

Both Alec and Grace grabbed one before Double D dropped all three on the deck.

Grace took a sip. "A Moscow mule. I'm impressed you knew what to do with our ingredients."

"You'll come to see that I'm useful to have around."

"Night Fever" by the Bee Gees began to play over the outside speakers.

"And you delivered on the tunes, too," Grace said.

Alec took a sip of the lime-flavored drink. "Not bad. What's the hard stuff?"

"Vodka," Grace answered. "So, go easy if the sway of the boat will eventually get to you."

Missy and Stephie joined them, sporting long sleeves and buffs around their necks, the stretchy nylon tubes of fabric bunching beneath their chins in a splash of vibrant color.

"I think we should nominate Double D for trip bartender," Missy said, a drink in hand.

Alec picked up his empty plate from the bench and scooted closer to Grace, who took his plate and stacked it onto hers as Missy and Stephie sat in his now-empty spot.

"I can handle giving the ladies drinks." Donovan let the railing support his weight as he stretched his legs out before him and crossed one foot over the other.

Brad and Fowler appeared from the outer walkway and stepped into the group. Brad sat on a storage bin that likely held life vests and took a drink of his beer. "You ready to deploy the buoys?" he asked Grace.

"I will be. I'll work on the calibration tomorrow."

"How did you both come up with the idea for the imaging system?" Fowler asked, looking from Brad to Grace.

Grace's gaze settled on Brad with the look of a viper considering her prey.

Either Brad hadn't seen it, or else he chose to ignore it. "We both worked as interns at the Shark Lab in the Bahamas when we were in college. Missy was there, too."

Missy watched him with an expression of bemused detachment.

The girls seemed to have a different viewpoint but didn't speak up.

Alec knew of the Shark Lab, the well-known shark research facility at Bimini that was started by Dr. Samuel Gruber.

"You developed the array there?" Alec asked.

"Yep," Brad answered. "We did preliminary testing on lemon sharks. Then CMI picked up the project and the rest, as they say, is history."

Grace remained silent, and Missy gave a slight shake of her head.

There was more to the story, but no one seemed inclined to elaborate, so Fowler let it drop, as did Alec.

CHAPTER 8

Grace awoke with a start, the boat rocking gently back and forth, the hum of the motor reverberating in the distance. Why weren't they anchored at Guadalupe as planned?

Then she remembered. The *Mercado* had encountered rough seas during the night, and Captain Bellamy had said they'd likely be delayed because of it.

A dim gray light filled the small cabin she shared with Missy. Dawn wasn't far off. Grace rubbed her face and lay in her bunk, deciding whether she should try to go back to sleep. She'd likely just toss and turn, so she might as well get up and face the day. She wanted to work on the interface for the buoys anyway, and another day at sea offered the perfect opportunity.

She crept from her bed, not wanting to wake Missy in her berth on the top bunk. Grace quickly changed into a pair of dark-blue quick-dry pants and the fleece she'd worn yesterday, layering it over the t-shirt she'd slept in. She pulled a buff over her head and settled it around her neck, then secured her hair into a haphazard bun with a hairband. She grabbed her thick-soled water shoes and slipped them on her feet, liking the traction they offered while on the deck of a swaying boat.

Snatching her sunglasses from the narrow desk, she stepped

quietly into the corridor. The only sound was a sharp click as she shut the cabin door. Making her way to the salon, she flipped on a light at one of the work spaces and then turned on the main computer. As she waited for it to boot up, she gazed out the window at the dark ocean and the dusky sky, the boat moving along at a steady clip.

The shadow of a man moved on the outer deck. Grace assumed it was either Erik or Pete, but then recognition made her stomach do a somersault.

Alec.

She pushed open the self-shutting door and stepped outside.

"Good morning," she said.

Leaning over a large black case, he glanced up at her. "Morning. You're up early."

"I could say the same for you. Any idea on our ETA?"

He flipped open the lid to the case, revealing some kind of flying apparatus tucked into foam inserts. "Probably early evening. How'd you sleep through all that wild chop?"

"Like a baby." She peeked over his shoulder. "What's that?"

"A drone. I want to get some footage today as we're cruising along."

She uncrossed her arms. "Can I help?"

"I thought you'd never ask." He stepped to the side. "Help me take it out by grabbing one of the mounts."

Together, they pulled the circular drone free.

"It's huge," she said as she shuffled to a nearby table and carefully set it down, while Alec did the same from his side. It had to be at least four feet in diameter.

"It's gonna get bigger," he said. "I still have to mount the stabilizer and then the camera."

She rested her hands on her hips. "This must be very expensive."

His eyes flicked to hers. "Very, so please don't break anything."

She threw her hands up. "Now you tell me. I'm not touching it anymore."

"I can still use some help."

The new day beckoned as the sun crept closer to making an appearance.

"How were you planning to do this alone?" she asked.

Alec crouched and removed a large black frame from another case. "I can get by, but since you're here...."

"It looks like you're going to build a bicycle."

He laughed. "Can you balance the drone on the edge of the table, so I can connect this to the bottom?"

Grace paused and took a deep breath. "Yeah, I suppose."

She held tight to the drone as Alec dropped to the deck and scooted beneath the flying apparatus, his legs extended, creating a boundary around her feet. He attached what looked like a roll cage.

"Stay put," he said as he crawled on all fours to a third case and retrieved a complicated-looking camera.

Grace's muscles flexed as she gripped the high-tech flying machine, her rear end pushed back at an awkward angle. Alec shuffled on his butt back underneath and swiftly attached the camera, then came to stand opposite her, grabbing the drone at the center. "Let's set it down now."

"It won't tip over, will it?"

"Nah, there's a small base at the bottom of the stabilizer."

Once it was steady on the boat deck, Grace stood upright and shook out her arms.

"Wanna fly it?" Alec asked, grinning at her.

"No!" She'd be horrified if she crashed it.

He started extending the drone arms, snapping all six into place, and then went to work on the rotor blades, which had been folded inward for storage. When all twelve were flipped into position, he looped a lanyard over his head and picked up a rectangular box, securing it to a clasp at the end of the lanyard.

"Stand back," he said.

Her chin snapped up. "What? Are you launching it from here?" She stumbled backward. From where it sat on the deck, it wouldn't be able to rise straight upward. Visions of being mauled by the numerous spinning blades flashed through her mind.

Alec snapped several switches on the drone, the camera, and the controller, then stood back as the behemoth began to whir, coming to life. Grace tried to merge into the corner, in case the thing became suddenly sentient and decided to take out all life in its vicinity.

"Haven't you ever seen a sci-fi movie?" she asked, annoyed that her voice was more of a shriek. "These things always go crazy."

Alec chuckled but kept his eyes on the controller screen, his long fingers working the toggles. The contraption lifted into the air and slowly moved horizontally until it had cleared the boat, then climbed higher and went out over the wild blue sea.

Grace breathed a sigh of relief.

"You swim with sharks," Alec said, still watching the control panel that hung from his neck, "and yet you cower from something man-made."

Grace stepped closer to him. "You nailed it. Humans scare me far more than sharks."

"Check it out." He beckoned her closer.

"You can see the film in real time?"

He nodded.

She came close enough that her arm brushed against his, and she caught a whiff of laundry detergent from his t-shirt, giving him an appealingly clean aroma.

The video screen on the controller displayed blue ocean and the rising sun cresting the shoreline to their port side.

"And then there was light," she murmured.

"And the light was good."

She briefly met his gaze as he flashed her an amused look.

"I went to Sunday school," he said, "until my dad decided surfing was a better way to commune with God."

"I have to agree with him. My dad worshipped the ocean and little else."

"And you?"

She watched the swell of the waves as they caressed the sandy beach on the video screen. "It doesn't make sense to me to sit in a building and talk about the salvation of the world when I'd rather *be* in that world. If I have a purpose on earth, I'm damned well going to go out and find it."

"I think you have, Grace."

For a moment, the flirty intimacy filled the space between them and surrounded Grace like a caress of warm Caribbean water, igniting a pleasant feeling in her belly.

She gave a shy smile but stepped back. "The first time I dived with sharks was when I was four. Each summer my dad took our family on vacation in the Bahamas, and while he would take us to aquariums and teach me and Chloe endlessly about the creatures of the ocean, he really believed that being up close and personal with them was of the utmost importance. I learned to hold my breath while swimming with nurse sharks."

"Well, that explains everything."

"What's that?"

"You're part shark."

She smirked. "They're just my happy place, that's all."

He fiddled with the drone controls. "You're a strange woman, Grace," he murmured.

Before she could offer a retort, the buzz of the drone overhead signaled its return, and she considered dashing into the salon as Alec landed it in case something went terribly wrong. She didn't know why the big buzzing apparatus made her nervous, except that it looked like it was secretly spying on them, providing information to pirates or maybe shark hunters.

Alec guided the drone expertly onto the table, the stabilizer mount gently making contact, then shut down the motor.

"Now what?" she asked.

He let the controller dangle from his neck as he stepped closer and removed a memory card from the camera. "I'll download the footage on my laptop and see how it looks." He turned, focusing on her. "But first, how about I buy you a coffee for being such a good assistant?"

"Are you offering me a job?"

"The door's always open." As if to emphasize his statement, he held open the salon door as she walked inside. "I was just telling Double D that we should hire a shark-obsessed computer scientist."

"You don't know my demands." She headed down the narrow, spiral stairs that led to the galley.

"Try me," Alec said from behind her.

"I need at least three weeks of vacation each year, preferably in the Bahamas."

"Done."

She reached the small dining area with two tables flanked by bench seats, one beside the other like an old-fashioned diner, and waved at Chris in the back. A tattoo of an octopus ran along his right arm, the tentacles wrapping around the veins and muscles of his forearm, flexing as the young brown-haired cook organized something for breakfast.

"I've got coffee ready," Chris said, raising his voice over the din of his busywork and nodding toward a countertop.

Alec got there first and grabbed the silver coffeepot.

"Decaf for me," she said, before he poured her a cup. "I try to keep my caffeine to a minimum when I'm diving."

He reached for the second, smaller pot and soon deposited a mug into her hand.

She sat at one of the tables, and Alec took a seat opposite her.

"I also don't ever want to run the drone," she added, resuming their previous conversation.

Alec took a sip of the hot beverage. "Which reminds me—how would you feel about a go-pro attached to your chest?"

Grace stopped stirring the cream and sugar into her cup and looked at him. "I draw the line at wearing it in the bathroom. But will it work? You told me the setup wasn't viable with Bertie Nichols."

"I know, but we were trying to get him and the sharks and his abalone harvesting all in one shot. Double D and I'll be shooting you, and Stephie will be taking photos, so we'll have the long shots covered. But you'll be face-to-face with the sharks, so we might get something worthwhile."

"With hope I'll be face-to-face," she interjected. "If it's not too cumbersome, I'll give it a try."

"Fair enough. And I'd like to put one on Missy and Tony as well."

She nodded.

Alec went quiet, running a thumb along the rim of his cup. Just as the silence veered toward awkwardness, he spoke again. "I hope you don't mind me asking, but what's going on with you and Michaels?"

Huh?

Alec knew that she and Brad had been a couple. Was he asking if they were *currently* dating? Confusion swirled in Grace's head, and words logjammed her throat.

She managed to croak out, "Pardon me?"

"With the imaging system."

Oh. She expelled a relieved breath and hoped he couldn't hear the rapid beating of her heart. Chatting about her ex with Galloway was at the bottom of her to-do list. "Right. The imaging system." But then, discussing her and Brad's history in developing the sonar array was also a sore topic.

"What really happened at the Shark Lab?" The fluorescent dining area lighting made Alec's eyes appear a dark hunter green.

Grace considered how much she should say. None of it was a secret, except for maybe the specific content of the algorithm she had developed. And for now, she was bound by the confidentiality agreement she'd negotiated with the board of CMI two months ago, so mentioning the details of it was off-limits. Not that she trusted Galloway enough to confide that part to him anyway. The depth of his friendship with Brad was still up for debate, and she didn't want to confront Michaels about the sonar array until she knew that her code worked. If it did, then the array project would be transferred to her supervision, and she would be able to cut Michaels out once and for all.

"Brad and I met at the University of Miami. We went to the Shark Lab to work on an early version of the sonar array, to identify lemon sharks. When he graduated, he got a job at CMI, based on what I thought was his field of study."

"And what was that?"

"Polyandry."

At the questioning look from Alec, she added, "When a girl shark has more than one husband."

He raised an eyebrow. "Polygamy for chicks?"

She smiled. "Something like that. But it turned out that Brad had sold them on the array idea. And they took it. And they ran with it."

"And Brad didn't give you any credit."

"Bingo."

"Could you take legal action against him?"

Well, she had, of a sort; but instead of elaborating, she continued explaining what she could.

"Not really," she said, bracing her shoulder blades against the back of the bench seat. "A shark imaging system is a broad idea, and in that sense, can't be patented. My work at the university was open-sourced, so technically, he could take the concept anywhere he wanted."

"Did you follow him to CMI?"

She could appreciate the puzzled look on Alec's face, but the slight derision in his voice pissed her off. She yanked the buff over her head—she'd begun to perspire—then took a sip of coffee to quiet her anger. Releasing a frustrated breath, she said, "Look, shark research positions aren't that easy to come by, and the idea for the array goes back to my dad. He was never formally trained in computer coding, but he'd always dabbled in it. Chloe and I grew up writing logic paradigms for how to sort a basketful of marbles or all the buttons in my mom's sewing basket. My dad put a lot of thought into a way to track sharks, but back then, the technology didn't exist to implement it."

Alec's expression had changed from skepticism over her deci-sion to work with Brad to one of quiet fascination. Or perhaps he secretly thought she was in over her head. It had certainly crossed her mind a time or two.

"I guess you could say I'm a bit attached to this project," she said. "CMI was willing to fund it, and I had a way to get hired."

Lines creased Alec's forehead. "Because Brad brought you in?"

"Hell no. I'd already broken up with him, and he had no desire to share the glory of his great new project. But the early stages of the array were fairly rudimentary. At the Shark Lab, we only had two layers of deep learning—find the blob in the water, then identify if a fin was present. With that data, you couldn't even be certain it was a shark, since large fish often looked the same. To take the array to the next level required many more layers and much more coding to handle all the data. On top of that, the program had to be taught what a shark looks like, along with the differences between shark species—so far, I've only added I.D. markers on great whites. All of this requires massive amounts of data input, and it's a process we're continuously updating. So, Brad quickly hit his wall of incompetence."

"Couldn't he have hired another coder?"

"Maybe. But it was *my* project, so I went to CMI and offered my help. Unbeknownst to Brad, I had a rough algorithm already written to handle the next ten layers."

Alec leaned back and grinned. "He has no idea what you've done, does he?"

"Tony's pretty up-to-speed, but if I get eaten by a shark on this trip, Brad's grief won't be because he's torn up over my demise. He'll never get the imaging system working without me."

"And he knows this?"

Grace shrugged. "I think he's beginning to suspect. I think it's making him more desperate to hold onto his dictatorship." She worried her lower lip. "Look, can you leave all of this out of the film? Because in the end, what's important is the array and how it will help swimmers and sharks stay alive."

Alec regarded her, his gaze contemplative. "He could still just get another programmer."

She narrowed her gaze. "I've made provisions for that."

Laughing, he said, "Damn. Remind me never to play poker with you." He ran a hand through his short hair. "You know what you are?"

She gave him a questioning look.

"A card shark." He chuckled over his own pun.

She gazed into eyes the color of an ancient forest, lush with life and the promise of something more. It would be so damned easy to fall for Alec. But she'd played in that sandbox with Brad and was still paying the price for it. She wasn't sure she was ready to do it again.

Dealing with sharks was so much easier.

ALEC STOPPED TINKERING with his video cameras and placed them, one at a time, into the hard cases sitting in a corner of the salon. Once they were secured, he stacked the containers to keep the throughway clear. With the Wi-Fi signal the strongest in this location, it got crowded with everyone tending to their computers, books, and paperwork.

Grace stepped inside with Missy and Stephie. The three had been chatting out on deck for the last hour.

"We should be at Guadalupe in a few hours," Grace said.

Double D looked up from where he sat working on his laptop. "It'll be dark by then, most likely."

"Unfortunately," Grace replied. She looked at Alec. "Is all your gear ready?"

"I think so."

"Chow's on," Brad said as he walked through and headed down the stairwell to the galley.

Everyone filed down for dinner, and soon enough, Alec was packed into one of the booths, Double D beside him and Missy on the end. Across from him sat Tony, Stephie, and Grace, who faced Missy. In the other booth were Erik and Pete, along with Brad and a pasty-faced Fowler.

Grace glanced past Alec to the booth beside them. "Frank

shouldn't eat this if he's seasick." Using her fork, she stirred the spaghetti noodles and meat sauce on her plate. "I really don't want to see this meal on the floor later."

"Chris is a bold chef." Donovan took a long drag on his bottle of beer. "I think it's a test to see which one of us has the strongest stomach."

Grace slurped up noodles, then wiped her mouth with a napkin. She pointed at Double D. "I'm guessing you win."

Donovan shrugged, set his bottle on the table, and then asked Missy, "How did you and Grace become friends?"

"At the Shark Lab," she answered. "Somebody had to teach the Ice Queen how to party. No better place than the Bahamas with its balmy weather and gently lapping waves."

Double D laughed. "Damn. I think I missed my calling. It would be nice to stay in one place instead of constantly traveling. Lemon sharks, right?"

Missy nodded, her mouth now full of salad. She waited until she'd swallowed before answering. "But we also studied tigers and hammerheads. Grace started working on her imaging system with these makeshift sonar detectors on broomsticks. We'd stand in knee-deep water with the lemons and try to get readings."

"You were a good sport," Grace said, looking at the other woman. "That's when I got you hooked on freediving."

Alec scooped up the remaining sauce on his plate with a piece of bread. "Did your dad teach you to freedive?"

"Yes, kind of. We often swam in shallow water with no scuba or snorkeling equipment except for a mask. But it wasn't until I went to college that I learned more properly how to extend my breath-holding."

"That's one thing I'd like to master," Double D said. "There's no better place to be than in the ocean."

"Except for all the shit that can kill you," Tony said.

"Anatomy is destiny." Stephie spoke without emotion, her words flat and final.

Everyone paused and looked at her.

Alec was accustomed to the austere young woman and her pragmatic view of the world, but expedition crews generally didn't warm up to Stephie. That had made Alec only more protective of her, eliciting the older brother tendencies that Ty and Brynn usually responded to with a *shove it*.

"Sigmund Freud said that," he said, trying to save the conversation. "He was talking about gender, but we know now that environment plays as big a role. I'd guess all that freediving you three do," he nodded toward Tony and Missy, but his eyes landed back on Grace, "has affected your ability to be in the water. It's likely given you an advantage."

His attention slid over to the counter where Chris had placed plates filled with some kind of chocolate cake, but he was helpless to reach it, boxed in as he was.

Grace stood and snatched one. "But not as big as I'd like. I can't seem to stay down longer than five minutes. I've trained specifically to get past that barrier, but I just can't do it." She leaned across the table and handed the enticing confection to Alec. "Your eyes gave you away."

He grinned and took it. "Thanks." He grabbed his fork and shoveled a large bite into his mouth. Damn, it was good. He had a weakness for cake.

"What's the record depth for freediving?" Double D asked.

Grace brought over more plates of cake and passed them around the table. "I believe it's over eight hundred feet."

Donovan shook his head. "That's insane. Your lungs would be the size of peas."

Taking her seat again, Grace picked up a spoon and dove into her own dessert. "But you forget that we came from the sea. When we're in the water, our bodies remember."

"Right back in your mama's womb," Tony said.

"And the whales are my brothers." Double D did his best to hide a burp.

"When we go back to the sea, we're going back from whence we came," Stephie said, glancing at Grace beside her.

Grace gifted her with a smile. "John F. Kennedy. One of my favorite quotes."

Stephie beamed, and again, Alec marveled at the change in his usually serious photographer. Being around Grace was good for her.

With dinner winding down, everyone migrated to the upper deck, and Tony started mixing rum and cokes. It was the best part of the day, as far as Alec was concerned, with a cotton-candy colored sky decorating the horizon. He wore a light jacket to counter the breeze, and he had the perfect view of a pretty girl as Grace chatted with Missy across from where he stood. Life was good.

Brad climbed up the ladder, holding a bottle of tequila. "Time to commemorate the trip with a shot of confidence." He filled paper cups, and they were passed around. Erik and Pete joined in, but Stephie stuck to her coke without rum.

Brad raised his cup, and everyone did the same. "Here's to a successful expedition."

Alec downed the liquid, the shot warming his insides. A feeling of contentment overtook him.

In the distance, a dark outline signaled the impending appearance of Guadalupe Island, but it would still be a few hours before they made anchor. It would likely be pitch-black by then.

Fowler joined them, his face sporting a bit more color than at dinner. He took a seat beside Grace and surprisingly accepted the paper snifter of tequila that Brad offered. Alec imagined that alcohol was the last thing Fowler needed, but he really didn't care if the asswipe got sick over it.

When Brad offered a second shot, Alec declined. He didn't want to overdo it the night before a dive.

"Who'd have thought we'd end up here together." Brad leaned against the railing on the other side of Alec. "You were into underwater photography back in our surfing days, and look at you now. Where'd you end up going to school?"

"UC Irvine, but I didn't study film."

"What did you study?" Grace asked, obviously eavesdropping despite the chatter from Donovan and Missy.

"Mechanical engineering."

"Really? Why don't you work as an engineer?"

"I kinda do. I haven't been on an expedition yet where something mechanical didn't go wrong. I like tinkering."

"Maybe you can help us with the imaging system," Brad said.

Alec crossed his arms. "Grace seems to know what she's doing."

"There's room for innovation in protecting people from shark attacks," Brad said. "Much of what's out there is either cumbersome or ineffective or both."

"I don't like those chainmail suits," Stephie said. "If a great white wants to bite you, that type of suit isn't going to stop them. I think it might do the opposite and attract them. What I'd rather have is a wristwatch that emits a frequency that would deter sharks."

"You want to place your life on the line with a wristwatch?" Fowler asked, incredulous.

Stephie's face remained serene. Alec couldn't recall the woman ever losing her temper. "I would rarely activate it," she said. "I don't like to repel sharks, but it would be nice to have the option to press a button and get them clear of me in case they became too aggressive."

Grace nodded. "That actually would be fantastic. There's something like it sold in Australia, but it's not practical for surfers or for young children."

"What about aerial photography?" Missy asked. "Spot the sharks from a low-flying plane. A lot of beaches do this."

"It's only about twenty percent effective," Grace said. "And cloudy days or sun glare present problems. There've been beaches that erected barriers to protect swimmers, but this doesn't help surfers. And it also can entangle other creatures, such as dolphins, leaving them to die. It's not a good solution. If we can get the imaging system to work, the data can be fed to the local lifeguard station, which in turn could be updated in real time on social media. Beachgoers would only need to check their phone for the latest on sharks in the area."

"What about all the tagged sharks?" Fowler asked. "They're already being tracked. Can't we feed that info to the public as well?"

"Definitely, and some groups already do that. The problem is that not every shark is tagged, or can possibly be tagged, so the information is limited."

The boat lurched to the right, and Fowler's face blanched as he grabbed the railing. "The answer is obvious—stay out of the water."

"You're talking to the wrong group," Brad said. "Gracie's like a fish. Being on land slowly drives her crazy."

Fowler abandoned his cup of tequila and sat. "Are you a mermaid, Dr. Mann? We can break that news in the doc."

"Would anyone believe you?" Grace asked, baiting him.

Fowler sighed. "You're probably right. I've got a theory that the aliens have been here for a while, but people have seen too many movies and simply dismiss it outright when some news outlet reports it."

"But don't you sell projects that are sensational?" Grace asked.

"Damned right I do. The public gobbles it up. It doesn't mean they believe it, though."

"You should make fictional films then."

"Basically, he does," Alec said under his breath.

"I don't sell fiction," Fowler countered.

"But you do twist the truth," Double D said. "Either way, it's irresponsible."

"Is it?" Fowler appeared to get his bearings again, anger flashing in his eyes.

Brad leaned against the rail and crossed one ankle over the other. "The public can figure it out."

"No," Grace said. "Look at the PR damage from the movie *Jaws*. People have been vilifying the great white ever since. Even the author of the book regretted what he'd done. Peter Benchley spent the rest of his life trying to save the species he'd made as famous as The Beatles." She shook her head. "Sharks are on a path to extinction. We have to educate people. It's no longer good enough to have them sit by and twiddle their thumbs, claiming ignorance. And people need to enter the water armed with knowledge. Not only will it reduce shark attacks, but it will *save* sharks. There's simply no reason to be so afraid of them."

Brad huffed and looked away. "She's on her soapbox again."

She stood and approached Brad and Alec. "You know, Brad, the difference between you and most researchers is that you view the sharks like some amoeba that needs quantifying rather than as living, intelligent creatures."

"The problem with you, Grace, is you practice pseudo-science based on how you feel about your subject. It's not scientific. When you submit papers for review and talk about the love connection between you and Sally Shark, how does that work out for you? *I looked in her eyes and knew she had a soul,*" he mimicked in a woman's voice.

Grace narrowed her gaze. "Believe me, the only soulless eyes I've ever looked into are yours."

CHAPTER 9

G race awoke with a jolt. A quick glance at her digital watch told her it was 5 a.m. Excitement coursed through her.

I'm here.

She bolted out of bed and quickly dressed in her usual attire—sports bra, t-shirt, and quick-dry shorts. She switched out the lavender fleece for a navy one.

Missy stirred and looked down at Grace from her perch on the upper bunk. "God, you wake up early." She snuggled her face closer to her pillow.

"The sun is about to rise," Grace said around the toothbrush in her mouth. "Time to look for sharks."

Missy ran her fingers through her hair, then closed her eyes. "Okay. I'll be along in a bit."

Grace spit in the sink, then rinsed her mouth. She grabbed her sunglasses, hat, and buff, and slipped her cellphone into her pocket. Not that she'd be making any phone calls, but she liked to have it handy for any impromptu photos or videos. She'd found that it was the best way to document anything important. She didn't need some fancy camera, especially not on this trip, since Alec was along to make her and Brad movie stars. Michaels would eat it up, she had no doubt. Her argument with him the previous night threatened to dampen her enthusiasm, but she shoved it aside. He'd backed off, and she'd ended up with Alec, Missy, Stephie, and Double D on the back of the boat, swapping expedition stories for several hours. It had proved to be a boon to the friction that Brad always stirred up between the two of them.

Leaving the cabin, a smile stretched her lips wide, and her heart pounded with a charged expectancy. She knew full well there'd be no sharks frolicking around the boat, that instead she'd be greeted by deep blue ocean and the rocky escarpment of Guadalupe Island in the background. The whites would likely be shy, even standoffish at first, and finding them would take patience. But it didn't matter. Just the idea that she was in the same vicinity as the iconic great white was enough to make her want to skip to the railing in glee.

Resisting that urge, she left the salon and stepped into the alcove on deck where she'd helped Alec launch his drone yesterday morning, half expecting to see him. But the area was empty, giving her a slight pang of disappointment.

It was early, and the alcohol had flowed for several hours last night. As near as she could tell, she'd been the only one to hold back. Well, maybe Stephie Kim had as well. That girl was all business. If Alec ever let her go, Grace would seriously consider trying to get the girl a job at CMI.

Grace didn't want to waste one precious morning while she was here, especially nursing a hangover. It was important to stay focused on the goal: the whites. She was on their timetable, not her own, and she didn't want to miss a minute of it.

Moving to the starboard side of the boat as it bobbed gently in the placid water, Grace released an audible sigh.

Hello, my sweets.

The briny smell of saltwater greeted her, triggering all the happy places in her head and heart. It was such a relief to be out of the office and in the bosom of Mother Nature once again.

It made her so damned happy.

She gazed at the barren outline of Guadalupe Island—a volcanic remnant—and located North Head jutting from the water, its presence a beacon to the sharks. Well, not really. It was the Northern Elephant Seals, the Guadalupe Fur Seals, and the California Sea Lions that drew Jaws here every fall, and the barking and clamor of those animals could be heard in the distance. A dense fog had amassed in the upper elevation, waiting for the impending sunshine to trigger a cascading waterfall of vapor.

Truly, they had entered another time and place, a Jurassic Park filled with ancient great white dinosaurs swimming around them.

She climbed the ladder to ascend to the higher viewing platform and was startled when she found Alec there, camera in hand and pointed toward the island.

"I didn't expect anyone up this early." She came onto the deck, her cheery countenance buoyed more by his presence.

Turning, he took several photos of her. She bounded closer, forcing him to stop.

He lowered the lens. "It's hard to sleep in a place like this."

She placed her hands on the railing. Erik and Pete moved about on the deck below. "I know. I have the most vivid dreams when I'm on the water. We're in the realm of the unknown."

"Do the sharks whisper sweet nothings in your ear?"

She bent forward and laughed, scanning the water for any sign of movement. "I don't know you well enough to tell you my dreams."

He snapped several photos of the island slowly coming to life with the rising sun. "I hope that will change one day."

She briefly let herself bask in Alec's flirting, then gave a nod toward the shore. "That's known as Prison Beach." She pointed toward it. "To the left, on that rocky slope, are the remains of an old prison."

Alec squinted. "It's difficult to see."

"It's pretty broken down and blends into the hillside."

He switched his camera lens with a longer one sitting on the table. "This seems a remote place to have a prison. Who was it for?"

"The only story I've heard is that it was built for one man in the

1860s who was caught having an affair with the President's wife, but I don't know if that's true."

Double D appeared, balancing a tray with several cups of coffee in one hand while he hauled himself up the ladder with the other. "I thought I heard voices."

Grace quickly took the beverages from Dan so he could use both hands. "Thanks," she said. "What great service. I was sure you'd finished off the rum last night. How are you even awake?" She set the tray on the table but resisted the urge to grab a mug, despite the compelling aroma. When freediving, it was important to keep her heartrate down.

But she had to give Chris, the bohemian chef, credit—he somehow managed to make a fantastic pot of joe each morning. She'd need to dash downstairs to grab a cup of decaf.

Double D sank onto the cushioned bench seat, sweat beading along his brow, his breathing heavy. "I'm pretty sure I just used up all my energy for the day getting that to you."

"Did you finally exceed your rotgut limit?" Alec asked.

Double D exhaled. "Bite your tongue." He took a large gulp of coffee. "I'll be better. Just give me a minute."

"Maybe I should grab a bottle of something," Grace said. "Isn't there some theory that you need to keep drinking to cure a hangover?"

Alec reached around her, grabbing a mug. "Says the woman who drank sparkling water last night."

"The hair of the dog, but I'll be fine," Double D said, waving a hand at them. "I'm ready to stare into the jaws of death."

"I think your stench will scare all the fish away," Alec said. "Let's grab breakfast."

Dan moaned. "Don't mention food again."

GRACE SIPPED HER COFFEE, her belly somewhat filled from half a bagel slathered with a thin layer of cream cheese. Too much food made diving difficult, so she'd get the majority of her calories at the end of the day. She gazed out the window of the salon at the flaming yellow ball cresting the horizon, biding her time until they could deploy the buoys or until a shark showed up. As she booted up her computer, her eyes kept landing on Guadalupe Island, sitting right at their front doorstep.

The ever-present grin took control of her mouth once again.

Someone let out a whoop. Grace slammed her coffee down and dashed out of the salon.

Tony stood on the upper deck with Missy and Stephie, leaning over the railing and pointing. "We've got a shark!"

Grace spun around and smacked into Alec. "Sorry." His hands steadied her, but she ducked around him, leaning into the salon and grabbing the binoculars on the desk. She looped them around her neck and bolted outside, running down a set of stairs and to the fore of the boat. Alec was already on the pulpit that jutted over the water, a small handheld video camera capturing the ruckus. Grace came up behind him, scanning the water.

"There!" Tony yelled.

Grace concentrated on where Tony was pointing. A dark mass swam just under the surface, creating a sizable wake. The nearly black torpedo-shaped fish rose higher, and its skin revealed cobalt and turquoise hues against the blue sea. Grace's heart pounded. She laughed aloud, shaking with giddiness. All her imaginings didn't compare to that first moment when she spied these formidable and extraordinary creatures.

She brought the binoculars to her eyes. The dorsal fin—an object of terror for an entire generation raised on *Jaws*—broke the surface as the shark moved parallel to the boat and toward her and Alec's position.

She squealed with delight.

"Old friend?" Alec said.

"I'm checking."

"It's the Professor," Tony bellowed.

Grace studied the jagged edges of the dorsal fin, but it wasn't until she saw a notch missing in his caudal fin that she agreed with her graduate student.

"We first saw him last year," she said for Alec's benefit.

"He looks to be about fifteen feet."

She nodded. "He's a beauty. We frequently caught him in the company of two females. We called them Mary Ann and Ginger, but they usually chased him off."

"From what I hear, the females do seem to dominate around here."

The Professor glided beneath the narrow walkway that held them. They both whirled to the other side.

Grace kept the shark dead-center in the binocular eyepiece as it swam away, awe swelling her chest, increasing the pounding of her heart. "They're so powerful. It's breathtaking really."

"So, did you ever find out?" he asked.

"What's that?" She strained to keep the Professor in her sights as he glided farther away from the boat, finally disappearing.

"Who he preferred—Ginger or Mary Ann."

She let the binoculars dangle around her neck and looked at him, taking a deep breath as the excitement of the moment dissipated. "It was hard to tell. Maybe we'll solve that puzzle this time."

"My money's on Mary Ann," Alec said.

"Nah," Double D said from behind them. He'd obviously heard their conversation. "If the Professor is the stud I think he is, then he'll definitely go for the flashier woman."

Amusement danced in Alec's eyes. "Too much work. A man prefers his woman to be more down-to-earth."

"Depends what you want that woman for."

Grace glanced into the distance, mentally tracking the Professor's path. She wanted to believe it was a good sign he'd come by to greet them. If fortune was shining down on them, they would identify new sharks on this excursion. Never-before-identified sharks were always a welcome harbinger of a healthy Pacific great white population.

"Maybe we'll find us a Gilligan," she said, uttering the thought aloud.

ALEC GRIPPED the edge of the buoy and grunted as he and Double D lifted it, and then carried it across the deck. They set it down on the swimming deck with a thud.

"Sonuvabitch, these are heavy," Donovan exclaimed.

"We want them to be stable in the water," Brad huffed, shuffling across the deck with a second buoy, Erik and Pete helping him. They deposited their load with a definitive bang.

As the five men moved the last one to the lower deck for easier deployment, Fowler strode up. "What's the plan?"

Brad wiped sweat from his forehead with the side of his forearm. "Captain Bellamy will get us into position, then we'll push them into the water and secure an anchor."

Stephie stood off to the side, filming the activity since Alec and Donovan had their hands full.

Fowler examined the apparatus from several angles. "Does anyone have to be in the water for this?"

Brad rested his hands on his hips, trying to catch his breath. "No. Not unless something goes wrong."

Frank looked up. "Where's Dr. Mann?"

"Grace is inside, booting up the software and making sure it's working," Brad continued.

Alec nodded at Donovan and walked back to the salon. He wanted to grab a second video camera. As he stepped into the makeshift office area, he saw Grace sitting at one of the computer desktops, her fingers flying over the keyboard, her attention on the data scrolling on the screen.

He paused at the table where Missy sat, flipping through a book filled with photos of great white sharks. "Easy reading?"

"It's the MCSI shark I.D. book," she answered. "Just wanted to get familiar with who I might meet out there."

Strain marked Missy's face, her lips spread into a tight smile. Alec had no doubt that if Grace were perusing the contents, she'd be like a kid glued to a toy catalogue at Christmas time, her eyes wide with delight. But he would bet a hundred dollars she already had the thing memorized.

The Marine Conservation Science Institute had been studying the whites at Guadalupe Island since 1999, controlling the identification and naming of all the sharks, although scientists like Grace and Brad often employed pet names. It was expected that Alec's footage would be added to the database that tracked the appearance of sharks to the island. Each year a new edition of the book was released for scientists, recreational divers, and arm-chair enthusiasts.

If one of the whites happened to be a new visitor, then Grace might get the chance to choose a moniker for her find. He wondered if Gilligan was at the top of her list.

Alec looked at Missy's pinched face. "You okay?"

The dark-haired woman's staccato nod said otherwise. She resumed her perusal of the spiral-bound, waterproof book containing photo after photo of great white sharks, and Alec respected the dismissal. Whatever weighed on Missy was none of his business. He turned and peered over Grace's shoulder. Computer code filled the desktop screen.

"What are you doing?" he asked.

"Just a few last-minute tweaks," she replied.

Alec leaned closer and squinted. "Your code is...."

She stopped typing and glanced up at him, shifting to block the screen with her torso. "My code's proprietary."

Amused, Alec said, "I'm not going to steal it. I just wanted to watch the master at work."

"Wow." Her eyes widened. "And I thought Fowler was the only kiss-ass on board."

Double D stepped forward and handed Alec a large video camera. "Now, now, Galloway. Quit hitting on the pretty programmer."

Grace's cheeks flushed pink, and she spun back to face her computer screen.

Alec grinned and hoisted the camera to his shoulder. As he headed to the door, he said to Grace, "You about ready? The boat's headed to the first buoy position."

She nodded, keeping her eyes on the computer screen. "Yep. Be there in a sec."

Alec followed Double D outside. He turned his ball cap backwards and positioned himself on the main deck. Donovan secured himself to the viewing platform with a tether and a carabiner, his grip firm on his camera, which was also attached to him via a safety harness. Stephie sat nearby, fiddling with the settings on her camera.

The *Mercado* came to a stop, and the captain cut the engines. Grace and Missy joined everyone. Fowler sat off to the side smoking a cigarette.

Erik operated the crane from the upper deck as Brad, Tony, and Pete secured the buoy to two lead lines. Alec filmed from the starboard side, while Donovan shot from portside. Stephie snapped photos nearby.

With the engine whirring, the crane lifted the apparatus and lowered it into the water. Since it was weighted at the bottom, it quickly sank. A hushed anticipation ensued as Alec continued to film. He knew that once the equipment reached the ocean floor, the upper portion would detach and rise to the surface, dragging a line behind it. At incremental positions along that line were small sonar-emitting and receiving devices.

A conical white beacon broke the surface, and everyone cheered. Grace's face split into a wide smile. Her face was mostly hidden by a hat, sunglasses, and a neck buff, but Alec zoomed the camera in on her anyway. She exchanged a high-five with Tony and Pete and noticeably avoided Brad.

He stopped filming. "I want to be in the water for the next deployment," he said.

Grace shifted her attention to him. "I'll get in with you."

"We're goin' in, Double D," Alec yelled over to his partner. "You too, Stephie."

"Roger, boss," she replied.

Alec looked at Grace. "Will you freedive?"

She stepped closer to him. "No. I'll use scuba." She turned to the captain, who stood off to the side. "We're gonna need to get the cage in the water for the next one."

Captain Bellamy nodded and gave instructions to Pete.

"Time to get wet," Missy said.

While the captain drove the boat to the second deployment position, Alec returned to his cabin to strip out of his clothes and pull on nylon swimming trunks and his black wetsuit. By the time he returned to the deck, Double D and Pete had assembled the scuba tanks, masks, regulators, and flippers. He checked the camera equipment Donovan had brought out—two video cameras were nested in waterproof housings and ready to go.

The captain cut the power, and a clanging sound echoed as he dropped anchor. Grace and Missy walked on deck, and Alec did a double-take. "What the hell are you wearing?"

It wasn't the contours of Grace's curves now in full view that had his jaw swinging in the wind—although it was damned nice to finally match his imagination to reality—but rather the audacious color of her wetsuit, as well as Missy's.

Alec squinted from the bright yellow neoprene hugging Grace from neck to ankles. Missy's attire was even more confusing—hers showcased black and white horizontal stripes.

Double D lifted his buoyancy vest and scuba tank to the bench, and then froze in his tracks when he caught sight of them. "Hells bells, I've always wanted to dive with a banana and a zebra."

"Do you like it?" Grace asked, genuine enthusiasm shining in her eyes.

"Not really," Alec uttered. "You're like a homing beacon to sharks."

She scrunched her brows together. "That's the point. I want to attract sharks, not drive them away."

Brad shook his head from where he was preparing the next buoy. "There's no definitive proof that the color yellow draws sharks."

Grace glared at him. "And there's no definitive proof that it doesn't. Sharks are color blind, so contrast should draw their attention."

Missy buckled a weight belt around her waist.

Bewildered, Alec said, "And the stripes are because...."

"Unlike Gracie, I prefer not to flash like a neon sign. I'm supposed to look like a deadly sea snake."

He scrubbed a hand down his face. "So, while Grace is attracting sharks you're repelling them?"

Missy scrunched her nose. "Not repelling exactly. I just don't want them getting too close to me. I'm guessing they're smart enough not to eat lethal prey."

Donovan gave a nod of approval. "It's an interesting experiment. And Bulldog here," he flipped his thumb in Grace's direction, "will stand out like liquid sunshine on film."

Alec glanced around, bewildered. "I can't wait to see Tony's suit."

"He's not getting in the water with us for this one." Grace grabbed a pair of fins from the pile of gear. "He's gonna stay back and monitor the array, but his suit is camo blue."

Double D let out a hearty laugh. "Perfect. He'll be fucking invisible on film."

Missy ran both hands through her brown hair and secured it with a ponytail holder.

"Do you have an extra tie?" Grace asked her.

Grace's blonde tresses flowed past her shoulders, making her look reckless and sexy, filling Alec with a new tension that had nothing to do with her safety in the water. Against his will, his gaze skimmed the swell of her breasts and the lush curve of her hips.

Missy pulled an elastic band from her wrist and handed it to Grace, who began scooping her hair back with her fingers. Alec sucked in a breath, his lust kicking him to the curb. Maybe to the next street. Hell, probably to the next town.

Shit.

He turned away and ran a frustrated hand through his short hair. Sitting on the bench, he slipped his arms into his buoyancy vest, the pockets already weighted to his specifications.

Shit.

He'd been doing pretty well at keeping his attraction to her under wraps. Until now. He secured the vest by clipping the buckles and then grabbed his mask and fins.

Shit.

He headed to the aft of the boat. Double D and Stephie joined him, both suited up and carrying the video and photo cameras. They made fast work of donning neoprene hoods to cover their heads and ears.

Grace and Missy caught up and did the same.

Alec tested the regulator inside his full face mask. "We'll all get in the same cage for the sake of time. Grace, Missy, and Stephie take the downstairs, Double D and I will be up top."

Frank leaned over the railing from the upper deck. "Why don't you use the hookah system?" he asked, referring to the topside hoses that supplied air to divers in the water, eliminating the need for the cumbersome scuba gear.

"What if we wanna leave the cage?" Donovan asked.

"Are we in the cage or out?" Stephie asked matter-of-factly, stuffing her hair into a black hood. "Because we shouldn't take our fins if we're in."

"We're in," Alec said. "But bring them. It's better to be mobile, just in case. Our goal is to only get footage of the deployment, nothing else. This'll be our warm-up dive."

"There probably won't be any sharks," Grace said. "The noise from releasing the array will likely deter them."

Alec chanced a glance her way. Now that she was suited up, her female parts were sufficiently covered by the buoyancy vest, bringing his temperature down a notch. Except for her yellow arms and legs, she looked like the rest of them, her flaxen tresses safely hidden away from his carnal thoughts that had stampeded out of the gate without warning.

"We'll be on Channel A," he said and motioned for Grace and Missy to get in the cage that now dangled in the water portside.

Grace pulled the large mask over her face and gave him a thumbs-up. She tucked her fins under one arm, and Alec grabbed her other hand as she sat and scooted to the opening in the cage.

Grateful to fill his mind with an activity that didn't entail Grace naked and on her back, he got the girls into the cage, then yelled up at Pete, "Give us twenty minutes to get set up before you deploy."

Pete gave a nod, the second apparatus already connected to the crane.

Alec pulled on his mask. "Testing," he said into the comm.

"Copy." *Grace.*

"I read you." *Missy.*

"Aye, boss." *Stephie.*

"Roger dodger." *Double D.*

Sitting on the edge of the cage bobbing in the ocean, Alec pulled on his fins then took the camera that Donovan handed him. He sank into the water and held onto the second camera while Double D joined him.

Once they were all settled—the girls on the lower deck and Alec and Donovan on the upper deck—Alec signaled Erik that they were good. Erik activated the winch, and the cage sank slowly below the surface and into the clear blue that characterized the water around Guadalupe Island. Alec held onto the side of the cage and began adjusting the inflation valve to add gas to his buoyancy vest so that he remained in a neutral location and didn't float upward. He swung his gaze between his legs and saw the girls below, bubbles from their equipment shooting past him.

He realized it was a good thing after all that each woman had a very different wetsuit color. It made it easy to know who was whom.

As the submersible cage continued its descent downward, Alec breathed in short and then out long, the only sound the rhythmic cadence of his regulator. He scanned their immediate surroundings and saw nothing but gradations of blue hues that reminded him of Grace's eyes.

There were no sharks.

The movement of the cage stopped. Alec checked the depth on his dive watch. Thirty feet. That was as far as the submersible went.

They hung suspended in an entirely different world, an environment alien from the one humans inhabited, a saltwater paradise free of gravity. As spatial references fell away, a sense of peace overtook Alec.

Did the giant blue whales—the largest species on earth at over fifty feet long—fathom their own size?

Life here was experienced entirely through a different sensory system. A world filled with sonar.

With humans' inability to process such signals, the depths of the oceans appeared cold, disorienting, and just plain scary. At a thousand feet, there ceased to be light.

But the sonar array would penetrate this world and hopefully illuminate it in a far greater degree than imagined thus far. If Alec understood what Grace was implying about her neural network, then it could be trained to document far more than sharks.

But the array transmitted and received signals. How would marine life feel about this intrusion into their cosmos? Would it be nothing more than an annoying blip to them, or would the signals blast wide and far, reverberating in ways Grace and her team couldn't predict?

"Buoy two deploying in five." Erik's voice in the headset brought Alec back to the job at hand.

"Copy that." Alec checked his camera. "Double D, I'll move to the right, and you film from the left."

"Locked and loaded," Donovan replied.

"You ready, Steph?" Alec asked.

"10-4."

"Just don't photograph my crotch, thank you very much," Donovan said.

"No crotch. Got it." Stephie's voice held no hint of sarcasm.

A muffled thump echoed through the water, and Alec focused the camera on the apparatus as it rocketed toward them, on a path approximately fifteen feet away.

The device zoomed past and hit the seabed some distance below, dispersing a cloud of sand. A white missile popped free and careened back to the surface, elongating a rope with sonar devices tethered to it.

"I'm leaving the cage to get a shot of you all," Alec said.

"Make sure you get my good side," Double D remarked.

Alec removed his flippered foot from the cage slat he'd been using as an anchor and swam away from the suspended enclosure. As he twisted around to focus his lens on the others, a shadow passed overhead.

"We've got a shark," Grace said as Alec jerked his head up to get a visual.

His heartrate sped to sprint-race level.

Holy Mother of God.

A great white shark glided above him, its triangular, torpedo-shaped head swaying back and forth to the motion of its tail and strong caudal fin. Its white belly blended into the light that filtered down from the surface, offering camouflage, but there was no mistaking the gargantuan girth, as if the white had recently eaten a small car. As it moved overhead, the wake pushed against Alec, and he struggled to steady his camera so he could film it. With a clear view of the shark's underside, he verified no claspers present—the extension of the pelvic fin on males. It was a she, and a colossal one at that.

"That is one big fucking fish." Donovan's voice was nothing more than a whisper.

"Are they all this big, Gracie?" The tension in Missy's voice was palpable.

"No. I'm coming out."

"Nice and easy, Grace," Alec said, continuing to film while

trying to get a grip on his nerves. If he could get the shark in relation to the cage, it would help to frame the shot.

From the corner of his eye, Alec saw Grace exit the cage and swim upward. She passed Donovan and proceeded slowly to the opposite side of Alec's position. He appreciated that she was considering film angles, but he didn't like her being out there alone, her yellow arms and legs and black buoyancy vest making her look like an octopus.

The large female white inspected the rope with the sonar transmitters, and Alec wondered if that was what had drawn her in. He also wondered if she would attack the devices. As he kept his camera rolling, the enormous fish came around for another pass.

Her size was beyond anything he'd ever seen in a great white, and while fear sizzled along every nerve ending in his body, her languid movements and calm demeanor were, oddly enough, quietly reassuring.

She was magnificent.

The muscles in Alec's legs strained as he used his flippers to control his position so that he could track her.

"Oh my God!"

Grace's declaration jolted through him. He snapped his attention to her, certain another shark had appeared.

"What's wrong?" Missy asked, her voice filled with panic.

Grace gasped and her breathing became erratic. Alec started to move toward her.

"No, no, I'm sorry," Grace said. "I'm fine. I just can't believe it."

"Believe what?" Alec's tone was harsher than he intended, but for a split second, she'd scared the living shit out of him.

"That's Bonnie."

Alec looked over his shoulder as the massive female disappeared, having lost interest in them.

"Are you sure?" he asked.

What sounded like a sob filled the airwaves. "Yes."

CHAPTER 10

As the sun set against a sky of orange sliding toward pink, Alec stood on deck and drank a beer. He'd abandoned his ball cap since the wind had picked up, small whitecaps marching across the ocean's surface as if headed to battle. He gripped the railing as the boat swayed back and forth.

The third array buoy had been deployed, and they were now anchored within close proximity to the sonar triangle. Telemetry readings had started coming in, and Tony had been stuck at the computer the remainder of the afternoon, performing quality control on the incoming data.

Once Grace had seen Bonnie—or rather a shark she *believed* to be Bonnie—she'd been glued to Alec's laptop with a focus that bordered on obsession, combing through the footage and stills he, Double D, and Stephie had taken. A glance through the salon window confirmed that she still sat at the table, watching and freezing the footage, and sketching into a notebook. Alec guessed she was marking every dorsal notch, scratch, wound, and birthmark she could find.

Another boat had moved in, about a mile away. It didn't look like the tourist variety. Alec was about to find the captain and ask him about it when Brad left the salon and joined him.

"How's it look?" Alec asked, nodding toward Tony.

"Good so far. We're getting readings. Tomorrow we'll work on coordinating with visuals. Hopefully this weather will die down a bit, and Gracie can start skinny-dipping with the whites."

Alec pushed that image aside, especially since he had no desire to envision it with Brad in the mix. "Who's the other boat?"

"Researchers. Grace knows them. They're based out of Woods Hole. We're gonna take the outboard over later and say hi, if you want to come."

"Sure."

A gust flattened Brad's dark hair against his forehead. "You really think that shark you saw today was one that frequents the Farallones?"

Alec finished his beer and shrugged. "Even if it's not, it was an impressive female. I hope we see her again."

"Grace might have a mental breakdown if you don't."

Bristling over Brad's condescending attitude toward Grace, Alec watched the sea lions and seals that occupied the rookery in the distance, a collection of dark spots on the ecru-colored sand. Dusk was shark hunting time, so only the truly bold or the utterly igno-rant pinniped would be beyond the breakwater. The youngsters played in the shallows, while the adults seemed to be bedding down for the night, though not quietly. Barking and howling and cackling sounds filled the air. The males were no doubt fighting over territory.

"Why'd you date her?" The question slid from Alec's mouth before he could stop it.

Brad leaned his forearms onto the railing and released a low chuckle. "Shark Lab is pretty intense, with all the interns crowded into a tight living and work space. All you do is hang out with each other." He shrugged, appearing relaxed, as if he and Alec were the best of friends. "Grace was the best-looking of the bunch. She's not bad in the sack, but she never puts you before her work, and she never shuts up about her dad and his research." He shook his head. "It gets old fast."

"I heard *she* broke up with *you*."

To Brad's credit, his expression of surprise looked genuine. "Is that what she said? Yeah, well, we were pretty much done by then. I guess she just needed it tied in a neat little bow."

"It must be awkward working with her now."

Brad made a sound of resignation. "I can deal with it. Sometimes I'll be dating someone, and they won't like it, especially since Grace's viral photo. She's kind of famous now, and other girls don't seem to like that we're still friends."

"Are you?"

"Am I what?"

"Friends."

"Sure, why not."

Alec figured he may as well go the full monty now. "But the sonar array began as Grace's Ph.D. dissertation, and when you left Shark Lab, you took it with you to CMI without telling her."

"Is that what she told you? We both used it in our research at UM. She didn't own it. It wasn't proprietary. She assumed we'd peddle the project together to a private facility, and she's just angry that I managed to get hired because of it."

"But she was hired, too."

Brad snorted with disdain. "She was more aggressive than I thought she'd be, but lesson learned. Like I said, don't ever stand between her and her work."

Alec thought of Grace's cryptic remarks about protecting the contents of the deep learning code she'd written for the array, and he suspected that Brad's future would hold more lessons laid down at the hands of Grace Mann.

"Do you remember that really shitty day when we were tow surfing at Mavericks, and you were supposed to drive the jet ski and get me when things turned bad?" Alec asked.

Brad watched Guadalupe Island, his gaze pensive. "That was the day Paulie McWilliams disappeared."

"Yeah, and I thought I was going to join him since you chickened out and never came in to get me. I got pretty banged up in the Boneyard." Paulie was eventually found, but barely alive with a broken back. It easily could have been Alec's fate that day as well.

"I didn't bail on you. I was looking for Paulie. And you survived."

It was bullshit. Tow partners had to stick together. It could be the difference between life and death.

It was the same spiel Michaels had told him back then, when they were a couple of eighteen-year-olds filled with a reckless drive to meet the power of Mother Earth's big waves and walk away smarter and cooler because of it. But Alec had talked to some of the other guys that had been there on that ominous day, the black-clouded sky pressing over them, stirring the pitch-black ocean water into a swirling abyss. They said Michaels had choked.

In the end, Alec hadn't really blamed Brad—that day had been damned scary, and what had happened to McWilliams shook everyone up—but any amount of trust in Michaels-the-boy had disappeared. Listening to how Michaels-the-man had screwed Grace over, both figuratively and literally, was leaving the same bad taste in Alec's mouth all over again.

"I did," Alec said. "My mother held me extra tight when she saw me later that evening. Just a word of advice, Brad. Trust is a delicate thing."

Brad swung his gaze to Alec, his brows knitted together. "You don't trust me?"

"I think you handled Grace wrong, and it just might bite you in the ass." Alec walked away before Michaels could reply.

Did Brad really deserve the warning? Maybe. Maybe not.

If Grace hadn't managed to get put on the team at CMI, would Brad have kept going with the project anyway? Was her coding work really that unique, or would Brad have been able to find another programmer to develop it? And if he had, would he have at least included Grace's name on it? If Brad was still the Brad of old, then the answer was undoubtedly no.

Not that any of this was Alec's business.

He stepped into the salon—Tony was still focused on the desktop, and Grace was busy scribbling into her notebook. For a split-second—with her hair loose and in disarray, and her dark-rimmed glasses resting low on her nose—Alec caught sight of a little Gracie Mann. He could imagine her sitting at the feet of her father, soaking up his knowledge, formulating a determination to follow in his footsteps.

And that was when it became crystal clear.

Gracie wasn't an emotionless bulldog—or an ice queen—about her work. It was quite the opposite. She was passionately trying to impress a man who had obviously meant everything to her—her father.

She looked up, startling Alec from his stupor.

"So?" he asked, trying to sound casual, as if he hadn't been staring.

She grinned, young-Gracie alive and present in the glow of her Caribbean-blue eyes. "It's Bonnie."

GRACE BRACED herself as Brad drove through the choppy water, the outboard tossing around like a bath toy. A steady rain beat down on them. She wiped water from her eyes and tightened the hood of her windbreaker around her face.

Brad brought the small watercraft flush against the *Wallflower*, a large research vessel contracted by the Woods Hole Oceanographic Institute based in Massachusetts. Alec grabbed a rope and jumped onto the boat, pulling hard as the outboard bumped against it. His water shoes slipped, and his leg muscles bulged as he compensated. He still wore shorts, but Grace had changed into lightweight nylon pants. Two men appeared and helped Alec secure the runabout.

Grace grabbed Alec's outstretched hand, and he hauled her onboard with a burst of strength. The others quickly followed.

Despite several people moving about, Grace immediately caught sight of Sylvie Alexander. The older woman greeted her with a wide smile that brimmed with the exuberance of a young girl, contradicting her age. She folded Grace into a warm embrace. "Gracie, it's so good to see you. Quick, come inside and get out of this weather."

They were ushered into a lounge area similar to the salon on the *Mercado*—computers, books and papers filled the countertops, and a handful of people crowded the space. The boat rocked from side to side, and the aroma of coffee and too many bodies filled the air.

As Alec, Dan, Brad, Stephie, and Tony crowded behind her, Grace pushed the hood from her head and shook the water from her jacket before proceeding any farther into the room, not wanting to track it all over the floor.

A familiar face appeared through a door on the opposite side of the room. "It's my darlin' girl," Harry Alexander's voice boomed. It had been a few years since Grace had last seen the Alexanders, but Harry still sported a shock of crazy gray hair that put her in mind of Albert Einstein, along with a bushy beard to match. A few more years—and a few more pounds—and he'd give Santa a run for his money.

Grace was soon caught up in a hearty hug from Sylvie's husband. She inhaled the comforting scent of sunscreen and saltwater and the man she considered part of her family.

"I don't want to get you wet," Grace said, stepping back, a grin stretching her lips from ear to ear. "I'm so glad we were able to cross paths. I wasn't sure if our expeditions were going to match up."

"I'm pleased as punch that your array is getting off the ground," Harry said. "We've been here a week now. I've got lots to tell ya."

Filled with anticipation, Grace peeled off her jacket and hung it on a nearby hook while the others in her group did the same. "I want you to meet Alec Galloway. He's filming a documentary on our work."

"Pleased to meet you, sir." Alec shook Harry's hand, then Sylvie's.

"Harry and Sylvie were good friends of my dad."

Grace also introduced Double D and Stephie. Harry knew Brad and Tony, and Missy and Frank had stayed back on the *Mercado*—Missy from fatigue and Frank from another bout of seasickness.

Grace and Stephie crammed around a table with Sylvie and Harry, while the men stood, leaning on counters and against walls.

Harry introduced two young men named Joey and Martin, while a girl with shoulder-length black hair and tan skin handed out coffee in Styrofoam cups. "Don't worry, it's decaf," Harry said, then gave a nod toward the girl. "This is Mackenzie. I've got myself three grad students this time around."

"Lucky you," Grace said. "What are you working on?" She took a sip of the freshly-made brew, grateful as it warmed her insides.

"It's exciting, Gracie," Harry beamed. "Remember our shark cam idea?"

She gave a nod.

"It's a go. We're just waiting to get a tag on a great white."

"When you get it, let me know," Grace said. "I'm dying to see your footage."

Alec knocked his ball cap back a bit. "Are you attaching a camera to a shark?"

"No," Sylvie answered. "There's a lot of issues with that scenario, as you can imagine. What we're doing is attaching a clip-on transmitter to the dorsal fin. Once it's in place, it will provide a homing beacon to a remote monitoring unit, which is shaped like a long torpedo so that it can shadow the shark as inconspicuously as possible. As it follows the shark, we should be able to see hours of activity in real time. Unfortunately, we had some problems earlier in the week when one of the whites attacked the AUV in the water."

"Was there damage?" Grace asked.

"A few toothmarks, but it's still functioning." Sylvie opened a laptop, tapped on the keyboard, and then spun the computer to face Grace. "We've ID'd several sharks so far. Lucy, Mau, Legend, Geoff Nuttall, and Gianna. We think it was Lucy who gave us a love bite."

Grace scrolled through the photos, admiring the male and female great whites that frequented Guadalupe Island each fall. She glanced over at Sylvie. "I saw Bonnie today," she said quietly.

Both Harry and his wife stopped and stared.

"Are you sure?" Harry's bushy eyebrows came together to form a hedge below his forehead.

"Yes. We were deploying the sonar array, and Alec got her on film, but she didn't hang around for long. I studied the footage all afternoon, and the markings my dad had recorded were present. Have you seen her?"

Harry shook his head. "That would be a damned sight. Wouldn't that be something? I don't think she's ever been ID'd down here. She's always been at the Farallones. Why would she come here instead?"

"Who's to say she hasn't been coming here all along?" Alec said.

Brad shook his head. "She'd be hard to miss. Somebody would've reported her—a biologist, a grad student. Hell, a tourist."

Harry sat back and stroked his beard. "I don't know. If it is Bonnie, she'd be big." He raised a bristly eyebrow-hedge in Grace's direction.

"She was," Grace confirmed.

"And I have a theory about those big females," Harry continued. "They're careful. How else could they have survived for so long?"

A derisive snort escaped Brad. "I'm sorry. I just can't buy this self-aware shit."

Harry narrowed his eyes at Grace's ex. The Alexanders were aware of her history with Brad. "We know that elephants and whales are highly social and very intelligent," Harry said. "Sharks have been on this planet for millennia. I'd say they've learned a thing or two during their time here, and who are we to presume their level of consciousness?"

Time fell away, and Grace was back in her childhood home, her father and Harry having one of many similar conversations around the dinner table. Grace would eat meatloaf smothered in ketchup or her mom's homemade tamales while listening intently to theories behind shark behavior and ways to understand it.

"Well, in light of what you've told me," Harry said, "I've got a story to tell. We made a trip to the island a few days ago and met up with several locals. Did you know there are about thirty families on the island?"

Grace shook her head.

"The men are all fishermen," Harry continued, "and they know the whites quite well, so it's always good to talk to them. They traded us a bunch of prawns for all the soda, batteries, and chocolate we had." He chuckled. "Anyway, there was this one fella. What was his name?" He looked at Mackenzie.

Grace shifted her gaze to the woman, noticing that she was quite pretty.

"Ricardo," the girl answered, casting a glance at Alec.

"Yep, that was it. He said that a lot of the fishermen talk about a massive shark that has come to these waters many times."

Grace's attention on Harry's words wavered as she became aware that Mackenzie had positioned herself beside Alec.

Harry ran a hand through his wild hair. "Some say she lives here year-round, but that can't possibly be—we know the sharks leave by January or February. But nevertheless, the idea persists that this massive female, and of course it *has* to be a female if she's as big as they say, is tied to this place like a guardian of some sort."

Mackenzie said something to Alec, who gave a nod and a half-smile.

"And now you tell me that Bonnie is cruising around." Harry let out a laugh. "God, I hope we see her."

The boat lurched, and Mackenzie fell against Alec. He caught and steadied her. Grace's irritation reached a flashpoint, annoyed that the little tart had managed to get Alec to touch her.

"How big do you think she is?" Sylvie asked.

Trying to ignore the pretty grad student and Alec, Grace said, "We estimated twenty-two feet."

"Holy hell," Harry burst out. "Did you get a permit to freedive?"

"Yes," Grace replied.

"If we get some downtime, can we join you in the water?"

"Of course."

"Mackenzie is an excellent freediver," Harry added.

Swell. Grace pasted a smile on her face. "We're only allowed three freedivers."

"If someone backs out, maybe she can fill in." By Harry's open expression, you'd think the girl were his granddaughter, except that the Alexanders were childless.

She hesitated. Normally, she wouldn't pin the success of an expedition on a diver she hadn't worked with, but she trusted Harry too much to doubt that the girl's credentials were solid. Grace hadn't known Alec's skills before jumping in the drink with him, so she'd already broken her own rule on this trip.

"I'll let you know," she said, a sudden bout of fatigue swamping her.

For one brief moment, she allowed a pity party to engulf her and slumped against the backrest of the bench seat.

She needed to keep her eye on Brad and the array, she needed to trust that Alec would present her and the work in a positive light, she needed to remain focused on being in the water among great white sharks. And now she needed to worry that Mackenzie might steal the affection of her favorite man on the boat.

Enough of that.

Harry and Sylvie continued chatting, and Grace straightened her spine and took a sip of coffee, suppressing the urge to scowl as Mackenzie struck up a conversation with Alec.

CHAPTER 11

G race stepped out on deck, padding along on bare feet. A simple black one-piece bathing suit covered her torso, and she'd pulled her bright yellow wetsuit up only as far as her waist. For a moment, she'd considered wearing the one bikini she'd packed but then backed off. Thoughts of snagging Alec's attention with a bit of cleavage had crossed her mind, only to trigger an immediate irritation for acting idiotic and insecure.

I've got nothing to prove, and if he wants to flirt with Mackenzie-who-also-freedives, then I can't stop him.

Still, there was nothing like a little breast exposure to solidify one's standing with the male species. She and Missy had often joked: *When in doubt, whip the boob out.*

It was late morning. She'd taken her regimen of vitamins and eaten a bowl of oatmeal with cinnamon and turmeric nearly three hours ago, so it should be well-digested by now. It was important that her digestive tract not hog all the blood since other organs in her body would need it during the freedive, organs such as her brain.

She'd also left her wetsuit half on in case she needed to use the lavatory because she'd also been consuming a low-sugar electrolyte drink all morning to stay hydrated.

A glance at the sky—no clouds, endless blue expanse, and the peaceful flat water—filled Grace's chest and belly with eagerness. With the whim of a moody woman, Mother Nature had gifted them with a calm and placid sea after the maelstrom the previous night. It was as if the ocean were giving its blessing for a successful outing.

Be professional, she thought. Don't jump up and down like the time her dad had gifted her a pair of binoculars on her birthday. She'd been eight years old, and it had made her feel like a grown-up and full-fledged member of his research crew since she could finally search for dorsal fins in the water along with the other scientists.

She smiled and suppressed an excited giggle.

"We've got three sharks in the water," Tony yelled from above her.

Sweet. She did an imaginary fist-pump in her head, and then indulged in a little side-step shuffle, lifting her arms up and giving a boogie-shake of her hips.

"She dances," Alec said from behind her.

Startled, she gasped and spun around. Alec's wetsuit molded his body and showed every sleek, muscular contour.

"Just burning off some nerves." The words tumbled out in a breathless rush.

"It's good to know you *have* nerves."

"I never claimed to be superwoman."

He grinned. "That's a relief."

He moved past her, carrying a large camera encased in a water-tight housing.

"I just hope those sharks Tony sighted stick around," she said. Whites could be notoriously bashful. She trailed Alec to the diving deck, still bobbing her head to an imaginary beat.

"Let's get in the water," Alec said. "Gather your team, Dr. Mann."

"Yes, sir." She glanced at the upper deck. "Tony, let's go," she yelled. "Find Missy."

Alec handed the camera housing down to Double D, who was

already in the water, then grabbed a pile of straps and approached Grace.

"This is a chest harness," he said.

She slipped her arms into her wetsuit and pulled it onto her upper body, the back open. Alec stepped behind her and zipped it closed, then reappeared before her. He lifted her arms as if he were dressing a young child and looped the harness around her shoulders, clipping it just below her breasts. He tugged on the straps so that there wasn't any give.

"This is the on/off button." He pointed to a flat silver knob on the small waterproof camera now resting against her ribcage. "If you can, try to have the camera running only when there's a shark in the vicinity. Press it once to turn it on." As he spoke, he performed the action, and a red light activated. "Press it again to turn it off. Got it?"

"I think I can handle it," she said in a cheeky tone.

"Just do the best you can."

When his eyes met hers, the heat in his gaze caught her off-guard, and her breath bottlenecked in her throat. Then he turned away and began rigging the same setup onto Missy and Tony.

A flush of heat filled Grace, jumpstarted by Alec's obvious interest. With her nerves flitting about like teen girls at a Taylor Swift concert, she jumped up and down and shook out her arms, rolling her head back and forth, attempting to burn off a bit of energy with calisthenics.

When Alec finished securing the cameras, he went to work strapping on his rebreather and assembling the rest of his gear. "Give us ten minutes, then get in the water," he said to her.

"Are you going in the cage?" Grace asked.

"Yes, but we'll exit as needed for more mobility."

Stephie appeared, suited up and looking more like a deep space astronaut with the bulkier and more complex rebreather equipment engulfing her small frame. "I'll be with Double D."

"I'll be portside," Alec added. "Also, the cages have six go-pros each strapped around the perimeter. Don't forget that the extra air tanks and scuba gear are stashed in the starboard cage."

Brad joined them, also wearing a rebreather. "I'll be with Alec," he said.

Frank ambled forward, clad in a black wetsuit. "I'm gonna hang out in the surface cage."

Grace hoped the sharks wouldn't be overwhelmed by such a large audience.

Alec entered the top of the cage and slipped into the water, his mask in place. Once Brad joined him, he gave a thumbs-up, and Erik engaged the winch, lowering the cage into the watery depths. Then Erik did the same for Double D and Stephie in the opposite cage.

Tony and Missy donned masks with snorkels attached, but Grace preferred to be as unencumbered as possible, so she went without. She buckled a belt around her waist with two-pound weights disbursed evenly on the outside, giving her a total of twelve pounds to assist in hovering once she reached a desired depth. Sitting down on the edge of the diving deck, she positioned a neoprene hood over her braided hair and pulled extra-long fins over her scuba booties.

Frank entered the surface cage anchored to the aft deck where it bobbed in the water alongside Pete, the hookah system sending air to them via hoses. They wouldn't be encumbered with scuba gear and, thanks to the large air-holding tank, wouldn't need to run the noisy generators while they were in the water.

"Remember," Grace said, looking at Missy and Tony to her right, "if a shark comes toward you, don't make a hasty retreat. Affirm your position in the water. Hold your ground."

They both gave a nod, but Missy's pale and pinched face prompted Grace to say, "Just have fun. You're part of a very small club of adventurers who have done this."

Missy visibly swallowed, and her chest rose up and down in rapid succession. She looked like she might vomit.

"You don't have to go," Grace said sincerely.

Tony gently nudged Missy, pushing her toward Grace. "You're not experiencing woods shock, are you?"

Missy's shoulders remained taut as her feet dangled over the side of the deck. "What in the hell is that?"

"It's when people get disoriented in the wilderness."

She shook her head, rapid and firm. "No. I'm fine. Just a few jitters."

Grace reached for Missy's hand and gave it a squeeze. "We'll all keep an eye on each other. Any problems, just come to the surface." She held her friend's gaze. "We're not shark bait."

Missy released a shaky laugh. "I hope the sharks got the memo."

"Besides," Tony cut in, "you're a venomous sea snake. The sharks will *hate* you. It will probably be a total mean girls' snub, so try not to be too disappointed when Dr. Mann gets invited to all the shark parties."

"Initially, shoot for maybe one minute of down time," Grace said. "Then gradually start increasing it." Grace's heart chanted its rapid song of fear and excitement; the initial anxiety of a dive meant decreased dive times. "It could take us up to an hour to get acclimated. And don't forget—once you start going deeper, give yourself at least three minutes at the surface before diving again."

It was an odd thing, but even freedivers could get decompression sickness or risk blackouts if they didn't allow oxygen and carbon dioxide levels to rebalance periodically.

Missy silently agreed.

"Collapse your lungs and extend your spine," Grace continued. "Imagine that you're an underwater missile."

Missy's chest inflated as she took a deep breath and straightened her back, expelling air from her lips as if she were puffing out circular smoke rings.

They each began the pre-dive breathing exercises. *Inhale one, hold two, exhale ten, hold two.* Repeat. After twenty repetitions, Grace placed her mask over her eyes and nose, and she entered the water. Missy and Tony silently followed.

Grace moved along the surface to clear the boat and get a visual on whether the three sharks were still present. She dipped her face into the ocean. Visibility was more than fifty feet in the crystalline blue water. No sharks.

Initially, she would take it easy, with shallow dives of fifteen to twenty feet; then with hope, when a shark was in the vicinity, she'd be warmed up for deeper and longer dives.

She, Missy, and Tony needed to keep an eye on each other, but they each had different freediving abilities and would need to honor their own pace. And this was the first time Tony and Missy had dived with whites in this way—anxiety could shorten their breath-holding.

Grace brought her head out of the water, breathed up, and dove, her butt coming up and out of the water.

Moving like a mermaid, her arms by her side and her body undulating up and down, she descended, sighting one of the submersibles. Alec was already on the upper portion of his cage, his camera at the ready. Grace cleared her ears repeatedly by trapping air inside her sinus cavities as she moved deeper into the stunning abyss.

About fifteen feet above the submersible cages, she stopped and hovered in the weightless environment. Tony and Missy were right behind her.

Excellent.

They all paused, their backs to one another, maintaining a 360-degree view of their surroundings, and Grace scanned the crystal-clear water for sharks.

If only Bonnie would make an appearance.

Grace took in the blue world where there was no up or down, a place defined by its lack of definition. A slight pressure began to build in her chest, the barest hint of a convulsion. Then, a flush of energy filled her as her spleen—in response to the lack of air—released fresh, oxygen-rich blood into her system. Her heartrate slowed, and a surreal calm settled over her.

One of the best natural highs on the planet.

Suspended in this other world, the only contrast was prismatic rays of sunlight from the surface. Grace checked her dive watch. One minute had elapsed, but her brain told her it had been much longer. Down here the march of life slowed and time elongated. Did the sharks and whales and dolphins experience this as well?

Missy and Tony began to ascend, so Grace did the same. With a steady pace, they glided to the surface, drawn to the light, like mankind seeking God and the bone-deep desire for enlightenment.

At around seven feet below the surface, she exhaled the remainder of the air she'd been holding, bubbles flowing upward from her mouth. This prevented shallow-water blackouts, which Erik would be on the lookout for from the boat, and Pete, from the surface cage; but the bigger benefit was the ability to inhale much-needed air immediately.

Grace burst through the surface and took in a lungful of sweet oxygen.

"I feel good," Tony exclaimed. "But where are those sharks? You need to get to work on your magic elixir, Shark Lady."

Grace laughed. "I'll crank my shark-o-meter up." She looked at Missy, who coughed as she treaded water. "You good?"

Missy gave a thumbs-up.

For the next twenty minutes, all three of them repeated this routine of descending and ascending, gradually increasing their down time to over three minutes.

During a break topside, a dorsal fin cut through the water about a hundred yards away. Grace filled her lungs with air and dove, this time going deeper, until she neared the submersible cage.

Alec was completely covered in neoprene and rebreather equipment and held a camera in front of him. Double D looked the same in the opposite cage. The only way to tell them apart was the eyes in the dive masks. Still, Grace knew which one was Alec by the way he held himself. With his tall frame, he curled his shoulders slightly forward, while Donovan didn't. She knew Brad's location, too, since he was the only one beside Alec, and Stephie was easy to spot because she was the smallest.

Grace pointed to her left, and Alec acknowledged her with a

nod. With deliberate movements, she activated the camera on her chest.

From beyond, a feathery movement hinted at the approach of the shark. Then a small shadow began to build in size, finally materializing into a magnificent great white shark.

A jolt of adrenaline zapped Grace. With a conscious effort, she steadied herself in the water, waiting until the momentary, terror-stricken urge to flee passed. Her heart, so calm during the past thirty minutes, began pumping in earnest.

The white shark swam straight toward them, its fins angled down and its mouth open, revealing a collection of deadly white triangles ready to consume the flesh of seals and sea lions, or perhaps a human by mistake. While this angle of approach was disconcerting, Grace had always liked it, because the sharks appeared to be smiling. And she knew it could see her. With its angular head and narrow snout, white sharks possessed monovision.

Like a giant airplane, the shark glided closer, hardly flicking its tail but moving with speed and dignity. Grace caught a glimpse of the underside. *No claspers.* This big beautiful creature was a female.

The white didn't change course. Missy and Tony had moved closer to the submersible, but if Grace did the same then Alec wouldn't have a good shot. And although the instinct to beat a hasty retreat pressed on her, Grace willed herself to stay the course, and instead, shifted closer to the fish, farther from the safety of the humans. Using her fins with the barest amount of movement, Grace held herself steady, never taking her eyes from the great white almost upon her.

The shark's skin glistened brightly, the gray tone shining with silver from the sunlight that filtered from the surface, the white underbelly putting Grace in mind of whipped cream.

The massive female continued to approach and, about ten feet away, turned to its right and swam past, its wake slamming against Grace and pushing her back. At once, Grace noticed several things: the freckles on the shark's snout, the ampullae of Lorenzini with which the white could sense the electrical current of Grace's beating heart, a scar near the five gill slits (*this is Mary Ann!*), and a fishing line that was wrapped around her dorsal fin and trailing a twine of rope behind her.

Mary Ann moved away, her caudal fin scarcely swaying. It never ceased to amaze Grace how little effort sharks exerted to move through the water.

She looked at her dive watch: 3:56.

She'd reached her limit and needed to ascend.

At the surface, Tony let out a whoop. "It's Mary Ann!"

"Oh my God!" Missy gasped for air. "Did you see the size of her?"

"She's looking mighty fine," Tony added, as if he were sizing up a potential female companion.

"How big do you think she is?" Missy asked.

"We estimated about seventeen feet last year," Grace said. "But did you see the fishing line?"

"I know what you're thinking," Tony said. "And I'm not sure you'll be able to get close enough."

"It doesn't matter. One way or another, I'm cutting that damned thing off her."

ALEC WATCHED the impressive white female circle the water, trailing fishing line from her dorsal fin. It didn't look like it had created much of a problem for her, but it was still a reminder of the obstacles these animals faced from human interaction.

He'd gotten good footage of Grace and the shark. As Grace, Tony, and Missy had surfaced, the white had continued to patrol a wide perimeter but, thankfully, kept her distance.

With his camera still targeted on the shark, Alec grinned. Regal and calm, the great white watched them. It was hard not to be awestruck while in her presence.

"That's Mary Ann." Brad's voice filled the radio headset. "I'm surprised to see her. The females usually visit every other year."

"I'll bet she's looking for the Professor," Double D said.

"She's checking us out." Stephie's voice cracked with static.

"Oh shit. This can't be good." Donovan's voice had Alec searching for Grace.

Her lithe form slipped down to them as if she were a fish herself. She held something in her hand.

A knife.

She was going to remove the fishing line.

Just like the water pressure at this depth, concern began to squeeze Alec on all sides. But he kept filming her.

"She'd better hope the Mexican Navy never catches wind of this, or we're all screwed." Brad's voice dripped with scorn.

Grace paused about thirty feet away as Mary Ann briefly blocked Alec's view of the woman in yellow. Tony had come down as well, but Missy was hanging back, remaining closer to the surface.

Alec ran several scenarios through his head; all of them involved abandoning his camera and getting to Grace as soon as he could. If she startled Mary Ann in any way....

Grace angled herself to swim parallel to the shark, then kicked her fins to match the white's speed. At the last second, Mary Ann turned and spun away, leaving Grace in her wake.

But Grace was determined. As she positioned herself again, Tony came to her side.

Good. It might help if something went wrong.

Time stretched as Grace and Tony attempted to engage the shark. About every four minutes, they rose to the surface to regain oxygen, and then returned. They went through this cycle again and again, and surprisingly, Mary Ann remained.

Alec spied a few sharks below them, but Mary Ann—clearly the dominant shark—held court, and those males and females never rose any higher. She seemed very interested in Grace and continued to glide effortlessly through her aquatic world, a collection of striped pilot fish hovering near her mouth in a daring display of bravado.

But great whites of her size didn't waste time with fish—that was for the pups and young of the year. Alec recalled viewing the carcass of a one-year-old white shark. At that age, whites had tri-cusped shaped teeth that were more suitable for grasping fish. As whites grew and matured, their teeth broadened out, allowing them to literally saw their prey in half. Somehow the pilot fish knew that Mary Ann was interested only in seal or sea lion meat with their high caloric content.

Alec hoped Grace wouldn't suddenly be added to that list.

Other groups of fish came and went—fusiliers with pale purple hues and striking yellow stripes along their bodies; a fast-moving group of grayish wahoo, their elongated bodies flashing as they moved in unison through shafts of sunlight; and tiny jellyfish that were best avoided, due to their sting.

Alec continued to film as Mary Ann returned for yet another pass. Very quickly he knew this round would be different. Instead of attempting to swim beside the shark, Grace had positioned herself directly before the sharp-toothed lady leviathan.

What the fuck?

He expected Mary Ann to turn at the last minute like she had previously. Or rather, he prayed that she would. If the shark became aggressive toward Grace, the bloody fallout would be upon them before they could react.

Tony appeared to lose his nerve and moved to the side, and Missy was nowhere to be seen.

"What the hell is she doing?" The strain in Double D's voice strung Alec's nerves even tighter.

"She's shark whispering," Stephie said quietly—almost rever-ently—as she continued to snap photos.

Stephie's comment seemed to stop time, holding them all in limbo as the shark closed the gap to Grace. Alec kept the camera running, but looked up from the viewfinder to watch the event unfold in real-time.

Grace raised her left arm forward, palm faced outward. In the blink of an eye, the shark's nose butted against Grace's hand, shoving her back, but somehow Grace held her ground.

Then the shark did something extraordinary. It slowed itself and paused, and Grace's gloved hand once again touched the snout.

Stunned, Alec witnessed Grace push against the shark, its head angling up slightly from the pressure of one tiny, puny human hand, putting Grace literally face-to-face with dozens of knife-edged teeth.

Alec's heartbeat ricocheted in his ears.

He knew about tonic immobility but this…this was….

Who the hell would ever try it on a great white shark?

Grace looked like a piece of lint beside the massive beast.

And somehow, it was working.

Grace swung her body up and over Mary Ann and grabbed hold of the dorsal fin, and then shark and woman merged into one as they glided through the water.

Alec had forgotten to breathe and gasped in panic, his body ready to mutiny and shoot to the surface before it suffocated. The one thing you never did in a rebreather was to stop breathing.

Count it out.

He closed his eyes for a moment as he sought to regain a rhythm.

Steady. Keep it together.

This was how accidents happened.

Breathe in, breathe out. Make the exhalation longer.

As he reclaimed his equilibrium, he went back to the camera, and despite his shaking hands, he made sure he was getting the shot.

Grace had grabbed hold of the knife that dangled on a lead from her wrist and was working on the fishing line.

The shark moved away, and Alec debated whether to follow, but then just as quickly, Mary Ann turned back. Grace was still taking a free ride, sawing at the line, swapping her hands back and forth to push the offending rope away. When she'd gotten it all, she released her hold and angled her body so that her momentum carried her upward. Alec didn't know how much time had elapsed, but Grace no doubt was precariously close to blacking out.

Mary Ann continued a leisurely trajectory as if a human hadn't just hitched a ride. Alec stopped recording and watched Grace's long fins oscillate back and forth as she ascended, Tony accompanying her. Once she was at the surface, some of the tension left him at last.

"I think we're done for the day," Brad said.

"Agreed," Alec replied. "Erik, are you there, over?"

"I'm here, over," the deckhand answered.

Alec's heartrate finally began to settle down. "Bring us up."

"Roger that."

Mary Ann made another pass, this time quite close, and without warning thrust forward and bit the cage.

"Oh, shit!" Alec scrambled back, dropping his camera. Luckily, it landed at the bottom of the metal slats.

Brad chuckled from where he'd retreated to the opposite far corner. "She's just curious about us."

As Mary Ann gifted them with a dentist's view of her mouth, the cage jerked up and down. One of her serrated, razor sharp teeth came loose, and Alec caught it in a trembling hand before it floated away.

As the shark departed into the never-ending fluid world, the winch began to raise the cage.

Sweat dripped down Alec's forehead, stinging his eyes. He blinked rapidly to maintain his vision in case Mary Ann came back to play one more time. He slipped the tooth into a pocket on his vest and retrieved his camera.

He knew that Mary Ann hadn't been attacking them. While her mouthing of the cage had certainly startled him, raising his blood pressure to stroke level, he couldn't help but feel that there was a sense of gratitude from her.

Had she known about the line wrapped around her dorsal fin?

It was possible.

Did Mary Ann approach Grace because she'd sensed that this

human woman could help her? Did sharks have gut feelings, a sixth sense, an ability to read the body language of other creatures around them?

With her capacity to sense prey across great distances, Mary Ann had most assuredly known of Grace's presence. She'd tolerated it. Hell, she'd practically played tag with Grace.

Missy's words echoed in his head. Marine creatures naturally gravitated to Grace. Perhaps they sensed something in Grace's energy—a subtle perfume of love and compassion and a drive to protect them.

If so, he understood. He wasn't immune to Grace either.

For as many times as Alec had been in the water with great whites, he'd never filmed a freedive. And despite the terror of watching Grace approach a white head-on, it was a breathtaking display of elegance and curiosity between humans and sharks.

Grace Mann was quite possibly the bravest person he'd ever known.

CHAPTER 12

G race pulled herself onto the dive deck and cast off her mask. She was utterly spent. Tony began shedding his wetsuit, but Grace didn't have the energy. Frank and Pete exited the surface cage, but where was Missy? She'd have to look for her later to reconnoiter the dive.

No one spoke. Fatigue permeated the atmosphere.

Eric worked the winches, the noise from the motors blaring in Grace's ears. She hung her head and waited for the annoyance to pass. As she continued to sit at the edge of the deck, her legs dangling in the water, an image of laying her head down on her pillow made her feel drowsier.

Peripherally, she was aware of the submersibles coming level with the boat. She sensed rather than witnessed the commotion of Alec, Double D, Stephie, and Brad stripping out of their rebreather equipment.

"Very impressive, Dr. Mann."

Grace glanced up at Stephie, although the girl seemed far away, her voice muted.

Stephie's expression immediately became serious. "Alec?" she yelled, her tone stern and all-business.

Grace frowned and tried to locate him. Without warning, he was beside her.

"Grace, your lips are blue," he said. He pulled her up, then held her firmly around the waist as he guided her into the salon.

"Wait," she said. "I need to take my wetsuit off."

"We'll do it inside." His tone was firm, almost brusque, which irritated her. She wasn't a baby. She could do it herself.

As they neared her cabin, she began to shiver. She reached for the door handle but the weakness in her arms surprised her, as did the lack of control over her fingers.

The shaking intensified.

"No," Alec said. He dragged her farther down the hallway.

Crowding her into the small bathroom space that everyone shared, he shut the door. Reaching around her, he turned on the shower and within seconds steam began to fill the room.

He unclipped the camera harness and dropped it to the floor, and she wondered if he'd broken it but didn't have the energy to ask him. He put his hands on her shoulders and turned her away from him, and then unzipped the wetsuit. As if she were a doll, he peeled the neoprene away from her body, tugging to get it off her arms. He knelt and yanked the fabric down her legs.

The few times her mind had dared imagine Alec undressing her certainly weren't like this.

He lifted each of her feet in turn as he pulled the diving garment completely free, leaving her only in her black swimsuit.

He stood. "Get in, Grace."

She stepped under the stream of hot water. Alec, still wearing his wetsuit, remained beside her while she closed her eyes and let the liquid flow over her head.

Slowly, the chill began to diminish, replaced with a delicious warmth that seeped into her muscles. Finally, the shaking abated.

Wiping water from her eyes, she looked at Alec, his gaze fixated on her. "Thank you." She crossed her arms and tucked them beneath her breasts. Although she wasn't naked, and her bathing suit was unprovocative, she suddenly felt exposed, aware of the tight space they both occupied. They'd never been alone before. Not really. There always had been other people around.

"It was quite an afternoon," he said.

"Did you get some good shots?" she asked, her voice unsteady.

"What I got was incredible. What you did was...."

"I know what you're going to say." She didn't want to leave the hot water, but they didn't have an endless supply. She shut off the stream and shakily sluiced water from each arm. "It was stupid, right? Reckless?"

Her towel was in her room. She'd need to make a dash for it, but it would probably be more like a snail's pace.

"I wasn't gonna say that, but you did make my heart stop a few times."

"I had to help her."

"I know. I'm glad you got the line off her. Brad said it was Mary Ann."

"Yes."

Alec's eyes softened. "Then maybe she remembered you."

It was an outrageous notion, but she appreciated the suggestion nonetheless.

She started to shiver. "My towel's in my cabin."

"Right. Sorry." He stepped back and opened the door.

She slowly walked to her cabin and grabbed her towel. As she wiped her arms and legs, she faced the door—still ajar—not wanting to miss Alec as he passed by.

He didn't disappoint her.

He took one step into her room. "I'll hang up your wetsuit. Meet me in the galley once you get dry, and I'll buy you a beer."

She started drying her hair with the towel. "I'd rather have a giant bowl of buttered noodles. Could you ask Chris if he'd make it for me?"

"Sure." Alec paused, and his gaze became serious. "I have two things to say to you."

She waited. Her heartbeat went pitter patter. Anxiety mounted as she wondered if he were about to ask her on a date or tell her she was too nutso for him to ever hook up with.

"What you did was fucking amazing. But please don't ever do it again."

ALEC SAT in the galley and took another long swig from the bottle of Sam Adams. Not his favorite beer, but it would do. He was finally beginning to feel calm, or maybe it was the alcohol. He was on his second. He definitely needed something to take the edge off.

He'd been here for fifteen minutes, his only company the cook. And Chris hadn't been too talkative as he prepped sloppy joes for dinner, along with a generous helping of pasta. Alec had put the request in, not only for Grace, but also Missy and Tony. All three of them were likely in need of a heavy dose of carbs.

Grace Mann was straining his boundaries. He was a man who welcomed the out-of-the-ordinary, loved going to the edge. It was in that place that he'd always found a hidden reserve, a new and different leap in his personal evolution that he naturally craved. His mother had said he was an odd combination of restlessness and obsessive focus. He'd worked his ass off to build a career in underwater photography and filmmaking, not for ego, but because he liked to push himself. To excel at something required hard work, and he was fascinated with honing his skills to the point where he was good enough to stop worrying about his abilities, embedding them into his blood, into his very DNA.

It was at that point that the struggle to survive in a creative field ceased, and instead, the act of conceiving became everything.

He was now standing on a precipice—on the cusp of a film that could elevate him to that next level. It all had to do with Grace and her connection to the sharks. And not just any shark, but the most-feared monster in the ocean—the great white.

If Grace could interact with such a formidable predator, what would this do for shark conservation efforts? It could change the face of it. And her 3-D imaging system could save lives while, at the same time, easing the terror humans had of sharks.

Grace was out to change the world.

She had most assuredly shifted his.

Double D slipped into the seat opposite Alec, sporting a beer as well. "Footage is good."

Alec gave a nod. He shouldn't have looked away from the viewfinder. They needed to capture every shot possible. It was such a rookie move. That was how much Grace's behavior had rattled him.

"My mom went to the office and found our contract," Alec said. "She scanned it and emailed it to me this morning."

Donovan took a long swig from his bottle. "And?"

"Everything we shoot belongs to the Institute."

"Even the footage we scrap?"

Although Chris was far enough away that he couldn't hear them, Alec kept his voice low. "Technically, yes."

"We've really got to get that bullshit clause out of our contracts," Double D huffed, shaking his head.

"I agree. The big question will be just how much pull Fowler has with the CMI Board."

Donovan scratched his cheek. "Don't you have a friend there?"

"I know Stewart Smith through my dad and Uncle Simon."

"If we get into a pissing match, maybe one of them can do us a favor."

"Maybe," Alec said. "Are you still uploading everything to the cloud?" Galloway Films maintained its own offsite data storage in the event that something catastrophic occurred, like the boat sinking.

"Yep. Been using the SAT phone. That bill's gonna be a bitch."

Alec leveled his gaze on his partner. "If any of this goes south, we'll wipe the cloud if need be."

Donovan held his gaze for a long moment, then sighed, muttering obscenities under his breath. "I'll take care of it myself." He drained the remainder of his beer.

Captain Bellamy entered the galley, got a cup of coffee, then turned to them. He pushed his ball cap up a notch, then took a sip from his mug.

"I heard about what happened," he said.

Double D let out a bark of laughter. "Dr. Mann touched Mary Ann smack dab on the Flintstone. Hypnotized her right on the spot." He stretched an arm along the back of the bench seat and grinned at Alec. "I don't know about you, but I'm pretty sure my balls shriveled to raisins right then."

The captain folded his arms across his chest, becoming contemplative.

"What is it?" Alec asked.

"Shark-touching is strictly forbidden," he said quietly. "I trust in Dr. Mann's abilities, and I'm prepared to let some of this slide, but if you think at any time the situation down there has deteriorated, then I need you tell me."

Alec understood. If Grace lost sight of her objective and began making unwise decisions, then it would be up to Alec to tattle on her.

"I have the authority to shut it all down," Captain Bellamy added. "I don't want anyone dying on my watch."

Alec nodded. "Agreed."

Alec admired and respected Grace, but just how far would she go in the water? And just how far would he go to film her?

"I CAN'T DO IT." Missy hung her head, avoiding Grace's gaze.

Grace sat beside her friend on the lower bunk in their cabin—Grace's bed. She'd been resting since Alec had stripped off her wetsuit and planted her under the hot shower. She'd been spent from pushing herself too far with Mary Ann and had inadvertently fallen asleep. Not only had she missed the beer with Alec, but she was now ravenous. She needed to head to the galley before she started eating her bedsheets.

Missy had woken Grace when she'd come to change into long pants and a jacket.

Grace reached over and covered Missy's hand with hers. "It's okay."

Grace knew giving up was hard for her. Missy wasn't the type to back down from a challenge, having spent nearly as much time in the ocean as Grace.

But freediving with great white sharks was a different ballgame.

Missy glanced up, tears in her eyes. "The longer I was down there, the more panicked I became." She disengaged her hand from Grace's and swiped at the wetness on her cheeks. "They're so damned big, Gracie. I didn't think I'd be afraid, but I was. Like *completely terrified* afraid." The last part was barely audible as Missy's voice cracked.

Grace leaned over and wrapped her arms around her friend, pulling her into a hug.

"I'm sorry," Missy whispered. "Does this ruin everything?"

Grace stayed quiet and considered how to answer that. It had been decided in the early planning stages that there needed to be three of them freediving, for safety reasons. Even with Alec, Double D, Stephie, and sometimes Brad, in the cages, the freediving left Grace and her team vulnerable. As a precaution, no one would freedive alone, and even two divers offered less than ideal protection. It was important to keep eyes in all directions as much as possible. While Grace truly hadn't felt threatened while participating in her viral photo in Hawai'i, or with Mary Ann this afternoon, she knew enough from her adventures with her father in the Farallones that white sharks—like any wild animal—could never be considered tame or completely under control.

They were ambush predators, and it was always the one you didn't see coming that you had to worry about.

"We'll figure something out," Grace finally said.

No one else on the boat freedived. She'd tried to get Brad to do it when they'd been a couple, but he'd quickly developed cold feet after a few breath-holding exercises and static dives. When the inevitable convulsions hit him, he'd freaked and never wanted to try again.

Grace could use scuba equipment, and she would certainly do that if needed, but there was one other option. Unfortunately, it meant inviting a cute grad student into the water who also seemed to have her eye on Alec.

"There's a girl on the Alexanders' boat who freedives."

Missy pulled back. "Really?"

Yeah, really. "I'll invite her to join us."

Missy's shoulders sagged in relief. "I hope she says yes."

Grace didn't have the heart to share her potential love life woes with her friend. "I have a feeling she will."

In the end, the sharks were more important than getting cozy with Alec Galloway.

They always had been.

GRACE FOLLOWED Missy to the galley, her stomach grumbling as she caught a tangy whiff of something that likely involved barbecue sauce and meat. For a moment, she envisioned herself knocking Missy down and running straight for the stove, eating it directly from the pot, like some wild she-animal.

She fought the impulse with difficulty.

Everyone was already crowded into the booths, the tables packed with plates of food, bottles of water, and beer. As soon as Grace entered the room, the raucous chitchat went quiet, startling her into immobility.

Her hand flew to her hair. *I should've brushed it.*

Double D broke the awkward silence. "Three cheers for our shark lady."

The chatter resumed with congratulations. Erik patted her on the back as he passed by. Her gaze caught Alec's—he was crammed into a corner of one of the tables—and he saluted her with his bottle of beer. She wanted to apologize for not meeting him, but Double D and Tony formed a testosterone obstacle beside him.

She waved at Galloway then immediately scanned for food.

Chris deposited two bowls filled with buttered noodles onto the counter, and she rushed over.

"I got your request," he said. "Anything else?"

Grace grabbed one bowl and handed the other to Missy. "Yes. Give me tonight's dinner, too."

He soon handed her a plate with a sloppy joe on a crispy brown bun, coleslaw, and sweet potato fries. Grace inhaled the mouth-watering aroma, certain she'd never had a better meal in her life. She took the seat recently vacated by Erik, beside Brad and across from Tony. Missy took a spot at the table with Frank, Stephie, Captain Bellamy, and Pete.

Grace started shoveling pasta into her mouth.

"How'd you do it?" Tony asked, watching her intently.

She knew he referred to the moment she had slowed Mary Ann with a hand to the shark's snout. "My father," she mumbled around another forkful of buttery carb deliciousness.

"At least your appetite wasn't affected," Brad said.

Grace ignored him.

Tony's eyebrows pinched together. "You learned that from your dad?"

Grace frowned, wiping her lips with the back of her hand. "Why are you acting so surprised? We've put sharks into tonic immobility before."

"Not a great white," Tony said incredulously. "And not a great white swimming straight at us."

The pasta bowl was empty, so she scooped up the sloppy joe and took a large bite.

God, she was in heaven.

She grabbed three fries and made fast work of them. "Same principle," she said around her food.

"Face it, Tony-boy," Double D said. "Gracie's got nerves of steel."

"Maybe it's just the ice in her veins," Brad uttered under his breath as he tilted his beer bottle for a drink.

Grace was too intent on her food to defend herself or bother explaining. In truth, she'd simply done it. There hadn't been much time to think it through.

"Well," Double D said, "we've seen the Professor, and now Mary Ann. If Ginger doesn't show herself soon, the Professor is gonna shack up with the only lady in town."

"What about Bonnie?" Alec asked.

Double D grinned. "I didn't say he had to be exclusive."

Grace reached for the ketchup bottle and squirted a generous portion onto her plate, then immediately started dragging her remaining fries through it.

Brad turned toward her. "While you were napping, Tony and I ran diagnostics on the array. We're collecting data, but we're getting some weird readings. There were some dolphins in the grid this afternoon, along with a few seals. It seems to be making the results a little wonky."

Grace nodded. This was to be expected. She'd need to tweak the code, but she didn't feel like reassuring Brad. Let him sweat it out for a while.

She finished her fries and went to work on the coleslaw.

"I don't think I've ever seen a woman eat so much food so fast," Double D said. "I had no idea a sumo wrestler was secretly hiding inside of you, Dr. Mann."

Now that she was beginning to feel more herself, she flashed a smile at Donovan.

Alec pushed his plate over to her. He'd left a handful of fries on it.

"Thanks," she said, including him in her circle of appreciation.

"The Alexanders will be here in a bit," Brad continued. "They heard about your escapades and want to see Alec's footage."

She silently acknowledged him once again, but her priority was Alec's plate of food.

"And a tourist boat dropped anchor about a mile away. I radioed them to stay clear of the buoys, but they'll likely be chumming the waters tomorrow."

Frank turned and asked over his shoulder, "What exactly is chum?"

"It's usually tuna heads," Alec said. "Whites love them."

"And why is Dr. Mann refusing to use any?" Frank asked.

"She wants a natural interaction with them," Brad said. "In some ways, chumming changes their behavior."

Grace stacked the empty plates and bowl, finally feeling satiated.

"So, they're being trained?" Frank asked.

"I wouldn't say trained as much as conditioned," Brad said. "Great whites are as wild as any animal. There is no training one. That implies predictable behavior. I would never presume to predict a great white's behavior."

"That shark that Grace interacted with today," Frank continued, "was she pregnant?"

Grace stood and grabbed a bottle of water from a mini-fridge. "Female whites have wide girths, but she could be pregnant. We don't have any good way to tell for certain."

"How many babies?" Frank asked.

Grace shrugged and sat down again.

"Maybe we'll film a birth while we're here." Frank's tone was hopeful.

Grace took a long drink of water, then said, "Doubtful. No one has ever filmed a white delivering her pups, and this isn't an optimal nursery. We think they deliver in the Sea of Cortez. The young of the year later appear on the coast, all the way up to California. I really think the sharks come to Guadalupe to eat, since there's a big fat buffet of seals littering the beaches."

"It would make a great ending to the doc if we filmed a live birth," Frank said.

Grace was skeptical about obtaining such footage, but she couldn't disagree that it would be amazing to add it to the film.

"Shark babies have been known to eat their siblings in utero," Alec said.

"Can you blame them?" Grace asked. "I don't know about you, but my sister drives me crazy sometimes."

"I'm the oldest," Alec said. "It's my job to look after my brother and sister, not serve them up on a bed of rice."

"We've got company," Erik yelled down from the upper deck.

Grace deposited her dirty dishes in a bin and headed out of the galley, feeling much more vigorous than when she'd entered. If the company was Harry, then she needed to ask him if he'd loan them Mackenzie for their future dives.

She'd inform Alec of the change in Missy's status once she worked out all the details.

ALEC STOOD on the upper deck of the *Mercado* with Harry Alexander, the dark silhouette of Guadalupe Island filling their view in the distance. The night sky was clear of cloud cover, revealing a canopy of stars that reminded Alec of childhood campouts with his folks and Ty and Brynn in the Sierra Nevadas.

Harry and several of his crew had motored over this evening from their ship to have dessert—Chris had whipped up two chocolate cakes—and to chat about the days' activities. Double D had shared their footage of Grace and Mary Ann, and Harry had sung Grace's praises while harboring a definitive glint of worry in his gaze. Harry's wife Sylvie had *oohed* and *aahed* while nervously laughing at the same time.

Alec couldn't help but feel a kinship to the Alexanders, at least when it came to Gracie Mann.

"I'm glad that Mackenzie can join your team," Harry said.

"Me, too," Alec replied, but he had to wonder why Grace hadn't informed him of the change in divers until the switch had been completed.

Maybe she had thought he would argue against it. Maybe she'd thought he would shut down the expedition, at least the freediving portion of it. He was loath to admit it, but Brad was probably right about her. Work came first. Always.

It was fortunate having the grad student available since Alec was fairly certain that Grace would have freedived anyway. It was better to have three in the water rather than two.

But Alec hadn't missed Mackenzie's attentiveness to him this evening, and while it was flattering, he had no interest in reciprocating. So now he had to walk a fine line between friendliness and encouragement. And to top it off, he'd picked up a frosty vibe from Grace when she'd caught him talking to the girl.

The dark-haired intern held little allure for him beyond professional acquaintance, but somehow, he'd ended up in hot water without having done anything wrong. Just another complication that he could do without.

"Still thinking about today?" Harry asked.

"It's hard not to."

"Grace loves those sharks. She always has."

Alec leaned his forearms on the railing. "Because of her dad?"

Harry nodded. "Eddie Mann and I went way back. Still can't believe he's gone. Grace and her sister, Chloe, would visit him at the research station on the Farallones. Have you ever been there?"

"Not to the islands, but I've been in the surrounding water."

"Caged?"

"No," Alec replied, attempting to laugh. He gripped the railing and stretched out his arms, scanning the inky water buffeting the boat. What were the whites doing right now? Preparing to enter a few slumbering minds tonight? Alec had equal number of sublime ocean dreams and nightmares.

Harry raised an eyebrow. "It's human nature to be afraid, but I'm impressed. It's certainly not a place for the faint of heart. San Francisco is only thirty miles away, but it might as well be a thousand—the islands are barren and incredibly isolated. When the weather turns bad, and it often does, there's no coming or going, no supplies delivered. A lot of folks can't cope with it and leave as soon as they can." He chuckled. "Even I didn't like it. I lasted two months the first time and only returned once more for three weeks.

"But not the Mann girls," he continued. "They loved it. They scrambled all over the rocks, watching the birds—the cormorants, the egrets, and the albatross. That island is dangerous, with steep drop-offs and loose gravel everywhere. If I'd had kids, I wouldn't have brought them there. But Eddie loved two things—the whites and his baby girls. Chloe didn't take to the sharks, but Gracie is just like her daddy. She knew all the whites by name, could identify them easily, and would watch them kill with intense curiosity and little apprehension.

"I guess what I'm trying to say is that she's got white shark in her blood. She'll never be able to separate herself from it. And I can tell that it bothers you."

Alec glanced at Harry. "I just worry that she'll overreach. I don't want her to get hurt."

The older man watched him with a speculative gaze. "Her father, bless his soul, never let that consume his thoughts. In some ways, it was the purest kind of parental love I've ever seen. He wanted Grace—and Chloe too—to find her destiny, her heart's passion, that one thing that would propel her life forward. And Gracie did. Not many men can stand beside a woman like that. That Michaels fella" —he flicked his head in the direction of the salon one level below them— "couldn't stand not having Grace's undivided attention. But you're different. I can see it."

Alec tried to hide his shock.

Am I really so transparent?

He thought he'd been doing a fair job of keeping his attraction to Grace hidden. He was pretty sure even Grace didn't realize how much she'd gotten to him.

Alec decided to feign ignorance. "Sir, I'm not sure what we're talking about now."

Harry grinned. "I was a young man once. I've seen the way you look at her." He clapped Alec on the back.

Needing to change the topic before he got himself into trouble, Alec asked, "How long have you and Sylvie been married?"

Harry thought for a moment. "Hell, it's been so long that I forget."

"I imagine it helps that you both share the same passion for your work."

"Yep. She's the brains. I just get to tag along."

That could be a description for him and Grace.

CHAPTER 13

Grace stared at the computer screen, sipping a cup of chamomile tea as she monitored the data input from the sonar array. She'd spent all morning adding a subroutine to parse out readings that *weren't* sharks, and so far, the generated output wasn't freezing up.

Thankfully, when it came to shark readings, the results were looking good, but she kept her excitement to cautiously optimistic. Just as the neural network was like an onion peeling away the levels of shark identification, debugging her program was a process that wouldn't be solved in only one pass.

She also wanted to cross-reference the output with visual sightings, footage from Alec and Double D, and digital photographs from Stephie. She'd just begun this tedious process with Fleetwood Mac streaming in her earphones, when her music player showed the battery to be nearly dead. She suppressed an irritated snarl. Music helped her tap into the creative side that was oftentimes needed for coding, and she'd acquired an affinity for 70s music from her dad. Chicago, Cat Stevens, Styx, and Elton John both soothed and inspired her.

Missy and Tony had been on visual lookout for sharks and were on the viewing platform, clad in long-sleeved shirts, hats, and sunglasses, with binoculars in hand. Frank had complained about boredom and settled into the TV room to watch a movie. When the foreboding music from *Jaws* had echoed back into the salon, Grace had cranked up the volume of her personal tunes. While she loved the movie—the character of Quint could have been modeled after her dad with his nerves of steel and admiration of sharks—she never watched it while she was actively on the water and engaged with great whites. A superstition maybe, but she was very careful to keep her head space in the right place.

Frank must have brought the DVD on board with him, because the TV room was usually stocked with more generic fare—Jason Bourne and Mission Impossible flicks the popular viewing choices.

Brad was helping Alec and Donovan with the drone as they sought to film the whites preying on seals at a beach area north of their position. A steep underwater drop-off made it possible for the sharks to lurk in the deep and attack with surprise, a feat that was about fifty percent successful.

It wasn't a place to plan her next freedive.

Grace frowned as the Doobie Brothers suddenly went silent. She tried to remember where she'd put her charging cord.

Missy burst into the room. "One of the tourist boats lost their shark cage."

Grace pulled the earphones from her ears and set the spirally mess of cords onto the desk. "How could they lose it?"

"A shark bit through the ropes holding it. Apparently, it was a big mess. The thing broke loose and floated to the bottom. Now it's wedged in some rocks. They need help."

"Can't their crew get it?"

"It'll require divers outside a cage, and while they're waiting for permission from the Mexicans, they wanted to know if we'd help since we've already got a permit."

Grace stood and followed Missy out on deck. Captain Bellamy had already pulled anchor and had the *Mercado* motoring toward a boat in the distance.

Grace donned her sunglasses. She estimated they had about ten minutes. Alec, Double D, and Brad had begun assembling diving gear on the lower deck.

Grace doubted that Missy would be keen on entering the water sans cage, so she turned to Tony as he hopped down from the upper-deck stairs.

"We should go down with them," she said. "They'll need eyes in the water while they work." Tony silently agreed.

Stephie appeared with her camera already encased in its water-proof housing. "I'll come, too."

Grace nodded and dashed back to her cabin. She quickly changed into the only two-piece suit she'd brought, not for Alec's sake, but because she would need to stop by the bathroom first, and it would make it easier to do her business. The practical peach top was made for swimming, not sunbathing, and there was nothing skimpy nor sexy about the navy bottoms. She'd hardly woo Galloway with it if his interest were in Miss Grad Student.

When she finally made it to the diving deck, all three men were gathering gear. Alec's wetsuit only covered his bottom half, revealing a lithe, muscled, and tan torso with just a smattering of chest hair. Double D, on the other hand, was a hairy mass, putting Grace in mind of a St. Bernard dog.

Alec glanced up and his gaze rested on her. She pretended not to notice and grabbed a black wetsuit hanging from the rack.

"You joinin' us, Gracie?" Double D asked.

"I'm not gonna let you guys have all the fun." She stepped into the suit, giving the gentlemen a nice view of her butt. It was either that or turn toward them and flash a bit of cleavage. No reason to be obvious.

When she stood straight, Alec was behind her, reaching for the zipper on her suit.

"Thanks," she said, throwing him a smile over her shoulder but avoiding his eyes.

He zipped her into place. "With you and Tony coming, Double D is going to film it." His hand lingered a smidge too long at her neck. Despite the thick neoprene, her skin reacted with a hot flash.

Then it was over, and he stepped back, leaving her flushed from head to toe. Rather than look at him, she made herself busy strapping an air tank into her buoyancy vest.

The *Mercado* came abreast of the *Argonaut*, a sleek white ship designed for paying customers. It undoubtedly had a larger salon, a spacious upper deck with maybe even a hot tub, and elegant rooms with double beds and en suite bathrooms. The steady clink of the anchor dropping into the water echoed back as Captain Bellamy parked the requisite fifteen hundred feet away from the other vessel.

Alec and Double D jumped into the outboard, and Grace helped transfer the air tanks to them. Once all the gear was stowed, she scrambled into the craft, Alec grasping her elbow. As the current bounced the boat, she fell against him, plastering her shoulder to one of his pecs. Once again, she pretended not to notice, although he was fast becoming the mother of all distractions.

Brad, Tony, and Stephie followed, along with Missy.

"I'll monitor from above," she said when Grace gave her a questioning look.

Alec started the engine and guided the watercraft to the larger boat, bringing it close to the swimming deck on the back end.

Three men stood there.

"Hey, thanks for coming," one yelled, wearing a wide-brimmed straw hat, shorts, and a torn t-shirt.

Alec brought them closer and cut the engine. Double D jumped off with a rope and secured it, but they all stayed in the boat since they'd enter the water from here.

"No problem," Alec said. "What happened?"

"A shark named Felix, a male juvenile, got agitated then got tangled in the air hose and pretty much bit his way through everything."

"Was anyone hurt?" Grace asked.

"No, thankfully. We only had two people in the cage. As it started to sink, they escaped through the top."

Grace glanced at the surface. No shark fins. "Was Felix hurt?"

The man sighed. "I don't think so, but our head diver said the damned shark really went to town on the cage, biting and attacking it, so it's probably damaged."

Grace considered the behavior. "He was likely just overly curious, but glad to hear everyone got out. We'll swim down and see what we can do."

"Thanks. We appreciate it. We've got a hook we'll send down with you. If you'll attach it to the cage, then we can haul it up." He nodded over his shoulder toward a short, stout man. "We're gonna send Tom down with you." He took a deep breath. "I know we'll have too many people in the water, but if we do this quick, the Navy'll be none the wiser."

Grace nodded and donned her gear, as did everyone else.

Alec reached around her to grab his tanks and regulator. "Double D will film while Brad, Tony, and I work on the cage with Tom." He looked at her. "Your job is to watch our backs." He glanced at Stephie. "You hang back a bit and take pictures."

"If we're trying to keep this under wraps from the authorities," Stephie said, "should we be documenting this illicit dive?"

"It's not really illicit," Grace said. "I think the Navy dudes will come through. Better to have the footage just in case."

Alec grinned at her. "Spoken like a true star."

Grace wrinkled her nose.

One by one, everyone went into the water. The men on the *Argonaut* dropped a hook attached to a rope into the water that Tom retrieved and took with him as he began descending. Grace positioned herself on the far right of the men while Stephie took up the left side.

Grace scanned the area, but didn't see any sharks. Schools of fish darted out of the way as they slowly entered the dark-blue depths illuminated by shafts of sunlight. The only sound was the regulator as Grace took slow and steady breaths. She longed to freedive, so she could hear the nothingness of the fluid world. Scuba gear always made her feel as if she was one step removed from the environment.

Her eye caught movement in the distance. A great white neared, but then turned and departed before getting too close. This was typical white behavior—reticent and circumspect. With seven people in the water releasing bubbles from their regulators and generally making noise, the sharks would be drawn to them as well as display wariness of the interlopers.

Two whites approached from the north. Grace watched them as she continued her downward descent. Up ahead, Alec turned his head, and Grace knew he'd sighted the sharks as well, but he kept swimming.

The cage became visible, wedged into a jutting rocky protrusion. Alec, Brad, Tony, and Tom descended to its level and began an inspection while Double D filmed. Grace could see that it was a composite cage—it had been assembled once they'd arrived at the island. This made it easier to store, but also inherently weaker than a cage welded as one complete structure. On the left side, the metal bars caved inward. Felix had been a busy little shark.

Alec gave the contraption a shake, but it was wedged and didn't come loose. Grace suspected that Felix had chomped on it much like a puppy might go after a shoe, and in so doing, had exerted enough pressure to jam it into the jagged shelf.

While the men worked to free the mangled contraption, Grace hovered nearby. Every time Stephie snapped a photo, the flash illuminated the surroundings, a beacon announcing their presence to all the marine life in the area. While the light wouldn't necessarily attract sharks, the electromagnetic energy from the camera equipment—and from the divers themselves—surely would catch their attention.

Two whites approached. Grace's heartrate picked up speed like a ball rolling down a stairwell. There was no doubt the sharks sensed the presence of them. As the whites neared, Grace sought to identify them.

Both were females and both were large, maybe eighteen feet in length.

Not Bonnie, though. Grace hoped her father's favorite shark would make another appearance before the expedition ended.

The two sharks swam together, making a circular path around them. Although whites were known to be solitary animals, in locations such as Guadalupe Island, Seal Island in South Africa, and the Neptune Islands in Australia, the sharks appeared to co-mingle.

Did they hunt together? Did they enjoy a bit of camaraderie? No one knew.

Grace remembered a study she'd read about out of South Africa that had concluded great whites didn't work in groups, and that they favored no one white shark over another. Their groupings were random and filled with territorial behavior rather than love or apparent attachment.

Still, Grace had a feeling there was far more to the sharks and the hierarchy they displayed. She knew body language was a strong form of communication, and these two females, so similar in size, seemed to accept that neither one was dominant. At least for the moment.

A third, smaller shark appeared, swimming quickly and darting around. Claspers in the genital region indicated a male, and he was clearly agitated.

Grace suspected he was the cage attacker.

Hello, Felix.

The females seemed to pay him no mind, although, in a display of dominance, they moved above him and lowered their pectoral fins.

Their message was clear to the young male. *Get lost.*

But like a teenager ignoring his elders, Felix instead came closer to Grace.

As he slowed to skim past her, she made eye contact. He immediately shot off at a breakneck pace.

This wasn't good.

Felix was posturing, despite the two females above. It was as if he'd decided that the cage was his, and he didn't like the humans touching his stuff.

While Grace honestly felt no threat from the females, neither of which she'd been able to identify yet, Felix was a different story. He seemed belligerent, ignoring the much larger and more dominant females clearly telling him he was acting like a punk.

Grace chanced a glance back at the men and the cage. Alec had moved to the bottom and was trying to push the contraption from the rock, stirring up sand and creating cloudy puffs, which were swiftly reducing visibility.

This put Felix at a distinct advantage.

Grace brought her attention back to the male shark still circling them, passing closer each time. His rapid and nimble movements put her on edge.

A hand touched her arm, and she turned to see Alec beside her. The cage was free. With the hook in place, it began a slow upward glide.

Felix darted past and bumped Grace's shoulder. Her heart slammed into her chest as Alec yanked hard on her arm, pulling her toward him. Stunned by Felix's aggressiveness, she sought to steady her breath since this was no place to hyperventilate.

Alec brought his face to hers, watching her, obviously assessing her level of panic.

She nodded and gave a thumbs-up.

Felix had startled her, that was all. It would be highly illogical for the male white to attack any of them.

Alec released her, and they began to ascend along with the others.

Grace slowly spun around as she went, seeking to locate all the sharks in the water. The two females had gone deeper, proceeding at a languid pace and giving Grace and the others a wide berth. But great whites had excellent upward sight, and Grace sensed that the ladies still had the situation in view.

Suddenly, Felix shot up from the depths and attacked the bottom of the cage, clamping his massive mouth on the bars, the sound of twisting metal echoing in the water.

Everyone swam to the left to avoid the shark and his intense interest in the cage. Felix shook his head back and forth, his powerful body pushing the cage upward. As he continued to fight the metal as if it were prey, Grace swam closer to get a better look, fascinated by his tenacity.

The shark's torpedo-shaped snout was stuck between two metallic slats. Great whites couldn't swim backwards. Felix was now good and stuck.

Alec's hand on her arm stopped Grace's movement. She looked at him, annoyed. He shook his head. She pulled her arm free and pointed at the shark.

They needed to help Felix.

Alec directed his finger upward. He wanted her to go to the surface.

She shook her head and waved beyond him to the others who had stopped and were watching the unfolding situation of the trapped great white.

Alec's gaze held frustration. Grace waved him forward, along with the others, trying to indicate they should all grab hold of the cage.

Tony left them and went to the surface, and soon the winch that was dragging the cage upward stopped.

Felix still whipped his tail in a frantic motion to get free. Grace gave one last look of admonishment to Alec, then swam around him and toward Felix. Thankfully everyone followed. Grace couldn't do this alone.

She pumped her fins in strong strokes and swam beneath the cage to get to the other side. Alec was right beside her. When she tried to grab the metal bars near Felix's snout, Alec pushed her aside so that he was between her and the shark. The others surrounded the cage and grabbed hold, Felix jerking it so much that it was difficult to keep a grip.

Together, they attempted to pull the cage free from the shark, but Felix jammed himself more snugly into the slats.

There was only one thing to do. Before Alec could stop her, she swam upward and entered the cage through the top, which was luckily still accessible. As her air tank scraped along the metal sides, she moved straight down into the face of Felix. She didn't dare look at Alec, but imagined anger clouding his face.

With its cornucopia of spiky teeth, Felix's mouth faced her like a beast from a horror movie.

She wanted to be gentle, but the shark was frantic in his captivity. As fish and cage performed a macabre dance, it became a challenge for Grace to get close.

She pumped her fins in short, quick bursts—straining her legs—and placed both of her glove-covered hands against his snout. She prayed that his excessive body-whipping wouldn't accidentally bring his very sharp incisors into contact with her fingers.

She pushed hard as the others attempted to yank the cage upward.

Felix fought her, his strength impressive. She screamed into her regulator as she gave everything she could muster to shove the shark back.

Suddenly, the top slat holding Felix in place snapped free and a thousand pounds of shark lunged upward and straight into her. Knocking her mask and regulator off, he slammed her into the side of the cage. Saltwater gagged her and burned her eyes. She fumbled for her regulator and put it back into her mouth. With her mask gone, visibility was poor, but it was clear that she and Felix were both trapped in the cage. Luckily his mouth was far above her. Unfortunately, she was now parallel to his whipping tail.

Still stunned, she flattened herself against the side, but the damned air tank kept her too close to the frenzied fish. Her heart hammered in her chest. She was peripherally aware that the others were surrounding the prison in which she now found herself, but all she could concentrate on was Felix's thrashing body.

He slapped one way, then another. Grace shifted to avoid it, then moved quickly in the opposite direction.

Felix couldn't exit the cage. The opening she'd come through was too small, and she could no longer reach it herself, and she suspected the top couldn't be flipped wide because of the earlier damage.

She hoped Alec and the others would find a way to free Felix, because she had no way out.

While she knew that one direct hit from Felix could crush her ribcage, her bigger fear was that he'd render her unconscious. If that occurred, she'd likely drown.

But worse than her impending death was the fact that Felix wouldn't last much longer. And she didn't want him to die for his reckless behavior, because it had also included reckless human behavior. Nothing was worse than being the cause of distress in—or death of—the animals one studied.

Felix jerked again, and the force pushed the cage up. With a jolt, Grace smacked the bottom, perilously close to Felix's caudal fin, a veritable knife slashing in all directions. It caught her in the face and knocked out the regulator again, and for a confused moment she tried to remember where she was. She struggled to find her mouthpiece again and shoved it between her lips, then huddled in the corner, hiding her face this time.

The cage lurched and began moving again as the winch re-engaged. Two divers hovered below Grace, but she had to shut her eyes. The saltwater stung too much. Between painful blinks she identified the divers as Alec and Double D.

Double D swam up to the bottom of the cage and inserted what looked like a crowbar between the slats of the floor and one of the walls. Alec came level to her, concern in his eyes. His hand covered hers where she gripped one of the metallic bars. She gave a nod to tell him she was all right. In return, he squeezed her hand, but Felix thrashed again and shook Alec free.

Alec quickly swam to Double D and began to yank on the weakening cage connection.

With a pop, the contraption broke open.

Felix's tail struck her on the back, hitting her air tank, and the pressure in her regulator dropped. He continued pummeling his metallic jail, causing bone-jarring shakes, and panic filled Grace.

She was losing air.

She wanted to signal Alec, but he and Double D were working like madmen to wrench open a bigger hole.

If she shed her scuba gear, she might be able to squeeze out.

She needed to act fast because once she abandoned the air tank, she wouldn't have much time.

Grace ripped off her gloves. Her fingers fumbled along the diving vest, unbuckling the clips as she located them. She inhaled the last bit of air trickling into her mouthpiece. In one fluid motion, she pushed the tank apparatus from her shoulders and let the regulator pop out of her mouth. Making her body straight, she used the cage to push herself feet first through the opening. Double D and Alec noticed and tugged on her legs.

Without warning, Felix's tail clipped the back of her head and everything went black.

CHAPTER 14

The powerful blow of Felix's tail slammed Grace against the cage. Alec felt her go limp and frantically pulled her out before the shark nailed her again. Holding her against him, he pumped his legs hard to take him to the surface, reaching deep for a burst of energy from his already exhausted body.

She didn't have much time.

They surfaced, and he positioned her face up. He spit out his regulator. "Somebody grab her!" He swam toward the swim deck, pulling Grace's lifeless body with him, panic roaring in his head. With Felix still thrashing around in the cage, most of the crew and passengers were watching the shark, but the general commotion was soon directed toward him.

Missy rushed to the edge and dropped to her knees. Stephie and Tony, still in the water, swam to Alec's side.

As he neared, Missy grabbed Grace's limp body and hauled her out with a grunt. Alec threw his mask aside, pulled off his tank and heaved it onto the deck, then hauled himself out. Shaking, his arms collapsed. Donovan was suddenly behind him, giving him a push, and Alec all but crawled onto the platform.

Missy had Grace on her back, her hands performing compressions on her chest. The black wetsuit didn't rise or fall, and Grace's face was as pale as her matted hair.

Tony and Stephie hoisted themselves out of the water as Alec scrambled over to Grace's lifeless body. Alec pushed Missy aside and began CPR himself.

Thirty compressions.

Pinch her nose.

Elevate her head.

Breathe into her mouth.

Breathe into her mouth again.

More compressions. One, two, three...he counted them out, focusing on the repetition.

Don't get it wrong.

Keep going.

He blew two more breaths into her mouth. Her chest rose, then rose again. Back to compressions. More breathing.

Again.

And again.

Don't die on me, goddammit!

Grace coughed. Alec turned her to the side, and she ejected a good amount of seawater.

He bent over her, trying to catch his breath, while she continued to hack. His face rested against her neck and his hand gripped her hip. "Sonuvabitch, Grace," he whispered, suddenly aware that his eyes burned with tears.

"Gracie, thank God." Missy knelt opposite Alec, pushing Grace's hair away from her cheek, the movement forcing Alec to lean back.

Without warning, Grace shot up. "The shark." She pushed to her knees.

Alec struggled to stand on unsteady legs, then helped her to her feet. She took the stairs as he, Tony, Stephie, Missy, and Double D, who had been standing off to the side, followed.

A crowd clustered at the railing, the cage in the water below them. Yelling and swearing filled the air as several of the men, including

Brad, were attempting to use long sticks with hooks to unlock the top of the cage, but it was still jammed. Alec, along with Double D's help, had already tried in vain to lift the damaged top while it was still in the water after Felix had gotten trapped with Grace.

"He'll die." Grace's voice cracked.

Alec glanced around. Spying his goal, he ran back to the diving deck and snatched up the crowbar that rested beside the gear he'd abandoned moments ago in his desire to get to Grace's inert body as quickly as possible.

He jumped into their outboard and crashed into Grace as he reached for the rope anchoring it to the *Argonaut*.

"I'll do it!" She shoved him toward the captain's seat.

He started the engine, and then pushed the engine throttle hard. Grace stumbled back.

"Sorry!" He spun the wheel and brought the boat around in a tight turn, bracing his bent leg against the seat while the boat rocked erratically back and forth. Just as quickly, he cut the engine so he wouldn't overshoot the cage bobbing in the water, housing a very unhappy shark.

To edge closer, he gave the motor the slightest bit of thrust, but left the engine idling.

"Grace." He indicated for her to change places with him. She bumped into him as she took hold of the wheel.

He grabbed the crowbar from where he'd tossed it on the floor and went to the opposite side of the boat, having angled it perpendicular to the still-thrashing shark and the cage that was loath to let anything escape it.

"Be careful," Grace warned. "Don't hurt Felix."

"I know," he said, almost laughing that she wasn't worried about him or the fact that she'd nearly been killed by this contentious fish.

Alec took a deep breath and leaned over the side of the outboard, waiting for a lull in the action from the frantic shark. When Felix paused and sank beneath the surface, Alec wedged the crowbar between the now uneven slats and yanked hard.

Felix thrust upward, banging his nose against the cage. Alec reared back, losing his grip on the metal lever.

Fuck!

Alec quickly scrambled forward. Luckily the crowbar was still where he'd jammed it and not sinking into the ocean. He grabbed hold again. It was only a matter of minutes before the damned shark drowned. Filled with frustration, Alec released an angry groan as he tugged with every last ounce of strength he had.

The cage top sprang free and Felix burst forward, heading straight toward Alec. Grace thrust the outboard into reverse, and they slammed hard into something, throwing Alec into the driver's chair and Grace on top of him.

"Shit, I'm sorry!" She pushed off him and cut the engine.

Alec came to his feet, standing behind Grace, and they both searched for Felix in the water.

"He's free!" someone from the *Argonaut* yelled.

Grace gasped and pointed. "There he is."

Twenty feet away, Felix's dorsal fin broke the surface as the stressed shark shot away with rapid speed.

And then he was gone.

Alec braced his hands on the captain's chair and the console, effectively boxing Grace in, as he sought to calm his breathing.

How had such a simple task gotten so completely out-of-control?

He leaned his forehead onto her shoulder, the fear he hadn't had time to acknowledge finally seeping into his limbs. He needed to sit down, but more than that, he needed to be near Grace.

He was forced to lift his head when she turned to face him.

She touched his arm and her eyes locked onto his. "Are you all right?"

"Am *I* all right? Jesus, Grace, you were unconscious."

She gave a slight nod and a bewildered expression crossed her face. Then she smiled. "Holy shit." Laughter bubbled out of her. "What the fuck just happened?"

Startled by her response, Alec stared at her. She was so near that he wouldn't have to move far to kiss her. "I think you might have a concussion," he said.

The boat rocked, and she fell toward him. He wrapped his arms around her and didn't let go. She didn't respond in kind, but he didn't care. He was so damned glad that she was alive.

And then her arms circled his waist, and she returned the hug as a muffled sob escaped her, her face pressed against his wetsuit. He folded her into a tight embrace and she clung to him.

He brought his hand up to her neck, shocked when something red trickled down his fingers.

"You're bleeding." He lifted her hair. A two-inch gash just below her hairline oozed bright red blood. "It doesn't seem bad. Let's get you back to the boat."

She stepped out of his arms and wiped at the tears on her cheeks, her eyes puffy and red. She appeared embarrassed, her gaze sliding to just past his shoulder. "Uh oh."

He followed her line of sight to a big dent she'd inflicted on the *Argonaut's* hull when she'd hit reverse.

"Don't worry," Alec said. He reluctantly released her as she stepped aside so that he could have full access to the captain's seat. "The *Argonaut* won't sink."

He started the engine so they could begin the process of retrieving their crew and gear to head back to the *Mercado*.

"At least Felix is free." Her gaze swung to the mangled contraption being lifted from the water. "But they'll never use that cage again."

GRACE SAT ON HER BUNK, her head bent forward and her hair pinned up so Missy could put a few stitches into the gash on her neck.

"I can't believe you were in that cage with a great white," Missy said.

Grace hissed. Missy's handiwork stung.

"Yeah, me neither." Bundled into a fleece jacket, black nylon pants, and thick socks, she finally felt warm and safe, but her body from head to toe was beginning to ache in response to the ordeal.

Missy exhaled a deep breath which served to dry Grace's injury, then gingerly dabbed ointment on it. "Your wound is gooey, but I think I can bandage it up for you to dive tomorrow. Are you really going back in the water so soon?"

"I don't want to waste a day lying around. Besides, I don't want to psych myself out worrying about this. It was just an unfortunate accident."

"Instigated by a wild great white shark." Missy covered the laceration with gauze and began taping it down. "Those unpredictable beasts."

Grace laughed. "If it were easy, everyone would be doing it."

"True, true," Missy replied in a singsong voice. "So, what's going on with Alec?"

"What do you mean?"

"Has he made a move on you?"

Grace frowned. "No. Why?"

"He fought like hell to get you out of that cage. After it was all over, he seemed a bit shell-shocked to me."

"He's been in dangerous situations before," she said, remembering his story about Bonnie and the Farallon Islands, as well as the gruesome death of Elliott Marsh. "I'm grateful he was there today."

"And now his reward is sex."

Grace snorted. "You're terrible. You set women back a hundred years."

"It's not that, Gracie." Missy smoothed her fingers over her handiwork, and then stood. "Alec's different. Not your usual 'King of the Hill' beefcake. He actually seems *in touch* with what he does. He's not out trying to conquer the sharks to build up his own ego."

After Alec had released Felix, he'd pulled her into an embrace, both startling her and melting her resolve. The way he'd held onto her…as if he cared…it had knocked the composure right out of her.

Had it meant something? Or had she imagined it? Although

Missy had concluded that she didn't have a concussion, she'd been more than a bit traumatized.

"He does have great social media accounts," Grace said. "He's a very eloquent writer."

"I knew it. You're not immune to him." Missy placed the items she'd used to treat Grace's injury back into the medical kit on the desk.

"Are you?" Grace blurted out, needing to know.

Missy leaned a hip on the edge of the desk and crossed her arms. "I'm not chasing Alec."

"I think Mackenzie is."

Missy's brows shot upward. "Really?"

Grace's shoulders sagged. "I really don't have time for this."

"And now she's going to dive with you." Missy's expression turned crestfallen. "It's all my fault. I should get back in the water with you and Tony."

Grace expelled a grunt of exasperation. "No, you won't. This is crazy. I'm not going to rearrange my professional life for a guy. If he's interested in Mackenzie, then so be it."

"If it's any consolation, I think you're wrong. I've seen the way Alec looks at you."

Warmth filled Grace's belly. "How does he look at me?"

"Like there ain't no other girl on his radar. Seriously, I saw the glint in his eye that night at the fundraising gala."

Grace shook her head, uncertain about getting involved with Galloway. "Maybe after the expedition."

"Because of Brad?"

"It's worth considering."

Sleeping with Brad had created one long complication after another. Did she really want to go down that road with Galloway? And if Brad caught wind that she and Alec had become more than friends, she honestly wasn't sure what he would do. Would he make life more hell than it already was? Brad certainly didn't miss having her in his bed, but his pride would be pricked, and he'd likely make her pay for that.

"I really need to date someone outside of the workplace," she said.

"And how will you meet this person when all you do is work?" Missy teased. "C'mon. Dinner awaits."

∾

ALEC TOSSED BACK the shot of tequila Double D placed before him as they waited for dinner in the galley.

Just one.

He needed to calm his nerves. Since returning to the boat, Grace had gone to her cabin with Missy for a medical exam, and Alec's mind had gone into replay mode of her near death.

Fuck.

He waved at Donovan to pour another shot.

Just one more.

His friend obliged, and Alec let the liquor slide down his throat. He leaned back and rubbed a hand down his face.

"I looked at the footage that Stephie took," Double D said. "It's good, if we wanna use it."

Alec nodded. He wasn't ready to view it himself. It would just remind him how differently this day could have ended.

Double D swallowed the tequila in his glass and smacked his lips together. "That was one mean mother of a shark."

"Thanks for your help," Alec said.

"I've always got your back, Galloway, and there was no way in hell I was letting Dr. Mann go to the big ocean in the sky."

A grimace stretched across Alec's mouth. "I don't think Felix was mean. He was just trapped and panicked." *And easily could have killed Grace.*

Brad slid onto the bench seat beside Alec. "Grace was stupid to have gone into that cage."

Alec's tenuous hold on his emotions snapped. "And where the hell were you when we were trying to get her out?"

"I went onto the *Argonaut* to help them get the top free. That seemed to be the best course of action."

"Obviously, it wasn't." Alec sought to quiet the flash of rage coursing through him; Double D seemed to sense it and poured him another shot. Alec threw it back, swallowing it in one gulp.

Brad shook his head. "She's lucky to be alive. Honestly, this makes me question her decision-making abilities."

Alec bristled. "Are you serious?"

A quick glance in Double D's direction, and Alec knew his friend was giving him an unspoken warning. *Shut up.* He was right. Alec would only make things worse for Grace by arguing with Michaels. She would hardly appreciate his interference.

"It was reckless," Brad continued.

Alec fiddled with his empty shot glass. "She was just trying to help that shark."

"And she was the only one with the balls to get in there and try," Donovan said. "I think it would've worked if that bar hadn't snapped."

Grace descended the stairs into the galley, her gait stiff. Alec could only imagine how sore she was. A body-wide ache had spread through his own limbs, once he'd returned to the *Mercado*, although the tequila had taken the edge off the worst of it. He resisted the urge to jump up and help her since Brad blocked his way, although the thought of shoving Michaels to the side made Alec feel all warm and fuzzy.

Double D stood and let Grace slide into his seat. Alec caught sight of her bloodshot eyes and didn't miss the discomfort straining her half-smile. Missy sat beside her, and Stephie and Tony filed in as well.

"Any stitches?" Alec asked, enjoying the fact that she was only inches away from him. Something in him relaxed now that she was close, a reassurance that she was indeed alive and that he hadn't imagined it.

"Just a few."

"Concussion?" Donovan asked.

"I don't think so," Missy replied.

"In that case, we've got tequila, darlin'." Double D pushed the bottle across the table toward her. "And if anyone deserves a shot, it's you. You cage-wrestled a great white. There's not many who can make that claim to fame."

Alec filled his glass with the amber liquid, and then pushed it across the table to her. She took a deep breath and then swallowed it in one gulp, closing her eyes. She coughed, and her cheeks turned pink. It was a beautiful sight, considering that a few hours ago, she'd been as white as a ghost, and maybe just as dead.

He smiled and poured her another, but she didn't drink it.

"Well, if there's a silver lining," Tony said, "we detected Felix with the sonar. We also got a nice hit on you all with the cage. The imaging system is working well."

"That's great," Grace said. "I'll have a look at it later."

"It can wait until tomorrow," Tony said.

"Well, I plan to be in the water tomorrow."

Alec watched her closely, concerned about the dark circles under her eyes. "Are you sure about that?"

"I'll be fine."

"That saltwater is gonna hurt like hell," Double D said.

Everyone laughed.

"I didn't get a chance to thank you both." Grace's gaze flicked from Alec to Donovan. "I probably wouldn't have gotten out without you."

"Stephie got some fantastic fucking footage," Double D said.

"You're gonna use it in the doc?" Brad asked.

Alec's eyes locked with Grace's. "I don't know. We'll wait and see."

"Fuck that," Brad said. "You know we're gonna come out of this looking bad, Grace. The whole thing was a giant nightmare of a lawsuit waiting to happen. We probably should've stayed out of it. You know that several of the passengers on that boat were filming the whole thing on their phones. This will hit social media, and it's gonna be a cluster."

"Bullshit," Alec muttered. Grace could have died, and this was what Brad was harping about?

Grace's weary expression was suddenly lined with anger. "You're just worried that somehow you'll be blamed for it."

"You're damned right I am," Brad said, raising his voice. "I care about my career. I'm sorry to see that you don't feel the same about yours."

Grace looked like she wanted to roll her eyes. "Oh, I know all about you and your love of your precious reputation."

"What if you're vilified in the press?" Brad bit out each word like he was talking to a child. "Or badgered by the public outcry of endangering a shark? You work for me, remember?"

"How could I forget?" Grace said under her breath.

"I really don't think Grace comes off looking reckless," Double D said. "And the captain of the *Argonaut* and I had a little chat with all the passengers who were filming on their phones. They all agreed not to post anything public, at least until tomorrow. We didn't add that the captain shut off their Wi-Fi access for the evening. I've already uploaded something. I've got a buddy at the Washington Post, along with some blogger connections. The right story is out there."

"The right story?" Brad asked, incredulous.

"That would be the truth," Donovan said flatly. "Or were you looking for a lie?"

"Isn't that why you suppressed all the tourists' videos?"

"No. I asked them to wait because, to be quite honest, none of them would have the most accurate information. They were only topside. They didn't see what was happening down below. And I really think Grace's bravery will go a long way to showing how *some* humans will do anything to save this species. The people on board were pretty agreeable. Some even let me download what they'd shot, and I incorporated it into my footage. It's pretty good stuff, if I do say so myself."

"Thanks, Double D." Grace smiled at him.

"You, little lady, are my hero."

Grace took a sip of tequila, and then slid the glass back to Alec. "I'm already feeling it."

So was Alec, so he didn't drink more. If he kept at it, he might embarrass himself by telling Brad to go jerk off, or worse, tell Grace that he was seriously falling for her.

"You really should've cleared it with me first," Brad said.

"Sorry," Double D replied, his voice edged with sarcasm. "I'll be sure to do that next time."

Brad leveled his gaze at Donovan. "There won't be a next time."

For once, Alec had to agree with Brad. But still, if this behavior was any indication, Michaels must have been the biggest asshole boyfriend ever.

"I still want to see the footage," Brad added.

Double D's expression took on an innocent glow. "Of course."

"There is one way to fix this," Grace said.

All eyes shifted to her.

"We need to find Felix again and shoot footage of him, to reassure everyone that he's not any worse from his ordeal."

"It's a good idea," Alec said. "It would be nice to know if he sustained any permanent injuries."

"Dinner's ready," Chris announced.

General commotion ensued as everyone filed toward the cooking cubbyhole and loaded up on fettucine alfredo. Alec slid into a seat beside Grace, her plate piled high with pasta, salad, and two pieces of bread.

"I'm taking this to mean you're not feeling sick," he said, crowding closer to her. With so many people, it was a tight fit.

"Not yet," she replied. "I'm pretty starved, actually."

Donovan grinned from across the table. "The more you eat, the more tequila you can have. And then we can go skinny-dipping."

"Let's not scare the sharks with your big white ass, Double D." Alec grabbed his fork and started digging in.

Donovan laughed. "I'll take any female attention I can get."

To Alec's right, Stephie gave an unladylike snort.

"So," Tony said, sandwiched between Double D and Missy, pinning Grace with an expectant look, "give us all the gory details."

Grace chomped on a large mouthful of noodles, then said, "Well, let me tell you. Felix brought wine and offered me his finest tuna dish. Then we curled up in the cage and watched *Free Willy*."

Alec's fork hovered halfway to his mouth. Was Grace cracking a joke? Had that whack on her head changed her personality?

Tony laughed.

"Don't be so easy next time if he comes around for a second date," Missy admonished.

Grace shrugged and dug into her salad.

"Did Felix knock some of your marbles loose?" Alec asked. He immediately regretted it when Grace looked affronted.

"Why would you say that?" She reached past him for the plate of butter, her arm bumping his hand.

"I know why," Tony said. "He's only seen workaholic-Grace."

Alec raised an eyebrow. "You mean there's a non-workaholic-Grace?"

Grace narrowed her gaze. "I'm really quite funny."

"Well...." Missy hedged.

"I'm not?"

"We humor you because you're the shark whisperer." Missy stuffed a forkful of lettuce in her mouth.

Grace caught Alec's eye and shook her head. "Please don't call me the shark whisperer in the documentary. Good grief, look at Felix. He wasn't too happy with me."

"Yeah, but it's strange," Tony said, his gaze on Alec. "We get in the water, and creatures just come to her, including the sharks."

Grace slathered butter on her bread. "Felix was there because he really liked that cage."

"Maybe, but he also liked *you*." Missy pointed her fork at Grace, who shrugged.

"Grace is no marine magnet," Brad said, dropping his used utensils and dinnerware into a nearby plastic bin. "The animals aren't that self-aware."

"Says who?" Stephie countered, surprising Alec. She rarely interacted with other divers when they worked on a project, but ever since they'd come on this expedition, she'd been more opinionated. Alec was beginning to think it was the Grace Mann effect.

Brad picked up his bottle of beer from the other table and looked down at Stephie. "You're anthropomorphizing."

"You're saying you've never felt connected to the animals you study?" Stephie asked.

"Not enough to cuddle up and watch a movie with them."

Stephie turned to Alec. "What do you think?"

Alec pushed his empty plate away. "I think we have no idea of the depth and complexity of creatures like whites or how they communicate. And who wouldn't like Grace?"

"True." Missy nodded in agreement.

"Whether we're anthropomorphizing or not," Grace said, "the truth is that making animals more relatable helps in conservation efforts."

Brad tipped his bottle and took a swallow of beer. "It's easy if you're trying to save panda bears. No one is going to love a great white."

"I think you underestimate people," Grace said. "The important thing is to educate and get the word out to the public."

Frank stood and cleared his plate as well. "But the public still only sees *Jaws* when they think of sharks."

"Maybe," Grace replied. "But beliefs can change."

Frank's plaid shirt stretched tight across his slightly protruding belly. "All I know is that I'm not feeling too inclined to get in the water tomorrow."

"The cages are safe," Grace said.

"Oh really?" Frank chuckled. "Your recent escapade doesn't calm my fears."

"That was an anomaly."

"Isn't that what every person says before they're eaten alive by one of those monsters?"

CHAPTER 15

S tiff and sore, Grace forced herself out of bed. She'd slept in her clothes, so after a quick sniff in the armpit region to assure herself that she could get by in the same outfit, she brushed her teeth, grabbed a navy windbreaker, and slipped on a pair of flipflops.

She gingerly ran her fingertips over the bandage at her neck, the gash stinging, and headed to the galley for tea. Once she had a cup in hand, she went to the upper deck.

Climbing the steep steps—no easy feat while balancing the steaming mug in her right hand—she found Alec fiddling with his drone. His pale blue t-shirt stretched across his broad shoulders, hinting at a coiled physicality, and a flash of deep kisses and sweaty sheets filled her head.

For God's sake. She wasn't that starved for a man.

Just for Alec.

"Morning," she said.

He glanced up, and a grin split his face, warming her much more than the hot tea.

"How you feelin'?" he asked.

Hot and bothered…for you.

"Like I went ten rounds with Muhammad Ali." She sat on a

nearby bench as she tried to get a naked Alec out of her head. It had to be the life-threatening experience. Weren't sex and death linked somehow?

Leaning over the black flying camera, Alec fiddled with a small screwdriver and a bunch of wires. "Maybe you should stay out of the water today."

Grace sipped her drink and took in the picturesque, cloud-mottled lavender sky and the glassy ocean surrounding them. She couldn't have crafted a more perfect moment. The pull of the water and sharks below made the thought of spending even one day topside and not down in the peaceful sea unbearable. Grace almost screamed in frustration.

"No." Her gaze caught Alec's.

"You want to talk about it?"

She gifted him with a quizzical tilt of her head, the muscles in her forehead bunching together. *About Felix or about us?* Was Missy right about Alec's interest? Uncertainty made her hesitate. But then there'd been that hug after they'd rescued Felix. Surely Alec didn't embrace every scientist he worked with as if he were desperately happy they were alive.

In the end, she chickened out and opted for the safe route.

"Okay, yes, I'm a little unsettled by the incident yesterday, but I wasn't afraid to die then and I'm not now. I know Brad thinks I was reckless, but Felix might not have made it otherwise. I could never stand by and watch an animal die, especially if there was something I could do to help it. I'll always feel this way, until the end of my days."

"You want to give me a hand?"

She set her mug on the bench seat and kneeled beside Alec.

"Can you hold that covering in place while I secure it?" he asked.

She nodded and did as he asked, moving close enough that she could feel his body heat. She caught a whiff of soap-showered skin and freshly-laundered t-shirt, the pale blue material emphasizing his tan arms. They were nice arms—taut and lean, not too muscular.

She liked his hands, too—steady and sure as he twisted the screws into place.

Her lips scrunched into a grimace. She really shouldn't sit so close to Alec while the word *screw* flitted through her head.

"Don't worry, almost done," he said, misinterpreting her response.

She quickly schooled her features.

"What's it like to be in a cage with a great white?" he asked, his attention still on the drone.

She swore under her breath, mostly because she was starting to get annoyed by the way her feminine parts came to life around Galloway. "All right, you've beaten it out of me," she said, needing to release some of the frustration. "I *was* afraid. The power in Felix humbled me right down to my toes. I knew I was up shit creek the moment he blasted into me."

Alec looked at her, close enough that she could see the changing hue of his eyes—not blue, not green, but something in between.

"You were lucky, Grace." There was no reproach in his quiet tone, instead the statement sounded almost reverent.

"I was lucky because of you. Don't think I don't know that."

"You should take care," he added. "Post-traumatic stress and all that."

Concern gripped her. "Did you have that with Elliott?"

Pain flitted across those lush blue-green eyes that reminded her of an underwater garden. "Yep." He shifted his focus back to the drone. "I'm done. You can move your hand."

She reluctantly sat back on her heels.

He shifted to a crouch and examined a different part of the apparatus, taking him farther from her. "If you ever have a bad dream, come find me. We can have a hot chocolate and talk about it."

It wasn't exactly a request for a date, but the sincerity in his voice filled Grace with warm anticipation. "Thanks. I'll remember that."

Fortunately, she'd slept soundly during the night, her body in need of deep recovery rather than a recounting of the incident that had nearly killed her. She usually never dwelled on the scary encounters she'd had over the years, and her reward was a relatively tame dream world when it came to the sharks. But she didn't mention that to Alec. She'd never had a friend killed right before her eyes. A chilling reminder that her beloved sharks were, always and forever, wild animals.

But she also knew the truth. Man was the wildest animal of them all. And by far the most lethal.

ALEC DIDN'T GET in the water with Grace. While he worked the drone topside, Double D and Stephie went down to record the free-dive, which included Tony and Mackenzie. Frank and Missy were in the surface cage, and Brad monitored the array. Three sharks came to visit—two males and a small female—but no Bonnie or, thankfully, Felix. Maybe Felix had decided he'd had enough of human interaction for a while.

The lighting was good, and Alec got a chunk of usable footage of the boat, the rocky shoreline of Guadalupe Island, and the sharks while they were at the surface.

He had just landed the drone when Mackenzie surfaced and climbed onto the diving deck.

"That was amazing," she said, setting down her mask and snorkel, and then squeezing water from her shoulder-length hair.

"Where's Grace?"

"She and Tony wanted a few more dives." She stepped closer to look at the drone. "I'm pretty beat. I'm not quite at their level." She grabbed a towel and wiped her face. "Did you get some good footage?"

"I think so."

She stepped closer still, bumping against him. "Could you unzip me?"

She easily could do it herself with the cord attached in the back, but Alec obliged, then returned to inspecting the drone.

Mackenzie wasn't an unattractive girl, but he was more interested in a certain canary yellow diver currently swimming with great whites below the boat.

He'd been gripped with more than a desire to get sky footage this morning—he'd stayed out of the water because he'd honestly needed a break from worrying about Grace.

Yesterday's incident kept replaying in his head.

He oscillated between gratitude that Grace was safe and wanting to chew her head off for putting herself at risk.

I could never stand by and watch an animal die, especially if there was something I could do....

It seemed better if Double D filmed her today.

"Did Grace really almost die yesterday?" Mackenzie asked, shedding her wetsuit and standing before him in a fairly provocative purple bikini.

He should really tell her to stop trying so hard. Maybe Brad would be interested. Alec glanced through the window of the salon. Michaels sat at the computer, engrossed in whatever was on the screen.

Returning his focus to the drone, Alec replied in a flat tone, "Yes."

What if she hadn't come back?

He turned to Mackenzie. "How was she down there?"

The girl seemed a bit taken aback by the intensity of Alec's gaze. "She seemed fine. It was impressive, actually."

"What do you mean?"

"The sharks always came to her. I've never seen anything like it."

Shit.

He turned and entered the salon, popping the memory card from the drone into his computer. He sat down and started pulling up the playback, so he could review his footage.

He was an underwater filmmaker, for crissakes. Grace's love of sharks should inspire him. And it had, in the beginning, at least. He needed to get a grip on this irrational fear he had of her getting hurt.

Irrational? That was rich. She'd nearly been killed yesterday.

His fear was completely *rational*.

Fuck.

Mackenzie trailed after him. At least she had the good sense to wrap a towel around her, although it was probably because of the air-conditioned office more than a need to be modest.

Mackenzie turned to Brad. "Could you see us?"

"Yeah. And I got a good read on human versus shark. Grace'll want to cross-reference it with Donovan's footage, but...."

Brad's voice trailed off, and the tone snapped Alec out of his angry stupor.

"What the hell?" Brad stared at his computer.

Fear crept up Alec's spine. He stood and looked at the grid outlined on Brad's desktop screen. "What is it?"

"This can't be right." Brad shook his head. "I'm showing twelve sharks right below us."

Alec slammed open the salon door and ran to the diving deck. Two sharks skimmed the surface near the cage. Erik and Pete were watching the hookah system sending air to Missy and Frank. "Brad says there's twelve sharks in the water."

"That might be right," Erik said. "There was a lot of activity all of a sudden."

"Where's Grace and Tony?"

"They just dove again."

Alec grabbed the radio receiver. "Donovan, do you copy?"

"Roger that."

"What's happening?"

"There's a shitload of sharks down here."

"Signal Grace and Tony to come up."

"Roger that."

"Are they boys or girls?"

"We've got one girl, and the rest are males."

Not good. The males might jockey for position with the female. No one had ever witnessed white sharks mating, but Harry had mentioned that several of the girls they'd seen in the last few weeks were sporting fresh bitemarks, a sure indication of sharks copulating.

"Keep shooting, but get Grace the hell out of there."

She probably had about three minutes remaining before she'd need to surface, but when sharks were concerned, anything could go wrong in a matter of seconds.

"Are they aggressive?" Mackenzie asked over his shoulder. "I was just down there, and everything was fine."

Alec was about to grab his wetsuit and a tank when a violent thrashing of caudal fins and sharks created a whirlpool, slapping Alec with water.

Grace's head, clad in a yellow hood, surfaced just beyond the brouhaha.

"Get out of the water!" Alec yelled.

Tony pulled himself onto the diving deck, sitting as he tried to catch his breath. "There's a bit of a tussle going on." He yanked off his diving mask.

Frank and Missy had started to exit the surface cage, Erik and Pete focusing on them. Panic coursed through Alec. He ran along the side of the boat and jumped into the outboard tethered to the *Mercado.*

Please let the key be in the ignition.

He cast off the lines both fore and aft, and thankfully the key was right where it needed to be. He revved the engine and made a sharp right turn, then crashed through the water toward Grace and cut the engine so hard he fell against the steering wheel.

He moved to the back of the boat and leaned over to reach for her, but a large white moved directly between them, a violent torpedo in the water. Grace's eyes widened through her mask.

"C'mon, Gracie. I've got you." He extended his hand as far as he could without falling in the water himself.

She spun around when another shark bolted behind her, then bumped her hard, shoving her through the water at least five feet.

"Grace, get the fuck in the boat!"

He was about to jump in the water, knowing it was the worst possible move he could make, when Grace came to her senses and swam quickly to him. He grabbed her hand and yanked her over the side, so hard that she hit the floor head first. He gripped under her shoulders and pulled her upright, her overly-long flippers snagging on the driver's seat. He wiggled one and then the other off her feet, then sat beside her, breathing heavily.

Coughing, she pushed her mask and hood off and wiped a hand down her wet face. "Wow. That happened fast. I've never seen anything like it. I think they were trying to mate." She paused, her chest rising and falling in rapid succession. "I hope Double D gets it on film."

Alec reached behind her to unclip the harness that held the go-pro camera between her breasts. She helped remove the straps from her arms and he set the camera aside. Turning, she leaned over the boat.

"I wonder if we could see anything from here," she said.

The outboard bobbed back and forth in the current, the sun setting as the afternoon began turning to night. Alec watched Grace as she searched the frothy water for sharks. Her face was red, her hair was stuck to her forehead in a clump, and her nose was running.

"You have a booger," he said.

"What?" Her hand flew to her nose. She turned away from him and started swiping at her nose, first with her fingers and then the back of her hand. When she acquired the culprit, she hung over the boat and washed her hands in the water. She looked back at him and laughed. "Sorry. Didn't mean to gross you out."

"You could never do that."

Another bout of thrashing occurred at the surface, diverting Grace's attention. She shook her head, mesmerized. "Damn. I wish I could've stayed down there. Double D and Stephie got lucky, being in the cage."

"They're no doubt close to their bottom time limit."

"You're probably right."

She rolled her shoulders and stretched her neck from side to side.

"How's your wound?" he asked.

"Good. We had a fantastic day. I wish you'd been there."

He was glad he hadn't been. Who would have plucked Grace out of the water before a few white sharks roughed her up, or worse?

"I didn't think the sharks mated over here," he said.

"This might not have been mating behavior. Maybe it was just a territorial thing. But wouldn't it be awesome if they're out there right now, fornicating? I wonder if she's an opportunist and goes at it with more than one guy? You know she can store the sperm for later."

Alec released a long, deep chuckle. As the tension seeped out of him, he sat back and extended his arms along the gunwale, putting an arm around Grace in the process. "This is the strangest conversation I've ever had with a woman."

"You've never talked to anyone about sharks doing their sharky thing?" She shifted to a sitting position but maintained her proximity to him.

"You're gonna be the death of me, Grace Mann."

"Why would you say that? You've surely logged more hours in the water than me."

"Why didn't you go to the backup tanks in the submersible?"

She shrugged. "I didn't think I needed to. It all happened fairly quickly."

"And you were the common denominator."

Her blue eyes stared at him. "What's that supposed to mean?"

"Mackenzie said the sharks love to come to you."

She worried her lower lip. "I guess. What's so bad about that? I think my yellow wetsuit is working."

She glanced down at herself, and Alec's gaze followed, enjoying every curve and contour she possessed.

"Yeah, that must be it," he murmured, thinking how her modest breasts would fit perfectly in his hands.

"All right, I'm going to tell you a secret." She squinted toward Guadalupe Island as she spoke. "I don't have nightmares about sharks, even after something dicey or dangerous occurs, like the

Felix thing. But I do dream a lot about them, and more so when I'm in a place where they are, like here. It started when I first went to the Farallones with my dad, when I was a young girl, but it still continues to this day."

"What are you talking about?"

She looked down at her hands. "I dream about the sharks."

Alec's forehead furrowed, and his gaze became fixed on her profile.

She peeked up at him. "I talk to them, Alec," she whispered. "That's how I know them."

He hesitated to answer, sensing that if he gave the wrong response, he'd inadvertently push her away.

"I know what you're thinking," she continued, her voice back to normal, then switched to a mocking tone. "She's so shark happy, she thinks she can talk to them in her dreams."

She straightened and angled her body towards him. "I'm not crazy, and I'm truly not *that* shark-obsessed, but I've always had some deep kinship with them. I talked to a shaman once, and he explained that some people have an extra ability to hear the wild creatures of the earth, and that, over time, this ability can grow. And no, I can't chat with great whites while I'm frolicking with them in the water, but I do have some extraordinary dream encounters with them. I used to think they were just dreams, but I'm not so sure now. It's really weird, but when I dive, I feel like I know them. Or at least some of them. And I think they know me."

She paused, twisting her hands together.

"I probably shouldn't have told you that," she added.

Alec would have kissed her if they weren't clearly visible to the occupants on the *Mercado*.

"I'm glad you did. Your sonar array employs deep learning. Maybe we could hook something up to one of the sharks, and you could converse with it?"

She narrowed her gaze and slapped his ribs with the back of her hand.

He laughed. "What?"

"Now you're teasing me."

He continued to chuckle, enjoying the levity between them.

"I've never told anyone about it, except for the shaman, and my mom, and my sister, Chloe."

"You never told Brad?" But he already knew the answer.

"Are you kidding? He'd call me a mutant and tell me it was all in my head."

"What did you ever see in him?"

She slumped back against the seat. "The truth is, I've never had much experience with boyfriends. In college, I was usually too busy studying to date. I suppose I was easy pickings for someone like Brad. To be honest, I was flattered by his attention in the beginning." She shrugged, looking embarrassed.

It was getting dark, and they needed to return to the *Mercado*, but Alec rather liked having Grace all to himself, her near-miss with the sharks notwithstanding.

"You didn't want to hire me because I was friends with Michaels." It was a statement, not a question.

Her gaze softened. Stripped of her armor, her interest in him was raw and stark.

"In the beginning, yes," she said.

Somebody yelled in their direction from the larger boat, and while Alec couldn't quite make it out, he knew his time with Grace had come to an end. Reluctantly, he tore his eyes from her, looked past her shoulder, and gave a nod. He stood and went to the captain's seat.

"I take it you still don't want me here," he said over his shoulder.

She laughed. "Now it's for an entirely different reason," she said, her voice lower, huskier, the longing unmistakable.

He started the engine and took it slow this time as he drove the outboard back to its berth beside the larger vessel.

But he was in no mood to go slow with Grace any longer. Unfortunately, privacy was in short supply on the crowded *Mercado*.

CHAPTER 16

Grace helped herself to extra portions of dinner. It was Casado night, a traditional Costa Rican meal of white rice, black beans, plantains, salad, and fish. Chris also added a potato picadillo hash and sliced avocados, along with flour tortillas on the side.

After Alec had returned her to the *Mercado*, they'd viewed Double D's footage, and while it had been a rather aggressive melee of white sharks at the end of her dive, no mating had occurred. But Grace couldn't help thinking the display might have had something to do with courtship territorial rights and not which shark was entitled to first dibs on the island's food chain of elephant seals.

A quick shower to wash off the saltwater was followed by a new bandage for the gash on her neck. Missy told her the wound was too moist despite the tightly taped dressing, and she suggested Grace stay out of the water the following day. Grace had no intention of skipping an excursion in the deep blue if she didn't have to but didn't argue the point. She was still distracted by her private powwow with Alec. She had opened up more than planned and was now wondering if it had been too much.

And Mackenzie had managed not only to remain for supper, but had also squeezed into place between Alec and Double D across the table from Grace. It would have been enough to make her lose her appetite if she wasn't famished. She always needed an extra-hefty dose of calories after diving.

"I still can't believe you were in the water with all those sharks as they played out some turf war," Missy said, spooning a helping of fish and rice into her mouth. She was sitting between Grace and Stephie, and the scent of lilacs wafting from her freshly-washed hair overpowered the delectable smell of dinner.

"I got out just in time." Mackenzie's chocolate-colored eyes widened. Her dark hair was swept away from her face, emphasizing her olive complexion. "We were with the female for a while. She was quite calm." Her gaze flicked to Grace. "I'm glad you're okay."

"Me, too." Grace popped a piece of fried plantain in her mouth, savoring it. Plantains were one of her favorite foods. "The female was Lucy. She's easy to spot because she has a damaged caudal fin. And I recognized a few of the boys—Mike, Monkey, and Legend."

"I really thought she was already pregnant. She seemed so gigantic in the girth."

Double D shoveled a big spoonful of rice into his mouth, and then said around the food, "Maybe that's why she didn't fool around."

"Is there any way to be certain if the females are pregnant?" Stephie asked.

"Unfortunately, no," Grace said. "Some researchers have used sonogram equipment on sharks, but you have to catch and briefly detain them. That would be impossible with a white that size."

"She'd hardly sit still for it," Mackenzie said.

"Oh, I don't know," Donovan said. "I'd give her a little hug and hold her in place."

Grace flashed him a bemused smile.

"Did you know that sex is the most dangerous thing an octopus can do?" Missy said, buttering her tortilla.

Everyone looked at her.

She glanced around, then chuckled. "Females are big and hungry, and cannibals too, but of course the males can't resist them." She rolled the tortilla and took a bite. "The anticipation of sex renders them a bit stupid."

Double D grinned. "I think we boys can all relate."

Missy swallowed her food. "To avoid being eaten, they've learned to sneak up on the female, preferably while she's busy doing something else like foraging for groceries, and quickly nail her."

Donovan laughed. "No foreplay?"

"It's too tricky. Copulation requires that he insert one of his tentacles into a hole in her head, the same one she uses to breathe with as well as to defecate from."

Double D crossed his arms. "All right, now you're just being gross."

"To avoid getting too close, the males perform a 'reach.'" She mimicked it by stretching her right arm out toward Donovan. "Some have even developed an adaptation in which the male detaches his sperm arm, so he can escape before she decides to dine on him."

Bewilderment settled over Donovan's face. "He severs his own penis? Jesus, those dudes will do anything to get laid."

Alec chuckled and took a drink of his beer.

Missy retracted her arm. "Sex in the wild isn't for the faint of heart. I wonder if great white canoodling is just as dangerous. When those sharks started swarming today...." She shook her head and looked at Grace. "I was really worried about you."

Grace gently knocked shoulders with her. "You know I was in my happy place, right?"

Missy shook her head again and said quietly, "You know you're crazy, right?"

"She just channels her fear differently," Stephie said matter-of-factly. "You don't face your fears while sitting comfortably at home. You must actively engage them."

"I don't know," Missy replied, "I'm afraid of poltergeists, but I don't think shacking up in a haunted house would make me any less frightened."

"Ghosts can't bite you," Donovan said.

"Are you sure?" Missy countered.

Alec pushed back his empty plate. "Whites occupy a rare place in our minds filled with shadows and monsters and things that scare us shitless," he said. "They trigger that ancient primeval part of our brain that screams *run*."

Missy bobbed her head in agreement. "Yes, that."

"Maybe that's why I swim with them," Mackenzie said, her expression serene. "To show that they aren't monsters but are simply themselves—a pure and perfect predator. They really are quite sweet most of the time."

The girl's insightful answer surprised Grace. Damn. She was beginning to like Mackenzie. Scratch that. Grace had already developed a grudging respect for her pretty rival. While Mackenzie wasn't as strong a freediver as Grace would have liked—Missy was better—the girl had still held her own today.

"Thank you, Mackenzie, for diving with us. I'm hoping we can get in the water tomorrow, if the weather holds. Would you be available?"

"I can do that." The girl nodded, shifting so that she leaned into Alec.

Grace made a concerted effort to keep her expression neutral and not let the frown tugging at her face make an appearance.

"Do you have any extra room on board?" Mackenzie asked. "Maybe I could just bunk here for a few nights to make it easier, in case you want to dive in the mornings."

"She could stay with me," Stephie said.

As luck would have it, Stephie was the oddball third female on the boat and had ended up with a double-bunk room to herself.

"Perfect." Grace forced her lips into what she hoped was a welcoming smile. Fearing that the green-eyed monster rumbling around in her chest would suddenly burst forth like some creature from *Alien*, she nudged Missy, prompting her friend to move. Missy transferred the nudge to Stephie and Grace started scooting.

"We've got poker on the agenda later," Double D said.

"That sounds like fun," Mackenzie responded, her voice full of enthusiasm. "Could you take me back to my boat, so I can grab a few things?"

Grace didn't need to glance up to know that the girl's question was directed at Alec. She bolted to the spiral stairs and departed the galley before she could listen to more of the conversation between Galloway and the attractive grad student.

Reaching the upper deck, she sucked in a lungful of fresh air, angry over letting Galloway get under her skin.

ALEC MANAGED to pawn Mackenzie off on Double D, claiming he needed to review the footage from today. To appear on the up and up, Alec had settled himself into the salon with his computer, all the while wondering where Grace had disappeared to. When he finally went in search of her, Missy told him Grace had fallen asleep in her bunk.

He was disappointed and considered asking Missy to wake her, but he couldn't abide his selfish feelings. Grace had dived all afternoon and was likely exhausted.

He returned to reviewing footage, and Stephie joined him as she edited the photos she'd taken that afternoon. Brad worked on the array but soon left in frustration, claiming he needed Grace to help him with some new glitches that had appeared in the identification of the elephant seals. Amazingly, the pinnipeds sometimes appeared in the water with the whites, swimming circles around the sharks.

Brad left for the galley, dragging Tony with him to help set up the poker game.

Donovan stepped into the salon carrying a duffel bag, Mackenzie behind him.

Stephie stood. "C'mon. I'll show you where you're staying." She waved Mackenzie to follow.

Once the girls were gone, Alec turned to his partner. "Thanks."

Double D folded his thick arms across his chest. "Normally I'm glad for your castoffs, but that poor girl has no interest in me." He paused for effect. "And a lot for you."

Alec blew out a breath. "If she sneaks into my bunk tonight, will you protect me?"

"If she...." Double D couldn't finish his sentence; his face flushed with disbelief. "Am I missing something here?"

"Yeah, Grace." Alec had barely said the words aloud, but Donovan heard them.

"I didn't think Dr. Mann was giving you any return signals. And why would you turn down a sure thing for something that's likely never gonna happen? And I should also remind you that you could screw with our job if you start screwing around with our boss."

"But you want me to go after a grad student?"

"Well, keep it discreet, of course. I'm just trying to help you out, buddy."

"Thanks, but I can manage my own love life."

Double D leaned against the desk. "I knew you liked Grace, but I had no idea it had gotten to this level. What're you gonna do?"

Alec shut his laptop. "That's none of your damned business."

Donovan held up his hands. "All right, all right. I was prepared to give you privacy in our cabin with Miss Grad Student, but the offer's still there if you can woo Dr. Mann."

An expedition fling was bad on so many fronts, but Alec was too far gone. His only problem now was where and when to make his move. He pinched the bridge of his nose and smiled with little humor. "Thanks, I think."

"Jesus, you're so damned stressed. Get laid and get it over with, but for God's sake don't detach your junk after."

Alec chuckled over the octopus reference.

Mackenzie and Stephie reappeared.

"C'mon, girls," Double D said, his voice booming. "You two ever play poker?"

~

GRACE AWOKE IN HER BUNK, surprised that she'd fallen asleep. A quick check of her watch told her it was after 10 p.m. She lay back on her pillow and debated whether to return to sleep, but thirst finally drove her to search for her water bottle on the desk.

It was empty.

A glance at the upper bunk showed it to also be empty. The poker game must be in full swing. Grace didn't feel like company, so she crept into the salon and grabbed a cold water bottle from the mini-fridge as chatter echoed from the galley below. She slipped out the door and headed to the upper deck for a few minutes alone with the stars.

Miles from any town, the darkness was absolute as they bobbed on the gentle swell of ocean currents. The Milky Way in its full glory spilled across the sky, a thousand pins of light, reminding her of the humble position of humankind in the scheme of the universe.

She tucked the bottle into her jacket pocket and climbed the steps to the upper viewing platform. A quick scan confirmed she was alone. She moved to the railing and stared at the endless black sea. A light wind blew her unbound hair away from her face, and she inhaled the moist, briny scent, making her feel at home. She had no doubt that saltwater ran through her veins, mixing with her blood, making her a creature of two worlds.

Grace Mann, mermaid.

The childhood fantasy resurfaced, and a sharp longing squeezed her heart.

I miss you, Daddy.

Eddie Mann had dreamed of the sharks, had even told Gracie on more than one occasion that he'd dreamed *with* the sharks. She'd never really understood what it meant until she'd started doing the same thing while she was in high school. She apparently had inherited that peculiar quirk from her father.

What were the sharks doing in the murky depths below? The elephant seals didn't venture out after dark, so the sharks had nothing to hunt. How did *Jaws* sleep? Did they sleep?

Grace ran possibilities for research projects through her mind.

"Not a card shark after all?"

Grace jumped and spun around, the bottle of water falling out of her pocket. In the far corner sat Alec.

With her hand at her chest, she gasped, "You scared me."

"Sorry."

"How long have you been sitting there?" She reached down to grab the bottle.

"Not long. Just enjoying the view."

A flush of heat filled Grace, because it was clear that he wasn't referring to the night sky.

"I thought you'd be hanging out with everyone else." *With Mackenzie.*

"I was kind of hoping to hang out with you, but Missy told me you'd crashed. You wanna count the stars with me?"

As the adrenaline drained from her body, she gave a nod, crossed the deck to the other side, and sat beside him.

"What were you thinking about?" he asked.

Grace didn't feel like rehashing her mystical connection with the sharks. It seemed prudent to keep her weirdness on the down low. "What kind of sleep cycle do great whites adhere to?"

"Well, they have to keep moving or else they'll die, so I'm guessing it's similar to dolphins—half their brain rests while the other half keeps them alive."

Alec wore a red fleece zipped to his chin, dark pants, and sneakers. He offered his beer to her, which she declined with a shake of her head. Uncapping the water, she took a drink.

He reached into his pocket. "I almost forgot. I wanted to give this to you." He handed her a big beautiful great white shark tooth.

His hand was warm where her fingers made contact.

"Where did you get it?" She touched the serrated edges, a deadly weapon of the great white.

"Mary Ann. After you cut the fishing line off her, she came by the cage to show off her pearly whites."

"Really?"

"I think she was trying to say thanks. Or else get lost. I have to admit that shark-speak isn't my strong suit. She left that behind, and I've been meaning to give it to you ever since."

The gesture warmed her heart. "Thanks."

"I knew you weren't a flowers and chocolate kind of girl."

She made a sound of agreement, admiring the triangular cuspid.

"Harry told me about your dad," Alec said. "He must've been an amazing guy."

She looked up. "He was."

"How old were you when you saw your first white shark kill?"

"I was six."

"That must've been unsettling."

"Oddly enough, it didn't scare me. My sister, Chloe, was there as well. She was four, and she hated it. She started shrieking and crying."

"But not you?"

Grace settled her gaze on the inky outline of Guadalupe Island in the distance. "Don't get me wrong, it's difficult watching death, especially of adorable seals, but at the same time, I was mesmerized. It was quite bloody. The sharks slice those poor seals clean in half, then they thrash around in a frenzy, a veritable stew of blood and death. It's the stuff of nightmares."

"What *are* you afraid of, Grace?"

"Well, don't tell Missy, but even before her story of octopus sex, I wasn't too fond of them."

"Really? Why?"

She scrunched her nose and gazed upward at the thousand-light canopy. "I know they're smart as all get-out, and when they look you in the eye, they're like little people sizing you up. But my dad took Chloe and me to an aquarium once. He knew one of the guys in charge, so we were allowed behind the scenes. I was standing near the octopus exhibit, and although I didn't have my hand in the water, the damned thing shot out a tentacle and took hold of me. It dragged me into the tank."

Alec's face shifted to a horrified look. "Holy shit. What kind was it?"

"A Giant Pacific Octopus."

"How did you get out?"

"I was about seven at the time, but I could hold my breath for two minutes and thirty-six seconds." She flashed a look of mock pride at him over her childhood feat. "I would practice in the community pool each week after my swimming lessons. It drove my mother crazy because the lifeguards kept telling her that I was trying to kill myself. But it saved my life that day."

"How did they get you free?"

"It let me go, I swam to the edge, and my dad hauled me out." The memory of her father whacking her on the back to expel the water she'd swallowed surfaced, the sting of those swats sending a ghost tingle between her shoulder blades.

"Did he want to sue the facility?"

Grace laughed. "No way. You know what he said to me after I practically vomited tank water all over the floor?" Changing the tone of her voice, she mimicked Eddie Mann. "Gracie, you've been initiated, my girl."

"Initiated into what?" In the dark, Alec's features were all angles and shadows, but she could sense his bewilderment over her father's behavior.

"To the world of ocean creatures. He considered the entire event a good omen." She fiddled with the shark tooth in her hand. "My dad was a little rough around the edges and brooded at times, but he was very charismatic. My mother told me once that loving him was entirely out of her control. She was just happy to join him on the ride."

"Like father, like daughter." Alec stretched his legs out, settling close enough to her that his thigh bumped hers. "I've never met a woman like you, Grace."

"I hope that's good," she teased.

"Yeah. It's good."

The heat in his voice was unmistakable, and it warmed her from the inside out, causing her skin to perspire beneath the sweatshirt she was bundled into.

"Tell me something crazy about you," she said.

"I have a dog."

She lowered her eyebrows. "Okay. I guess that's crazy, since I doubt you're hardly ever home."

"True. She stays with my parents. She really adores my mom."

"What kind of dog is she?"

"A golden lab."

"What's her name?"

"Grace."

She released a bark of laughter. "You're full of it."

"No, it's true. Her name is Grace Kelly. I could introduce you one day. I think she'd like you—kindred spirits and all that."

She couldn't shake the smile from her lips as she turned her gaze back to the ocean that shimmered under the crescent moon, pleased that Alec dangled a future between them.

And then she remembered that maybe he was saying nice things to get her in the sack, that maybe he had no intention of following through with such suggestions, that maybe, in the end, he'd be like Brad. The smile left her face.

"You're overthinking it, Grace."

"About what?"

"Us."

Her eyes locked with his. "You're awfully sure of yourself."

"Around you? Hardly. But there is one thing I *am* sure of."

"And what's that?"

"I'm not going to let a chance with you go by."

Ah, hell. It worked for her.

She held his gaze, letting him know that he had a free pass to first base.

He leaned forward and kissed her, his lips warm and inviting, his skin smelling of sweat and sunscreen. He scooted closer and kissed her again, and she slanted her mouth against his, sinking into the delicious sensations that had lived only in her daydreams until this moment.

She brought a hand to his cheek, her fingertips brushing along the stubble, and then slid it to the back of his neck. The kiss changed, deepening, as Alec pulled her into his arms.

When she surfaced for air, she thought to say something funny, but he'd literally knocked the wind from her. Like flash lightning, her body was on fire everywhere. She brought her mouth to his again and let loose the desire coursing through her. Lack of sex for well over a year apparently wasn't good for a person, and she suddenly wanted to remedy that. With Alec.

She plundered his mouth, her hands groping his face, his shoulders, his chest. He shifted her onto his lap, and she straddled him, wanting to feel him against her. Wrapping his arms around her, Alec swept her mouth with his tongue, leaving a lingering taste of beer and onions.

His hands slid beneath the layers of her clothing, burning her skin as they held onto her hips, and then began an upward climb.

Fumbling with the zipper on his jacket, she attempted to yank it down when voices erupted on the deck below.

Grace stopped her attack on Alec, her mouth near his, her breath jagged and uneven.

"Let's go to my cabin," he said quietly.

"What about Double D?"

"It'll be okay. He'll stay away."

While Grace's body wanted nothing more than a release at the hands of Alec—a shudder passed through her at the very thought— worry gripped her. Surely they'd be caught. And the boat was small. The gossip would spread faster than a mako on attack.

Damn.

"We can't."

"You can't leave me like this, Grace," he whispered. "I *need* to have you."

Another wave of longing nearly undid her.

Damn again.

"Okay," she agreed. "But meet me in the bathroom."

She climbed off him.

Standing beside her, he leaned his face close to hers. "That's not necessary."

"No one will barge into the bathroom," she said. "I'll go first. Wait five minutes and then follow."

She turned to leave, but he grabbed her hand and held her in place. "Just for the record, I never voted for the john." He kissed her then let her go.

Doing her best to regain her composure, she descended to the lower deck and tried to slip past the small crowd, catching sight of Captain Bellamy, Erik, and Double D.

"Hey, Grace," Tony said upon noticing her.

Not wanting to be bothered by distractions, she gave a wave and kept moving. "Good night."

CHAPTER 17

As Alec waited on the observation deck, he ran a hand through his hair and down his neck. Shit, he was sweating.

He gripped the railing and watched the water. Laughter and conversation echoed from below. In the murky ocean beyond the boat he saw a dorsal fin glide across the surface. From the size, it could be one of the big girls. Was it Lucy, the female from earlier who'd had to beat off a passel of males? Were they still chasing her? As with many species, white shark females were bigger than the males. He had to think the females were picky about who they mated with, allowing only the males they felt were worthy. Coupling was likely a violent affair, if the bitemarks the females frequently sported were any indication—deep cuts and gashes just above the head.

Had Double D and Stephie gotten close today in documenting a white shark sex romp? Either way, Alec sympathized with the males that were probably always attempting to gain top dog status.

His own powerful urge to mate throbbed painfully in his shorts.

Some tiny part of his brain still functioning acknowledged that this was probably stupid. Professionally, he needed to keep things aboveboard with Grace. But he'd been sliding toward her ever since that night he'd sat in the auditorium in Monterey and listened to her presentation about sharks. No, scratch that. His fascination had begun even before meeting her, when he'd read about her work and seen the viral photo of her freediving with a great white in Hawai'i.

Every night since embarking from San Diego, she'd entered his nightly slumber, filling him with desire and enticing him with her intellect and her passion.

And after nearly watching her die in the cage with Felix, his resolve was stretched a bit thin.

Grace wants me.

He wasn't about to look a gift horse in the mouth.

Her bright lemon wetsuit had teased him with her perfectly proportioned shape. When he'd stripped her down in the shower after she'd spent too much time in the deep trying to free the fishing line from Mary Ann, he'd been angry—in less time than it would take to blink, the large female shark could have bitten Grace into two separate pieces. It hadn't helped his temper that Grace had been exhausted and practically dead on her feet, the evidence in her pale face, blue lips, and shivering limbs. At the same time, Alec had been gripped by something else altogether—the curve of her hips and the swell of her breasts, hidden only by a bit of nylon and spandex, had triggered a primal instinct, a territorial need to lay claim to her.

The urge to bite Grace and leave a mark had coursed through him.

He wasn't so different than those white male sharks that literally mauled the females during coupling.

But he'd held back then. He'd never had any intention of forcing the issue; he'd never been entirely sure how she felt about him.

But now he did.

Whatever thread of chivalry he'd been clinging to had just gone up in a puff of smoke.

Grace was the girl of his dreams, and now that he knew she wanted him, staying away from her was no longer possible.

He had waited long enough.

Suppressing a growl of frustration, he pushed back from the railing.

He dropped from the ladder, skipping all the steps, his legs bending to absorb the impact.

"Hey, Alec," Double D said from the diving deck where the others sat in a crowd. "Bring me a beer, would you?"

Alec gave a nod and waved half-heartedly before heading straight into the salon. He'd be damned if someone stopped him from getting to the head. Without slowing his pace, he opened the door to the cabin he shared with Donovan. In one swift motion, he removed the red fleece jacket he'd been wearing, leaving him in a gray t-shirt. He knelt and pulled a duffle bag from beneath the lower bunk. He unzipped several pockets before he located his goal —condoms. He didn't always travel with them, not like some of the guys he'd gone on expeditions with who always plotted to bed something of the female variety if given half a chance. Michaels had been such a plotter.

But at the last minute, Alec had tossed a handful in his bag. Grace had been on his mind at the time. It didn't hurt to be prepared, and he hadn't wanted to count on bumming one off Double D or Brad. He doubted Grace's ex would be happy to know that Alec was chasing her.

Alec really didn't give a shit, but he suspected that Grace did.

He quietly left the cabin. A glance confirmed he was alone in the hallway. He went to the bathroom door and knocked softly.

Grace's bright blue eyes and rosy pink cheeks appeared on the other side. She tried to look past him, but he blocked her view as he stepped inside and closed the door behind him.

"No one saw me," he said.

She nodded and took a deep breath, looking bashful under the harsh bathroom light. Her eyes dropped to his chest. "I like your shirt."

He glanced down, having paid little attention when he'd pulled it on this morning.

The lettering read: *Hurricane? You mean surfing weather.*

"You must be pretty good," she said.

"I do all right."

"You're a big wave surfer, right?"

Alec reached for her. "If you want to learn to surf, all you have to do is ask." His mouth lowered to hers. "I'd be happy to teach you."

"We should be quiet."

He kissed her lightly. "Whatever you say, Grace," he whispered against her soft lips, then captured her mouth with more intention.

She yielded and he pressed closer, consuming her as if she were a lush, ripe peach. He wrapped his arms around her, bringing her against him. He couldn't stop the shudder that coursed through.

Not much time.

Shit.

Bathroom sex was more of a turn-on than he'd anticipated.

She backed up against the sink, tugging him with her, and her hands groped at his waistband and then higher, her fingers raking his bare skin. He lifted her onto the sink's edge, and she wrapped her legs around him.

She fumbled with the zipper on her jacket, yanking it down. Alec helped her finish, then pushed it from her shoulders and arms. Beneath she wore a thin white tee stretched across her breasts.

He kissed her again, and she matched his frenzy, removing his shirt and exploring his chest with her mouth and hands.

He pushed his fingers under her shirt and didn't stop until he found his goal, cupping her breasts in his palms. Grace leaned back and yanked her shirt over her head. Next came the white sports bra.

Seeing her bared pushed him to a new level of need and restraint.

He stifled a growl, but it escaped his mouth anyway.

Almost there. Don't blow it now.

She slid to her feet, and in one movement, Alec burrowed his hands past the waistband of her stretch pants and pushed them down her legs. She kicked off her water sandals, and he yanked the pants from her, kissing the cleft between her legs. He paused, caught in the exotic scent of Grace's readiness for him, but she urged him to stand.

Thank God.

He didn't have the patience to dally in Grace's playground. That hopefully would come later.

With hands on her hips, he lifted and perched her on the edge of the sink once again. Her mouth found his, hot and frantic and determined, and he unbuttoned his pants and shoved them down.

Grace reached for him.

"Wait," he said.

Bending down, he pulled his pants free of his feet and searched the pockets. As soon as his fingers found the condom he tore open the packet. Grace's mouth nipped along his bicep as he got the damned thing on as fast as he could.

"You're prepared," she murmured.

Her coral-tipped breasts stared back at him.

"I only brought them because of you."

She let out a low, throaty laugh. "You were pretty sure you were going to get laid."

"No, I wasn't." He put his hands underneath her knees and stepped closer to her. "Just hopeful. A woman like you doesn't come along every day."

He watched her face as he pushed inside her. Her breath caught, then rattled. He cupped her buttocks as she wrapped her legs around him.

Jesus, she felt good.

He held himself still to prolong the pleasure for just a moment longer. That was about all the willpower he had.

In a wild frenzy, Alec repeatedly drove into Grace, unable to slow the act, his body driving single-mindedly to completion. Grace gripped him tightly, her body taut as she met him thrust for thrust. When a cry slipped out of her, he covered her mouth with his. The intensity of his release continued in waves, and he rode the aftermath while clutching Grace against him.

He buried his face into her neck, sweat glistening on her skin and his, and bit the skin on her shoulder, then gentled it with a kiss. He could at least soothe his love bites, unlike the sharks.

DEEP BLUE

Her legs gripped him tighter, and she hugged him against her, breathing as if she'd just run a very fast mile.

He brought his face to hers and kissed her. "Not really how I envisioned our first time, but it'll do."

"You think?" She grabbed his lower lip between her teeth. "I'll never be able to use this bathroom again without thoughts of you."

He glanced down, aroused all over again at the sight of their joined bodies. He cursed his lack of foresight—he'd only brought one condom.

A knock on the door startled them both.

"Is there someone in there?" Missy.

"Yep," Alec answered. Grace was no help as she started to nibble on the underside of his jaw. "Give me a minute."

Grace snorted a very quiet giggle. "She'll think you're wrecking the place," she whispered.

"Isn't that what we just did? Come back to my cabin."

Grace sighed against him, running her hands along his ribcage. "Okay. I'm not ready to stop touching you."

He sure as hell wasn't ready to be done.

He kissed her long and hard, then untangled himself from her. In the tight space, they searched for clothing and attempted to tidy up.

"I'm gonna find Double D first and tell him to stay away," he whispered into her ear as he stood behind her, "then I'll join you."

He pulled her back against him, and she leaned her head to the side so he could nuzzle her neck. He stepped around her to open the door, in case Missy was still there, so she'd see him first, but the corridor was empty. He exited his and Grace's love shack and walked toward the salon without looking back.

Eager to get Grace alone and naked again, he pulled a beer from the mini-fridge and went out onto the deck, a chill rippling through his overheated body as the cooler air washed over him. Donovan still sat with Captain Bellamy, Erik, and Tony. Brad and Mackenzie also sat in the circle, her eyes visibly lighting up when she saw him.

Alec avoided her gaze and handed Double D the beer.

"Thanks. Took you long enough."

"I got sidetracked." How was he going to tell Donovan to stay away from the cabin for a bit with an audience staring at him?

"You joining us?" Double D asked.

"Nah. I'm gonna crash."

Double D nodded and held up the beer bottle in salute. "We've got a busy day tomorrow. Can't wait to see what new shark story Grace will bring us. Tell her another mating skirmish would be ideal."

Alec released a laugh and a half-smile. "Shark porn?" He preferred the mating skirmish he'd just had with the Shark Lady herself.

Brad leaned back, his portable canvas chair stretching tight. "I've never seen her kiss a shark, but I'm sure it's coming."

"Ah, but I heard she kissed you, Michaels," Donovan said. "So she *has* already smooched a shark."

"Asshole," Brad retorted, but there was no real heat in it.

Unexpectedly, jealousy wound tight in Alec's gut, and an urge to punch Michaels pulsated hotly in his veins.

"Sleep tight," Alec said, and turned away from the group.

He'd lock the cabin door in case Double D returned before Alec was finished with Grace. And he'd make damned sure any memory of Brad Michaels was gone from her mind, her heart, and while he was at it, her soul.

CHAPTER 18

Grace grabbed her jacket off the bathroom floor and headed to her cabin, her body still buzzing from the encounter with Alec.

He'd broken her man drought, and the only thought her brain could retain was...*holy shit.*

She hadn't realized how much she'd needed to get laid. She hadn't remembered how good it felt to have a man want her again. And she *really* hadn't comprehended how much Alec would turn her world upside down. But he had. And then some.

Missy lay on the top bunk reading a magazine. She glanced at Grace. "Where have you been?"

"Just hanging out." Grace's voice sounded as if she just had the wind knocked from her. She dropped her jacket on the desk chair then smoothed a trembling hand along her hair, trying to appear nonchalant.

"What's wrong?" Missy propped herself up on an elbow, her brows jammed together in worry, and then her forehead smoothed out and her eyes widened. "Oh, shit. You're fooling around with Galloway, aren't you?" She sucked in a breath. "Were you in the bathroom with him?"

Good grief. Was it written all over her face? Grace opened her mouth to deny it, but she didn't want to lie to Missy.

Missy's mouth stretched into a wide grin. "I didn't think you had it in you. How was it?"

The worry and tension drained out of Grace like a balloon deflating. "It was...*wow.*"

"Has he professed his undying love for you?"

Grace frowned. "No. And God, I wouldn't want him to. Do men do that with you?"

Missy gave a grunt of agreement. "There've been a few."

"And how did those work out?"

"Okay, I get your point."

Grace grabbed her hairbrush and began working on her knotted tresses. "I'm leaving in a minute."

"Gracie, don't lose your head over him."

The brush caught on a tangle, and Grace winced. "Seriously, you're telling me this now?"

"All right, all right. Are you headed back to the bathroom? Because I gotta say that you're gonna get a lot more interruptions."

"No. His cabin."

"What about Double D?"

Grace shrugged. "I don't know." She went back to working on her hair. "Look, Missy, I really don't want anyone to know."

Missy chuckled. "Famous last words." Her expression quickly sobered. "Sorry. People aren't surprised if I have some torrid affair while on expedition, but Dr. Gracie Mann is all business."

Grace gave up on her frizzy tresses, tossing the brush on the desk. "There was Brad, of course."

"Yeah, but I'm chalking that one up to naiveté. You're not naïve anymore."

"What if I still am? Do you think I'm making a mistake?"

Missy swung her legs over the edge of the bed and jumped down. "You swim with great white sharks, and you're worried about some guy breaking your heart? He should worry that you'll break *his* heart."

Grace hadn't considered that, but deep down she knew it was an absurd notion. "Missy," she said, her voice low for effect, arching her right eyebrow, "have you met Alec Galloway?"

Missy's eyes flashed with mischief. "Yes," she answered, her lips stretching into a grin. "And there's not too many like him. You'd better use every trick you've got to keep him interested."

Anxiety did a painful somersault in Grace's belly, and she inwardly groaned. "I don't have many tricks."

"I'm kidding." Missy grasped her shoulders and gave her a light shake. "Relax. He wouldn't pursue you if he didn't want to."

"Oh, God." Grace sank into the chair and hunched over, her face in her hands. "Is this just an expedition fling?"

Missy crouched beside her. "Maybe," she said, her voice soft and empathetic. "Gracie, you're totally overthinking this."

Grace lifted her gaze. "That's what Alec said."

"And already, he knows you too well."

Grace sat up straight and expelled a deep breath. "Screw it. I like him. Probably too much, but it is what it is."

Missy stood. "Then in the spirit of screwing, I give you permission to rendezvous *here*."

Grace shot up from the chair.

"I know," Missy said before she could speak, "My altruism is shocking. I'll leave until," she glanced at her watch, "midnight, okay?"

As Missy spoke, Grace caught a whiff of alcohol on her friend's breath. "Missy, you're tipsy."

Missy giggled at the rhyme. "Just a little."

"You don't have to leave."

"I know. But I'll do it in the name of lust."

Grace wrapped Missy into a hug. "Thank you. I'll return the favor."

"I'm not finding any prospects on this boat."

"Maybe a Mexican sailor will swim up and require our assistance?"

Missy's eyes lit up. "Hmm, that has possibilities." She grabbed a sweatshirt. "I'm gonna go find the captain and ask if he's heard any distress calls from gorgeous men lost at sea. And of course, they would've had to survive the sharks."

"That's how you'll know he's the one."

Missy smirked as she shut the door behind her.

GRACE WAS ABOUT to leave for Alec's cabin to tell him of the change in location when someone knocked on the door. She swung it open.

Alec stood with a dangerous gleam in his eye. His tan face with its five-o'clock shadow put her in mind of a man who'd spent days in the wilderness with nothing but his instincts to survive. She wobbled on her feet.

Had that been the boat swaying, or was she lightheaded from the male specimen standing before her?

"I saw Missy," he said, the intensity of his gaze putting her in mind of a kelp forest, filled with shadows and hidden places.

"Do you want to come in?"

"Yeah, I want to come in."

She stepped back and shut the door behind him. His tall, lithe frame appeared coiled and ready to strike. "Did something happen?" she asked.

He rubbed a hand behind his neck in agitation, then looked down at her. "Did you love Michaels?"

"No," she replied without hesitation. Maybe she'd wondered in the beginning if she had, but it was crystal clear to her that she'd never felt that depth of emotion for her ex. "Did he say something?"

Alec stepped closer to her. "He's just a dickhead."

"You don't have to tell me twice."

When Alec didn't say anything, or make a move to touch her, she grabbed hold of his shirt to bring him closer. She didn't have a repertoire of feminine wiles in her wheelhouse, so she followed her instinct to soothe his edges, to let him know that he eclipsed Brad in every possible way.

"I'm really not thinking about Brad or anybody else."

Alec's gaze met hers. "Good."

His kiss was hot and filled with carnal promise, and she was completely panting for him, despite that it had been only about twenty minutes since their first encounter.

He tugged off his shirt then made quick work of disrobing her down to her birthday suit. He ran his hands along the length of her, exploring and branding her skin with his touch. Despite that he'd just taken her, and quite thoroughly, it was shocking how much she craved him again.

He met her hunger with equal demand, and she soon had him naked, reveling in the strength of muscles that flexed and rippled beneath her hands. Everything about him kicked her libido into overdrive.

"Which bed is yours?" he asked.

"The bottom one."

He had her flat on her back and covered with his body in one swift motion. Pleasure rippled through her.

"I'm close, Alec." Her words came out in a breathless plea.

He suddenly left her, leaving her disoriented. He jammed a hand in the pocket of his shorts again and retrieved another condom. As he put it on, Grace enjoyed the view—his powerful legs and flat stomach, the hair that ran down his chest and further.

"You're beautiful," she whispered.

As his body blanketed hers, he said, "You're just trying to get me into bed."

"Is it working?"

He shifted and she slid her hand down to guide him. When he pushed completely into her, she wrapped her legs around him and met his thrusts with her own.

He drove into her, her release coming fast, furious, and all-consuming. He reached his climax with a groan and held her tight, his arms wrapped around her as if she were a buoy, the only thing saving him from being swept out to sea.

For a long moment, Grace *was* swept away, thinking of nothing but Alec and her intense need for him. As the crest of her orgasm abated, Alec continued to cling to her. Her mind whispered epitaphs in her ear—*wow* and *holy shit* on repeat. She needed to expand her vocabulary. If she died right now, her tombstone would say: *She passed peacefully from amazing sex.*

She held Alec close, her lips nibbling on his shoulder, tasting his salty skin as the earthy scent of their coupling filled the space around them.

She closed her eyes and relaxed, Alec still inside her, still holding her like she was the very air he breathed. Her hands drifted from his shoulders to his buttocks.

"I still want you," he said.

She laughed as his hot breath tickled her neck, then squirmed until he raised his head. "That's good. I was hoping this wasn't just drive-by sex."

"I meant I still want you right now." He pulled his arms free so he could brace himself over her.

"You can have me until midnight."

He glanced at his watch—the only thing he still wore. "We've got an hour." He kissed her. "This was awfully nice of Missy. I'm not sure Double D would've stayed away from our cabin for that long."

Grace raked a hand through Alec's hair. "Missy thinks I should've jumped in the sack with you weeks ago."

"You should listen to her." He leaned down and bit her neck.

Grace arched her back, and her body tightened with anticipation. She released a contented sigh, swirling in her own satisfaction.

Alec pillaged her mouth with his lips and tongue. She wrapped her arms around him, snuggling into his warmth, happiness suffusing her like a kid on Christmas morning.

He shifted slightly, and Grace was surprised he was still hard inside her. As a new wave of lust overtook her, Alec stilled and his expression became serious in the harsh glow of the desk lamp illuminating the room. "This isn't drive-by sex."

She smiled, rubbing her fingers on the stubble on his cheek. "That's too bad. I just love random sexual encounters."

He stared at her, his face frozen in shock.

"I'm totally kidding," she blurted.

His broad shoulders sagged slightly. "I'm gonna need to get used to your sense of humor."

She kissed his chin. "Yes. Because I'm very funny. I keep telling people, but they seem to think I'm just this crazy, driven shark lady."

He nuzzled her neck again. "You *are* a crazy shark lady."

But it apparently didn't deter his ardor, because he made love to her again, and her body responded eagerly, leaving her spent and satiated in his arms.

ALEC LAY on the narrow bunk with Grace's naked body pressed against his side, her leg draped over his and her head resting against his chest. They had less than twenty minutes before Missy would return. He wished they could have the entire night together, but he'd take what he could get.

And he'd managed to *get* Grace three times.

He'd turned off the desk light, and they lay together in semi-darkness. She smelled of sun and ocean and sex, and he periodically buried his nose in her hair and inhaled.

"Are you sniffing me?" she asked after the fourth time he'd done it.

"You smell good."

He twined the fingers of his free hand with hers. He could easily fall asleep but made an effort not to. Once he left, he wouldn't have this Grace available to him—wanton and relaxed and sexy as hell. He'd have to pretend they were business associates for the sake of the others. It would suck being unable to touch her whenever he felt like it.

She laughed. "I don't think I've had a real shower in days."

"I like a woman in her natural scent."

Grace snickered. "How did you get started in filmmaking?"

He pulled the sheet higher to keep Grace from getting cold. "When I surfed competitively as a kid, I was always fascinated by the photographers and video guys who filmed the competitions. In high school, I started monkeying around with my own equipment. At that point, my brother and I had started big wave surfing with our dad, and there weren't a lot of filmmakers in that arena, so that's where I started cutting my teeth and getting footage that other people wanted to see and were willing to pay for."

"That's when you hung around with Brad?"

He fiddled with her hand. "Yeah. I'd known him from the competition circuit, but not well. We both started hanging out at the big swells—Mavericks which is just south of the Bay area and Ghost Tree near Carmel—so we became friends. But I use that term loosely. I know he made it sound like we were tight, but it wasn't like that."

She gave a soft snort. "He likes to say whatever suits him. That type of surfing sounds dangerous. Do you still do it?"

He ran his other hand along her hip to the swell of her buttocks, enjoying her smooth-as-butter skin. "Not as much as I did back then. It was my dad's thing, so once Ty and I were old enough, tall enough, and strong enough, we thought we could do it." He laughed. "Big waves will humble you right from the start. And if not the waves, my dad always made sure we were never too big for our britches. He's a tough son-of-a-gun, but he has no patience for ego. He made sure we knew why we were there."

"And why were you there?"

"To honor the power of Mother Nature but never to think we had her figured out. No matter how good you are at what you do, you must always approach with a beginner's mind."

Grace went quiet, nodding against his shoulder. "That's how I feel when I'm with the whites. What's it like to surf a big wave?"

He took a deep breath. "Well, it's like nothing else I've ever done. You can't focus on anything but the wave. All your other senses fall away, and you're completely in the moment. If you've hit your mark and can hang on and can enter the barrel, then you've hit the sweet spot. In a big wave, the energy is at such a giant level that, if you can survive, it's a high that can easily become addictive."

"Was it that way for you?"

He sniffed her again, and she rewarded him with a nudge. "For a while," he said. "But it's also dangerous as hell. After a few close calls, I started focusing more on filmmaking."

"Why didn't you study film in college?"

"I thought engineering was more practical. While I was in school, I freelanced a lot in underwater footage and interned with a well-known cinematographer based in L.A. When I graduated, I formed Galloway Films and have had a good run with projects— knock on wood. I don't take it for granted. I know I'm a lucky son-of-a-bitch."

Grace craned her head to look at him. "I believe luck and hard work go hand in hand. Lucky breaks only occur if you're positioned to grab them."

"Speaking from experience?"

She resettled her head in the niche between his collarbone and shoulder, pressing her curves more tightly against him. "Maybe."

"What was it like with your dad? Did you live on the Farallones?"

"Chloe and I did on a few different occasions. My mom really didn't approve, but she still let us go. I was six the first time we went, the same time I saw my first kill. It was a short trip, only about a week. My mom came with us, but she never went out on the boats. She always got really seasick. That first time I was on the ocean with my dad, with the wind whipping around us, the water in whitecaps, and the ocean saying in no uncertain terms that this place was dangerous, it just mesmerized me. Chloe, on the other hand, hated it."

"Why?"

Grace chuckled. "My dad would tow a carpet decoy in the shape of a seal behind the boat to attract a shark. One time, one of the giant females—one of the sisters—showed up. What an incredible specimen she was. She came up beside the boat, and she was *bigger* than our boat. Chloe freaked out. I'll admit I was shaking too, but I still loved it."

She ran a hand along his bicep and squeezed, her voice picking up in velocity. "The sister lifted her head out of the water and looked at us. I mean, she *really* looked at us. Her eye was so blue, not pitch black like I'd always thought. I was awestruck. I could literally feel her awareness, her intelligence. I had no idea it would be like that, and it blew me away. The sister circled our boat repeatedly, and Chloe was convinced we were about to become her next meal. My dad told us otherwise, but she was too upset. Finally, Dad had to turn the boat around and head back to shore to take her to Mom. But just before he did that, he looked at me and said 'Gracie, always keep your wits and pay attention, but remember, the sharks have souls, too.'"

"So, your dad was a believer."

"What do you mean?"

"The wild places were his religion." He played with Grace's hair.

"Hmm. I never thought about it like that before, but that's a good way of putting it. The Hawaiians believe that the dead return to the water and become sharks."

"Then maybe your dad is out there."

She rested her chin on her hand and gifted him with a serene expression. "That's a nice thought. I think he'd like that. He loved the ocean, and he loved sharks."

"I'm sure he loved you and your sister more."

Her eyes narrowed. "You didn't know my dad."

"I'm guessing you're a lot like him."

She laid her head back on his chest. "Maybe. Well, probably. My mom likes to say so, especially when she's mad at something I'm doing that could be dangerous."

"She worries about you. I can relate."

She lifted her head. "You're worried about me? But you probably know sharks as well as I do. You know it's ridiculously safe."

He released an exasperated huff. "I don't really think you can use the phrase *ridiculously safe* in the same breath with a great white shark. And while I agree with you in principle, there will always be Elliott."

"I know," Grace murmured. "I'm sorry, but his death was such a rare occurrence. White sharks don't usually attack divers. They're more apt to go after surfers."

Alec sighed. "I know. Mavericks is a notoriously shark-infested area. Tyler got bumped from his board once by a great white. He literally rocketed ten feet in the air."

"Was he okay?"

"Yeah, but that was the beginning of the end at Mavericks for him. He started spending more time climbing in the mountains."

"And you spent more time *in* the water than above it."

"I guess I was destined to stay in the ocean one way or another."

She scooted closer to bring her face closer to his. "I'm glad."

He pulled her atop him, taking her weight against him from her breasts clear down to her toes. "If you'll teach me to freedive, I'll teach you how to surf."

She grinned against his mouth. "It's a deal."

They let their bodies do the talking for the short time they had left.

CHAPTER 19

G race awoke early after a sound sleep. Her thoughts turned to Alec—and the previous night—and her body reminded her of every delicious thing he had done to her. On the heels of that thought, anxiety began to chew around the edges of her bliss.

Two weeks remained in the expedition. Had she just made an awkward mistake? Would sleeping with Alec make their work easier or harder? How would she keep her cool around him? Would spirals of lust shoot out her eyes every time she looked at him?

She buried her face in her pillow to stifle a groan. It smelled of him. She inhaled deeply, just as he'd done with her hair. It reminded her of want and need and yearning.

Alec Galloway was the perfect male storm: physically appealing, mentally equal, and an impassioned soul. It was that last point that drew her while, at the same time, setting off alarm bells—no man in her life had ever met that criterion, except perhaps her dad. Certainly not the boys in high school, and not Brad, although she couldn't deny that his work with sharks had given her false hope that he shared the same connection to the deep places, to the ancient pathways that the sharks embodied.

She rose from bed and started to get dressed, reaching for her one-piece to take it to the bathroom with her. She'd be freediving again today.

"Wrong choice." Missy's sleepy voice drifted from her perch.

Grace turned to her bunkmate who was visible in the gray light filtering in through the small window.

"You just rocked Alec's world," Missy said, propping her head up with her hand. "Well, I'm assuming you did."

"Of course," Grace retorted with mock sarcasm. "I used all my tricks."

"Then don't wear your one-piece today. Break out the bikini, Gracie."

"Really?"

"Yes, really," Missy admonished her. "It will give you leverage."

Grace's mind went blank. "Why do I need leverage?"

Missy yawned and rolled onto her back. "I don't know, but it doesn't hurt to stock up."

Grace considered her options. "But he's already seen me in my two-piece."

"Oh, right. The one you'd wear if you were swimming the English Channel."

"It's not that bad." Grace frowned, affronted by Missy's assessment.

"Look in that top drawer." Missy pointed across the cabin. "I've got a purply one that's clean. You can borrow it."

Grace rustled through Missy's belongings until she found a pretty, mauve-colored top that didn't have much fabric to it. She hesitated.

"At least try it on," Missy murmured.

Oh, hell. Grace grabbed the top and the matching bottoms and headed to the bathroom.

ALEC MADE his way to the galley on the lookout for Grace, but she was absent. She might still be sleeping. Yesterday had no doubt been a long day for her, but on the heels of that thought, he pondered how he might get her alone again.

Brad and Tony were eating eggs and toast and discussing politics. Alec had no desire to enter that conversation, so he grabbed coffee and a plain bagel and headed out on deck. In the morning sunshine, he saw two dorsal fins cutting along the surface of the glassy water. He climbed up to the observation deck. At the railing stood Double D, Eric, and Pete, but they weren't looking at the sharks. Alec shifted his gaze to where they stared, about to bring the bagel to his mouth, but stopped the action mid-air.

Grace and Missy were one level below at the fore of the boat, faced away from them and watching the water, clad in fairly revealing swimwear.

No wonder the guys weren't watching the sharks.

Double D caught sight of him. "A lot of sharks out this morning."

"You're all acting like you've never seen one before," Alec said, trying to clamp down his irritation over them ogling Grace.

But, damn, she had a nice ass, and he'd had his hands all over it the night before. He took a bite of bagel and indulged the view along with the others.

"It's about time they broke out the bikinis," Pete said.

His comment broke the spell that even Alec had succumbed to.

These little shits were enjoying it too much. What was Grace thinking?

"It's a little cold out, isn't it?" he muttered under his breath and headed down the steps to the lower deck.

Grace saw him approach, and her smile boosted his ego several notches. The front of the suit revealed the nice curve of her breasts and an enticing amount of cleavage. He resisted the impulse to pull off his fleece and drape it over her. Double D and the boys would wonder what the hell was wrong with him, and they'd probably revolt over him covering the merchandise.

"Morning," he said.

Missy beamed. "Good morning, Alec." She wore a rather skimpy fatigue-green string bikini, but his eyes immediately homed in on Grace's curves, which both piqued his jealousy and made him want to drag her back to the head.

He stepped around them both and stood to Grace's left side. "There seems to be a lot of action out there." He nodded toward the water.

"We should probably get in," Grace said.

That was fine by him. The sooner she covered up all that skin, the better.

He took a swallow of his coffee. "I can be ready in ten minutes." *Or now, if she wants a quickie.*

"Did you sleep all right?" she asked.

He faced forward, aware he was being watched from behind as well as from the side by Missy. "Yep. You girls realize you've got an audience, right?"

Grace looked over her shoulder and waved, but when she turned back to the water, a frown pinched her face. "It was all Missy's idea," she grumbled.

"Not that I'm complaining," Alec said.

"Gracie needs to let loose," Missy said.

"She did. Last night," he added quietly.

Missy raised an eyebrow and grinned. "Touché." She pushed back from the rail. "All right, Dr. Mann, cover yourself. It's kinda chilly anyway. And you're welcome, Galloway." She walked away.

"She thought you'd like to see me in something less frumpy." Grace's frown deepened. "I don't usually parade around in skimpy bathing attire. It's so unprofessional."

Her nipples puckered in response, and Alec forgot to breathe.

"Just so we're clear," he said in a rush, trying to keep his voice low, "I've never thought of you as frumpy." He swallowed against the dryness in his throat, allowing his eyes to skim her breasts then drop lower to her flat belly and long legs. "And I like the bikini. I like it a lot."

"Really?" She smiled. "I'd kiss you right now, but...well...you know that wouldn't be a good idea." She bit her lip, as if she were considering it anyway. "I'll go get my wetsuit. I'm eager to get in the water."

I'm eager to get inside you.

She turned on her heel and left, her bare feet padding along quietly. Alec looked out at the water, afraid that Donovan and the boys would see his tongue hanging out and know that he was good and whipped. If Grace snapped her fingers right now, he'd follow her in a heartbeat.

Staying away from her was going to be hell.

"Why'd you scare 'em off, Galloway?" Double D grumbled from above.

"Gear up. We're going in the water in ten."

Alec bit into the bagel.

He'd need the energy to keep up with Dr. Mann.

GRACE SANK into the water and began a steady descent, undulating her body like a mermaid, the extra-long flippers on her feet making her feel like a dolphin. Through her face mask, she spied Alec atop the starboard submersible with a camera pointed at her, while Stephie floated in the cage below, snapping photos. Double D was once again in the portside cage. Three sharks swam in the periphery, moving farther away as Grace, Mackenzie, and Tony entered their domain.

She went deeper, adjusting the pressure in her ears. The first thirty feet were always a struggle, requiring constant paddling, and then, as if some magical line had been crossed, with her lungs half their normal size, the ocean would suck her in, drawing her into its watery bosom. At this point, she no longer needed to use her fins.

This response of the human body in the water was known as the Master Switch of Life, and it was a nod to the connection humans had to the creatures of the sea. It never failed to give Grace a sense of belonging to her marine brethren. Humans evolved from the sea, and this Master Switch was the proof.

Two females and a male surrounded them. Grace hovered in place, watching them, but they kept their distance.

Mackenzie and Tony had already ascended for air, and Grace looked back at Alec. He gave her a thumbs-up, and she ascended.

On the third descent, the sharks came closer. The first female was Mary Ann, and Grace was glad to see that she'd managed to remove everything from the big girl. The male was probably new, about twelve feet in length. He swam lower than the females, since he clearly wasn't dominant, and they appeared to tolerate him. He seemed inquisitive, but the females' presence kept him from approaching Grace or Mackenzie or Tony.

Suddenly the three sharks disappeared. Visibility was good, but they still slipped away in the blink of an eye. Grace ascended and met Tony and Mackenzie at the surface.

"Why'd they leave so fast?" Tony asked.

"Bigger shark," Grace said. *She had a feeling....*

She dove again since talking would waste energy. Plus, she didn't want to miss whatever had caused those other sharks to flee.

As she came close to Alec's depth, his eyes bulged, and he pointed behind him. Grace looked past his shoulder and a shadow began to materialize, growing with each passing second.

Alec had pivoted and was aiming the camera in the direction of an approaching shark. Grace could see it head-on, the Mona Lisa-smiling face of a great white becoming clearer. The tail swished slightly back and forth, and Grace's heart started to pound in her chest. The shark's mouth was slightly agape, revealing a range of sharp teeth, an endless collection of savage mountain peaks.

Alec craned his neck back to film the massive female as she moved over him, headed straight for Grace.

Easily eight feet across, she was a submarine in the water, and Grace felt the shockwave of the water she displaced.

Grace hung suspended in the watery dimension, wafting like a jellyfish on the currents the shark generated, and tried to find identifying markers.

It has to be Bonnie. It would be surprising if there was a multitude of giant females around the island.

The shark angled slightly, preparing to pass by with only a few feet separating them. Calm and confident, the female's blue eye watched Grace.

The great white's conical snout glided past, the pectoral fin almost touching Grace, before the shark's displaced water pushed Grace backward. The enormous gill slits worked in a steady rhythm, extracting oxygen from the water that flowed constantly into the shark's mouth and out the openings.

Grace finally caught sight of the countershading pattern, where the dark dorsal side met the white ventral underside. Bonnie's unique markings stood out.

She's my Bonnie-lass. Her father's voice echoed in her head.

This was his shark. His baby. His favorite.

Time slowed as Grace waited for the lunar tail of the shark to glide by. If Bonnie decided to make a meal of Grace, she could do it easily in one giant inhalation.

Bonnie moved away and then circled around for another pass, this time bringing a friend. Unbelievably, a large yellowtail amberjack dashed in and out of Bonnie's mouth, likely performing this suicide behavior to gain bits of food that might still linger. Bonnie tolerated it, probably because it was the best way to get a tooth cleaning.

Mesmerized, Grace drank in the sight of the most perfect predator she had ever seen. Although Bonnie's girth was so thick as to be almost comical, as if she'd been unable to stop eating ho-ho's, Grace had a strong feeling that the majestic female was pregnant.

And then out of nowhere, a Guadalupe fur seal joined them, swimming an elegant underwater ballet. Bonnie moved her head back and forth like a sprinkler, but made no other indication that the seal had caught her attention.

The adorable pinniped approached Grace, its wide eyes soulful, its behavior playful. It advanced toward Tony and Mackenzie, then dashed away, but Grace noticed that it always kept its eye on Bonnie.

Bonnie continued her cruising, sliding along as if she hadn't a care in the world, and Grace sensed the shark's curiosity about them, her demeanor calm, almost serene.

For a moment harmony reigned, a flawless convergence of human and shark and seal, all sharing one world.

And then Grace was forced to surface before she blacked out.

"We should get a biopsy," Grace said, leaning against one of the desks in the office, her arms crossed. "And then we should tag her."

Everyone was crowded into the room. Missy, Stephie, and Tony sat at the table looking at Double D's computer as he loaded footage from his and Alec's cameras, as well as the chest cameras each of the divers wore.

From across the room, Alec watched her with laser intensity. He ignored the chatter and said, "Please don't tell me you want to be in the water when that happens."

Grace drew her brows together. "Probably."

"Who knows how she'll react."

"I doubt she'd even feel it. Did you see how big she is?"

"We all did, Grace. And we all just about shit our pants."

"Except Gracie," Missy said, staring at the computer screen. "Are you missing the fear gene?" Missy glanced up at her. "I think you missed your calling. You should be a Marine in one of those elite forces. You're like some steely-eyed robotic warrior, afraid of nothing." Her eyes shifted back to the footage that Double D was screening.

Grace wanted to view it, too, but she'd wait until the others had had a chance. "Tony and Mackenzie were there, too." She nodded at the two grad students like a proud mother. "You both did well."

Mackenzie sat on a stool near Alec. After last night's escapades, Grace no longer felt as threatened by the young woman, but it would be nice if Grace could inform her that Alec was off the market. Unfortunately, she'd have to tell everyone else as well and couldn't see any good reason to for now.

"She was scary," Mackenzie said, "but she was way more interested in Grace than either of us."

"And then that seal showed up." Tony shook his head. "I've never seen one play with a shark like that before."

Brad shifted from his stance near Grace, leaning down to grab a bottle of water from the fridge. "Maybe I'll get her from the outboard."

"How many sharks did you tag today?" Grace asked. Brad and Fowler had been gone all morning around the north side of the island, chumming in an effort to attract sharks.

He took a long swallow from the bottle. "None."

"We've seen her twice now in this area," Grace said. "Maybe she'll continue to hang out here. I want to have a spear with a tag ready from now on."

"How big would you say she is?" Fowler asked, positioned in the corner beside Alec.

"Well, looking at the footage," Double D murmured, continuing to watch his computer screen, "I'd say twenty-two feet, based on comparisons against Grace and Mackenzie, but the angle was never that great."

"That would put her as the largest female sighted at Guadalupe," Brad said.

A chill ran like wildfire along Grace's spine. She rubbed her hands along her upper arms, enjoying the warmth from her fleece jacket and the pants she now wore. She had freedived all afternoon, but Bonnie hadn't returned. Grace was feeling the usual fatigue and lowered body temperature she always did after hours in the water.

"I think she's pregnant," Grace added. "And if I were to guess her age, I'd say she's pushing 80 years old."

A look of disbelief crossed Frank's face, the creases around his blue-gray eyes more prominent due to expedition fatigue. "Do sharks really get that old?"

Grace nodded. "We can't know for sure. To determine her exact age, she'd need to be dead and dissected."

"Interesting thought," Frank replied.

Grace didn't bother to hide her scowl. "It's a disgusting thought, Fowler. Imagine what Bonnie has seen in her life. Think of all the pups she's given birth to. How many eighty-year-olds do you know that are still having children?"

"Can we try to get the biopsy and tag her from the outboard?" Alec asked.

"But then we'd need to chum," she said, "and I'm not entirely convinced it would work on a shark like Bonnie. The big females often stay deep. Besides, I'd like to keep it clean."

She meant that in regard to both the handling of the shark as well as literally. When chum was in the water—ground up fish and tuna heads and blood—the divers were covered in it. It usually took weeks to get the aroma of fish guts and entrails from her hair.

"Let me try," Grace said quietly, looking only at Alec. "And you'll film it."

He didn't answer, instead gifting her with more of the brooding countenance that had been gathering steam the longer they talked about Bonnie. If they had been alone, she liked to think she could have kissed away those rough edges.

But maybe she was overestimating her effect on Galloway. Best to stick with what she knew—sharks.

CHAPTER 20

Grace spent the next few days swimming with the white sharks. Despite no sign of Bonnie, she was in heaven. But alongside that bliss was a growing frustration. Although Alec was always in the water with her, they hadn't been able to find much time alone. He'd hinted a few times about the bathroom, but Grace was nervous they would be caught, and while she thought about asking Missy to vacate their cabin again for a few hours, it hardly seemed fair. Everyone was physically spent as they tried to get as much underwater footage as possible. Missy was especially tired, since she'd taken to accompanying Brad on the outboard in his attempts to tag.

They were more than halfway through the expedition, and energy had started to wane. Tempers frayed easily in such tight living quarters, nausea and a general malaise had afflicted just about everyone at some point, including Grace, and now bad weather was about to hit.

Her opportunity to get in the water today had just disappeared.

It was late morning, and Captain Bellamy had pulled anchor and was now steering the boat to a more protected cove. Grace took the opportunity to hunker down at her computer to assess the progress of the array. With so much time in the water, she'd neglected it.

There were bugs, but not anything that wasn't fixable. She needed to concentrate, which had proved to be a challenge. It wasn't just the gorgeous white sharks that were distracting her.

There was also a gorgeous filmmaker.

It was disconcerting how he addled her thoughts. She really needed to drag him into the bathroom again.

She tapped a key on her laptop to bring the screen to life. Her email was open.

What the hell?

She glanced over at her grad student. Tony was busy inputting shark dimension data, a never-ending task. "Did you send something from my computer?"

He didn't look at her. "No, but Brad wanted to look at the code."

Bullshit.

A few keystrokes later confirmed her suspicions.

The rat bastard.

She left the salon, barely acknowledging Alec and Double D on the diving deck, Mackenzie nearby like some groupie. The men were hunched over their camera gear, removing pieces from a bucket of fresh water and drying each one with a noisy air gun.

The boat tilted as a gust of wind pummeled her, forcing her to grab the stepladder leading to the observation deck. She turned her head to get a clump of hair out of her eyes and climbed up.

Brad and Fowler, both clad in windbreakers, were watching something on a personal device in Frank's hand.

"Can I talk to you?" Grace said to Brad, her t-shirt billowing and flattening as the *Mercado* surfed the choppy water. She gripped the railing to keep her footing, her bare arms immune to the chilly wind. Her anger had superheated her core.

He glanced up. "Yep. What's up?"

She flicked her gaze to Frank and in a flash decided she didn't care if he stayed. "Did you copy my code?"

Brad squinted, his face stone-cold. "You don't own it, Grace. Your work belongs to the Institute."

"Who did you email it to?"

Sitting up straight, Brad averted his gaze.

"You're so stupid," she continued. "You sent it to yourself and someone named Bill Holmes straight from my computer. Who the hell is Bill Holmes?"

"He's a friend of a friend," Frank interrupted. "He's a computer programmer, like you."

She ignored Fowler. "Care to explain, Brad?"

Brad made a choking noise in his throat. "Your code isn't performing perfectly. I don't know if you can even make it work. Frank gave me a contact. This Holmes guy is going to look it over. Maybe he can help."

"And you cleared this with Stewart?" she asked.

Brad's lip curled. "I don't have to clear every decision with him."

"Who's paying this guy?"

"I'll push it through when we get back."

Grace's breath rattled in her chest as she fought the urge to punch Brad in the nose. "Everything we're doing is *proprietary*."

"Your code isn't copyrighted, Grace." Brad's cheek flexed. "I don't need your permission to have someone else work on it."

That's where you're wrong, asshole. But until she could deliver a fully-functioning array to the CMI Board, she couldn't invoke the closed-door contract they had agreed to with her.

She spun on her heel and headed back to the salon before she said something she'd regret, or worse, that might incriminate her in the event she and Brad ended up in court.

First, a password change on her computer. Tony could no longer be trusted. Second, a prayer. *Please let the encryption hold.* The entire file required a decoding key to view it. This Bill Holmes would know this as soon as he tried to open the layers of programming, but he apparently had not yet conveyed this stumbling block to Brad.

As she dropped down to the diving deck, Alec caught sight of her, concern immediately crossing his face. "You okay?"

Mackenzie was now helping them dry out their equipment, the

girl's annoying nearness to Alec plucking Grace's irritation like a deeply embedded splinter. "Just dandy," she said.

"We could use another hand." Alec's voice was hopeful.

No, you couldn't. Grace would just be in the way.

"I have work to do." She turned her back to them and headed into the salon. Grabbing her laptop and charging cord, she didn't stop until she was tucked into her cabin. Missy was gone—probably in the galley playing cards—so Grace could work in solitude.

Once she was alone, she slumped into the chair and rubbed her forehead, the aftermath of her anger leaving her shaky.

She couldn't fucking believe it. Brad had stolen her work. *Again.*

No matter how hard she tried to protect what was hers, she was fighting an uphill battle. For every two steps she took, she kept sliding back down the hill.

And what about Galloway? Could she trust him? Was it only a matter of time before pretty Mackenzie turned his attention away from her?

Chin up, Gracie. Her father's words echoed in her head.

If Eddie Mann had ever found fault with his daughters, it was usually in one area—self-pity. He'd had no tolerance for it.

If what she suspected was true, that Galloway had stolen something far worse than Brad had from her—her heart—then she'd somehow deal with it if he ended up breaking it.

Opening her laptop, she found solace in the only thing that mattered—her work.

ALEC TOOK a bite of his turkey on rye and glanced at Brad and Fowler sitting across from him. They were alone in the galley, and while Alec was glad to be free of Mackenzie and her annoying hovering, he wasn't sure the switch had landed him in better company.

And where was Grace? She had disappeared into her cabin a few hours ago.

"So, what's up?" Alec asked.

Brad was working his way through a ham sandwich, but Fowler was eating saltines and sipping ginger ale. Alec suppressed a smile. Seasickness was a bitch, and the galley was probably the last place Fowler should be with the constant swaying from the growing storm slowly enveloping the boat.

"I got an email this morning from Ruschart Media," Frank said. "They're very interested in this doc we're making."

Alarm bells went off in Alec's head. "Why am I not surprised that you're in bed with them."

The boat rocked, and Fowler blanched. "What's that supposed to mean?"

"They're behind a lot of the shock-and-awe programming that surrounds wildlife filmmaking."

Fowler shook his head. "Your holier-than-thou attitude is admirable but doesn't necessarily make any of us money. Ruschart has a huge reach, and they've offered a substantial amount for worldwide rights to the film you're making."

Alec took a long drag from his water bottle. "But?"

"We need to up the danger quotient."

Alec shook his head. "It's been plenty dangerous already."

"I know," Brad chimed in. "And we've got excellent footage. But we either need more shots of Felix, and preferably him going after Grace again, or we need a new story."

Alec couldn't believe what he was hearing. "You're saying you want to *provoke* Felix into aggressive behavior?"

Brad shrugged. "He's already aggressive. Let's just shine an extra spotlight on it."

"Grace'll never go for it."

"That's why I'm talking to you. And honestly, you don't have to do much. That shark is already on some sort of personal warpath. So, that brings me to plan number two. Bonnie."

Alec abandoned what was left of his sandwich, his stomach beginning to sour the more Brad flapped his lips.

"We need a narrative around this shark," Brad continued.

"Something dark and mysterious. We already have shots of Grace with her, but maybe we can dig up some footage of her dad? Wouldn't it be great if we could find old film of him with Bonnie? Maybe you can ask her if she has any home movies."

Alec clenched his jaw. "Why don't you ask her yourself? And for the record, I won't put Grace in danger just to get an exciting shot."

Michaels shifted the ball cap on his head. "Shit, Galloway, have you not been paying attention? She gets herself into dicey situations all the time. Just make sure you catch it on film."

Alec didn't like the turn this was taking. He couldn't disagree about searching for an angle for the film, and he'd been toying with several ideas this past week, but he wouldn't know what he had until he and Double D got to work in the editing room. But Alec also knew that CMI could take any film he produced and re-cut it if they chose to. He wasn't about to voice that aloud, however.

Alec slid out of his seat and stood, gathering his lunch plate. "It will be a good film, Brad. We don't need to manufacture any drama. Why don't you trust me on this?" Alec glanced at Frank. "Grace has a presence on film. It'll be enough."

Fowler wiped at his forehead, having sprung a leak of sweat. "I hope so."

"You look like you need to use the john, Frank."

Alec left the men with his most amiable smile, but the knot in his stomach returned. Grace and Felix and Bonnie just didn't strike Alec as a friendly threesome.

CHAPTER 21

Grace left her cabin only because Missy came by to tell her that Harry and Sylvie and some of the crew from the *Wallflower* had come aboard. Bad weather left everyone with nothing to do but twiddle their thumbs, so naturally it was a good time to socialize and get caught up.

It was late afternoon, and an iron-gray sky was visible through the salon windows. Whitecaps danced around the boat, and Guadalupe Island was barely visible through the haze and mist.

"Gracie." Sylvie warmly embraced her.

Grace returned the hug, enjoying the motherly smell of the woman. "Any news?"

She beamed. "Harry and I've got something we want to show you. But first, I want to introduce you to Albie Corcoran."

An older, slender man clad in baggy clothes stepped forward. His long sandy hair was pulled back in a ponytail, revealing sharp cheekbones and a tan face. He extended a hand. "Please call me Corky."

"It's nice to meet you," Grace said, clasping his hand in greeting.

As he was introduced around—nearly everyone had crowded into the small space—familiarity nagged at Grace.

"Corky is a biologist as well," Harry said, settling his gaze on her. "He worked with your dad."

Now she remembered. Her father had mentioned Corky on occasion. Before she could ask him about his history with Eddie Mann, Sylvie ushered her to sit at the table while Harry pulled a laptop from a waterproof case, set it before them, and pulled up a video file.

Missy crammed in beside Grace, and Stephie slid in from the other side. Alec and Double D hovered behind them, watching over their shoulders. Mackenzie situated herself beside Alec. Grace's inner green monster grumbled, but she chalked up her short temper to still being pissed at Brad. But the girl was tenacious. Surely Mackenzie wasn't getting any encouraging signals from Alec. Was she?

Maybe she liked Alec as the brother she'd never had.

Grace impulsively spun around to face the girl. "Do you have any siblings?"

Stunned by the odd question, Mackenzie stared at Grace for a moment, then finally said, "Yeah, I've got three brothers. Why?"

Huh. "No reason," Grace murmured and faced forward but not before catching a glance of Alec's confused expression.

"We managed to get a transponder on one of the sharks," Sylvie said.

Grace's attention shifted to the only thing that could break her territoriality when it came to Alec Galloway—*Carcharodon carcharias*. "Which one?"

Sylvie's grin made her look like a giddy ten-year-old with silver hair. "Mary Ann."

Excitement filled Grace as she watched the video that had begun playing. With the transponder attached to the big shark, the monitoring unit had been able to shadow Mary Ann, tracking her movements while filming her the entire time. The greenish-tint to the footage made her look like she was swimming in a pond.

"How deep?" Grace asked quietly, since the entire room had

gone silent, the only sound the pelting of rain on the hull of the *Mercado*.

"She hugged the island, but in some places, she got down to two hundred feet," Harry said. "She spent the night swimming into the current."

Grace stilled and rested her gaze on Harry. "Oh, my God," she whispered, flicking her eyes back to the screen. "She's sleeping." Sure enough, Mary Ann's movements were minimal, steady, and rhythmic. Her eyes were also different, as if she'd shut down brain activity.

"Isn't it fantastic?" Sylvie's voice vibrated with elation.

Grace sighed, keeping her gaze on the footage. "Yes."

Such a sight had never been recorded. No one knew what the white sharks did when they weren't busy stalking the seals of Guadalupe, or any of the known food sources elsewhere in the world for that matter.

Grace's throat clogged with emotion, and tears threatened to stream down her face, but she blinked rapidly to keep them at bay. "This is amazing. Thank you for showing this to me."

For the next ten minutes, they watched the remaining footage in silence although nothing more happened. Mary Ann rested while continuing to swim, her ability to breathe dependent on constant and lifelong movement.

When the video ended, Grace hugged both Harry and Sylvie while congratulations were exchanged and beers dispersed

"Just think of what you'll learn from your shark cam," Grace said.

Sylvie's eyes sparkled. "We've already got ideas for upgrades. You can bet we'll be back next year."

"What brings you down to Guadalupe, Corky?" Grace asked the man sitting on a stool across from them.

He tipped his bottle for a swallow, then smiled. "I'm on one of the tourist boats." He held up his hands. "I know, I know. Don't shoot me. I brought my granddaughters. They're both in high school and wanted to see the sharks, and I figured a commercial trip would be more comfortable for them. When I found out the Alexanders were here, too, we made plans to get together. And then I heard you were here, so I knew I had to meet you."

"Did you work in the Farallones?" Alec asked, still behind Grace.

"Yes, sir. I was there in its heyday with Eddie, when there wasn't a definitive shark program to be found, just anecdotal evidence." His warm brown eyes settled on Grace. "Did you know your dad was instrumental in rewriting a lot of what we know about great whites?"

A happy, warm feeling suffused Grace. Maybe it was the beer she was indulging in, or maybe it was Harry and Sylvie's fabulous research breakthrough. Or maybe it was talking about her dad. Some days the pain of losing him cut so deeply that she didn't dare go near it, or else it would swallow her up. "I think my dad always considered the whites as kindred spirits."

"The apple doesn't fall too far from the tree," Sylvie said, glancing at Grace.

Corky nodded, a knowing glint in his gaze. "His fascination ran deep. People thought all along that the whites were nothing but mindless killers, but he found they hunted methodically, almost as if they had a plan, and a very cautious one at that. He also learned that they're visual predators. Their eyesight is quite good." He squinted, a sense of delight emanating from him. "I hear you've spotted Bonnie-lass."

Grace nodded.

He tipped his bottle at her. "That's a coup. I'm not surprised it was a Mann to discover a Farallones shark had migrated here instead. And why not? Those big females are like nothing else on this earth."

"How do you mean?" Alec asked.

Corky thought for a moment before answering. "For a shark to become that big—to become that unfathomably large—speaks of something altogether different than what most sharks are. Those females, well, they're the alphas—*the alphas of the alphas*, if you will

237

—and there's not many of them. They're smart." He paused. "I mean *really* smart. I came to the conclusion, along with your father" —he nodded at Grace— "that they know about us."

"About you and Eddie Mann?" Fowler asked from the other side of the room.

"Not specifically *us*," Corky answered, "but humans. When we'd see Bonnie, she'd swim by and watch us. She really hated the decoys. When we'd put a new one in the water, she'd suddenly show up, rip it to pieces, then disappear with a hard slap of her caudal fin, as if to speak her displeasure to us. Those decoys never fooled her. There was never any doubt that she was fed up with our presence, and she let us know in her own unique way. She patrolled a stretch of water off the east side of the island, and no seal ever got past her. The smaller sharks would take twenty minutes to eat their catch. Bonnie could eat a five-hundred-pound pinniped in three minutes flat."

"This isn't making me feel great about you swimming beside her, Grace," Alec said.

"I heard you were freediving," Corky said to her. "Your father and I never had the guts to get in the water with them, even in scuba gear."

"Visibility is better here," she said. "And as you said, whites are careful hunters. She's incredible, by the way." She craned her neck. "Alec, can you show Corky the footage of her?"

"I'd like that," Corky answered.

"Better yet, why don't you get in the water with us?" Double D said. "We've got room in the submersible cages. You might get a face-to-face with your old friend."

Corky considered the offer. "You know what? I think I'd like that even more."

CHAPTER 22

I t was late when Grace returned to her cabin, having visited with the Alexanders and Corky for several hours. Missy was missing, but Grace figured she would be along any minute. A knock at the door diverted her attempt to brush her teeth. She cracked the door.

Alec.

"Can I come in?" he asked, his voice low.

She nodded and stepped back. "Missy'll be back any minute."

Clad in a dark sweatshirt with *North Shore* stamped on the front, he entered the room and shut the door. "Actually, she won't. She's doing me a favor and agreed to give us an hour."

Alec's presence filled the small space, drawing her close like a shark on a blood trail, but she resisted the temptation. His growing reluctance for her to continue her freedives with Bonnie, spurred by Corky's comments, had annoyed her at first. Then, annoyance had grown to a full-blown aggravation as the evening had worn on. "What do you have to do in return?"

"Teach her to surf."

Jealousy flared. "That doesn't seem like a fair exchange," she said, scoffing to hide her discomfort. Mackenzie, Missy...how many women would she have to share Alec with?

239

He didn't crowd her, obviously sensing her petulant mood, but his intense eyes and stiff stance said something else.

"You're angry," he said.

"Irritated." She enunciated the word.

"About Bonnie."

Yes. No. "A little." She couldn't fault him for wanting to be careful while they were all in the water with great white sharks.

"Then what, Grace?"

Dammit. She knew better than to fraternize on expeditions. So much for sticking to her professional guns. Now her emotions were all over the place.

"Are you messing with me, Alec?" she blurted.

He narrowed his eyes, his voice uncertain. "What do you mean?"

"Did you nail me for sex? Is that your game?" She lifted her arms and slapped them against her sides in frustration, her voice getting shrill. "Have you moved on to Mackenzie?" Shit. She needed to stop right now before she said something she'd regret.

Alec's expression went from grimace to surprise. "Is that what this is all about?"

Grace didn't trust herself to speak. It had been a hell of a day. The boat had become claustrophobic for her, Brad was sneaking behind her back again, Mackenzie was stuck to Alec like a leech most of the time, and to top it off, listening to Corcoran talk about his time in the Farallones with Eddie Mann had ripped open a gigantic ache in her chest.

I miss you, Daddy.

She barely contained the sob that threatened to burst forth.

He moved closer to her. "I can't believe you're jealous."

"Yeah, I can't believe it, either," she huffed. "It really doesn't matter."

He looked at her, his hardened expression gone. "It does. It matters a lot."

He continued his forward movement until she bumped against the desk.

"And for the record, I didn't nail you for sex." His lips hovered near hers, his breath hot on her skin and smelling of peppermint. "And I'm not interested in Mackenzie. I just don't want to be rude to the girl."

"Did you eat a candy cane?"

His mouth stretched into a half-smile. "Gum." He pressed closer. "So, you admit you like me?"

She glanced up at him and gave a snort of disgust.

Of course, I like you.

That was the problem.

"You're not gonna say it, are you?" A sexy grin tugged at his mouth.

She pressed her lips together.

He braced his hands on the desk, confining her.

"I have no interest in any other woman. Ever since I saw you give that talk that night in Monterey, I haven't been able to stop thinking about you. And even before that, you were very much on my radar. When I had the opportunity to work with you, I jumped at the chance despite your reluctance about hiring me. And in case it's still not obvious, Dr. Mann, I'm crazy about you."

Grace flicked her gaze to his.

He kissed her, but she still wasn't ready to concede defeat.

"C'mon, Gracie," he murmured against her lips. "You can tell me you like me. You can tell me you want me exclusively." He paused and looked at her again. "It's what I want, too."

"This is going too fast."

"Maybe. Probably."

She grabbed hold of his sweatshirt. "You smell like Christmas, and I'm not normally a jealous person."

"You've never been romanced by Alec Galloway."

She gave him a playful shove.

He kissed her mouth lightly. "I've been known to drive women insane."

God, she believed it.

He pressed his advantage, pulling her flush against his body, and kissed her with no misunderstanding as to his intention.

Grace succumbed, her body craving all points of contact with him while her heart swelled with lust and longing and tenderness.

He lifted her onto the edge of the desk then slipped his hands beneath her shirt. He tugged it free and removed her bra. His mouth went to work on her bare breasts, inciting a frenzied response in Grace. She wrapped her legs around him.

Abruptly, he broke the contact, went to the door and locked it.

She stood and removed the rest of her clothes while he discarded his shirt and pants, then it dawned on her they didn't have a condom.

Grace nipped and kissed and touched him before he had to dash back to his room. Just as she was about to say something, a packet appeared in his hand.

"Do you always carry one with you?" she asked, breathless with anticipation.

He tore it open. "Since you? Yes."

Once he was ready, she dragged him to her bunk, and he covered her with his body.

"I want to take my time with you," he whispered.

"There is no time."

Grace lifted her pelvis to meet him. He thrust into her, and her body fully accepted him. Holding him tight with her legs, she gasped, finding completion almost immediately. Alec was right behind her, gripping her buttocks as he said her name then bit her neck.

Grace closed her eyes and held him to her, enjoying the recurring tremors of pleasure that continued for several minutes. Neither of them spoke, too spent by the coupling.

Grace startled awake, Alec still atop her.

She must have dozed off. Considering that Alec was still hard inside her, not much time must have passed. She turned her face to his—he'd fallen asleep against her pillow—and kissed him. He stirred, running his left hand down to her breast, and shifting slightly, he tested their still joined bodies.

"I know what you're going to say," he said.

As he moved, her breath hitched, a delicious wave of Alec-ecstasy washing through her.

"And what's that?" she asked.

"I need to leave before we get caught."

Grace sighed. She was close to no longer caring. It would be damned nice to snuggle up to Alec for the entire night.

He didn't fully make love to her again, but for a long while he enjoyed playing with her. And Grace was lost in the euphoria of it all.

CHAPTER 23

Grace oscillated her body into the blue abyss, becoming a part of the current, a wave blended with other waves. The morning had broken bright and clear, the remnants of the storm gone. The angry lashing of the wind and rain had moved out much the way Grace's bad mood had dissolved. She couldn't deny that Alec's touch held some kind of healing balm, her body calm and grounded after he'd satisfied her in ways she hadn't thought possible.

Somehow, he lessened the anguish of losing her dad. Only her work had ever done that.

Albie Corcoran had returned first thing and was now in the starboard submersible with Alec, along with a tagging spear that Grace could retrieve if Bonnie appeared. Double D and Stephie were in place in the opposite cage, while Fowler and Brad had gone off in the outboard for another day of chumming and, with hope, tagging.

Corky didn't have a rebreather, but Grace hoped the bubbles from his regulator wouldn't be a deterrence.

Tony wasn't feeling well and had decided to monitor the dive from onboard. Surprisingly, Missy had offered to take his place.

"I want to give it another try," she had said last night while

Grace was drifting off to sleep. "What do you think?" She'd leaned over the top bunk to look at Grace.

"I think it's a great idea." Grace had every confidence that Missy could manage the dives, and she was glad that her best friend was willing to face her fears.

It had made Grace think of her own fear of opening her heart to Alec. She could still smell him on her sheets. They hadn't had much time together before he'd left for his room, but the wall around her heart was already losing its strength.

She supposed at the end of the day, she couldn't be sorry about letting Alec into her life, regardless of how it might play out. While glad that he wanted to continue their relationship after the expedition ended, she also knew it could as easily go south once they were landlocked again. She really needed to prepare herself for that possible outcome. The demise of her relationship with Brad had blindsided her—she never wanted to be caught that unaware again.

When Grace and Mackenzie entered the water the next day with Missy, they did several practice dives first to get acclimated and to help Missy feel comfortable. Mackenzie had become stronger over the past several days and could now shadow Grace more closely.

Shadowing seems to be her forte.

But truthfully, if it weren't for the fact that the young woman mooned over Alec, Grace would have welcomed a friendship with the girl.

Grace had descended to forty feet when suddenly Felix appeared, exhibiting high energy and erratic movements.

He hadn't been spotted since the incident with the cage, not since the day Grace had drowned and come back to life thanks to Alec. While it was good to see that the shark hadn't sustained any serious injury from his imprisonment, Felix's behavior was immediately a red flag.

Grace spun around as he shot past her. Missy and Mackenzie turned in place as well, keeping him in their sights. He made a tight circle and came around for another pass.

He had fresh cuts on his head, but Grace didn't think these were from his time in the cage with her. He must have scuffled with another shark.

He was so close that Grace could reach out and touch him, but she held back. Not so much because the guidelines of the Biosphere stated that touching the sharks wasn't allowed, but it was probably a bad idea with this particular shark.

A school of mackerel scad danced in synchronized movements, avoiding Felix each time he slid effortlessly through the azure environment.

As he sped away, his pectoral fins were angled down, and Grace was pretty sure he was gaping.

Awfully aggressive, Felix, even for you.

They should probably exit the water, but Grace decided first to go on the offensive and began to swim after him. It was a technique her father had taught her. It basically told the shark not to mess with this particular human.

In an instant, her error was clear. Felix curled back, briefly looking like a shark donut, and headed straight toward her. She cut to the right and swam hard to avoid him. Out of nowhere Mackenzie's fin slammed into her face, knocking her mask off. Stunned, Grace fumbled for it, but it sank quickly.

Getting her bearings, she pumped her legs to ascend when suddenly Felix bolted toward her and attacked her flipper, clamping down on her foot. An inky pool of blood mixed into the water. With a hard yank, he began to dive, dragging Grace with him.

Grace pinched her nose with one hand to prevent saltwater from blasting into her sinus cavities while trying to bring the other hand to her heel to free her fin, but Felix was towing her too fast. And her foot was locked in his mouth.

As she bumped up against his side, she pummeled his scaly skin with a fist, trying to get him to release her. Efforts to wiggle her foot free from the plastic fin failed, causing a flash of pain.

Then without warning, she was free. Disoriented, the pressure in her ears told her she had gone much deeper.

She needed to get to the surface. If she blacked out, she'd drown.

A feeling overcame her. A sixth sense. *A knowing.*

There was a shark in the vicinity.

In Grace's narrowed and blurry vision, a shadow came close and a strong displacement of water pushed against her.

A big shark. A goliath submarine.

A sister.

As the mass neared, the girth grew in size with each passing second. And like a slow-motion sequence in a horror movie, the shark's open mouth became visible in the murky depths.

My God.

The leviathan moved away.

Was it Bonnie? Mary Ann?

Grace couldn't see beyond her hand, but her throbbing foot spoke volumes. Her blood was no doubt spilling into the salty abyss at this very moment, an offering that no shark could ignore.

Oh shit. Oh shit. Oh shit.

Grace started to swim, but she'd lost her spatial reference. It was impossible to tell which way was up or down.

Panic began to rise in her chest.

The great white bumped into her, and they came eye to eye. Grace didn't know how or why, but she didn't feel threatened.

It was as if the great white were trying to help.

Impossible.

Grace's lungs started to burn, and her awareness began to fade.

She was running out of time.

Without warning the nose of the shark slammed into Grace's chest and carried her forward. The momentum propelled Grace onto the shark's back, the sandpaper skin raking Grace's hands raw, but the giant dorsal fin stopped her and kept her in place.

With her mind mired in a muddy confusion, Grace clung to the shark and prayed with a desperate diligence: *please be moving upward and please, please don't bite me in half once we get there.*

The black void began to lighten, and shafts of sunlight angled down as if sent from the heavens.

Would she meet her dad on the other side?

With a violent thrust, Grace broke the surface and gasped desperately for air.

CHAPTER 24

"**D**id you get the shot?" Frank demanded.

Alec pulled a blanket around Grace. He knelt in front of her, still clutching the fabric at her neck—*to keep her warm*—but really, it was the closest he could get to scooping her into his arms. That's what he really wanted to do.

Grace's body shook as she gulped down air, and a tremulous smile flitted across her lips.

"What the fuck just happened?" he said under his breath, meant for her ears only.

She wiped at the water on her face, then winced and looked at her scraped-up palms, streaks of blood visible. "Which shark was it?" she asked, her voice barely a whisper.

Alec gave a shake of his head. "I'm not sure."

"Yeah, I filmed it." Double D answered Frank's question, his voice solemn.

"Thank God," Frank replied.

"Her foot's bleeding," Alec said. "And her hands. Missy, get the first aid kit."

Missy, still dripping water from her black and white diving suit, nodded and took off to grab the medical supplies.

Alec stared into Grace's eyes, so relieved to have her awake and breathing this time. He couldn't help himself—he reached out and placed a palm against her cheek, then he stood before he kissed her in front of the entire expedition crew.

Everyone was on deck, having scrambled on board amidst all the shouting and screaming while Pete, Eric, and Tony hauled Grace out of the water.

Missy knelt beside Grace and began cleaning her foot. As she did, more blood gushed out. "You're going to need stitches. Let me wrap it for now, and then we can go inside."

Alec remained beside Grace as she recovered from yet another near-death experience. He glanced at Donovan. "Thanks for grabbing the equipment."

Double D nodded, looking as shell-shocked as Alec felt. "That's why I'm the wingman," he uttered, but his voice echoed a sentiment of disbelief.

When Grace had been hauled like a bullet through the water by Felix, Alec had let go of the camera and started descending after her.

"I can't believe what happened." Missy secured a pad of gauze on Grace's ankle.

"I'm so sorry I kicked you in the face," Mackenzie said.

Grace's response was a curt nod as she grimaced from her foot wound.

"Did that second shark actually *help* you?" Missy asked in a hushed voice.

It sure as hell had. Alec didn't know what to say.

"This is gonna be the centerpiece of the documentary," Frank said. "I hope you got decent footage." He glared at Double D.

"Give me a minute, and then I'll download it." Double D unzipped his wetsuit and started removing it, but he appeared to be in no hurry.

Like everyone, Donovan clearly needed a moment to process what had just happened.

"Which shark was it?" Grace asked again, her voice a bit louder.

When Alec glanced down at her, her color was starting to look better. That was good.

"I saw her pop the surface with you," Tony replied. "She was so flipping big that I'm sure it was Bonnie, but we'll need to look at Double D's footage."

"Tell us what happened, Grace." Corky had remained silent until now, and even he looked shaken, despite a lifetime studying great whites.

Grace's breathing had finally quieted. "Felix came out of nowhere and somehow got hold of my fin. I tried to pull my foot out, but I couldn't. When he finally released me, I was disoriented. I'd lost my mask and had swallowed some water, and I was so deep that I could hardly see anything. I knew I wasn't going to last long. And then I felt a change in the water. I could feel the shark before I saw her, so I knew it was a big one. I'll admit, for a moment I thought that was it. My foot was bleeding and...well...I was easy pickings."

Alec crossed his arms as a slight tremor rippled through him.

Grace paused and swallowed hard. "Then she looked at me, and I wasn't afraid of her. But I was out of time." She pushed at her wet hair, her hand shaking and her voice filled with awe. "She caught me in the chest with her nose and brought me to the surface."

"Wait a second," Brad cut in. "You're saying this shark saved your life? This is stretching it, even for you, Grace."

"We can use this," Frank said. "I'd thought to get something more frightening, with a bit more blood and gore, but we can run with it. The shark that saved Grace Mann's life. This is perfect." He looked at Grace. "It's like they know you're a friend of the great white. It's as if they look out for you."

"Not Felix," Missy added.

"The matron admonishes the troublesome youth and protects her human friend." Frank gestured as if he were the ringleader at a circus.

Alec frowned. This was getting out of hand. While it was true that Grace was alive, had the shark actually saved her, or was it simply a coincidence?

"You're going to attribute an altruistic act to an aggressive apex predator?" Brad said. "This is going to backfire."

"Why?" Grace countered. "Why is it so difficult to believe that they have a brain and a complex one at that?"

"They travel alone," Brad said. "They give birth and swim away from their pups. They don't form relationships."

"I think you're wrong," Grace said.

"Because of your dad?" he countered.

"Yes. He studied the whites at the Farallones for years. Certain sharks *always* hung out together, even returning together every winter. They're not mindless fish simply under the control of their instincts."

"But they are, Grace." Alec couldn't stay quiet any longer. "Please don't ever forget that." *Because if you do, the next time just might kill you.* "This isn't scientific, it's anecdotal. Do you want to pin your professional credentials on it? How do we know that Bonnie, or whichever shark it was, wasn't just playing with you before taking a bite?"

Grace stared at him, and anger hardened her face. "Fine. Don't put it in the documentary."

"I'm afraid they might be right," Corky said, his voice quiet as if soothing a young child. "Predators often play with their food before a kill. Not that the white wanted to eat you, but it's likely that she saw you as something to investigate."

Grace didn't look at anyone as she spoke, a brittle edge to her voice. "Is it so hard to believe that she knew I was in trouble? Is it so hard to believe that she was smart enough to know that I needed help? Maybe when she first approached I was afraid, but then she nudged me, and then she looked at me." Grace stood. "And then she helped me." She hobbled her way into the salon.

Alec scrubbed a hand through his wet hair.

What if she's right?

The implication would point to an emotional intelligence that had never before been attributed to sharks. It was an astounding breakthrough.

252

If it were true.

But if he put this incident into the film, would she become a laughingstock? Would it ruin her professionally? Grace was deeply attached to her subject, her field of research a labor of love and obsession. Sometimes it was hard to see clearly. It was up to Alec to protect her, even from herself.

Frank sighed loudly. "All right, if we don't use that angle, then let's backtrack to the obvious. That giant mother-fucker of a shark was out to get Grace all along."

Corky levelled a cool gaze in Fowler's direction. "That's absolutely not true."

"You said it yourself," Frank rebutted. "The shark was out to investigate her."

"I *will not* use that angle in the film," Alec said.

"You have to turn all the footage over to CMI." Fowler's eyes glittered, his smugness evident. "Your *angle* is up for debate."

He knew about the contract clause. Fuck.

Alec's temper reached a flashpoint. "You're such a prick, Fowler. You'd either ruin Grace's reputation or vilify the great white. We should throw you in the water and see how *you* do."

"There's something else that hasn't been brought up." Tony stood off to the side, his gaze shadowed beneath a ball cap. "Dr. Michaels and Mr. Fowler were chumming right before all this happened."

"And what about it?" Brad asked. "We were trying to attract sharks."

"Near the *Mercado*?" Tony asked.

Brad stared at the grad student. "We weren't that close."

"Bullshit. I saw you a quarter mile away."

Alarm shot through Alec. "Were you really that close? We had three divers in the water."

"Which shark were you trying to tag?" Tony's tone demanded an answer.

"I don't know," Brad replied, his face stretched with incredulity.

"It was Felix," Tony said flatly. "I'd already ID'd him."

Alec faced off against Michaels. "What the fuck were you think-ing? Did you do that on purpose?"

"Of course not. I didn't realize we were so close to you guys."

"So you got him all riled up, and then he came back and attacked Grace."

"You can't blame me for the behavior of a wild animal." Brad aimed an arctic gaze at Alec. "And since when did you become so worried about Grace's welfare?"

"I'm not about to treat her the way you do."

"And what the hell does that mean?"

"Like some stepping-stone to further my career."

Brad released a bark of laughter. "That's rich, coming from you. You're here solely to piggyback off her so your film will get noticed."

Alec suppressed a flinch from the partial truth. "Stay away from her."

"Since when is my relationship with Grace any of your business?"

"It is now." The words were out before Alec could stop them.

"Jesus, are you fucking her?"

Alec stood his ground as Brad bore down on him.

"You son-of-a-bitch!" Brad shoved Alec.

Before Alec could land a punch, Pete and Tony grabbed Brad while Donovan planted himself squarely in Alec's face.

"Calm down," Double D said under his breath.

For one brief, wild moment, Alec almost pushed his friend aside to get at Michaels, his fist itching to crack the man's jaw.

Instead he gave a curt nod and headed inside, leaving a stunned audience in his wake.

So much for remaining professional.

CHAPTER 25

G race lay on her bunk, her foot elevated on a pillow, trying to rest now that Missy had pumped her full of pain meds. It hadn't been as bad as they'd feared, with only two lacerations that required stitches.

As Grace hovered in that place between waking and sleeping, she kept seeing the great white shark's eye.

It had been a transcendent moment. Even now, Grace's chest swelled with something akin to panic, but that wasn't an apt description. It was more like absolute awe mixed with a sense that something extraordinary had been exchanged between her and the shark.

Just thinking about it made her gasp in disbelief.

She knew it was real. She hadn't imagined it.

Tears burned her eyes.

I'm not crazy. I'm not.

Hadn't her father been labeled as such? Hadn't Grace's own mother accused him of taking stupid and unnecessary risks for a creature that could hurt him?

Had Grace turned into him?

Maybe Alec was right. And while she was loath to include Brad, maybe they both had a point: she was better off keeping her woo-

woo moments with the sharks private. Still, wasn't it better to relate her experiences in all their raw and authentic pathos to the public? Wasn't that what grabbed people's attention?

Grace didn't want to jeopardize her job. She'd worked too hard to get where she was. If the doc was too fluffy, too out-there, would the board decide she was a liability instead of an asset? Could this somehow jeopardize her work on the array?

The door opened, and Missy entered. "Well, you missed the show."

Grace dragged open her eyes. "What do you mean?"

Missy sat at the desk chair. "Alec all but spilled the beans about your relationship, and Brad went crazy. The two of them were about to fight it out like school yard bullies when Double D and the others stopped it. It was real caveman shit. All this talk about sharks and their instinctual nature—that primitive side still sits in us as well."

Grace closed her eyes. There'd be no dealing with Brad now.

"It's rather romantic, if you ask me," Missy continued.

Grace sighed and looked at her friend.

"I know," Missy said. "It's awkward, unprofessional, maybe a little unethical? Geez, Gracie, you're not a robot. And Alec was really sticking up for you."

"Is that how it sounded? That's not what I was getting from him. He agreed with Brad. I don't see how seconds later they were in a fight."

"Turns out Brad was chumming a little too close to us."

"What?"

"He was wrong to do it, but did it actually make Felix more aggressive?" Missy shook her head. "That's up for debate."

What the hell was wrong with Brad? "I'll tell Stewart when we get back. He'll want to know why I never want to go on expedition with the man again."

Missy nodded. "I'll back you up if needed. Tony saw it. I'm sure he'll speak up, too."

Grace remembered that Missy had taken a big leap to get in the water today. "How are you?"

"How am *I*?" Missy's aggrieved expression squeezed Grace's heart. "I'm just glad you're alive, Gracie." Her eyes filled with tears.

Grace reached out, and Missy scooted the chair closer and gently clasped her hand, which still stung.

"You got in the water with great white sharks," Grace said. "I'm *so* proud of you."

Missy laughed, then started crying, which she quickly clamped down on. "How are you so calm about all of this?"

"Haven't you heard?" Grace whispered. "I'm nuts."

Missy sobered. "No, you're not. And don't be so hard on Alec. Underneath it all, he was scared for you. It's so obvious. I don't know why you can't see it."

Glancing at the top bunk, Grace said, "It's going too fast. I'm not ready for it." She glanced at Missy. "It unsettles me."

"Sometimes I don't understand you. You brave great white sharks, but you're going to let a man like Galloway get away?"

Was she?

GRACE CAME AWAKE when a knock vibrated the door. The room was pitch dark.

"Come in," she said.

It was Alec. "Can we talk?"

She nodded. She must have slept for a while, because now her ankle was really beginning to throb.

He flipped on the desk lamp and sat in the chair that Missy had recently occupied. He'd changed into his North Shore sweatshirt and a long pair of black quick-dry pants. "How do you feel?"

"I've been better. I won't be getting in the water anytime soon."

Alec raised an eyebrow. "When has that ever stopped you?"

"I hear you got into a fight over my honor."

"Something like that. We're not a secret anymore, Grace. I guess I should apologize, but I really don't care. Well, I do care what you think, but I'm not sorry that we're together."

"Is life always so simple for you?"

He laughed. "No. What makes you think that?"

"We're *together*? Be real, Alec. This is an expedition fling, and as soon as you go on the next one, you'll find another girl to romance with your good looks and great personality."

"You think I have a great personality?" His eyes twinkled with amusement.

She didn't answer him.

After a long silence, she said, "You don't believe me about what happened today."

"That's not true."

"But...."

He rubbed a hand behind his neck. "I want to be careful how we portray it in the doc *if* we use it."

"If?"

He released a deep exhale. "We've got a bit of a problem in our contract. CMI has final say on the film and basically owns all the footage I've shot."

"I don't understand. What's the problem?"

"Brad's the problem. And Fowler. They've got a blood-and-guts vision for the film. Fowler claims he's already got distributors interested."

"But if CMI has final say, they won't approve a version that's not true."

Alec squinted. "Money does funny things to people. And I'm guessing CMI never has enough funding."

"That doesn't make them unethical."

"I agree. It's just that today's events could be slanted one way or another. If we showcase your interpretation, I fear your credibility might suffer."

Grace quieted. "And the other side?"

"That Bonnie—if it was actually her; Double D's downloading the footage now—was on the hunt for you. That she stalked you with the intention of killing you."

"That's absurd! Stewart and the Board would never go for that."

Alec's lack of response told Grace that he thought otherwise.

"So, we're damned either way," she said.

"Not entirely," Alec said quietly. "We have one other option. We can destroy the footage."

"No!" It was proof of a remarkable interaction. Grace was certain of it. Without the video documentation, it would always just be a funny story she shared at dinner parties.

"No, Alec, please don't." She shook her head in emphasis.

The sharks deserved better. Bonnie deserved to be seen as the intelligent creature that she was.

A knock at the door interrupted them.

"It's me." Double D's muffled voice reached them.

"Come in," Alec called out.

Donovan stepped into the room. "Sorry to interrupt you two lovebirds, but you really gotta come see this."

Alec stood and helped Grace to her feet. Although her ankle pulsated with pain, she could stand on it. Since she was wearing only a thin t-shirt and no bra, Alec pulled off his sweatshirt and offered it to her. Surrounded by his lingering body heat, she settled into the warmth it offered along with the heady aroma of Alec.

God, he smells good.

He wrapped an arm around her waist and guided her to the office crowded with bodies, nothing but black sky visible through the salon windows. Tony, Stephie, Missy, and Mackenzie sat at the table, crowded around a laptop computer screen. Brad and Frank stood to the side, hovering over their shoulders, their expressions unreadable. Corky was pouring a cup of joe from the small coffee maker tucked into the counter above the mini-fridge.

"She lives." Stephie's dry tone surprised Grace. She'd never heard the stalwart photographer crack a joke.

Grace gave a rueful laugh. "The sharks haven't gotten me yet."

Corky waved a finger at her. "You're like your father. He took ridiculous risks, too."

Grace had come to suspect as much. She hobbled into the room using Alec's arm for support.

"I'm glad you're okay," Corky added.

Grace smiled. "Thanks."

Tony jumped up, offering his seat, and Alec guided her into it.

Corky took a sip from his mug, then said, "You're drawn to the whites as much as your father was, and they to you. Despite the daredevil that seems to run in the Mann lineage, I can honestly say it was a privilege to be in the water with you, Grace. There aren't many like you out there."

"Careful, Corky," Alec cut in. "This might go to her head."

The older scientist shifted his gaze to Alec, who remained standing beside her. "You'd better do her justice in this film." Corky's easy-going countenance had been replaced with a hard-edged stance.

"I will," Alec said quietly. "I promise."

Missy spun the laptop towards Grace. "Your magnum opus."

A video was paused on the screen. Stephie punched the keyboard, starting the playback.

At first, the footage captured blue water and nothing else. Then out of the depths came a shark. And clinging to the top of the missile-made-flesh—or plastered might better describe it—was a tiny figure clad in yellow. She looked like a starfish hitching a ride.

Grace watched closely, goosebumps sprouting on her arms despite the warmth of Alec's sweatshirt. She was so tiny, and the shark was so big. Her bright wetsuit only served to emphasize the dichotomy of woman and the ancient predator of the deep.

The mouth of the beast was open, the teeth clearly visible in all their savage glory, and without proper context it certainly appeared as if Grace was about to become one more kill in a long list of predations.

Grace scanned the markings, and along with the notches in the dorsal and caudal fins, her savior was identified. "It's Bonnie." Her voice conveyed the reverence due to the Queen of the Deep Blue. No creature was her equal, not even man.

Grace swallowed against the lump in her throat.

Double D leaned across Alec and clicked a button, freezing the frame. "Using your height, I was able to extrapolate Bonnie's size."

She glanced at Donovan. "How long?"

"She's at least twenty-four feet."

"Holy shit," Grace murmured.

"Holy shit is right!" Double D bellowed. "She's the biggest shark ever recorded."

Grace glanced at Alec, willing him to read her thoughts. He couldn't possibly destroy this footage. It was simply too important from a biological standpoint, regardless of how the incident might be portrayed on film. He held her gaze, and she sensed his ambivalence.

He reached out and clasped her fingers, wrapping his large palm around hers.

"Bonnie helped me for no reason other than she wanted to," Grace said.

"It is curious," Corky said. "I heard about the fishing line you removed from Mary Ann, and there was talk that this shark was her, that somehow she remembered you and how you'd helped her. It sounded like a plausible explanation for why she would try to aid you. But Bonnie had no vested interest in any of this. It was almost as if she knew Felix was misbehaving and wanted to make things right. It implies a level of intelligence that has easily been attributed to whales and dolphins but never sharks, least of all great whites. I told you that your father and I had sensed this long ago, but we could never prove it. This could have far-reaching implications."

"*This* is your movie," Double D said, looking at Brad and Frank. "Not some preposterous notion that Bonnie was on a killing spree."

Alec's hand tensed.

Was he right? Should she be concerned about her reputation if she claimed that she and Bonnie were buddies, that maybe the shark remembered her from the Farallones when she'd sliced into Grace's neck all those years ago? According to that shaman Grace had spoken to, every scar she had was a mark, a bond between her and that animal, a symbol that she had been chosen.

Had Bonnie recognized a spiritual connection between them?

Would Grace be committing professional suicide by publicly making such claims?

Her sister, Chloe, in her pursuit of information on sperm whales, had recently told her of individuals who operated outside the rules of higher education and research. They jury-rigged apparatus and spent one-on-one time in the water with the whales, making huge strides in understanding the species, but no one in academia took them seriously. Everything they documented was ignored. Their only hope was to take it to the public and beg for funding.

Grace wasn't sure she was ready for her career to spiral in that direction.

And what of the array? She'd worked damned hard and couldn't walk away from it. She couldn't let Brad take credit for a project that ultimately should be attributed to her father. She had to continue to fight for ownership.

Brad shook his head. "You'll be laughed out of prominent journals. The Institute will probably fire you. You'll become a joke, Grace."

She inhaled a deep breath and released Alec's hand. "I imagine that would make you happy."

"Why would you say that?" Fowler argued. "We can cut the film to build to the moment when a great white shark becomes altruistic. It won't be as attention-grabbing as the 'Monster from the depths tries to eat young, nubile shark researcher,' but it should garner a lot of buzz."

Missy craned her neck to look at Frank standing behind her. "Nubile? Seriously? Who uses words like that anymore?"

As a heated, feminist discussion ensued—Stephie being the most vocal—Alec knelt beside Grace.

"Keep the footage," she said, her voice low. "Let's think about it before we do something rash."

He nodded. "We've still got one more week out here. What do you want to do?"

Grace considered the options. "Rest a day or two, then tape up my ankle and get in the water."

He shook his head in exasperation. "Yeah, I figured you'd say something like that."

"I need to tell Bonnie thank you."

"Any hope that you'll do it from the safety of a cage?"

"Nope."

His green eyes took on a brooding hue. "Then I've only got one thing to say."

"What's that?"

"I'll be right beside you."

CHAPTER 26

The Farallon Islands
November

Grace sat in the boat as it bobbed in the water. It had been three hours in Shark Alley and no sign of any sharks. She watched the wavy, frothy surface, looking for boils that would indicate a great white beneath the surface, or a dorsal fin ominously appearing—or even better, a collection of gulls on the water indicating a recent kill. But so far, zilch.

"I wish we got phone reception out here," Tony said, holding his cellphone up to the sky.

Half-asleep, Grace shook off her stupor and gave a nod, hiding her bleary eyes behind her sunglasses. She took a deep breath and glanced toward the rocky Farallon Islands nearby, jutting out of the water with their pointy granite peaks.

As she had nearly every day she'd been here so far, she felt her father's presence. And oddly, it didn't make her sad. For the first time since his death, she found herself at peace with the loss.

The weather was unusually nice today—blue sky, somewhat

calm seas, windy but not gusty. She wondered if the sharks were taking a siesta as well. Maybe when the sky was dark, then their mood darkened as well, turning to thoughts of mayhem and slaughter. She supposed it was easier to hunt in such conditions since the churning sea would hide the sharks from the elephant seals.

It would be great, though, if they could tag one damned shark today. She had thirteen transmitters with her, and so far, they'd only managed to attach one. That had been three days ago.

What didn't give her peace, however, was Alec. Her thoughts turned to him about every other minute. Idle time was the worst.

The remainder of the Guadalupe expedition had been anticlimactic, with Grace managing to avoid any more near-death experiences. Bonnie wasn't spotted again, although Felix reappeared three days later, missing the tip of his dorsal fin. A bitemark was evident. The prevailing theory was that Bonnie had disciplined the randy young male, and the ongoing joke was that it had been done on Grace's behalf.

Grace wondered if she would ever see Bonnie again and regretted that the shark hadn't been tagged or biopsied.

Accompanying that regret was uncertainty about her and Alec, compounded by the fact that research space at the Farallones had become available immediately upon her return. When Grace was offered the spot, she couldn't possibly say no. It was the first time she'd been to the island without her dad. Pride swelled in her chest that she had arrived, at long last, as a full-blown researcher.

I hope you're proud, Daddy.

But she'd barely had time to unpack from Guadalupe before heading out on this month-long assignment. Alec had returned to the Bay area, and while he'd promised to stay in touch, it wasn't always easy to get a signal out, and Grace had begun to wonder if distance had shown the sizzling chemistry to be what it was—an expedition hook-up.

"Let's just chum the shit out of the water so we can call it a day," Tony said. "I'm gonna make spaghetti tonight. I can't stop thinking about it."

Only Tony could relate chum to spaghetti sauce. She supposed it was only fitting since both were blood-red. While in residence on the Farallones, it was Tony who did most of the cooking. The other three scientists—one shark biologist and two bird researchers—were happy as clams to eat his cooking. Tony lived up to his Italian heritage.

"No chumming," Grace murmured.

The radio crackled with a connection. "Farallon Boat, this is the Sea Kelp, over."

Tony grabbed the handset from his reclining position on the bench. "This is Farallon Boat. Go ahead, Steve."

"Hey, Tony." Steve Markham ran a whale-watching tour company out of the Bay area and sometimes ferried supplies to them. "I've got a passenger needing transfer. I'll be near Mirongua Bay in about five. Over."

Tony looked over at Grace. "You expecting company?"

Grace shook her head. "The others must've forgotten to tell us. Maybe it's a young intern with a case of wine."

Tony sighed. "We can only hope." He clicked the transmit button. "All right, Steve. See you in a few."

Grace took a sweeping view of the ocean surrounding them with one last hope of seeing a shark as Tony started the engine. In short order, he guided the small boat out of Shark Alley to meet the *Sea Kelp*.

Grace sat in the bow as the tour boat came into view, and Tony angled their watercraft beside it. The passengers for the day crowded the railing, obviously curious about the transfer. Grace suspected that whoever was about to jump into their vessel had already shared stories with the tourists about the Farallones, the great white sharks, and the strange and hardy researchers who lived on this godforsaken island that was filled with barking seals and pungent, ammonia-scented bird poop.

Tony brought their boat parallel to the *Sea Kelp,* and one of the *Kelp*'s crew members threw down a nylon rope, which Grace caught and tied onto a cleat. Then she craned her neck to ferret out their pick-up.

Her eyes locked with Alec's.

Her heart jumped into her throat, and a jolt of adrenaline shocked her system, suddenly making her knees unsteady and her arms tremble.

"Dr. Mann," he said and grinned.

Damn, he looked good.

The ball cap covering his head and the red fleece jacket and long pants couldn't hide the physique that she decided was darn near perfect. She was glad for her sunglasses so he couldn't see her hungry desperation.

"Alec, is that you?" Tony said. "How the hell did you get a ticket here?"

"Friends in high places. I've got a permit for three days."

"To do what?" Grace finally found her voice.

"Film you. What else?"

He handed a duffel bag down to Tony, then several hard cases of equipment, which Grace was forced to grab. She'd never been fond of boat transfers. In choppy seas, the watercrafts would bang against each other, and Grace always feared she'd slip between the two vessels and be crushed.

But Alec made it look effortless as he hopped into their modest outboard under the intense scrutiny of the passengers. He brushed up against her, and she fought the urge to throw herself into his arms.

"Thanks, Steve." Alec waved up to the *Sea Kelp*'s captain.

"My pleasure," Steve said. "Have a good one."

Alec also waved to all the passengers, and they reciprocated, smiles covering their faces, unquestionably entranced by Alec Galloway. Handsome, compelling, and filled with tales of the sea—Grace had no doubt he'd had a rapt audience during the two-hour ride.

As Tony started the engine, she and Alec untied the boat, and they edged away from the *Sea Kelp*. Once they were underway, Alec sat across from Grace.

"Are we going in, boss?" Tony asked over his shoulder.

They could—they should—but she needed more time with the sharks.

"No. Take us back to Shark Alley." She turned her attention to Alec. "Sorry, you'll have to tag along for a bit."

"I'm easy." Alec adjusted his ball cap, his eyes flashing with dark desire and reaching straight down into her abdomen with the unmistakable pull that was reserved for Alec Galloway alone.

Grace wasn't sure what was more dangerous at this point—the sharks or Alec.

"How have you been?" he asked.

"I'm getting by." It was the truth. She should have added *barely*, but she didn't want to say more in front of Tony.

Alec gave a nod. "I told you I'd take you diving here."

"You brought scuba gear?" She glanced at his pile of bags.

He shook his head and laughed. "No. I'm not too proud to admit I'm a total chicken, so I came to tell you in person that I'm reneging on that promise. But I do have a rough cut of the doc that I'd like to show you." Then he added, his voice thick, "I've missed you, Grace."

Once again, she was glad for the sunglasses so he couldn't see her eyes filled with hunger and despair and an ache that had her clawing at herself during the long nights without him. Not trusting her voice, she bit her lower lip and snapped her chin in a clipped gesture.

"We've got a shark!" Tony whooped.

Grace stood and gripped the gunwale, peering over the side as Alec came beside her. An epic shadow cruised below them.

"That's a big one," Alec murmured.

Grace grabbed the tagging rod and double-checked that it was ready. "Bring us around, Tony."

Tony angled the boat in a circle, all of them keeping the shark in their sights. She hadn't deployed the decoy—a fiberglass shell that mimicked the shape of a seal—because lately, it hadn't really been working. Somehow, the sharks had become wise to the ploy to get them to the surface, probably from the cage-diving companies who frequented the waters and overused the decoys. Still, Grace debated throwing it in the water at this point, if it would keep the shark interested long enough for her to tag it.

Grace braced her rubber boots against the side of the boat, her foot wounds from Felix still healing and sore, and stood poised at the side, harpoon in hand, ready to lunge at a moment's notice.

The dorsal fin rose about twenty feet to port side, moving toward them. She saw a notch at the front.

"It's Ginger," she said, stunned.

"You mean the Professor's Ginger?" Alec asked.

"Yes."

Grace had seen Ginger in Baja last year and the consensus was that a big female such as her wouldn't return for two years, and most certainly not to the Farallones, when her usual pattern was to visit Guadalupe Island.

Not only had Bonnie changed her migratory route, but so had Ginger. Incredible.

"She must've heard you were in town, Dr. Mann," Tony said, on the other side of Alec and still at the wheel.

Ginger came straight at the boat and, in one powerful lunge, clamped her mouth on the outboard motor, knocking them all to the floor.

Grace screamed.

Alec fell on her. "Sonuvabitch!"

"She'll eat the fucking engine," Tony yelled.

Grace scrambled to stand, desperate to get a tag on her. As Ginger mouthed the motor, her pointy, freckled snout dripped water, and her magnificent rows of teeth were in full view.

"Alec, let me get closer." Grace gripped his arm.

"No. If you slip, she could bite you by accident. And you can't possibly tag her from this angle."

Grace grumbled loudly. Self-preservation held her frozen in

place, but hell…Ginger was a beauty, and she was right on their back doorstep. Grace made eye contact with the great white and grinned broadly at her. Opportunities like this didn't come along every day.

Grace glanced back at Tony, who thankfully was filming on his handheld video camera. Ginger lurched, rocking the boat back and forth.

"Let me poke her before she eats the boat," Grace said and pushed past Alec. She turned the tagging harpoon around and began to butt the tip at Ginger's nose, careful to avoid her eyes. "Git! Get away!"

Ginger took the hint and released her metallic prey, sinking back into the water and disappearing underneath the boat. Grace jumped to the side to get a visual. They waited, the boat undulating on the water, and the seconds stretched into minutes.

Tony hummed the theme from *Jaws*.

"Cut it out," Alec snapped. "This boat is too damned small to be out here with all these lethal fish swimming around."

Alec was rattled, if his taut shoulders and rigid jawline were any indication.

Grace took a steadying breath.

Truthfully, she was a bit shaken, too. She knew that Ginger didn't want to eat them, but that didn't mean Grace wanted to end up in the drink in shark-infested waters after the giant female disassembled their boat from her curious shenanigans.

Grace gripped the harpoon pole with sweaty palms. Feeling overheated in the sun's glare, she wanted to strip off her hat, buff, and fleece jacket but didn't dare let her attention waver.

"I don't think she's coming back," Tony finally said.

Grace's shoulders sagged, her body overcome with a sudden fatigue. She'd been out for the better part of the day and was exhausted. "I think you're right. Let's head back."

"I hope this thing starts," Tony muttered.

The motor puttered to life, but the boat didn't move.

"Is the prop engaged?" Alec asked.

"Yes!" Tony's voice rang with frustration.

"It must be jammed." Alec clambered to the stern. "Let me have a look." He leaned over to inspect the propeller.

Ginger flew out of the water in another engine attack.

"Jesus!" Alec bolted backwards, slamming into Grace.

They fell in a heap once again. Alec jumped to his feet and yanked Grace up.

Grace grabbed hold of his arm. It was covered in blood, and he'd smeared a fair amount on her. A quick inspection showed a large gash above his wrist. She grabbed a towel and wrapped it tightly around his arm. He sat down on the bench as Ginger sank back into the water again and moved along the starboard side.

Grace grabbed the harpoon off the floor of the boat, leaned forward, and stabbed the tip just below the dorsal fin. As Ginger left in a giant thrust, the boat rocked wildly back and forth.

"Did you get it?" Alec asked.

She spun around and knelt before him, checking his wound. The towel was soaked in red. "Yes," she answered, worried for him. "How do you feel?"

"I'm okay." His eyes were clear as he watched her.

"Tony, we need to get out of here."

"Put it in reverse," Alec said. "Then go forward. Maybe Ginger lost a tooth and it's jamming the prop."

Tony did as instructed, and the boat obeyed this time, careening forward as they headed to shore. Once there, Grace helped Alec out of the boat and guided him up the pathway to the house where the researchers lived, while Tony secured the outboard.

Once at the house, she opened the door and led him into the kitchen.

Barry Croft, an ornithologist, appeared, his round face wincing as his eyes widened. "Good lord! What happened?"

Barry's response made her look at Alec again. He was a bloody mess.

"This is Alec Galloway." Grace pulled out a chair at the table so

Alec could sit down. "It's just a little shark bite," she said, trying to convince herself that it was nothing. "Can you get the first aid kit?"

Grace spent the next half hour cleaning Alec's arm and stitching up the rather deep gash. To fend off infection, she started him on the antibiotics she had on hand.

The other researchers, Mickey and Carl, showed up and helped Tony carry Alec's gear to the house. Grace insisted Alec take some heavy-duty pain meds and put him in her bedroom upstairs, and he was soon asleep.

ALEC OPENED his eyes to darkness and a howling wind lashing the old house. It creaked and shuddered, and he wouldn't be surprised if the place were haunted. His arm hurt like hell, and the shark attack flooded his mind. Well, more like an accidental attack. Ginger had clearly been after the boat motor. But still....

He moved his other arm, and it bumped against something soft.

Grace.

She was curled up beside him, asleep.

Relief filled him.

If it took a shark bite to get her to come to him, then he owed Ginger a big thank you. He wanted to put his arm around her, but it was difficult without waking her. He rolled to his side, to face her, and brought his bandaged right hand to rest on her hip.

She opened her eyes.

"I suppose you let Ginger bite you to gain sympathy from me," she said quietly.

He angled his face to hers and kissed her. He'd thought of little else for the past four weeks. She kissed him back, and he pressed his advantage, letting his pent-up hunger for her loose. He nudged her to her back and gave full attention to a frontal assault on her mouth.

Her hands slid around his waist then clawed their way beneath his shirt up to his shoulder blades. He moved fully atop her, careful of his injury, taking his weight more fully onto his left forearm. He sank onto her, a shudder of anticipation rippling through him.

He was rock hard.

And he was desperate for her.

She clung to him, her mouth consuming him in a ravenous display of need, and when she arched her back, he nearly came in his shorts.

"Take off your clothes, Grace." He rolled away so that she could disrobe.

She made fast work of a long-sleeved white t-shirt and sports bra, then wiggled out of a pair of yoga pants. He watched her breasts in the gray light of the room, wanting to touch them, but only his injured hand was available at this angle. Instead, he used his mouth.

Grace gasped and pulled at his hair with her fingers. She pushed him to his back and popped the snap closure of his shorts, yanking them down. She gave up removing his shirt and instead pushed the bottom edge to his neck then leaned forward to bring her bare breasts to his chest.

He kissed her long and hard and deep, and she moved to slide onto him.

"Stop." Shit. He only had seconds. "Where's my gear? I have a condom."

She bit his lip. "Your stuff is here." She slipped off him. "Where?"

"My duffle bag. There's a pocket inside."

She unzipped his bag and fumbled through his clothing, then she was climbing back onto him and ripping open the square packet. He cupped a breast with his good hand while she encased him. Grace had great breasts, and he'd imagined holding, squeezing, kneading them until he'd been miserably aroused while separated from her.

Rolling her onto her back, he joined to her, and they came together in a flurry of heat and pleasure that bordered on pain.

He was lost in Grace.

He'd been lost since she'd left him.

But like Ginger who had relentlessly come after that boat motor, determined to understand what it was, even at the risk of hurting herself, Alec had come after Grace.

He couldn't live without her.

That much he knew.

CHAPTER 27

Grace lay nestled against Alec's left side. She had managed to remove his t-shirt, working it free over his bandage, so they were skin to skin. In the clammy chillness of the room, he'd pulled a tattered comforter over both of them.

She loved every hard plane of his chest and flat stomach, the corded muscles of his shoulders and biceps, and the sense of peace she felt in his arms.

She'd been a miserable fool to consider walking away from him and the inevitable hassle of a long-distance relationship.

If he wanted her, that was all that mattered.

A gale howled outside, a haunting sound that had always fascinated Grace when she'd visited as a child. Some researchers hated it here. Her father had sometimes spoken of a man or woman who'd gone plum crazy trying to live and work in such a barren, relentless, and isolated place. No more than eight people ever resided here at one time.

"Why didn't you answer my emails?" His lips brushed her temple.

Speaking of plum crazy—Grace was that and so much more for Alec. She was tired of fighting it. "I thought it was for the best."

His hand tangled into her hair, tickling her scalp. She sighed from his ministrations.

"Do you mind that I'm here?" he asked.

"No." She covered his leg with hers and skimmed her palm down his chest. "I'm glad."

"Were you just overthinking it?"

"Yes."

"Will you please stop?"

"Yes."

Silence stretched between them as the ebb and flow of the wind contrasted with the steady beating of Alec's heart against her ear.

She finally uttered what she'd been dreading to ask. "What did you decide to do with the footage of Bonnie?" She wasn't sure she wanted to know if he'd destroyed it.

She'd departed Monterey so quickly that she'd had little time with Stewart to discuss what had happened, except to show him the outcome of the array testing, which, by the end of the journey, had produced viable results, thanks to her continuous tinkering with the code.

Stewart had assured her that the terms of the closed-door contract she'd negotiated with CMI would be honored, and Brad would be taken off the project. In a way, Grace had been glad to be gone. She hadn't felt like having another confrontation with her ex, especially after he'd chummed the waters while she'd been diving. Was he that vengeful or just sloppy?

Either way, she wanted nothing more to do with him.

Stewart also assured her that he would deal with the fact that Brad had sent her code to another programmer. That alone was grounds for termination. No word yet on the outcome of it all, but Grace had set her worries aside, determined to enjoy the wonder of the Farallones.

"I didn't delete it, if that's what you're wondering. We had a guardian angel step in."

She craned her neck and looked at him. "What do you mean?"

"My Uncle Simon interceded on our behalf."

"I remember Stewart mentioning him. What happened?"

"He bought the rights to distribute the film, and paid the Institute nicely for it. CMI was happy, Fowler was out on his ass, and if you haven't heard, Brad is looking for work elsewhere."

Although she knew it was a possibility, she was still surprised. "Was he fired?"

"No. I think he saw the writing on the wall and left on his own."

Grace propped herself up on an elbow so that her gaze met Alec's. "What did your uncle say about the doc?"

"He's already seen a rough cut, and he likes it." His uninjured hand skimmed her buttocks. "Can I show it to you?"

"Right now?"

He grinned. "Yeah, right now."

He rose from the bed, and Grace enjoyed the view of his shadowed nude body as he retrieved a bag and carried it back. While she looked forward to more playtime under the sheets with him, she searched for her clothes and pulled them on, adding a sweatshirt for good measure.

"Can you help me?" he asked. He sat down without a stitch of clothing.

She complied and unzipped the carryall, removing the thick laptop. Alec booted it up, and the glow from the screen made his state of undress more distracting.

"Can you put something on?" she asked, her voice a bit breathless.

His response was a sexy, lopsided grin and a wicked gleam in his eyes. He leaned over and kissed her, then stood and donned his t-shirt and sweatpants with help from her.

She propped the pillows against the headboard, and they leaned back as Alec's film played, the computer sitting on his outstretched legs.

And she was stunned.

When it was over, he closed the laptop, engulfing them in darkness again.

"Where did you get all those photos and footage of my dad?"

she whispered, her throat still clogged with the tears she was unable to suppress.

"Susie Mann."

"You called my mom?"

He nodded. "I hope you're not mad. I can't take credit for the idea. It was actually Michaels who suggested it, although his slant was to tie Bonnie to you and your dad in a more sensational way." He paused. "Did you like it, Gracie?"

She sniffled and buried her face into his neck. "Yes," she choked out.

While he'd showcased the shark array and her work on it, the film was an ode to the life of Dr. Eddie Mann and the daughter who continued in his footsteps. Grace had never seen most of the footage he'd included. "My mom must've really done some digging in the attic."

"She did mention that she hadn't looked through a lot of it in years. She's a nice lady. I like her a lot."

"Did you tell her about us?" Grace asked.

"No. It was clear you hadn't mentioned me, so I kept my mouth shut."

She locked eyes with him. "I'm sorry. I just wasn't sure."

"And now?"

She leaned forward, her mouth near his. "I'm as certain as you are."

He pushed the computer to the edge of the bed. "And how certain is that?"

"I saw how many condoms are in your bag. You're at least thirty-times sure."

He tugged her forward, and she straddled him.

"You haven't seen how many are in my other bag."

EPILOGUE

Salt Lake City
January

Alec moved through the crowded expo in search of his brother. He ran into Double D near a table featuring the latest in high-tech wilderness video equipment.

"Have you seen Tyler?" Alec asked.

Donovan fiddled with the equipment, then set it down on the display table. "No. Maybe he's avoiding you. You know how he hates sharks."

"It's a lame excuse to get out of working for me."

"Maybe we should go to K2 with him." Double D raised an eyebrow.

"I hate the cold almost as much as he hates being underwater."

"How in the hell did you both come out of the same mother?"

"I've wondered that myself sometimes," Alec murmured. Except that he and Ty resembled each other too much for there to be any doubt they were related. "Find anything good?" Alec nodded at the gear.

"Yeah. But it's costly. Let's hope Sharkonator is gonna line our pockets. Speaking of our lovely movie star—where is she?"

"She went to grab a couple lattes before the show starts."

"She's at your beck and call. I love it."

Alec released a half-laugh and did a partial eye roll. "She wouldn't take kindly to that description, so keep your trap shut. I'm beginning to think she doesn't just study the sharks—she's actually one of them."

Double D let out a bark of laughter. "Does she disappear from your bed at night and return to the ocean?"

Alec shook his head and scanned the crowd again. "Smart ass."

"I never thought I'd see the day when you'd be good and caught by a woman." Donovan left the table and started walking beside Alec as they waded into the throng of people. "I really didn't think such a female existed. You were never that distracted by those other chickies you've dated."

Alec smiled, but he kept the truth to himself. From the instant he'd seen that photo of Grace swimming with a great white a year ago, he'd been propelled toward her by some nameless force. A part of him had known she was different and that his life had just taken a sharp turn.

It was too sappy to say aloud, least of all to Donovan. Alec would never hear the end of it.

He'd almost told Grace a few times, but he feared scaring her away. Their vagabond lifestyles concerned her, and she periodically ruminated over it. She also mentioned, only one time, but he suspected it weighed on her more than that, her concern that Alec would fall victim to whatever young, flirtatious intern happened to be on his next expedition, despite that Mackenzie had quickly backed off once she'd learned the status of his relationship with Grace.

And he had no intention of keeping his romance with Grace undercover again.

She was the one.

And he wanted to marry her.

She'd likely say it was too soon, that they were moving too quickly. He supposed she was right, but it didn't change the way he felt about her.

They found Ty talking to two men at a table featuring winter apparel.

Ty grinned when he spied Alec. "It's about time you showed up."

Alec hugged his brother. It had been over a year since he'd seen him. Stepping back, he eyed the suit and tie. "You're looking rather GQ."

"Well, I heard my brother was debuting a highly anticipated documentary about a woman who swims with great whites. I figured I needed to clean up for the press junket. You don't look so bad yourself."

Alec wore a dark gray blazer and button-down shirt, but he'd shunned a tie.

"Double D." Ty dragged out the syllables while shaking Donovan's hand. "It's good to see you."

"You gonna film a movie at K2 this summer?"

"I plan to shoot some footage but nothing formal. This is a fun trip."

Donovan laughed. "Only a Galloway picks one of the most dangerous mountains in the world for a vacation."

"So, where's this Grace?" Ty asked. "I want to meet the woman who domesticated Alec."

"Who says I'm domestic?" Alec asked.

Double D shook his head. "He's whipped."

Ty grinned. "Mom's gonna flip. Have you introduced her?"

Alec narrowed his gaze. "As soon as Grace gets a break in her schedule, we're driving up to the Bay."

Tyler's expression became serious. "Really? I was just kidding. Holy shit." He looked at Donovan. "He *is* whipped."

"Like an egg soufflé."

"All right," Alec cut in. "We're headed to the auditorium. Show starts in an hour. I've got seats in the front for you. Is there anyone with you?"

"You mean like a girl?" Ty asked, looking wide-eyed and innocent. "Let me see if I can round one up."

Donovan swore under his breath. "And you will. It's so fucking unfair. I wonder if I could get laid here as easily as a Galloway."

Ty exhaled, rubbing the back of his neck. "It's actually much harder than it looks."

Donovan looked at Alec. "Is he shitting me? And you think *I'm* a smart ass."

Alec blended into the crowd once again and headed to the auditorium.

GRACE LEFT the coffee vendor in the hotel lobby, two cups in hand, and walked along the corridor to the showroom where the expo was taking place. She hoped she remembered how to find the auditorium. She was probably late—she'd gotten held up by two women, both fit and athletic and probably some type of extreme athlete, when they'd recognized her from the press photos for the documentary.

She was also coming to realize that Alec was well-known at events such as these, having made the rounds with him the previous day. He'd literally been stopped at least twenty-five different times by people who had wanted to say hello.

She was nervous about previewing the film, but she had spent several twelve-hour days in post-production with Alec recording voiceovers and felt satisfied that he had struck a balance between her conjecture about the Bonnie incident and the possible display of altruistic behavior while keeping Grace's scientific research and findings at the forefront.

Once they had a final cut of the project, Grace had taken it to Orinda to show her mom, Alec accompanying her. She'd introduced him as her boyfriend, and her mom couldn't have been more warm and welcoming, later telling Grace that he'd reminded her of Eddie Mann in his younger days, and that Grace was smart to snatch him up.

I wish Daddy could have met him.

Ahead of her, a man with sandy-brown hair walked beside a well-dressed blonde woman in black dress pants and a tan top. Was that Alec? She picked up her pace to catch him, glad she'd opted for oxfords instead of heels with her light gray slacks and maroon blouse.

As she came abreast of the two, she did a double-take. The man's demeanor and walk was so like Alec's, but it wasn't her sweetheart. Then recognition dawned.

"Are you Alec Galloway's brother?" she asked.

"Guilty as charged."

"I'm Grace Mann."

The man's gaze softened. "Ah, the famous shark lady who caught my brother."

"That's me."

She would have shaken his hand, but hers were filled with lattes.

"It's nice to meet you," he said. "I'm Tyler. And this is Lindsey Coulson."

Grace smiled a greeting at the other woman. "Are you headed to the auditorium?"

"We are," Tyler said.

"Is it true that you swim with great white sharks?" Lindsey asked, her gaze warm and curious. Her perfectly straight nose put Grace in mind of an ancient Greek statue.

Grace nodded. "They're really just like puppies."

Lindsey laughed while Tyler shook his head, his face pinching into a mock scowl, and said, "I don't think so. Is that how you and Alec describe them while you're filming? *Let's go jump in the ocean with a bunch of sharp-toothed puppies?*"

"Yep," Grace replied. "That's about it."

"I hear you're headed to the Bay area soon."

I am?

"Our mother's gonna love you," Tyler added.

Alec was planning to introduce her to his parents? He hadn't mentioned it, not even when they'd gone to Orinda—just outside of San Francisco—to see her mom. Her stomach did a nervous flip, but her heart broke out in a happy boogie dance.

"I look forward to meeting her," Grace said. "And your dad, too."

"Try not to let him scare you. Big Jim Galloway is all bluster and no bite."

"I'll try to remember that."

"Do you surf?" Tyler asked.

"No."

He chuckled. "You will."

They entered the nearly filled auditorium, a steady stream of chatter humming in the background. As they made their way to the front, Grace caught sight of Alec at the podium speaking to another gentleman. When he saw her, he acknowledged her with a nod and a smile.

Double D was already sitting in the front row of reserved seats. "I've been craving a latte," he said, standing to join them.

"Oh." Grace felt bad that she hadn't gotten him a drink. "Here, take mine."

He threw up a hand in refusal. "No, I'm kidding. I see you found Ty."

"I did. And this is Lindsey," she added. Tyler had stepped on stage to talk to Alec.

Recognition lit Double D's face. "Coulson." He shook her hand. "I know who you are." At Grace's questioning expression, he added, "She's a famous mountain climber."

"Not really," Lindsey answered. "But thanks for the ego boost."

Double D tugged at his espresso-colored tie. "You climbing with Ty?"

"Well, the first part of my plan is working, and I tracked him here. I'm hoping if I trail after him long enough, he'll let me join his

K2 expedition." She shifted her focus to Grace. "Have you done any climbing?"

"No. I think I'd be out of my element."

"We've got a great little film about Grace." Double D winked. "What she does in the water will take your breath away."

The admiration in Donovan's voice took Grace aback. He didn't usually wear his emotions on his sleeve. "Thank you, Dan," she replied quietly.

"I look forward to it," Lindsey said.

"Have a seat, ladies." Double D ushered them to their places.

Tyler had stepped down from the stage, and Grace overheard Donovan say to him, "I can't believe you actually found a girl."

"She found me, Donovan."

"Even worse. But I'll bet she can outclimb you."

Grace settled beside Lindsey. "Are you and Ty...."

"Oh, no." Lindsey shook her head. "Nothing like that. I only just met him an hour ago."

If Grace was honest with herself, it had taken less than an hour to realize that Alec was going to be a problem for her, but she didn't share her insight with the other woman.

Alec jogged down the short set of steps and over to Grace.

She handed him his latte. "It's probably cold by now."

He leaned down and kissed her. "I don't care. Thanks." He extended a hand to Lindsey. "You probably don't remember, but we've met before. I was in Yosemite several years ago with some friends, and they introduced us. They said you and your sister left everyone in the dust that day on El Cap. You two were very aggressive."

"Maybe competitive was more like it," Lindsey replied, her expression a bit distant. "It's nice to see you again."

"I was sorry to hear about Alison."

"What happened?" Grace asked.

"My sister was killed at K2 two years ago." Lindsey cleared her throat.

"I'm so sorry." Grace thought of Chloe and how it would feel to lose her.

Ty joined them and with a somber tone said, "Lindsey's looking for a bit of closure. She wants to come to K2 with me. How about you and Grace come too?"

"Living in the Death Zone for weeks on end holds little appeal for me." Alec's gaze locked on Grace. "You up for snuggling in a tent for six weeks?"

"Are there any sharks there?" she asked.

"There can be," Lindsey said. "They're usually Russian."

Everyone laughed, and Grace sensed that Lindsey was glad to shift away from the melancholy atmosphere of talking about her sister.

The lights flickered.

"Gotta go." Alec leaned down and squeezed Grace's knee. "We should all have dinner later." He returned to the stage to prepare for the film's introduction.

Tyler took a seat beside Lindsey, and Double D sat one chair over on Grace's left, leaving an empty space for Alec.

Grace whispered into Lindsey's ear, "If you ever want to go shark diving, let me know."

"If you ever want to go to the top of the world, let *me* know."

A spotlight illuminated Alec, and he launched into facts about great white sharks and background on Grace's work. When the film started to play, he took his seat beside her and scooped her hand into his.

The opening shot was an aerial view of the *Mercado* and the clear waters around Guadalupe Island, courtesy of Alec's drone.

Alec rubbed the pad of his thumb on Grace's knuckle. She settled back and was transported to the place where she had always felt the most alive and connected. The sharks brought her close to the pulse of one of the wildest places on earth—the ocean, with all its inky depths and scary inhabitants.

Amazingly she felt the same when she was with Alec.

He knew the wild places, he knew the call, he knew the obsession. And he was willing to stand beside her.

She'd never expected to find anyone who could. Not after her father, but he'd been a little crazed from it. Maybe she was, too.

Gratitude welled up that she had Alec. He was a treasure. She needed to make sure she didn't screw this up.

She brought her mouth to his ear and whispered, "Thank you."

"For what?"

"For putting up with me."

He grinned. "It was either that or give all my condoms to Double D. And before I forget, I've got a job in Australia next month. I want you to come with me."

"You do?"

"There'll be sharks."

"Then I'm in."

Before she could move away, he nuzzled her cheek, his breath hot on her skin. "And I want you to meet my folks. I'm crazy about you, Gracie."

Happiness washed through her, and her body responded as it usually did around Alec—hot and bothered and yearning for alone time.

The lobby had a bathroom, didn't it?

An underwater world came to life on the screen.

Grace's voice filled the room. "My father always said we yearn for the ocean, because it's our one true home. Dr. Eddie Mann, a dedicated shark researcher, devoted his life to the great white shark. These extraordinary creatures aren't what we think they are, and perhaps they might be more than we ever thought possible. I'm Dr. Grace Mann. Come along as I take you on a journey into the deep blue."

THE END

Read more Grace and Alec adventures in A PATHWAY SHORT ADVENTURE COLLECTION, featuring the short stories *Deep Blue*

Australia, Deep Blue Réunion Island, and *Deep Blue Cocos Island.* Learn more at kmccaffrey.com/pathway-shorts-collection-one/.

Don't miss Missy's story in the novella SAPPHIRE WAVES, a second-chance romance in the gorgeous blue waters of the Bahamas. Includes a bonus short adventure with Grace and Alec - *Deep Blue Hawai'i.* Learn more at kmccaffrey.com/sapphire-waves/.

Sign-up for Kristy's newsletter at kmccaffrey.com/PathwayNewsletter/ to receive Pathway series updates, as well as a free digital download link to *Deep Blue Australia.*

If you enjoyed *Deep Blue,* would you consider posting a review? Not only does this help other readers discover a book, but it also aids an author in pursuing promotional opportunities. My heartfelt thanks.

~ Kristy

AUTHOR'S NOTE

When creating a fictional tale, I immerse myself in the subject. This usually entails research via books, but in the age of social media I'm able to connect to resources with the most current data available, which helped immensely in writing this book. Not only did I rely on wonderful nonfiction narratives such as *The Devil's Teeth* by Susan Casey and *Shark Trouble* by Peter Benchley, but I followed real-life shark photographers and researchers via Facebook, Twitter, and Instagram.

You may be asking: Is the shark information and behavior in my book accurate or fabricated? For the most part, everything my characters experienced was based on actual research and documented shark encounters. Grace's lecture at the beginning of the story was modeled on great white captivities handled by the Monterey Bay Aquarium in the early 2000s. Grace's imprisonment with Felix inside a submersible cage has also occurred with divers at Guadalupe Island, unfortunately more than once.

There is one scene, however, that I did dream up—Bonnie rescuing Grace by bringing her to the surface. In fact, I can't even claim the idea for my own since my husband suggested it one afternoon as I paced around, muttering about the need for a surprise outcome to the climatic end-scene of the book. So please forgive this deviance from known shark behavior, but during my months of investigation one thing jumped out at me—sharks, especially great whites, are not mindless predators at the mercy of their instincts. As I studied the work of researchers who regularly encounter these creatures, I was struck by the curiosity, intelligence, and even playfulness these giant fish exhibited. In recent years, altruistic behavior has been observed in creatures other than humans. One of the most striking has been humpback whales helping terrorized seals escape pods of hunting orcas. Bonnie's remarkable interest in helping Grace is farfetched, I'll grant you, but fiction as a predictive medium has borne fruit in the past. So, maybe....

A big inspiration for the character of Grace is a woman named Ocean Ramsey, a marine biologist and shark researcher. Amazing footage of Ms. Ramsey freediving with great whites can easily be found on YouTube. Based out of Hawai'i, she's a world-wide ambassador and advocate for shark conservation, and if you want to learn more about her work, she has a fantastic Instagram account (oceanramsey). You can also visit her website (oneoceandiving.com).

Another fictitious element in *Deep Blue* was the Shark Sonar Array. While sonar has been employed in tracking marine life for many years, to my knowledge apparatus possessing the complexity of Grace's array has not been attempted. Neural networks have been around since the 1960s, but it's been only recently that such technology has seen an unprecedented level of refinement. This has been due in no small part to the willingness of people to share their photos on Facebook, offering researchers the opportunity to test and "train" their tools to improve facial recognition through practice and learning. Deep learning algorithms have been applied to many diverse areas such as: determining whether a review on Amazon was positive or negative; differentiating between a British accent or a Southern drawl on an audio file; aiding Paypal in reducing their fraud rate by ten percent; and automating a process of tracking whales by the National Oceanic and Atmospheric Administration. According to Dr. Gregory Piatetsky-Shapiro, an expert on deep learning and machine intelligence, "Deep learning is probably the most important technical development since the invention of the Web in the 1990s."

Sharks today are in danger of disappearing forever. As the eminent marine biologist Sylvia Earle states: "Sharks are part of a healthy ocean." They are not the monsters that many of us have been led to believe, and it's only through continued research that we can understand and protect the domains that rightly belong to them. Humans are a far greater threat to sharks than sharks are to us.

I sincerely hope that you enjoyed Grace and Alec's story.

If you have further interest in learning about great white sharks and the ocean in general, I urge you to check out the following resources:

Dr. Neil Hammerschlag, Director of the University of Miami Predator Ecology & Shark Research Lab. (sharkresearch.rsmas.miami.edu)

Marine Conservation Science Institute, a nonprofit organization and leader in white shark research. They have been studying the white sharks of Guadalupe Island since 1999. (marinecsi.org)

Bimini Shark Lab, a world-famous shark research facility. (sharkdocsharklab.com)

Sea Legacy, a nonprofit dedicated to the protection of the ocean. (sealegacy.org)

Atlantic White Shark Conservancy. (atlanticwhiteshark.org)

Woods Hole Oceanographic Institution. (whoi.edu)

Ocearch. (ocearch.org)

AND IF YOU'RE on Instagram, the following accounts offer excellent marine-life photos and insights into shark behavior:

abc4explore
juansharks
michaelmuller7
drneilhammer
marinecsiorg
silenthunterpty

pelagic_life

rodrigofriscione

francobanfi

volunteerwhiteshark

teamsharkwater (its founder, Rob Stewart, died in early 2017 in a tragic diving accident, but his associates plan to continue his work)

mornehardenberg

iphotographsharks

mission_blue

sharkphotography_lalosaidy

hannah_gabrielson

biminisharklab

marine_biology101

duncan_brake

andycorbe

ACKNOWLEDGMENTS

A s a writer, I spend much of my time in solitary confinement and most days my only point of human contact is my husband (we both work from home). He isn't a writer, but he was tremendously supportive of this book and spent many hours troubleshooting plot problems with me. I came perilously close to adding him as a co-author. He even admitted that when he read an early draft, the ending brought a tear to his eye. After spending over a year immersed in this manuscript, I was too mired in the story to know if I'd hit the high points, so knowing I'd struck an emotional chord with my dearest was a huge confidence boost.

I also owe a debt of gratitude to another family member—my oldest son, Samuel. With a background in Physics and Computer Science, he was instrumental in helping me develop the underlying concept for the shark array, along with the education that Grace would need to realistically pull it off. This was the main reason I gave her a Ph.D. in Computer Science rather than Marine Biology. Sam and I had several lively conversations about neural networks, computer languages, and coding. Needless to say, one of our favorite shows is *Silicon Valley*.

This book marks a departure from my previous novels, all of which have been historical western romances. Switching genres is, in frank terms, an uphill battle in every aspect for a writer. I'm basically starting from ground zero in terms of readership and visibility. I knew I would need help in the editorial process, but I wasn't sure where I would find it. Enter the awesome author Ann Charles (if you haven't read her humorous Deadwood mystery series, you're missing out on some sexy, laugh-out-loud paranormal fun). Not only has she become a good friend and sounding board for all the craziness inherent in the publishing universe, she offered to contact a small group of her beta readers on my behalf. Their input has been invaluable in refining the manuscript to what you currently have in your hands.

I want to extend a huge thanks to Diane Garland for her insightful critique (and final proofread) that included catching my descriptions of Grace as petite, yet tall, and setting me straight on the true hue of hazel eyes (brown-green). All my life, I believed the term meant blue-green. Unfortunately, my driver's license has listed my eye color incorrectly for 35 years. I can only blame my mother for my lifelong confusion.

A big thank you to Becky Humphreys, also an author and a fellow shark-lover, for her in-depth assessment of the story. She questioned several of the shark facts I included, prompting me to dig deeper to ensure I was presenting accurate information.

My gratitude to Corie Carson and Vicki Huskey for flagging a minor reference I made about Disney princesses. Their knowledge and advice on the subject ultimately led me to delete the few lines of dialogue pertaining to it. (In an early draft, I had Brad's date Sidney state that she worked at Disneyland as a princess. Later, I changed her profession to exotic dancer. I was looking for an offbeat vocation, and I believe they both fit the bill!)

My appreciation to Michelle Davis for her careful perusal of the book, not the least of which was finding my inconsistent use of the term *freediving*. There are conflicting references depending on the source, running the gamut from *freediving* to *free diving* to *free-diving*. I ultimately decided to choose one form and remain consistent in its usage. If you happen to catch an error in the text then I applaud you, since I made every effort to clean it up.

Thank you to Lucinda Nelson, who admitted she didn't normally read this genre, but she liked the story and the characters, and was fascinated to learn more about sharks.

Many thanks to Bob Dickerson and Denise Keef for discovering numerous grammatical errors and to Heather Chargualaf, Dave Smithwick, and Ann Charles for enjoying the story, easing my mind that the book moved along at an entertaining clip.

Each and every one of you are worth your weight in gold.

Many, many thanks to my editor Mimi Munk for cleaning up both large and small issues within the manuscript. In return, I helped her discover the many uses of a buff, which she purchased after reading about Grace's. Every outdoor enthusiast should have this very versatile piece of apparel.

Much appreciation to my line editor, author Melissa Maygrove. I knew I could rely on her to find those pesky little errors that escape the revision process, no matter how careful I try to be.

Finally, thank you to the readers. My projects tend to choose me rather than the other way around, and they don't let go until I pay attention and give them their due. The concept for *Deep Blue* began over fifteen years ago (the original title was *Perfect Predator*), so this idea has been needling a part of my mind for quite some time. I'm pleased that you chose to spend time in my world, and I hope you'll continue to join me for romance and adventure in future Pathway novels.

After DEEP BLUE, join Alec and Grace in these three short adventures.

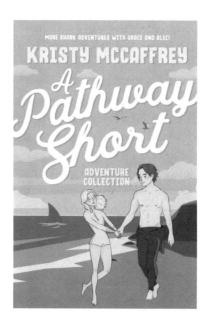

DEEP BLUE AUSTRALIA

When Grace accompanies Alec to Western Australia for a commercial shoot with great whites, she envisions relaxing days in the sun and smoldering nights between the sheets. But as Alec's mood becomes increasingly distant, Grace worries the chemistry they shared—so effortless in the beginning—was starting to fizzle. Is his reticence related to her, or something else? And can she find a way to help him get the footage he needs before his behavior places his life in danger?

DEEP BLUE REUNION ISLAND

Grace joins Alec on a trip to the French island of Réunion. Alec and his team—Dan "Double D" Donovan and Stephie Kim—are documenting the capture and relocation of mature bull sharks from the western coastline. For over ten years, shark attacks have terrorized the people of Réunion, essentially ruining the diving and surfing industry. The relocation program is a last-ditch effort to bring a peaceful coexistence between humans and sharks, but Grace's resolve is tested as she enters the water with these tenacious predators. Bull sharks didn't earn their name because they were polite.

DEEP BLUE COCOS ISLAND
Grace is invited to participate in a documentary alongside several distinguished female marine scientists, and Alec, Double D, and Stephie come along to film them in the waters off Cocos Island near Costa Rica. Grace is still dealing with recent criticism of the film Alec made of her last year diving with great white sharks, and in the company of such accomplished women, she struggles to keep her insecurities at bay. When differing viewpoints lead to friction, Grace must learn to stand up for herself, but a bright spot emerges when Alec makes a surprise decision about their relationship.

Learn more at
kmccaffrey.com/pathway-shorts-collection-one/

Don't miss SHARK REEF, a Pathway Short Adventure featuring Dr. Jen Fairfield, a friend of Grace's.

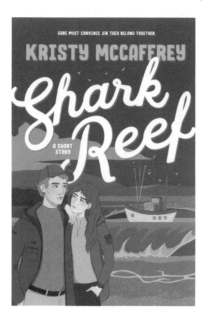

Dr. Gabe O'Grady has had it bad for Jen Fairfield since the moment they were introduced, but she had a boyfriend at the time, so Gabe stayed in the friend zone. When he learns she's about to spend three weeks in the remote Chatham Islands off New Zealand tagging great white sharks with a notoriously sketchy filmmaker, Gabe inserts himself into the project to protect her. But her indifference confounds him.

After ending her previous stalled relationship, Dr. Jen Fairfield is blindsided by her true feelings for Gabe O'Grady. After a night out with girlfriends and buoyed by their support, she makes her move with a very forward voicemail after a few drinks. But when O'Grady ghosts her for two months, Jen buries her hurt, certain she'll never see him again. Then he shows up on her expedition …

When Gabe learns Jen is single, he knows he can't let a chance with her slide by. But first he must rekindle the friendship that she seems determined to walk away from. He also needs to keep her safe from one of the most dangerous predators on earth.

Learn more at
kmccaffrey.com/shark-reef/

Read Tyler's story in
COLD HORIZON
The Pathway Series Book 2

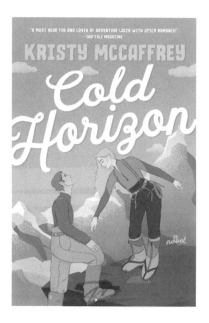

Lindsey Coulson likes to scale mountains. With her sister, Alison, she has made a name for herself climbing the tallest and most treacherous peaks in the world. But when Alison dies on a K2 expedition—the second highest mountain on earth—Lindsey stops climbing. Unable to shed her heartache, it becomes clear she must return to the wilderness and only one place will do—K2, the Savage Mountain. And to get there, she'll need handsome, enigmatic Tyler Galloway.

Ty Galloway welcomes Lindsey to his small crew with one hitch—to help with funding he wants to write about her for a magazine feature. In climbing circles, Lindsey and her sister had been famous for their mountain exploits, and her comeback story would be compelling. But he didn't account for how captivating the woman herself would be. Tackling K2 will test Ty's limits, but Lindsey Coulson will test his heart.

2021 National Excellence in Romance Fiction Winner

Learn more at
kmccaffrey.com/cold-horizon/

Read Brynn's story in
ANCIENT WINDS
The Pathway Series Book 3

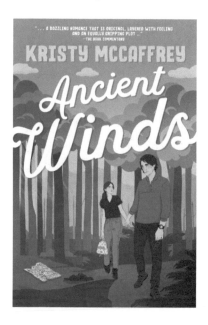

Brynn Galloway doesn't know it, but her academic career in archaeology is about to become a laughingstock. When a rare Sumerian artifact surfaces, her presence is requested in Bolivia, but nothing is as it seems. Soon, she's entangled in a desperate hunt not only for a valuable antiquity but also for answers to humanity that might stretch across time. And by her side is a sexy mercenary physicist with a maddening belief in space aliens.

Dr. Tristan Magee is in a bad mood. When his latest acquisition—an unusual and as yet untranslated Sumerian cuneiform tablet—is stolen right out from under him and spirited away to the Bolivian jungle, he'll do whatever it takes to get it back. Unfortunately, that includes partnering with a female archaeologist who proves to be the kind of distraction that brought down civilizations.

2022 Holt Medallion Finalist

Learn more at
kmccaffrey.com / ancient-winds /

ABOUT THE AUTHOR

Kristy McCaffrey has been writing since she was very young, but it wasn't until she was a stay-at-home mom that she considered becoming published. A fascination with science led her to earn two mechanical engineering degrees—she did her undergraduate work at Arizona State University and her graduate studies at the University of Pittsburgh—but storytelling has always been her passion. She writes both contemporary tales and award-winning historical western romances.

With the release of *Deep Blue*, Kristy is launching The Pathway Series, a project she's been developing for years. Each book will combine her love of animal conservation and environmental awareness, while also shining a light on unique and diverse locations around the world. Come along for high adventure with honorable heroes, determined heroines, and Kristy's trademark mysticism.

An Arizona native, Kristy and her husband reside in the desert where they frequently remove (rescue) rattlesnakes from their property, go for runs among the cactus, and plan trips to far-off places like the Orkney Islands or Machu Picchu. But mostly, she works 12-hour days and enjoys at-home date nights with her sweetheart, which usually include Will Ferrell movies and sci-fi flicks. Her four children have all flown the nest, so she lavishes her maternal instincts on Jeb, an American Bulldog her family rescued in 2021. He has his own Instagram account at @jeb_therescue.

"When we try to pick out anything by itself, we find it hitched to everything else in the Universe." – John Muir

Connect with Kristy
    Website: kmccaffrey.com
    Newsletter: kmccaffrey.com/PathwayNewsletter
    Facebook: facebook.com/AuthorKristyMcCaffrey
    Twitter: twitter.com/McCaffreyKristy
    Instagram: instagram.com/kristymccaffreybooks/
    BookBub: bookbub.com/authors/kristy-mccaffrey
    TikTok: tiktok.com/@kristymccaffrey

Made in United States
Troutdale, OR
06/18/2023

10668035R00179